# LIKE THE VERY FIRST TIME

"Let me guess, you are the type of person who will spend ten minutes toasting a marshmallow until it is perfectly browned on the outside, and all melted on the inside."

"How did you know?" Peggy threaded two of them on her long fork.

"You're the patient, deliberate type."

"And how do *you* toast a marshmallow?"

Clint took his fork and skewered a marshmallow, stuck it near the coals where it caught fire, blew it out, and ate it.

"It figures." Peggy laughed at him. "The impatient type."

"A man of action," Clint corrected.

"Some things are better for the waiting." She pulled a delicately toasted marshmallow off her fork and held it before his mouth. He held her wrist, slowly taking her fingers along with the marshmallow.

"You're right," he agreed, his voice husky.

His hand was strong around her wrist, his mouth warm and wet, his tongue sending delicious shivers through her fingers. His eyes held hers, dark with longing and promise. She felt like a virgin, being awakened to love for the first time.

## WATCH AS THESE WOMEN LEARN
## TO LOVE AGAIN

HELLO LOVE (4094, $4.50/$5.50)
by Joan Shapiro

Family tragedy leaves Barbara Sinclair alone with her success. The fight to gain custody of her young granddaughter brings a confrontation with the determined rancher Sam Douglass. Also widowed, Sam has been caring for Emily alone, guided by his own ideas of childrearing. Barbara challenges his ideas. And that's not all she challenges . . . Long-buried desires surface, then gentle affection. Sam and Barbara cannot ignore the chance to love again.

THE BEST MEDICINE (4220, $4.50/$5.50)
by Janet Lane Walters

Her late husband's expenses push Maggie Carr back to nursing, the career she left almost thirty years ago. The night shift is difficult, but it's harder still to ignore the way handsome Dr. Jason Knight soothes his patients. When she lends a hand to help his daughter, Jason and Maggie grow closer than simply doctor and nurse. Obstacles to romance seem insurmountable, but Maggie knows that love is always the best medicine.

AND BE MY LOVE (4291, $4.50/$5.50)
by Joyce C. Ware

Selflessly catering first to husband, then children, grandchildren, and her aging, though imperious mother, leaves Beth Volmar little time for her own adventures or passions. Then, the handsome archaeologist Karim Donovan arrives and campaigns to widen the boundaries of her narrow life. Beth finds new freedom when Karim insists that she accompany him to Turkey on an archaeological dig . . . and a journey towards loving again.

OVER THE RAINBOW (4032, $4.50/$5.50)
by Marjorie Eatock

Fifty-something, divorced for years, courted by more than one attractive man, and thoroughly enjoying her job with a large insurance company, Marian's sudden restlessness confuses her. She welcomes the chance to travel on business to a small Mississippi town. Full of good humor and words of love, Don Worth makes her feel needed, and not just to assess property damage. Marian takes the risk.

A KISS AT SUNRISE (4260, $4.50/$5.50)
by Charlotte Sherman

Beginning widowhood and retirement, Ruth Nichols has her first taste of freedom. Against the advice of her mother and daughter, Ruth heads for an adventure in the motor home that has sat unused since her husband's death. Long days and lonely campgrounds start to dampen the excitement of traveling alone. That is, until a dapper widower named Jack parks next door and invites her for dinner. On the road, Ruth and Jack find the chance to love again.

*Available wherever paperbacks are sold, or order direct from the Publisher. Send cover price plus 50¢ per copy for mailing and handling to Zebra Books, Dept.4326, 475 Park Avenue South, New York, N.Y. 10016. Residents of New York and Tennessee must include sales tax. DO NOT SEND CASH. For a free Zebra/Pinnacle catalog please write to the above address.*

# ON WINGS OF LOVE

## FAY KILGORE

**ZEBRA BOOKS**
**KENSINGTON PUBLISHING CORP.**

ZEBRA BOOKS are published by

Kensington Publishing Corp.
475 Park Avenue South
New York, NY 10016

First Printing: October, 1993

Printed in the United States of America

# One

*Peggy Jo Thompkins was running away from home.*

She had given it careful thought, and a great deal of planning. She even had a place to live and a job lined up where she was going. She was leaving behind Kansas, where she'd lived all her life, and everyone she'd ever called family. She was never going back—except to visit and show them all how wrong they'd been.

After eight hours of driving, the ghosts she'd brought along were becoming oppressive. "I'm not running away from home, I'm moving out!" she spoke out loud to outshout the ghosts. "I'm forty-nine years old, for Pete's sake. It's about time!"

The ghosts were guilty feelings. Although she vehemently believed in what she was doing, she couldn't exorcise her guilt about leaving her children, her grandchildren, even her parents, to pursue her own selfish needs. It didn't matter that her children were all grown, that her grandchildren had parents to be responsible for them, or that her parents were quite healthy and self-sufficient.

Being haunted by guilt was nothing new. Feeling responsible for those she loved was as much a part of Peggy Thompkins as her blue eyes or her blond hair, which was showing a great deal of white nowadays. She felt responsible for her family's happiness, their integrity, and even the consequences of their decisions. If one of them became unhappy she was sure it was somehow her fault. So vehemently did she believe this that her family had come to believe it also.

And that was the reason she was running away from home.

The state line lay across the highway, a clear line of demarcation between where she was coming from and where she was going. WELCOME TO NEW MEXICO, LAND OF ENCHANTMENT the road sign read. Peggy felt the bump under the tires, and swore she heard a door slam shut. You've done it now, the ghosts said. There's no going back.

*Of course not,* she told them. *This is the beginning of the rest of my life.* In spite of the depressing ghosts, a thrill of excitement coursed through her at the welcome sign. After four months of planning, she was finally in New Mexico.

The empty highway stretched across the flat expanse of desert to the horizon, where a blazing sun appeared to be sitting at the end of it. Peggy pulled the van over to the shoulder and got out. The fresh, warm breeze caressed her face, and she breathed in the clean, arid air.

*So vast,* she thought, letting her eyes scan the landscape around her. *So raw, untamed, untouched, and incredibly empty.* She was the only person for as far as she could see. In parallel lines from horizon to horizon ran the highway, the barbed-wire fence, and the silver rails of the railroad tracks. Though it was warm, she shivered. It was a novel experience, being alone.

*I'll get used to it. I'll relish it!*

The light sandy soil was dotted with low-growing mesquite, compact shrubs, and hostile cacti. The various grasses grew in tight yellow clumps, rather than the lush green expanses she was familiar with in Kansas. Now early August, there was little greenery in the desert. Most people would call it ugly, but Peggy experienced again the heightened awareness of communing with a soul sister. The sensation had struck her the very first time she'd seen the desert, four months ago.

The sun sank out of sight behind her, and a full orange moon rose out of the desert before her. *I'm not running away from home,* she said again, to herself, awed by the powerful beauty of nature, and the transformation the moonlight gave to the wild landscape around her.

*I've finally come home.*

The immense space, the fresh breeze, the bright moon rising higher in the darkening sky lifted her soul. After being married for twenty-seven years to a domineering, cheating husband, she'd finally divorced him two years ago. Her son and eldest child hadn't spoken to her for almost a year, since she'd disowned him for embezzling her investments. She had tendered her resignation as her elder daughter's nanny, and sold the family home out from under her younger daughter. She'd also finished college, earned her teaching certificate, and accepted the first job outside her home she'd ever held. Her battle-weary heart drank in the healing spirit of the desert around her.

*Land of enchantment,* she repeated. The moon-silvered highway beckoned and the iridescent phoenix she'd painted on the side of the van glowed softly. The vehicle had been the first of many purchases, once she'd made her decision, and she was still very proud of it. The mythical bird rising from its ashes to begin a new life, young and fresh, embodied all she hoped for with this move.

"Come on, my friend," she told the fiery phoenix, "let's go home."


Peggy rose early the next morning, while it was still dark. She filled her thermos with coffee and drove the twenty miles from Fort Sumner to the lake, where she would live, once the place was habitable. Sunrise over the lake was even more incredible than moonrise over the desert, and her fingers longed for a brush to capture the colors on canvas. She sat on the rocky formation at the edge of her property, drinking her coffee, and absorbing the peaceful tranquility of the morning.

When it was full light, she finished the last of the coffee with a sigh. Seeing the sunrise from her own front porch was definitely worth the lack of sleep. Now, there was work to do, and painting would have to be confined to interior and exterior walls until she got the studio organized.

A movement in the shadowed valley to her right caught her eye. Deer, several does with their half-grown fawns, were leisurely coming up the draw from the lake, stopping frequently to sample a clump of grass. With a lump in her throat, Peggy wished Shawn and Michael were here. Her grandsons would be thrilled to be so close to wild deer. She decided sending them a picture would be the next best thing.

*I'll be ready for you with my camera next time,* she silently promised the retreating herd. She waited until they were out of sight, then turned her attention toward the cabin.

The "cabin" was an ancient caboose, almost buried behind the additions that had been tacked on by its various owners. The front windows just barely peeked over the slanted roof of a lean-to shed. A screened-in porch wrapped around one end. A large addition had been added to the back. The cupola, with its observation benches, sat proudly above the mismatched hodgepodge reflecting the sky in its windows. It hadn't seen human habitation in over a year.

Peggy had fallen in love with it on sight,

seeing its potential, not its present state. It would be her own place, restored with her own hands, and unshared with another human being. It had to be unique.

Peggy went to the van and began unloading cleaning supplies. There were a few million nonhuman inhabitants to evict before moving day. Soon she was surrounded by enough stuff to outfit an entire janitorial service. Hoisting a broom and a thirty-gallon trash can, she entered the cabin by the back platform of the caboose.

An hour later, she came out for air, soaked with sweat and grimy with dirt and cobwebs. The early morning cool had rapidly given way to the heat of August, and the cabin wasn't air-conditioned. The bandana she'd tied over her hair had been retied, robber-fashion, over her mouth and nose to filter out the worst of the dust. She was untying it when a booming male voice brought her up short.

"You must be Dorothy!"

Peggy could only stare. The voice belonged to a big man, both in height and breadth, strong rather than fat. He had to be older than herself, if the dark silver hair was any indication. The most arresting pair of laughing brown eyes were taking full inventory of her from a breathtakingly handsome, sun-weathered face. Peggy's hand went reflexively to her hair, and she grimaced at the cobwebs she felt clinging to it.

"Clinton Howell," he introduced himself, extending a tan, work-roughened hand to her. "I own the cabin on the right where the road Y's. I couldn't help noticing the Kansas tags."

"Peggy Thompkins," she replied, somewhat overwhelmed by this big man with his booming voice and easy manner. She wiped her dusty hand on her shorts before accepting his.

"You're a long way from Oz."

"Actually, this is Oz," Peggy finally regained enough composure to remark. *And I must look like I've ridden in on a tornado.*

"Do you plan to live here, or make this your weekend retreat?"

"This is home." She moved around him and opened the sliding side door on the van.

"You have family here?" he asked, leaning against the side of the van.

"No, just me. I know it's early, but would you care for a Pepsi?" she asked, pulling one out of a cooler of ice.

"No, thank you. You drove here from Kansas? Alone?" He sounded incredulous.

14

"Yes," she answered warily, eyeing him. He didn't look dangerous, but you could never tell by appearances. He sounded more surprised than menacing, as if he couldn't believe a woman would do such a thing. She took a long drink from her can. Her throat felt like she'd inhaled more dirt than she'd swept out.

"How about yourself?" she asked him. "You have family here?"

"I run a large ranch south of here with my sons. I come out here to fish and retreat a little. I'm ashamed to admit I retreat more than weekends."

"Grandchildren?" Peggy asked, not sure why but sensing a kindred spirit.

"Yes," he remarked, surprised at her perception. "Now what would you know of grandchildren?" He walked with her back to the platform of the caboose.

"I have three of my own," she answered.

"You must have married in grade school and your children done likewise."

"Thank you. A pretty compliment considering I'm covered in dirt from head to toe." A self-conscious pass through her hair dislodged a few cobwebs. "Maybe it hides the wrinkles."

"Dirt becomes you."

"I don't know if that's a compliment or an insult," she replied, looking down at him from her higher step.

He was very distinguished-looking. He wore his run-your-fingers-through-it hair short and combed to one side. Laugh lines crinkled at the corners of his warm, intense brown eyes. His smile was easy, a slightly crooked incisor telling her that the strong white teeth were still his own. He wore a full mustache that retained some of the dark brown his hair must have been before it went gray. Looking at him made Peggy's heart skip strangely.

"Definitely a compliment," he assured her. "I like a woman who isn't afraid of hard work."

She laughed at that, trying not to allow him to see how nervous he was making her. "I think I went too far with this project. There is more involved than I can manage alone. Do you know of anyone local, with a truck and a strong back, who I could hire to haul off some of this junk?"

He was thoughtful a moment before he answered. "I think I can get you someone."

"Also, is trash burning allowed out here?"

"Yes. Be careful around all that old wood, though." He indicated the cabin.

"That's what I plan to burn." She laughed at his horrified expression. "Just the shed. It detracts from the caboose and isn't necessary."

"Is that old wood stove still inside?"

"Oh, yes. Is it original? I plan to keep it even if it isn't."

"It probably is. Why not make a wood pile out of the shed and use it for the stove?"

"What a good idea." She met his eyes and her smile faded.

The signals he was sending her were as powerful as they were unmistakable. Peggy wasn't naive. She'd received similar signals from other men, and had had no trouble ignoring them or making her lack of interest clear. The signal from Clint had found a receptor deep within her, refusing to be ignored, or discarded.

"So, what are the rest of your plans?" He said it in such a low, intimate voice Peggy realized he wasn't just referring to the cabin, and she attempted to get the conversation back on a safer track.

"I'm going to make a studio out of the largest bedroom."

"Are you an artist?"

17

"Yes," she answered with pride. "I painted the phoenix on the side of the van."

He gave an appreciative whistle and got up to examine the van again. "I am impressed."

"Thank you."

"I happen to know a decent carpenter, if you need one."

"Yes, I will. I need a lot more windows in the studio. I'd appreciate any references. Of course, I'd want to see his work first."

"I don't think that will be a problem."

The smile he gave her was filled with mischief, making his eyes sparkle. Peggy stood up and pulled her gloves back on, deciding the safest course of action was to put distance between herself and the charming Mr. Howell.

"It was good to meet you, Mr. Howell," she said, dismissing him. "I'd better get back to work. The carpet people are coming Monday, and the truck with my furniture will be here Tuesday.

"Oh!" She remembered the junk. "Could you call that man you spoke of, with the truck? I'd be so grateful."

"Certainly. I think he can be here in a couple of hours, if that's okay."

"Thank you. That will help a lot. I'll invite you back, when it's habitable," she said with a smile. "Perhaps I can meet your wife then." She knew she was being obvious, but, so was he.

"I'm a widower."

"Oh, I'm sorry. That was a stupid assumption on my part." She was ashamed of the relief that flooded through her.

"Not at all, considering the grandchildren." He didn't elaborate, and Peggy didn't press for more. "I'll go make that phone call."

He turned and walked down the hill toward his cabin. She could hear him whistling before she retied the bandana and reentered the caboose.

*Peggy Thompkins,* Clint thought as he returned to his cabin, his step lighter than it had been in years. She was obviously single, probably divorced, since she hadn't said anything about her status when he'd mentioned being a widower. Widows were always quick to let him know they understood what he was going through, having gone through it themselves. Divorce still carried a bit of a stigma with his generation, and so wasn't flaunted.

Peggy Thompkins, artist, adventurer, not

afraid to drive cross-country alone, or to tackle that abandoned relic, or to start over in a strange land. She embodied the pioneer spirit. Clint admired that. So far, he admired everything he'd seen of the woman. She was attractive. Dirt couldn't hide her deep, probing, dark blue eyes, or her full mouth. She wasn't too short, or too tall—not thin, but not too heavy. He thought she must be in her early forties. The grandchildren she spoke of must be babies, *or from stepchildren,* he thought on inspiration.

Her waist was a little thick, but her full breasts made that hardly noticeable. So did her full, shapely rear end. The shorts she'd had on exposed long legs that belonged in black stockings and high heels—or entwined with satin sheets.

He felt a surge of interest at the mental image. It had been a long time.


Peggy spent the next two hours after Clint's departure trying to work too hard to think about him. She was in the middle of vigorously sterilizing the bathroom, when a knock on the door interrupted her. Clint was back, wearing work clothes, and a wide grin on his face. He stepped back to indicate two

20

tall, rugged men who looked to be in their late twenties, obviously brothers.

"Peggy, I'd like you to meet my sons, Clinton, Jr.—we call him J.R.—and Justin. Boys, this is Peggy Thompkins, just moved here from Kansas."

They both wore straw cowboy hats to which they gave a respectful tug with their polite. "Pleased to meet you, ma'am."

"I'm pleased to meet you, too," Peggy returned, but with some irritation. "Clint, they are handsome men, but could I meet your family some other time?" She ran a quick hand through her hair, dislodging more than repairing, and a strand fell across her eyes.

"They are the men with the truck," Clinton explained, sounding hurt. "Just tell them where to start."

"Oh." Peggy was ashamed of her hastily formed conclusion. "I'm sorry, I didn't . . ."— she pushed at her hair again—"Come in, please."

She stepped back for them to enter. The three huge men completely filled the tiny caboose.

"Everything that isn't nailed down needs to be moved out. The refrigerator, the old furniture, everything. Also, the carpets out of the bedrooms."

The two boys went out to their truck for the appliance dolly. Clint stood in the center of the caboose, looking around.

"This place must have been filthy," he commented. "You've made a lot of progress this morning."

"I'm getting there," Peggy agreed.

The high observation windows in the cupola allowed beams of sunlight into the rather gloomy interior. Clint climbed the ladder and took a seat on a recently cleaned observation bench, once used by brakemen to survey the countryside as the train traveled over the rails. Now it allowed a breathtaking view of the lake on the east, and the other cabins in the community on the west.

"Isn't it great?" Peggy asked from below him. "It severely limits my available floor space, but adds such personality."

"It does have a certain charm," Clint agreed, climbing down. "So does the mistress of the house."

"You should see her cleaned up," Peggy quipped. Clint's appreciative smile was giving her a bad case of butterflies.

The boys came in, and Peggy and Clint went into the addition to get out of their way. It was slightly wider than the caboose, and had been divided into two bedrooms with a small bathroom between them.

"Are you going to remove this old linoleum?" Clint pushed at a loose piece of bathroom tile with his toe.

"Yes, I just haven't gotten that far yet."

"Do you have a scraper? I can do this while you supervise the boys."

She had known he was too good to be true. She had run away from home because of domineering men running, and ruining, her life. Now, less than twenty-four hours after crossing the state line, a new man was trying to take over.

"There's no need," she said. "I'll get to it."

"Suit yourself."

Peggy knew from his clipped response that he was taking her refusal of his help as a personal rebuff. She laid a restraining hand on his arm. "I do appreciate your offer, and especially your bringing your sons out here so quickly. I'd rather do all I can myself. It's a personal thing."

"I'd enjoy doing it, and enjoy even more saving a beautiful lady's hands from such abusive labor." He took her hand from his arm and stroked the back of it with his other hand. Her hands were already red and dry from her morning's cleaning efforts. "I am free for a couple of days, if you can tolerate the company."

Peggy assessed him for a moment, weighing consequences. The last thing she needed in her life right now was a man, especially an attractive single man who was warming her whole body through his touch on her hand. On the practical side, however, there was a lot to do, and his help would certainly make things easier.

"Your company is more than tolerable," she said withdrawing her hand from his. "Forgive my snarling. I've sort of been burned recently and am still a bit tender."

He knew she wasn't talking about a skin burn, and vowed to keep a comfortable distance. She must be recently divorced, he thought, curious, but knowing now wasn't the time for shared confidences.

"So," he rubbed his hands together, indicating readiness for action, "where are the tools?"

Peggy smiled at his enthusiasm and went to the van for the tools.

The boys carried out rusted iron bed frames, musty mattresses, warped pasteboard furniture, and dirt-encrusted carpets from the caboose and the two bedrooms. The floors of the addition were of particle board and in good shape under the worn-out carpet. The walls and ceiling had water damage from a previous leak. Since she had the manpower and the truck to haul it off with, she asked the boys to tear down the paneling and molded ceiling boards as well. Clint came to stand with her as she surveyed the bare wall studs in the bedroom.

"I suggest insulation before you replace the walls."

"Yes. At least in here. There will be so many windows in the studio, I don't know if insulated walls will make much difference."

"It will."

"Is it hard?"

"Insulating?"

"No, hanging drywall."

Clint gave her a quizzical look. He'd never heard a woman use the term "drywall." "Most people hire professionals to hang drywall."

"But is it hard to do?"

"Not hard exactly, just tedious and time consuming. Depending on how thick you want, the sheets can be heavy and unwieldy to manage alone."

Peggy had a distant look of thoughtfulness in her eyes. "I'll manage."

Clint opened his mouth to comment, then decided he really didn't know what to say, and kept silent.

When everything was out and loaded onto the truck, the two young men headed for the lake to cool off. Clint walked with Peggy back through the caboose, amazed at the difference. The floor was bare wide wooden boards. With the old furniture and most of the dirt and cobwebs gone, the open space in front of the cupola looked much more spacious. The front and back doors stood open, allowing a fresh breeze to purge the lingering smell of mildew and dust.

"Do you cook?" Clint asked her, surveying the tiny kitchen.

"Yes, but there won't be any Thanksgiving dinners served here. I came here to paint, not entertain."

"You're doing all this just for a place to paint?"

"Oh, no. I have a job teaching art at the junior and senior high schools, along with history."

"Why New Mexico?"

"Because Alaska didn't offer."

"Oh. I see." His expression said he didn't see at all.

"I needed a change."

Clint waited, but it soon became obvious he wasn't going to get any more than that for now. He cleared his throat to cover the uncomfortable pause. "I think the boys have the right idea with a swim in the lake. Come with me down to my cabin and we'll get some towels."

Peggy was sorely tempted. She'd never felt so gritty and sweaty in her life. "I have nothing to swim in," she said.

"Swim in what you have on. A little lake water can't do it any worse damage."

"And what do I change into?"

"Ah, don't worry about it. The humidity is so low here, you'll be dry by the time we walk back."

He was already walking down the hill toward his cabin; Peggy followed. A swim would be so refreshing, but swimming in her clothes and wearing them until they dried sounded more like something teenagers would do, not grandparents. *No,* she smiled, *teenagers would shuck their clothes without a thought. It's just like grandparents to swim fully clothed and suffer wet underwear for the sake of modesty.*

They walked along the road from the cabins down to a narrow sand beach. Several families were swimming in the shallow water along the shore, and the boat traffic was brisk, since it was a Saturday. Clint led her to a rock-rimmed cove past the beach that involved some tricky rock climbing to get to. The cove wasn't big enough for boats to bother with it, and the water there was deep enough for diving from the rock edge. Two piles of clothing confirmed Peggy's theory about the practicality of youth. She shaded her eyes against the glare off the lake, and saw Clint Jr. and Justin swimming back from the mouth of the cove.

"Ahh, to be young," she remarked to Clint, indicating the discarded clothing.

"I agree," he grinned at her as he pulled his T-shirt over his head.

"I didn't mean . . ."

Clint sat down and unlaced his shoes, apparently oblivious to Peggy's dismay.

"You gonna swim with your shoes on?" he asked, standing up. His shorts were all he still wore.

"I . . ."

"Don't be embarrassed. I'm sure you have beautiful feet." She still didn't move, paralyzed by the potential situation.

28

"Would you like my help?"

"No! I mean . . ."

Clint ran his thumbs under the waistband of his shorts, drawing her eyes to them, her heart racing. She quickly looked away, out across the lake.

"Join us when you're ready," she heard Clint say. She refused to look as he dove into the deep water, deliberating on whether to walk back to her cabin or not.

"Come on, Peggy!" Clint called. "The water's great!"

She gave him a quick glance, reassured that he was a safe distance out, then scrutinized the pile of clothing he'd left behind. The shorts were not there.

*So,* she thought, *he likes to tease.* She had to smile at herself as she realized how easily she'd been taken in. *I'll get you back for this,* she vowed silently, tugging off her shoes at the edge of the water.

As she pulled off the second shoe, she lost her balance and fell backward into the lake, screaming until her head went under. Immediately she swam deeper and into the narrowest part of the rocky cove, holding her breath and staying submerged until she thought her lungs would burst. She could

29

have stayed under a lot longer if she hadn't screamed, but it wouldn't have been as dramatic.

Silently she surfaced, as close to the rock edge as she could, trying not to gulp air as she assessed the location of Clint and the boys. As she had planned, all three of them were converging on the point where she'd fallen in. She remained hidden in the shadow of an overhang, waiting to see if any of them noticed her. She watched them diving under the water, searching frantically for her for several minutes before she took pity on them.

"You boys lose something?" she asked nonchalantly, swimming leisurely back to them.

Three startled faces turned toward her. The boys recovered quicker than their father.

"You scared me half to death!" he accused hotly.

"You deserved it." She laughed, pleased with the success of her ploy.

"I didn't cause you to age ten years!"

"Does that mean you're no longer young?"

She was treading water a few feet from him. He answered by plunging forward, swimming toward her with aggressive purpose. With a girlish squeal, Peggy turned to flee, swimming hard toward the opposite side of the cove.

He caught her as they reached the side, both of them laughing and breathing hard from the exertion.

"First . . . you work me . . . to death, then . . . you scare me . . . to death, now you're trying . . . to swim me to death," he panted. "Did my sons hire you?"

"Sons?"

"To knock me off for their inheritance."

"Oh. No, I decided to do this on my own."

"You're a heartless woman, Peggy Thompkins."

Peggy's racing heart belied his accusation as she looked into Clint's intensely warm brown eyes. What she saw there caught her mid gut, stifling the laughter. Although the water was cool, she felt the heat from his close proximity to her.

"We should be getting back," she suggested weakly.

"Let's take our time on the return trip," Clint suggested, but he didn't seem to be in any hurry to start back.

The boys had already dressed by the time they did return, and handed them towels as they pulled themselves out onto the rock ledge. Peggy noticed they both wore amused, knowing expressions. Their father was in for some teasing when they got him alone, she was certain.

"That was marvelous," Peggy commented shyly as they walked back up the road to the cabins. "I feel much better."

The boys were tying ropes across the overloaded pickup bed when they got back.

"Where are you staying tonight?" Clint asked.

"I have a motel room in Fort Sumner until I get moved in."

"It's a long drive back to town. The boys will follow you in."

"I drove five hundred miles alone from Kansas, Clint. I think I can handle twenty miles into town." She chided him gently, but he got the message.

"Of course you can. I just know you're tired. Anyway, the boys go back that way, and it's no problem."

"Thanks, but I'd like to do a few things before I head in," she told him, polite, but firm. "I'll be fine."

"Well, then." Clint considered inviting her to dinner, but suspected he'd be turned down flat. She was suddenly acting as if his presence was no longer desirable. "I'll see you in the morning." He turned away to help the boys finish tying down the load.

Peggy knew she was responsible for the irritation in his voice. It was a sorry pay-back for the backbreaking day he had just spent on her behalf, but he was the type of man who would take over if she allowed it, with the best intentions, but taking over nevertheless. Still, she didn't want him to think her ungrateful.

"Yes, I'll be back in the morning," she assured him. She got her purse to pay J.R. the money they'd agreed on for the work they'd done. "Thanks again. I really couldn't have done it without all of your help."

The boys drove off, the truck's springs protesting the load as they carefully traversed the rocky road down the hill and up the other side. Peggy and Clint listened to them until they reached the quiet of the blacktop.

"Well," he spoke finally, "if you don't need anything else, I'll head home."

"Thanks, Clint," she said again, knowing it wasn't enough, but not knowing what else she could say.

He disappeared down the hill, and she turned to look out over the lake. It was mirror smooth now, reflecting the warm colors of the sunset. A whippoorwill called across the gathering twilight.

*Clinton Howell,* Peggy thought, standing

on the platform of the caboose, watching the changing kaleidoscope on the lake's surface. *Did you have to land in my life the minute I set foot here? Couldn't you have waited until I got settled?* She had enjoyed the day with him, but she hadn't come to New Mexico to get involved with a new man. She'd come to get over one, two if she counted her son.

She sighed. *How do you say to a man, 'I really enjoy your company. Could you come back in six months when I'm settled in and ready to deal with a relationship again?'* She wondered how long he'd been a widower. If his easygoing attitude was any indication, it had been a while. If she discouraged him, he'd look elsewhere.

So? she demanded of herself. *What does that matter to you? You aren't looking for a relationship.*

But it did matter, and that made her sad, which in turn irritated her. She had come out here to prove she could stand alone, without a father, husband, or son managing her life, to teach art and paint. There was no place for Clinton Howell, but there he was anyway, stirring up emotions she had thought dead and grieved over too long ago to resurrect.

# *Two*

The next day was Sunday, and Clinton was dressed for church and ready to leave before he saw the red van with the brilliant phoenix on the side go past.

*She slept late this morning,* he thought.

Clinton was even more intrigued by Peggy Thompkins. Although he had spent all day with her, he still had little insight into what it was in Kansas that had driven her to move to New Mexico. A need to be independent seemed to be uppermost. It was implied with everything she said, her decisions regarding the cabin, and even her response to him. It wasn't a coy pretense of being hard-to-get. She had a skittish quality about her that reminded him of a hunted animal.

He'd decided last night that the best way to get to know more about her was to give her space. It was his theory that an ex-husband was somehow responsible for the over-crowding in Kansas. Nothing was better for anger and frustration than hard physical labor, and that cabin promised to provide plenty of that. And nothing was better for shared confidences than walks along the beach at twilight. Clint intended to arrange for that as soon as the opportunity presented itself.

Peggy passed Clint's neat log cabin with a thoughtful sigh. She had barely been able to stay awake long enough to eat something after her shower last night, but still she'd awakened several times with troubled thoughts of Clinton Howell. She'd overslept, waking finally to the unnervingly real sensation of him kissing her, his mouth warm and erotic against her lips. As she lay in the motel room bed, experiencing an unfamiliar tingling running through her body, she felt more disturbed than ever.

*You've been without too long, and this is a natural response to a handsome, virile male.* Even as she tried to explain it away to herself, she knew that wasn't true. She'd been divorced from her husband for two years, and the physical side of their marriage had been nonexistent long before that.

In the two years she'd been single, she'd dated several interesting men, and none of them had elicited such a powerful physical reaction. She'd even tried sleeping with a couple of them, when the ache in her heart was too strong to bear alone. The ache was still there the next morning, though, and she'd discovered that, at least for her, such intimacy without love was more embarrassing than fulfilling.

But Clint's haunting of her sleep had been almost as intimate as if he'd actually been there. She had seen his handsome, sun-weathered face, his brown eyes changing from laughter to desire as he watched her. Her skin imagined the touch of his work-roughened hands. The chest and shoulders he'd displayed, first during his teasing strip show, then in the water beside her, strongly denied the passing of the fifty-three years he'd assured her he'd lived. Her fingers even tingled, thinking about touching the brown-and-silver pelt that covered his broad chest.

*Grow up Peggy Thompkins!* she chided herself, unlocking the door to the caboose. *You're acting like a teenager in heat, and I know just the cure.* Surveying the conglomerate she had elected to make into a home, Peggy knew she had enough work to do to keep any wayward hormones under control for a long time.

Tomorrow the man would be here to install the carpet and floor tiles, which gave her exactly today to scrub the grime off the floors before it became part of the finished product. She wanted to wash the walls also. Painting would have been ideal while there was no carpet to be concerned with, but there simply weren't enough hours in the day.

Peggy heated water over a Coleman camp stove in an enameled steel pot, not trusting the small electric water heater that had sat unused for over a year. She had asked the boys to move the compact kitchen range out into the living room area so she could clean behind it. It would not be moved back until the carpet was laid in the kitchen.

She pulled on rubber gloves and started with the kitchen cabinets, using a scraper, assorted brushes, and rags. She didn't stop until lunchtime, taking a sandwich outside to eat on the steps, wondering why Clint hadn't come up yet. He'd said "in the morning" and here it was past noon.

*Stop it!* she commanded her idle brain. It was time to get back to work.

She had the floor of the caboose washed before he knocked on the door, looking fresh and rested. Peggy felt like something the dog had buried in the backyard.

"You've been busy," he commented, admiring the kitchen. He'd removed his shoes at the door out of respect for the freshly scrubbed floor. "What time will the man be here with the carpet tomorrow?"

"Around ten o'clock. They're coming out of Clovis." Her voice sounded so tired he turned to look at her. She was sitting on the floor, leaning against the wall. Every line in her face and body slumped in exhaustion.

"You're trying to do too much," he admonished her, dropping to his knees beside her. "You've set yourself an impossible time schedule here."

"Don't tell me how to manage my time schedule," she snapped, almost reflexively, and was immediately sorry.

"Don't mind me, I'm just tired and sore, and obviously out of condition," she apologized. "Would you like something to drink?"

"I'll get it." He was up before she could object. He went out to the ice chest in the van and returned with two cans of Pepsi, sitting down beside her on the floor.

"What's left for today?" he asked casually, not wanting to intrude if she didn't want him to.

"I wanted to do the walls in here before they installed the carpet tomorrow, but it isn't worth it. I'll do them later, when I'm ready to paint."

"More red?"

"No." She finally smiled, shaking her head. "There's enough red outside. The inside will be a very neutral cream, although it will probably take three coats to cover the old paint."

"At least," he agreed. "It'll make it much lighter in here."

"I wish there was a way to add more windows, but I want to retain the caboose look as much as possible from the outside, and adding windows will detract from authenticity. At least I have the screen porch, and the studio will be mostly windows when it's finished."

"Do you have a set plan in mind?"

"Only in my head. I was hoping the carpenter would listen to what I wanted and make suggestions."

"What do you want?" At her scrutinizing

gaze he flashed a guilty grin. "I wasn't going to bring this up until later, but I'm the carpenter I was going to recommend."

"Are you really a carpenter?" She sounded skeptical.

"I really am. I personally built every building standing on my ranch, including the house."

"And what's your consultation fee?"

"A steak dinner," he answered without hesitation. At her puzzled expression he continued. "There's a steak house in Fort Sumner that serves a decent T-bone. I give you my professional opinion on your building options here, and you take me to dinner tonight."

"Is this a date?"

"Of course not. This is a business transaction. You insult me. If this was a date, I would take you to dinner." *That should appeal to her independent nature,* Clint hoped.

Peggy considered his strange proposal. She wanted the studio finished as soon as possible, and school would be starting in two weeks, which limited her on time unless she was willing to allow someone to work while she was at school. If Clint was really a carpenter . . .

"When could you start?"

41

"I can do a rough sketch today, and take measurements. I can give you a cost estimate in a couple of days and start work as soon as the materials are available."

Peggy considered some more. Dinner was a small price for an estimate, and wasn't a commitment. She would ask the realtor for a couple of other names of carpenters and get quotes from them also. Eating alone was certainly getting tiresome and a business dinner wouldn't require that either of them play by dating rules, which would make it more companionable and less threatening.

"Agreed," she decided, feeling suddenly energetic at the prospect of starting work on the studio.

Peggy surprised Clint by having a sixteen-foot steel tape among her tools. They entered the hollowed-out future studio and began measuring the room, Clint making several rough sketches and writing down dimensions. He asked her how many windows she wanted, how big, whether she wanted them to open and have screens. They also discussed lighting.

"You're an electrician also?"

"Even with licensing it was cheaper to do it myself than hire it done."

"What other talents do you have, Mr.

Howell?" she asked suggestively, her head tilted to one side.

"Ahh, I only reveal what is needed at the moment. It's much more mysterious that way."

He gave her a warm smile that darkened his eyes and Peggy felt a delicious thrill run through her. "I can hardly wait to start."

"Does this mean I'm hired?" His voice was low and suggestive. Peggy flushed and broke the intense eye contact.

"On a consultant basis, for now," she hedged, leading the way to the door. "If you'll give me a thirty-minute headstart, I'll meet you in the motel lobby and conclude our business arrangement of this afternoon."

*Patience,* Clinton urged himself, walking back to his cabin. *Don't spook the quarry too soon.*

This was one nervous vixen he'd set his sights on, and action would have to come later. *When I have her in the sack,* he thought with a smile. He was whistling by the time he reached his cabin at the bottom of the hill.


Clint kept the dinner conversation lively and focused on the present and the future.

He observed her closely, noting that some subjects made her wistful, like grandchildren. He did discover they were all hers, and not all that young, the oldest being seven. She preferred to listen to him tell her as much as he knew about Fort Sumner.

"You'll have students who travel over an hour to school," he told her. "Some of the outlying ranches are quite a distance, but Fort Sumner is still the closest school system. As you can imagine, those students are provided with a vehicle on their fourteenth birthday."

Peggy was amazed. "Do the busses go that far?"

"Oh, yes," Clint assured her.

"Those poor kids."

"Mine did all their homework on the bus. Their grades suffered when they started driving."

"I'm excited about school starting, but there is so much to do at the cabin. On top of all that, I can hardly wait to set up my easel and start painting the desert, and the lake."

"It's good to have such purpose in life," Clint remarked somewhat enviously. Her face was animated with her excitement, her dark

44

blue eyes glowing, her cheeks becomingly flushed.

"Did I tell you how well you clean up?"

The flush deepened, and she was unable to meet his intense gaze. "Yes, but thank you again."

*Actually, you're quite beautiful,* Clint was thinking. He'd thought so when she was sweaty and covered in dirt, but seeing her with her pale blond hair soft and brushed back from her face, wearing a becoming sundress, just a hint of makeup to emphasize her eyes, and smelling of warm, clean skin was even more intoxicating than he'd imagined. He sat across from her, allowing all his male receptors to drink their fill, his approval evident in the warmth of his eyes.

Peggy felt breathless every time she met his gaze, her stomach full of butterflies that prevented her from eating much of the enormous meal they were served. She was much too warm, and knew she was blushing under his intense scrutiny. *So much for a companionable business dinner,* she thought, yet she had enjoyed his company and talking with him. He was intelligent and entertaining, alternately teasing her and making her laugh with his local anecdotes. When she talked, he listened intently, as if what she said was of the utmost importance, and his knowledge of the area was vast, having lived here all his life.

He walked her back to her motel after dinner, telling her about the owners of the various establishments along the town's main street. Although he hated to end the evening, he could see the fatigue in her face from her day as he stood with her outside her door.

"You should sleep well," he commented.

She felt the heat rise in her face, wondering if he would once again disturb her dreams. "Yes," she agreed, unable to meet his eyes.

"I'll come out tomorrow and help you clean out the lean-to before your furniture arrives."

"No, Clint. Thank you, but you've done too much already."

"I'd enjoy it."

"I really believe you would, but I need to do this alone." It was spoken gently, but firmly. She dared to look at him, pleading him with her eyes for understanding.

*Butt out, Clinton,* he upbraided himself. *You're crowding the lady again.* What he really wanted to do was crush her to him and kiss her until passion burned in those huge, frightened, dark eyes.

Peggy was sorely tempted to allow him to help, but her newly won independence was too fragile to allow any temptation. Clinton Howell was a strong, handsome, dynamic man, and he had "let me take care of you" written all over him. That was going to be as difficult to resist as his physical attraction, and resist she must. Her future as a person depended on it.

"I noticed you heating water," he interrupted her musing, clearing his throat nervously. "Is there a problem with the water heater?"

"To tell the truth, I'm afraid to plug it in, it's sat unused for so long."

"I thought I'd do some fishing in the morning," he stated casually. "Unless you had someone in mind, I'd be glad to come by in the afternoon and look at it."

Peggy thought about it. She needed the water heater, and someone had to look at it. It seemed harmless enough to let him do that. "What needs to be done to it before you get there?"

"It needs to be drained and refilled, if the spigot's not rusted closed."

"I think I can manage that." She smiled at him. "See you tomorrow."

"Thank you for dinner." He caught her free hand before she could escape inside, and gave it a warm squeeze. "Until tomorrow."

With a jaunty wave he climbed in his pickup and drove off. Peggy stood there, holding the doorknob, watching until he was out of sight.

The next morning she sat on the steps of the platform, drinking her coffee and watching the deer walk back up the draw from the lake, not even trying to curb her thoughts of Clint. She'd slept hard, undisturbed by dreams, awakening refreshed and energized in plenty of time to drive back to the lake to enjoy the sunrise. A lone bass boat cruised out across the lake, disappearing around the bend, heading toward the dam. From this distance she couldn't tell who the operator was, but assumed it was Clint. She added binoculars to her mental list of needed purchases.

It'll be fun to watch the deer, she thought, then laughed at herself. *Who am I kidding?*

She tackled the hot water tank first, having to use a wrench to turn the spigot at the bottom in order to drain it. She ran the water out through the window via a garden hose, turning on the cold water supply and allowing the tank to flush for a few minutes. Then she closed the drain spigot and allowed the tank to fill.

Once the tank was filled, she studied it for a few indecisive minutes. It was an electric appliance, not unlike an iron or a coffeepot, she thought. It either works or it doesn't. She had cleaned the outside of it, and the floor under it. The cord was undamaged. Plugging it in seemed a small act. Still her hand trembled as she held the plug in front of the outlet. She wished there was some way to do this by remote control.

*What a coward,* she chided herself, disgusted but unable to put the plug in the outlet while standing so close to it. So much for the independent woman. She needed a man just to plug in a water heater. She sat down on the bathroom floor to study the problem.

It wasn't long before she was up again, laughing at her foolishness. The plug-in wasn't the threat, the electricity was, and that could be controlled from a distance. She got her flashlight out of the glove compartment of the van and went to the breaker box, throwing the main switch. She'd learned about breaker boxes from the electrical volume of a recently purchased fix-it-yourself encyclopedia. With smug confidence she returned to the bathroom, and put the plug of the water heater into the now dead outlet. *Piece of cake.*

Still, her hand trembled as she stood before the breaker box. She took a deep breath, said a quick prayer, closed her eyes tightly, and shoved the switch back to On. Silence. Nothing exploded. Nothing even hummed. She opened her eyes and noted the lights were back on. Cautiously she approached the bathroom.

The water heater sat right where she'd left it, apparently oblivious to the drama it had starred in. The red indicator light winked at her. She relaxed. *Just an overgrown coffeepot.*

She went to the van for a Pepsi. It was definitely time for a break.

## Three

Clint waited until late afternoon to come by, cleaning his fish and organizing the components of a fish dinner, just in case he could persuade her to come. He found her sitting in the van, studying a book. The toilet was lying in the yard.

"Hello the camp!" he called out, startling her. "Must be an exciting book."

She gave him a tired smile and held it up for him to see the title. It was the plumbing volume of the fix-it-yourself encyclopedia.

"They had to pull the toilet to lay the bathroom floor," she explained. "It seems I now need something called a wax ring before I can put it back."

"Indeed."

"This may be old hat to you, buster, but I've never even heard of a wax ring."

He approached the prone toilet with a

stick, prying a nasty-looking yellow-and-black ring off the bottom of it, holding it out to her on the end of the stick. "Behold, a wax ring."

She wrinkled her nose in disgust as she came closer to look at it.

"This one's dead," he announced solemnly, laying it on the ground. "The new one will look better."

"Anywhere in town sell them, or does this mean a trip to Clovis?"

He assured her that the local hardware store carried them. She took him inside to show him the new carpet. Since there was no differentiation between kitchen, dining room, and living room in the nineteen feet of available floor space, she had chosen a high grade of kitchen carpet in a bright yellow, patterned with brown and dark green, and had covered the full length of the caboose. She made him take off his shoes before walking on it.

The kitchen cabinet sported a new bone-colored Formica top, and the bathroom floor was now covered with a tan Congoleum flecked with blue. She had not carpeted the bedrooms. They would wait until the remodeling was completed.

"I like it," Clint told her as they stood in

the bathroom. He pointed to the water heater, plugged in and in no apparent distress. "Did you also have a book on hot water heaters?"

"Well, sort of." Peggy flushed, but she was pleased with herself. She had drained it three times, and it had given her no trouble, dutifully heating each tankful without protest. She turned on the tap at the sink to demonstrate its production of clean hot water. Clint's lavish praise made her feel self-conscious.

"I've earned a college degree, and here I am making over a water heater like a silly kid," she said.

"Not at all," Clint assured her. "It's something you've never done before and you have a right to be proud. Now," he steered the conversation toward dinner as he followed her out of the bathroom, "I also have an accomplishment to be proud of, and I'd like your approval."

"What is that?"

They were back outside before he answered. "I caught five fine fish this morning, and would be most flattered if you helped me fry them."

"It sounds fantastic," she replied soberly, then smiled at his foolishness. "However, I came prepared today, and I plan to take a long swim."

He looked her over then. She was filthy, much more than fixing a hot water heater and supervising carpet layers warranted. "You cleaned out the shed," he deduced.

"Come see," she invited, pleased at his comprehension. She took his arm to lead him to the door of the shed.

The shed was a tacky structure attached to the side of the caboose, lean-to fashion. The inside was gloomy after the bright sunlight, lit by a single hanging bulb. There was no floor, no windows, and a corrugated tin roof.

"You worked out here in this heat?"

She shrugged. "It had to be done."

"Peggy! That's no kind of work for a woman!"

"It was just junk and trash. I burned most of it in the trash barrel."

Clint was upset, but her defensive tone warned him to let it go. "Any evidence of water leaking?" he asked, trying to calm down.

"I don't think so, but I think I'll put blocks under anything I store out here, and plastic over it. What I did see was evidence of mice. I need to pick up mouse poison tomorrow when I get the wax ring."

"How about a cat?"

"What?"

"A cat, you know, a mouser. We always have too many cats out at the ranch, and he could keep you company as well as take care of the mouse population."

"A cat," Peggy repeated thoughtfully. She had hoped for a dog, but there really wasn't room. "It would have to stay outside."

"They're used to that."

"I'll think about it," she promised. "Right now all I want is a refreshing swim. I've had enough of dirt and sweating and being hot to last a lifetime."

She locked up the caboose, and carried her clean clothes down to Clint's cabin, waiting outside in his porch swing while he changed and got a towel. Again they walked to the rock-rimmed cove. The water felt marvelous, washing away the filth, and leaving her pleasantly tired and refreshed. After their swim, they rested, the rocks pleasantly warm against their skin after the cool water.

Clint lay on his stomach, surreptitiously watching Peggy through half-closed lids. She was reclining back on her elbows, her face lifted toward the sun. With her hair still damp, her face void of makeup, her wet clothes clinging to her very feminine body, she could be twenty—thirty at most, he was thinking. Her skin was pale and smooth, and even the white hairs streaked through the blond added grace rather than age. As if sensing his scrutiny, she turned her head to smile down at him. Her dark blue eyes were clear and guileless, the lashes dark and wetly spiked.

"Do you fish?" he asked, feeling foolish at the way his heart reacted to her smile.

"No," she answered lazily, still smiling at him. *He really is a handsome man,* she was thinking, *and very sensual.* Sun-warmed, tanned, glowing skin stretched across the muscles of his broad back, shoulders, and arms as he lay with his head on his crossed forearms and watched her with sleepy eyes. She wished she had some oil, anything to give her an excuse to run her hands across all that warm skin.

"Would you like to? Fish," he reminded her. It was obvious she'd lost the thread of the conversation.

"Oh, I suppose." Then she shook her head. "No, not really."

"Maybe after you're settled, you'd like a boat tour. The cliffs are really something from out in the water, and it's hard to see the lake driving over the dam."

"I'd like that," she replied, feeling again the warmth in his eyes as he watched her.

They walked back to his cabin in companionable silence. Clint's cabin was built of logs with a wide covered porch on the front. The living area was dominated by a stone fireplace, the kitchen area was separated from it by an open breakfast bar. Peggy perched on a bar stool and sipped white wine while Clint deep-fried potatoes, fish, and hushpuppies. Store-bought cole slaw completed the meal.

"I thought I'd go into Clovis tomorrow and get prices on your windows," he said when he'd filled both their plates and had taken a stool beside her at the bar. "Is there anything I can pick up for you while I'm there?"

She shook her head, crunching into a fried fillet of bass. "No, thanks anyway. This is wonderful, Clint. My compliments to the cook, as well as the fisherman."

"When do the movers come?"

"Who knows? I'll be out here at dawn to await their call and give them directions."

"Excited?" It was a foolish question. Her eyes were sparkling in anticipation as she talked about it. She laughed, a delightful sound Clint thought.

"Do you realize this is my first house? I have always shared with someone, parents, husband, children. I helped my youngest, Erika, find an apartment when I sold the house out from under her." She laughed again. "She was pretty excited about her own place, too."

Suddenly Peggy's laughter changed to a wistful expression. Clint remained silent, encouraging, but not pushing.

"Do your sons live near you?" she asked, giving her attention to the cole slaw on her plate.

"Yes, in the same house, actually, with their wives and children. We built two more wings onto the main house when they got married. It gets a little crowded sometimes." Clint's expression also became wistful as he added, "And a little lonely. Maybe that's the real reason I retreat out here so often."

Peggy longed to hear more, but didn't want to pry. "Do the boys come out here often?" That seemed safe without totally changing the subject.

"When they can. There are no weekends, per se, on a ranch, so we share the responsibilities so that everyone has some time away. As you can tell," he waved a hand around the open room, "this is a fairly masculine abode. The women have always con-sidered this our retreat. They prefer to spend their free time in Albuquerque with an open expense account."

"With or without children?"

"Nursing babies go with their mothers," Clint stated firmly. "Otherwise, we take pity on them and let them go alone."

"Do your daughters-in-law get along well?"

Clint laughed at that, not answering for a minute. "They are identical twins. I'm surprised they allowed us to build them separate wings on the house." He shook his head, still chuckling, thinking about them.

"It's good to have family," Peggy stated softly. Clint sobered, studying her face. He thought he heard pain in her statement. She wouldn't look at him, so he wasn't sure.

"We depend on each other," Clint said. "I couldn't keep such a vast ranch without them."

Peggy smiled, but it was a sad smile.

"Would you like to come out Sunday, after church?" Clint invited. "We always have a huge dinner, and you could examine my previous carpentry efforts before you decide whether to hire me or not."

Sunday dinner with the family sounded a

bit too intimate to Peggy. She had just met the man, and preferred to keep their relationship neighborly for as long as possible.

"Are you going to tell me after building everything out at your ranch, you didn't build this place?"

"You've got me there," he confessed with a grin. "I built this place about fifteen years ago. Brought the boys up here to fish and swim when we could spare a couple of days. Usually had several of their friends at the same time."

"I bet you were a wonderful father."

The wistfulness was back in her voice, and Clint felt uncomfortable. He rose to clear the dishes.

"Let me do that!" Peggy jumped up. "You caught it and cooked it. The least I can do is clean it up."

"You forget this is a male kitchen," Clint remarked, opening the door of a dishwasher. "We probably have the only one of these out here."

"I can't imagine where I'd put one in that tiny caboose," Peggy agreed.

"Why the caboose? There are larger places for sale, most of them in a lot better shape."

"I love that caboose," Peggy smiled with

pride. "And it sits on the best lot overlooking the lake."

"You're right about that."

"I was told this was a retirement community," Peggy said. "Most of the cabins appear empty."

"It's probably about half retirement, half weekend cabins," Clint supplied. "The Wilsons live in that trailer closer to the lake, the one with the flower beds all around it. They asked me Sunday if I'd met you yet. They will come calling when you get settled."

"I'd feel better knowing some of my neighbors."

"You've created quite a sensation, arriving in that red van with the phoenix painted on the side. Everyone's wondering about you."

"And what do you tell them?" She smiled up at him. They were standing close together in the small kitchen.

*That you're mine,* Clint thought, letting his eyes reflect his thinking. Peggy appeared captivated as she returned his gaze. Out loud he said, "That so far the only time I've seen her, she's been covered in dirt."

His voice was husky, his eyes warm, and his mouth much too close to hers. Warning bells were sounding, and Peggy heeded them, sliding past him and out of the kitchen. "That's not very flattering," she chided him, trying to slow down her pulse.

She began to gather the damp clothes she'd swum in, rolling them into her towel. "Dinner was wonderful, Clint. Thanks again. I hate to eat and run, but I've got to be out here early in the morning."

"I'll walk you back to your van."

"It's still light out," she insisted. "I'll be fine."

He decided not to argue, but went with her out on the porch. "I'll leave the key under the mat for you. Feel free to come down here when you need to, and the movers also."

She gave him a puzzled frown, not understanding, which made him smile.

"I believe your toilet is still gracing your front lawn."

She called Megan, her middle child and oldest daughter, that night after she returned to the motel. Megan didn't seem particularly interested in her progress with the caboose, so after a few minutes Peggy asked about the boys.

"Michael has a black eye," Megan stated,

her voice accusing. "One of the other children at the day care hit him with a truck. It's a wonder he didn't lose the eye."

"Did you take him to the doctor?" Peggy asked, horrified. Michael was five, Megan's youngest.

"They didn't even call me about it. I found out when I picked him up, and it had already been four hours. They put ice on it."

"Oh, Megan," Peggy wailed. "He still needs to see a doctor."

"This wouldn't have happened if you'd been taking care of him, Mother. I told you that place wasn't safe."

Cold anger flowed through Peggy as she suddenly realized what Megan was doing. No wonder she hadn't been interested in the caboose. She couldn't wait to pounce on her mother about Michael's accident. Concern for her grandsons' welfare was Peggy's greatest weakness, and Megan used it ruthlessly.

Last summer, Peggy had told her she couldn't keep the boys while she did her student teaching. She had kept them since their births, even attending night classes when she decided to go back to school. But student teaching, done in the last year prior to graduation, had to be done during traditional school hours.

Since then, Megan had bombarded her with greatly embellished tales of abuse and neglect dealt out by the day-care centers she was now "forced" to put the boys in. The guilt had nearly given Peggy ulcers. Megan made sure she heard of every little event that happened, or could have happened, or should have happened and didn't. The boys, then six and four, hadn't needed much encouragement to join in the campaign to get Grandma back as their babysitter.

Overuse of the ploy had finally hardened Peggy to it somewhat, and anger and frustration had joined guilt. Even knowing what Megan was doing, even checking out the day care center personally on several occasions and finding it satisfactory, even knowing both boys would be in school this fall and in much less need of her care, couldn't totally free her of guilt. It was another of the reasons she'd "run away." Succumbing to the guilt and giving in was only a matter of time, so she'd moved five hundred miles away. And still Megan persisted.

"If you're dissatisfied with the day care, Megan, enroll the boys in another, or hire someone to watch them in her home." Peggy allowed Megan to hear her irritation.

"You know why I can't do that. We've been over it a thousand times."

"At least." Peggy dropped the subject. "I'll be at the caboose number from tomorrow on. The movers come tomorrow and I don't plan to return here to the motel."

"You're really enjoying all this, aren't you?" Megan accused.

Her anger made Peggy angrier. "I'm trying to, Megan," she replied evenly. There wasn't much to say to each other after that. They said goodbye and hung up.

Tomorrow was moving day. Peggy had been so excited until she talked to Megan. Now, the ghosts were back, throwing a wet blanket over the joyous day.

## Four

"There is no way, lady," the burly man announced baldly. It was noon, he'd just arrived with the moving van, and was already disgruntled after maneuvering the huge rig through the torturous gravel roads from the blacktop to the caboose. Now he stood in front of it, assessing the steep steps that led to the narrow platform and the even narrower door, his cap in the hand he was using to scratch his head.

His partner came back from walking around the place, hoping to find a wider, more accessible entrance. "This is the only entrance," he stated, "Except for the door to the screen porch. Same access into the caboose from that side, too."

Peggy chewed her lower lip in consternation. She had come too far to be thwarted by a narrow doorway. She wished Clint were here, then thrust the thought away instantly. Taking a deep breath, she allowed the movers to see how displeased she was with their negative attitude.

"I didn't move that much. Start unloading, and we'll take it one thing at a time."

Everything for the bedroom and the studio had to be put in the shed anyway, and it had an oversized door at ground level. The problem was, nothing over two feet wide would fit through the caboose door, and nothing over three feet in length would make the tight turn created by the high guard rail at the end of the platform. The doorway was further compromised by the cupola, which created a three-foot wide hallway out of the first eight feet. Temporarily at a loss for a solution, Peggy had them put the couch, her bentwood rocker, the dining room table, refrigerator, washer, and dryer all inside the screened-in porch.

When the movers drove away late that afternoon, Peggy stood in the middle of the caboose, trying to figure a way out of her dilemma. She could only see two options: smaller furniture, or widening the door into the caboose. Even a wider door didn't solve the problem of the short semienclosed platform. Now she understood the compact kitchen appliances.

The greatest disappointment was that she'd have to spend another night at the motel. She'd come out too early to purchase a wax ring for the toilet, and now it was too late. She'd also planned on sleeping on the couch until her bedroom was finished, but it was now sitting outside on the porch. Even the cardboard wardrobe boxes, which she'd planned to use as closets, were too big to bring inside, and were out in the shed.

"I will not give up!" she told the empty caboose. She went out to the shed to see what she did have. It would take some creativity, but what good was an artistic mind if not for creativity? She began to carry clothes into the caboose.

"Problems?"

"Oh, Clint!" Relief at seeing him flooded through her, then she was immediately disgusted with herself.

"I noticed the furniture on the porch. I wouldn't recommend your decorator."

"I could use a good carpenter, actually. Can you widen a door?"

He surveyed the two doors out of the caboose. "Which one? The cupola limits one and the other is surrounded by kitchen cabinets."

She sighed. "I know. I guess I go shopping for smaller furniture."

"Now, now, don't give up. Let's look at it first. By the way, I brought you a present." He handed her the box he was carrying.

"A wax ring!"

"Not as romantic as a box of candy or a diamond ring, but . . ."

He didn't finish. Peggy threw her arms around him in an enthusiastic hug, then released him before he even had a chance to return the embrace.

"I'm glad you like it," he murmured to thin air, disappointed in his slow reaction time. She was already out the door.

The toilet was back in its place in only a few minutes, and Peggy's mood was much improved.

"All that's left is something to sleep on. Do you think you could help me get the mattress inside?"

Clint frowned when he saw the twin-size mattress. "For the guest room?" he asked, hopefully.

"Nooo," Peggy drawled, suspecting the reason for his frown. "It's just me, so I brought Erika's bedroom furniture and gave her mine. At twenty-two, she's much more likely to use a double bed."

"That's too bad," Clint grumbled, not looking at her, and so missing her amused smile.

The flexible mattress made the tight turn into the caboose, but they were both laughing and out of breath by the time they got it inside.

"Time out," Clint wheezed, sitting on the floor. The dining room chairs that had made it through the door were covered in clothing. He looked around the caboose.

"Where are you going with the clothes?"

"They will go back in the cardboard wardrobe boxes the movers used, as soon as I disassemble them, bring them in, and reassemble them. That's what I was doing when you came in."

"What do you plan to do about the refrigerator?"

"Leave it on the porch, and buy a smaller one for in here, like the one we hauled out."

"How about double doors right there?" he suggested, pointing to the middle of the wall.

"They would spoil the side of the caboose, take away its authentic look."

"So does a screened-in porch and gold-

and-green carpet," Clint observed wryly. "Do you want to live here, or open a museum?"

Peggy studied the wall. Except for the cupola, there were only three windows across the front of the caboose. The back ones were obstructed by the addition.

"Or we can remove the railing on the back, widen the door, and build wider steps down to the screened-in porch."

"Hmmm. If we put the door in the center, could it be glass?"

"At least partially, or a solid door with a glass and screen storm door."

"That's a good idea."

"A good idea is supper," Clint stated, rising. "I don't have much, but I do have a can of tuna and some tomatoes. I'll tell you what I found for windows."

"That sounds wonderful."


An hour later Peggy was back in the caboose, unloading a few boxes and preparing to spend her first night in her new home. Clint had looked hurt when she rejected his offer to help, and she would have enjoyed his company, but she wanted to do this alone.

The first things she unpacked were the

stereo components. Alone, with darkness falling, the caboose was just too quiet. She arranged them on the coffee table, pushed next to the wall opposite the mattress. After ten minutes of searching, she finally found one AM radio station. She unpacked the tape player and got her tape case out of the van.

With the voice of Michael Bolton to keep her company, she unpacked and assembled lamps, found the box of linens and made up her mattress, set up the coffeemaker, and located enough bathroom supplies to allow for a shower. Wrapped in her robe, she sat on the mattress and made out an extensive shopping list, including window measurements, to use in Clovis the next day.

Finally, she turned out all the lights and tried to settle down for the night. She was tired, but sleep eluded her. The longer she lay in the strange darkness, the more nervous she became. Although she'd been alone in the motel, this was different. She'd chosen this lot because of its isolation from the other cabins. Now, she felt terribly vulnerable.

*You came here to be alone,* she reminded herself. *So—you're alone, and too old to be scared of bogey men.*

She got up and turned on a lamp.

"Baby." The spoken chastisement echoed through the empty rooms. Peggy shivered. *Okay, so we won't sleep for a while.*

She climbed the ladder up to the cupola, and sat in the seat that allowed the view of the lake. The waning moon was still bright enough to illuminate the landscape, its reflection splintered on the gently ruffled surface of the lake. She opened the window. The night air was cool and dry. Leaning against the corner, she listened to the sounds of the desert at night.

Once again, as she had on the night she'd crossed the state line, she felt the spirit of the desert healing her soul, feeding her, giving her confidence, assuring her that she belonged here. She sat there for a long time, just absorbing the sight and sound of the desert at night, letting the breeze caress her face, until she realized she was tired, and relaxed. She could sleep now.

Clovis, New Mexico wasn't Wichita, Kansas, but it was the nearest town of any size from Fort Sumner. Parts of it were quite old, and the flavor of the southwest permeated even the new areas. By lunchtime, Peggy had the van loaded to capacity and decided to take a break in the park with a boxed chicken dinner.

Two small boys played in a sandbox while their mother sat on a bench nearby. They were so near in age to Shawn and Michael, Peggy stayed to watch, a painful longing tugging at her heart. Since their births, they had been such a part of her life. Even after she'd given up taking full-time care of them, she'd seen them every day, or talked to them on the phone. Watching these boys caused a wave of homesickness.

The older boy was carefully sculpting the damp sand into a bridge for his truck to drive across. The younger one was flying a small airplane. As she watched, the younger boy flew his airplane into the older one's bridge, destroying it with all the accompanying sound effects of a diving aircraft and a loud crash. Outraged, the oldest boy punched his little brother, making him cry.

The mother ran to assist the youngest child and began scolding the older one in harsh tones, until he was also crying. Peggy couldn't bear to watch anymore. She dumped her uneaten lunch in the trash receptacle and left.

It was late afternoon when she got back to Fort Sumner. She stopped at the grocery store before driving back to the lake. Even here memories assailed her. The boys had always accompanied her to the grocery store, and she'd always kept special things for them. Now, there was no need to buy Captain Crunch cereal, Spaghettios, Kool-Aid, or Popsicles. Every aisle contained reminders of items she would no longer need to buy. She was totally depressed by the time she checked out.

Clint's truck wasn't parked beside his cabin, she noticed when she drove by, and she wondered if he'd gone home. She was as tired as she'd been on the days she'd cleaned, and was more disappointed in Clint's being away than she cared to think about. She could have used his booming optimism after the melancholy afternoon.

*You don't need a man, remember? There is plenty of work to do to keep your mind off Clinton Howell.* She carried her groceries out to the refrigerator on the screened-in porch.

"Hal-loo!" a cheery voice interrupted her, accompanied by an enthusiastic knock on the door. Without waiting for a response from Peggy, the visitor entered, negotiating the maze of furniture and boxes to the refrigerator.

"I'm Amanda Wilson. I live in the mobile just down the hill toward the lake. You must be Mrs. Thompkins. Clint has told us so much about you. I've been meaning to come up and say 'howdy,' but he insisted you've been too busy cleaning this old relic for visitors. Anyhow, I saw ya drive by when I was out walking so I thought now might be a good time. Welcome to Lake Sumner! Are you really an artist?"

Peggy had stood speechless with the refrigerator door open, wondering how long this animated woman would run on before she took a breath. There was sincere admiration in the question at the end, and Peggy smiled.

"Yes, I am—an artist that is. I'm Peggy Thompkins. It's nice to meet you."

"Wouldn't fit inside, huh?" Amanda indicated the wide, side-by-side refrigerator/freezer Peggy was loading.

"Not much of anything fit, I'm afraid," Peggy's gesture took in the porch full of furniture.

"You poor dear! What will you do?"

Peggy smiled at the distress in her visitor's voice. "Clint recommends a wide door in the center of the caboose."

"He is such a good man. A widower, you know? Three years, now." Her eyes sparkled.

"Yes, he told me." Peggy was amused at the woman's obvious matchmaking.

"Don't let me stop what you were doing," Amanda insisted. "Is there more to unload? I'd be glad to help."

"Everything else will wait." Peggy put the last of the perishable groceries into the refrigerator and stood up. "Would you like some coffee? I could certainly use a cup."

"Well . . . If you're going to make it anyway."

Amanda Wilson was a small woman, with deeply wrinkled sun-browned skin and short, straight white hair. There was a spring in her step and a sparkle in her light blue eyes that belied the evidence of age. Peggy served coffee and some store-bought cookies at the drop leaf table that divided the kitchen from the living room. Both women insisted on being addressed by their first names, and Amanda was fascinated by what Peggy planned for the cabin.

"You're so brave. If somethin' was to happen to Charlie, I don't know what I'd do. I'd hate to move to town, or in with one of the children."

"My mother and my daughter, Megan,

both thought that was exactly what I should do," Peggy shared.

"Live-in babysitter and housekeeper?"

"Of course. Actually, it was my house Megan wanted to move into, but the job was the same."

"That's so common. Not so long ago, when families stayed together, the women all worked together, sharing the duties of the household, the younger generations benefiting from the wisdom and experience of the older, the older being cared for by the younger."

"Do you really believe it was so harmonious?"

"Knowing the nature of women, especially how territorial some of them are about their kitchens, I doubt it, but theoretically, it sounds great."

"Most things do, in theory," Peggy agreed.

Amanda didn't stay long, promising to come back, and inviting Peggy to come visit her. After she left, Peggy made a quick supper of a chicken salad sandwich from canned chicken, changed into old clothes, put a Barbra Streisand tape on the stereo, and popped the top off her first can of paint. Singing along with Barbra, she applied a coat of bright yellow latex enamel to the inside of the kitchen cabinets.

Clint returned the next morning. He had gone home to collect additional clothes and some tools he would need to install the door in the caboose. He'd spent a pleasant evening with his family, but he was restless to get back. He'd stopped at the hardware store in Fort Sumner on his way through, and had carefully selected a door that allowed the most light through its frosted glass panes then a storm door with interchangeable glass and screen panels. After their talk, he was sure Peggy would be pleased.

The unmistakable sound of a skill saw could be heard when he started unloading groceries at the cabin, and he vaguely wondered who else was remodeling. It wasn't until his third trip that he was able to pinpoint where the sawing was coming from, since it was intermittent. His heart in his mouth, he took off up the hill to Peggy's at a dead run.

He saw her as soon as he topped the hill, kneeling on a two-by-four held off the ground by a kitchen chair, the skill saw in her right hand. She was lining up for another cut when he yelled her name.

The deafening whine of high-speed metal against the soft wood canceled out any chance of her hearing him, and he continued running toward her, shouting even louder. She jumped when he grabbed her arm before she could line up the next cut.

"What the hell do you think you are doing, you crazy woman?!" He grabbed the saw out of her hand, breathing hard from his adrenalin-fueled dash up the hill.

Peggy's eyes were wide with surprise through the safety glasses she was wearing. Then they narrowed and began to flash with anger.

"Give me back my saw!"

Clinton held it out of her reach. "Oh, no, not until you tell me . . . what you are trying to prove here. Do you have any idea . . . how far the nearest hospital . . . is?"

"Why? Are you having a heart attack?" She'd said it sarcastically, but the way he was gasping for air, it was a distinct possibility.

Already flushed with heat and exertion, his face grew redder at her sarcasm. "You could lose an arm or a leg using this thing!" He shook the saw for emphasis.

"I have no intention of losing anything, except a neighborhood carpenter if you don't give up that arrogant male attitude and *give me back my saw!*"

"You ever used one of these before?"

"I've been using that one for an hour now," she pointed to a pile of neatly cut four-by-four-by-two-inch blocks, "And I haven't so much as broken a fingernail!" She stood with arms akimbo and glared at him.

With the return of a normal pulse and respiration rate, Clint realized how his fear for her safety was being perceived. He carried the saw over to the steps of the caboose and sat down with it between his feet. Peggy decided to ignore him, and began to tug her box of wooden blocks toward the shed.

"Where did you learn to use the saw?"

Peggy stopped, noting the slight quiver in the voice he was trying so hard to control. He'd been genuinely frightened for her.

"It came with a detailed owner's manual." She had to smile as a groan came from behind the hands holding his head. "There's a lot of useful information in books," she persisted, her anger dissipating.

"Does experience carry any weight?"

"How can I get experience unless I do things?"

Clint groaned again. "I meant the experience of professionals."

"Of course. Who do you think wrote the book?"

Her guileless expression was too perfect, and Clint realized she was goading him. "That's twice you've scared me out of a large chunk of the precious little time I've got remaining," he scolded.

"I refuse to accept the blame for this one. I was in no danger. You jumped to false conclusions based on male prejudice."

Clint decided to change the subject. "So, what are the blocks for?"

"To put under the legs of the furniture, to keep it off the ground while it sits in the shed."

"Would you like me to slide them under while you lift?"

Peggy laughed then, and allowed him to do just that.

"How are we going to cut a door through this wall with all this furniture out here?" Clint asked. The shed was attached to the center of the side of the caboose, right where he had proposed to cut the door.

"We're not."

"What?"

"Come on, this is heavy!"

"Oh, sorry." Clint slid the blocks under the legs of the dresser. "What do you mean 'we're not?' "

"I did a lot of thinking last night. It's easier to cut a hole than patch one. I'll leave things status quo for the time being, until the bedroom and studio are finished, then I'll decide about the door."

"Oh." Clint decided not to tell her about his purchases.

"Will it be possible to add electrical outlets?"

"Where?"

"Everywhere. There are no wall plugs anywhere in the addition. If you need something electric, the plug is on the ceiling light. I'd like to run two-twenty for the dryer. I thought the bedroom would be the best place for that. And I'd like to install air-conditioning, although I'm not sure how. Then, in the studio . . ."

"What kind of books are you reading?!" Clint's mind was reeling.

"Electrical. I will confess to a slight nervousness around electrical things, so I thought maybe I'd have the wiring done before we hang the dry wall. Do you realize the entire caboose is on one breaker? I've already thrown that with the microwave oven."

"I doubt that this wiring has ever had to deal with a microwave oven. Are you soliciting my services as an electrician?"

"I guess I am."

Clint paused before answering. She was standing in the stuffy heat of a gloomy shed, smiling at him through sweat-streaked dirt. When she smiled at him like that, without her defensive guards up, he felt as helpless as a bass on a treble hook.

"Show me what you want," he conceded. He hoped Lloyd wouldn't give him too hard a time about exchanging the door.

# *Five*

"Two-twenty is just one-ten, twice," Clint explained as he instructed Peggy on which wires to attach where in the new breaker box in the hall between the bedrooms. She had insisted on learning how to do it, rather than watch him, and when he realized how closely they'd have to work for him to show her, it didn't seem like such a bad idea.

"Okay, that takes care of the dryer outlet. What do you plan for plumbing the washer?"

"I thought I'd tap into the bathroom plumbing . . ."

"You?"

"It doesn't look that hard," she informed him confidently. "I just have to cut a hole in the dividing wall and use T-connectors to tie . . ."

"Reading a book does not make you a plumber," he interrupted, somewhat sharply.

"This is all very hard for you to understand," Peggy said. "I could hire this whole project done. I could take out a mortgage and buy a nice brick house in town. I *want* to do this. I *need* to do this. I am capable of doing anything I put my mind to."

Her eyes had a faraway, defiant look. Clint had to ask, his voice quiet and unintrusive, "Who told you otherwise?"

Peggy looked at the tool in her hand then up at Clint. "Peter, my ex-husband." She gave him a wry smile. "Peter insisted I hire anything out that required manual labor, whether it was replacing a washer on a dripping faucet, or furnishing the living room. I was to hire only top-name companies, so the neighbors would see their truck at our house and know he had the means to hire only the best. It was never my house. It was never even his house." There was bitterness in her voice. "It was a monument to Peter Thompkins's success."

She glanced back at the wire strippers in her hand. "I'm complaining about what half the women in America would sell their souls to have. I must sound pretty spoiled."

"You sound frustrated," Clint said sympathetically.

"After he moved out, I no longer had the means to hire expensive workmen. When one of the grandsons got artistic on my living room wall with a magic marker, I thought, "I'm an artist with a college education. I can fix this myself." So, I did, and do you know what?" She looked at Clint expectantly.

"What?" he asked, his eyes merry with anticipation.

"I enjoyed doing it. It made me feel good." Peggy hugged her arms against herself, remembering. "Every time I looked at that wall, I felt proud of myself." She gestured with the tool in her hand, indicating the cabin. "I love this place. I feel at home here. I want to walk through it and around it and feel that pride of creation, that personal effort that makes it mine." She glanced at Clint, who was watching her intently.

"I guess I sound a little crazy."

"You're talking to a man who has either built or added onto every existing building on my ranch. No, you don't sound crazy."

His eyes were warm with approval, and something else. When he smiled at her like that, she felt warm inside, and her heart sped up, making her flush. Peggy tried to get the conversation back to plumbing.

"I had hoped to connect the kitchen plumbing to the hot water heater, also, but there doesn't seem to be an easy way to do it." She looked toward the bathroom, avoiding Clint's gaze.

"The washer won't be difficult," Clint told her, "since the bedroom and bathroom share that wall. If you want hot water at the kitchen sink, I'd recommend another water heater."

"I'll continue to boil water," Peggy decided. "I would like an air-conditioner, though. There aren't enough windows even when it's not all that hot."

"A water cooler," Clint suggested, then he smiled at her blank look. "The air is so dry here, we use water coolers instead of air conditioners. This place is small enough, you should be able to get by with just one."

"Where do I put it?"

"How about on the roof of the addition? Since it's lower than the top of the caboose, it won't show from the front. I can cut a vent hole over the doorway."

"That means cutting a hole in the side of the caboose."

"Over a hole that's already been cut.

Would you rather hang it in one of the front windows?"

"You think I'm being silly about defacing this old relic, but this caboose has a soul. I felt it the first day I saw it. A woman's soul, and I intend to do right by her."

Clint watched Peggy's blue eyes flash with the zeal of her conviction as she surveyed the area.

"How about right there?" She pointed up at the ceiling of the hallway. "It's a more central location."

All four rooms opened off the hallway, the two bedrooms, the bathroom, and the entry into the caboose. It was more a landing than a hall, since steps were required to get from the elevated floor of the caboose to the ground level floor of the addition.

"I'll look into it," Clint sighed, realizing arguing was useless.

They had started too late in the day to get much done, and Clint recommended a swim in the lake once they'd hooked the existing wiring into the new breaker box.

"It'll be a little more expensive, but I strongly recommend replacing the wiring in the caboose," he advised as they walked across the sand. "It's so old, it's a fire hazard."

"Did you know the electricity for the caboose was produced by a generator on one of the wheels? They only had electricity when the train was moving."

"You've done some research." The admiration in his voice was reflected in his eyes.

Peggy allowed herself to bask in the warmth of Clint's admiring brown eyes, in his smile. It had been a long time since someone had looked at her like that, her father, maybe, when she was a girl. Clint looked at her that way frequently, and she couldn't help but respond to it. She feared she could easily become addicted, and to more than just his approving gazes.

"When did you buy that place?" Clint interrupted her reverie.

"This summer," she answered. "I saw the ad for an art teacher shortly after Christmas, and wrote to the school board. I came for an interview over spring break and hired a realtor to show me what was available."

"I'm surprised he brought you out here. Most people consider twenty miles a bit far to commute."

"She," Peggy corrected. "And that's a strange statement from a man who lives an hour from town."

"Still, this is mostly retirement and lake housing."

"She explained that, but after two days of showing me everything Fort Sumner had to offer, and even Tiaban, she was getting a bit desperate."

"I doubt her commission off your place even covered her gasoline."

Peggy laughed. "Probably not, but the owner was certainly pleased in finally finding a buyer, so she may have finagled a larger commission out of him. I didn't buy it right away, not knowing if I had the job or not, so she had some time to work on him."

"She should have introduced you to me." Clint's voice became husky as he slid an arm around her waist. "I'd have doubled her commission and bribed the school board if I'd known."

They were standing at the edge of the water, and Peggy unconsciously licked parted, dry lips, mesmerized by the intense longing in his dark eyes, and the warmth of his hand on her waist. He was so close, and moving closer. Her heart was racing in anticipation, and panic. She slid her hands up his chest in a feeble attempt to ward him off. The intimate contact with his bare skin threatened her resolve, and in a half-hearted defensive gesture, she shoved him away. He stepped back, teetered precariously on the edge, arms flailing, then grabbed her as he fell into the lake with a yell and a loud splash.

"You did that on purpose!" she sputtered, regaining the surface. He was grinning, not even attempting to deny it. "We weren't that close to the edge!"

"Then why did you push me away?" he asked in a low, suggestive voice.

Peggy decided to ignore his interpretation of her question. The water hadn't cooled the warmth in his eyes, or in her belly. She swam toward the opposite shore with vigorous strokes.

Clint laughed, totally satisfied with her reaction. The last time a woman had shoved him away in panic had been high school. There was no doubt in his mind that she wanted him as much as he wanted her. It had been building all afternoon, and he intended to keep it building all night.

"I raided the freezer at home," he told her as they walked back toward the cabins. "I found two fillets that should be thawed enough for the grill right about now."

"After all the work you've done today, I should be feeding you."

"Let's compromise. I'll grill the steak, you provide the rest. How are you with apple pie?"

Peggy laughed. "I thought baked potatoes and salad went with steak."

"I'd rather have apple pie."

"I don't have any apples."

"I do."

"Just by coincidence, right?"

"I try to be prepared."

"Ever hear of Mrs. Smith's?"

"The widow with three teenagers that works at the courthouse? She baked . . ."

"The Mrs. Smith's pies in the freezer section."

"There's nothing frozen about that woman."

"You're hopeless." Peggy laughed and bumped him off the path with her hip.

"That's not true." He sounded insulted. "I'm quite hopeful, actually. Now, about that pie . . ."

"I surrender! I'll bake the pie."


"When does school start?" They were eating outside on Clint's picnic table. Peggy had thrown potatoes in the oven before she started the pie, then tossed a salad while it baked.

"August 15th. The teachers have two workdays before classes start on Monday. This steak is wonderful. Did you raise it?"

"Yes. It's sold under the label Clarabelle."

Peggy's fork stopped halfway to her mouth. "Clarabelle? As in organically grown, chemical free?"

"That's the one." His pride was obvious.

"You're quite famous." There was awe in her voice.

"The company is, actually. We are one of many suppliers. The company is out of Dallas."

"Still, I'm impressed."

"So was I, when I learned about them. There is a lot of money in anything organically grown, enough to offset any losses. We raise the feed also, which must be done without insecticides or chemical fertilizers. We recycle the manure."

"I'm fascinated."

"Enough to come out and see the place?"

"Well . . . in the interest of education."

"I promise it will be educational." His warm brown eyes promised more than that.

"I'd better check on the pie," Peggy said.

* * *

Peggy allowed Clint to complete the wiring by himself the next day while she finished painting the cabinets in the kitchen and bathroom, cut shelf paper, and unpacked boxes. Working inside the almost windowless caboose during the heat of August reinforced the need for the water cooler, and soon.

"I've got to go home tonight," Clint told her over dinner, a chef's salad on Peggy's screened porch. "The windows for the studio will be here Monday. I set up an account with Lloyd at the lumber yard so he could order everything you'll need and bring it all out on one truck." He sounded apologetic when he gave her the total she would owe on delivery.

"Clint," she laid her hand over his in reassurance, "I've got it. I knew remodeling would not come cheap. I've also been studying the book on dry wall. I thought if we did the walls and ceiling in the bedroom first, I can mud the joints while you're doing the windows for the studio."

"You're determined to do this, aren't you?" Clint was thinking she was more beautiful in her sloppy work shirt, a red bandana tied across her forehead, sweat band style, and paint speckles across her face than any woman he'd ever taken out on the town in high heels and makeup. As always when she discussed the remodeling, her eyes sparkled and her whole manner became animated. "Wouldn't painting the walls be satisfying enough?"

"Even you said it was more tedious than skillful," she reminded him. "It's just thin clay, and I'm no stranger to working with clay."

"Naive innocent. You'll sing a different tune soon enough. Then, the next time you see a smooth wall, you'll appreciate the dry wall profession.

"So, how will you spend your day tomorrow?" He pushed his chair back and picked up his bowl to carry it in to the kitchen. Peggy picked hers up and followed.

"Doing really exciting things. The laundry I've accumulated should take most of the morning. Then I thought I'd get the van washed."

"I bet you'll have trouble sleeping tonight, you'll be so eager to get started."

"Undoubtedly."

"You should go out to the graveyard while you're in town."

"I won't be *that* bored."

"Not the one in town," Clint explained. "The one out by the fort. It's a local tourist attraction. Billy the Kid and a couple of his cronies are buried there."

"If I have time," Peggy said vaguely.

"You were interested in local culture. Speaking of which," he grew serious, taking both her hands in his, "Would you come to church with me Sunday, then out to the ranch for dinner? I'll show you my chicken coop."

The suggestive tone at the end made Peggy laugh. "I've never had such a compelling proposition." She met his eyes then, and he saw the wariness.

"I can't, Clint. Not yet."

"Another time," he offered casually. "I wouldn't get any work done with you around, anyway."

Peggy knew his feelings were hurt, but it couldn't be helped.

"I'd better hit the road. It's an hour and a half drive from here, and I'm not packed up yet."

She walked him to the door of the screened porch. "Thanks, Clint, for all the wiring. You'd better be tallying a bill." The silence was uncomfortable. She wished there was something she could say to take that hurt accusation out of his eyes.

"I do want to see your ranch. Let me get settled first, okay?"

"There will be lots of Sundays," he agreed. "Thanks for dinner, and lunch." He held her gaze for a long moment.

Peggy held her breath.

"See you Monday." He gave her a smile and turned to start down the hill.

"See you Monday," she repeated.

"Stop by tomorrow and talk to Lloyd about that water cooler." He was already partway down the hill. "He can add it to the truck if you want."

"Thanks, I will. Good night."

"Good night."

*Thunderation! And blast!* Peggy restlessly paced inside the hot caboose, driven by frustration, as much physical as mental. *I send him every signal to keep his distance, then I'm disappointed when he does. I'm too old for these games.* She went outside. At least the air temperature was cooler.

Heat lightning played along the clouds obscuring the sunset, reflecting Peggy's mood. She decided to walk down to the beach. Maybe the exercise would clear her mind.

Not wanting to walk in front of Clint's

cabin, she took the steeper path down the other side of her cliff. It was much rockier, and soon she was too preoccupied with keeping her footing to stew about her tormented relationship with Clint. When the path, such as it was, leveled out, she was very near the cove where Clint always brought her to swim.

She sat on the warm rocks and took in the view of the lake, and the endless expanse of desolate scrub brush covered land to the north and east of it. From here, with the cabins blocked from view by the sheer rock cliffs, it resembled an oasis in the desert, manmade, but no less beautiful, or tranquil. The cove where she sat was darker than the rest of the lake, the high cliff wall casting it in shadow. She felt totally secluded, alone with nature. She wanted a closer relationship with this elusive spirit, and with a sense of touching the supernatural, she slipped out of her clothes and into the languid water.

She swam slowly, careful not to disturb the mood with noisy splashing, concentrating instead on the marvelous feel of the water caressing her skin with more intimacy than any lover. This lover was not a threat, and she gave herself up to the delicious sensations flowing over her. She dove, kicking down into the heart of the cove, thrilling to the greater pressure, the cooler temperature, the demands on her body to stay submerged. When she surfaced, she became aware of how quickly darkness had overtaken her, the distant lightning more eerie now with its contrasting brightness. A low rumble of thunder dispelled the last remnants of her sensual mood, and she shivered.

She quickly climbed out of the water and pulled her clothes over her still-wet body. It was safer to return to the caboose by the more familiar path along the beach than the steep treacherous way she'd come down. Clint should have left by now. It was totally dark before she left the beach, and Peggy was feeling a bit panicky, cursing herself for not bringing her flashlight. Each flash of lightning nudged the panic level a little higher, especially when a sudden gust of wind followed on the heels of a particularly loud rumble of thunder.

"Baby! Baby! Baby!" she chided herself, even as she broke into a run. The wind intensified, pushing her along even faster.

A blinding flash tore a scream from her throat, even as it illuminated Clint's dark cabin. Sand pelted her exposed skin and filled her open mouth as she gasped for air. She held the bandana over her face and prayed she could make the caboose before she was struck by lightning.

She made the platform of the caboose as the wind hurled the first cold drops of rain at her. She ducked inside the door to the crash of thunder that shook the illuminated ground around her. She stood gasping for breath in the middle of her living room, then realized she was in the absolute worst place in case of a tornado. Another crash of thunder shook the caboose, and she felt an overwhelming wave of homesickness wash over her.

Back home she would be surrounded by her family, reassuring the little ones that it was just a storm, secure in the knowledge that the radio and TV stations were on duty, and that the warning would be sounded the instant anything suspicious was sighted. Here, she and her caboose could be picked up and dropped in the lake tonight, and it would be Monday before Clint came back and realized it was gone, and then he wouldn't know who to contact back in Kansas. Just like Dorothy, she would be carried off on a tornado, only she would never be seen again.

It was several minutes before Peggy realized the wind had settled and the thunder was much more distant. She opened the door and went out to stand on the platform.

The clouds were well to the east now, and stars were actually visible toward the west. Thin clouds overhead scurried to catch up with the retreating storm. The breeze was cool and gentle, as if it hadn't been threatening to tear the place off its foundation only minutes ago. It hadn't even rained decently, just sprinkled, leaving a smell of wet dust in the air.

"All bluster and no show," she grumbled to the distant cloud bank. "All that wasted energy in panic, for nothing!" She propped the door open to allow the breeze to cool down the inside of the room.


The weekend passed quietly. Saturday Peggy took her laundry into Fort Sumner to the Laundromat, then stopped at the lumber yard. She met Lloyd, and he showed her water coolers and explained how they worked. They were quite simple in design, a fan blowing over water-soaked pads. She ordered one to be brought out with the rest of her order.

After leaving the lumber yard she drove

through the streets of Fort Sumner, remembering the things she'd seen when she'd come over spring break. She stopped at the bowling alley, intrigued by what she saw there. Two of the panels on the side of the building had been painted with bright murals, and a man stood on a ladder, working on a third one. Peggy parked the van and got out for a closer look.

The first panel was of Spanish conquistadors, mounted on horses in full armor, looking toward a tree-ringed lake. "Bosque Redondo Enters History, 1541," the caption read. The second panel was of a soldier in what looked like a Confederate uniform, standing guard over an Indian family cooking outside of their *wikiup*. Its caption read "Bosque Redondo Indian Reservation 1862-1868, Bad and Good Seeds are Planted." Peggy looked to the third panel that the man was working on, and found him watching her from his perch on the ladder.

"What's the Bosque Redondo?" she asked, since he'd already interrupted his work to look at her.

The artist was an older man, with white hair and a kind face. Instead of answering, he came down to stand beside her on the sidewalk, his intelligent eyes taking her in from head to toe. "You're new here," he finally stated.

"Yes," Peggy agreed. "I'm Peggy Thompkins. I've just moved here and was driving around when I saw your work. It's fascinating," she said sincerely.

"Bob Parsons," the artist introduced himself. "The Bosque Redondo is a natural oasis that became a major crossroad in a hostile country with little water, shade, or grass to feed horses or livestock. The Indians used it long before Coronado's group found it," he gestured to the first panel.

"There aren't any Indians around here?" Peggy asked, surprised.

"You may find an individual or two, but none of the tribes were from around here. They are all in the western and northern parts of the state."

Peggy studied the panel again. "What happened to the Comanche?"

"That is what the next panel is about," Bob said with a smile. "You come back when it's done." He gave her a slight bow. "It was nice to meet you, Peggy Thompkins. I hope we meet again. I always enjoy talking to people who are interested in history."

"I'm a history teacher," Peggy explained,

"and art. I will be teaching at the middle school and the high school."

"Then we have much to talk about," Bob said gallantly. "I taught history at the school here until my retirement. Good luck to you."

"Thank you. I should have guessed."

Bob turned back from his climb up his ladder. "Guessed what?"

"That you were a history teacher. You knew too many names and dates to be anything else."

Bob laughed with her and returned to painting the cowboy on the third panel. Peggy decided she'd had enough history for one day, and went home to paint the walls inside the caboose.

Sunday night Peggy called Megan and talked to the boys. She called Erika, her youngest, who always cheered her up. She called her parents, who'd spent the day with Kevin and his family. She begged for every detail of her son's family, especially about Hillary, his two-year-old daughter. When she hung up, she was too tormented to sleep.

She sat in the cupola, which had become her favorite place to think, and thought about Kevin. They had not spoken since the awful day she'd disowned him when she'd discovered him embezzling her investments. Actually, it was Kevin who refused to speak to her, blaming her for the resulting problems in his marriage.

She missed her son. She missed her daughter-in-law, Cheryl, but most of all, she missed Hillary. Just as she had with Shawn and Michael, she'd kept Hillary from her birth until last year, when she had given up care of the grandchildren to do her student teaching. Because of her fight with Kevin, she hadn't seen the child more than briefly since last Thanksgiving.

Five hundred miles away, the loss was even more acute. With a sense of "what-have-I-got-to-lose," she climbed out of the cupola and tried to call Kevin. He answered the phone, then hung up on her, just as he'd done every other time she'd called. Cursing herself as a fool, she cried herself to sleep, overwhelmed with loneliness and remorse.

## Six

Clint arrived with the truck from the lumber yard close to noon on Monday. "How do you feel about a sliding glass door into your studio?" he asked without preamble.

"A door?"

"Peggy, there is no way we can carry this stuff in through the caboose. You need another door, and since you won't cut one into the caboose, I suggest we cut one into the studio."

"I guess . . ." She looked at the loaded truck, then back at him. "You mean *now?*"

He answered her by pulling his skill saw out of his pickup. "Where would you like it?"

He followed her into the studio, and they decided to put it in the side wall, against the caboose. He pulled out his tape measure and pencil and began marking the exposed wall studs.

The lanky kid from the lumber yard was standing in the middle of the living room when she came back through, a bucket of spackling compound in one hand, a roll of tape in the other, a trail of dusty footprints on the new carpet behind him.

"Stop!" Peggy grabbed the stuff out of his hands. "Anything that can come through this way, leave on the platform, and I'll carry it the rest of the way."

He gave her a baleful stare, but she stood her ground. Finally he shrugged and went back outside. By the time the boxes of nails and other small packages were unloaded and the board lumber was stacked on the ground outside the studio, Clint had built the header for the sliding door and cut the hole in the side of the studio wall. He then helped carry the window units, bats of insulation, the plasterboard and the plywood through the new entrance.

The roofing shingles started another argument.

"I didn't order those," Peggy told the delivery boy when she saw them loaded on the truck.

The boy pulled out the inventory list and

showed her the shingles written on it, as well as several boxes of roofing nails. Peggy went to find Clint.

"Did you order shingles for the roof?"

"Yes, I did," he admitted.

"Without consulting me?"

"The addition was severely water damaged. It doesn't do any good to replace the walls and ceilings if you don't fix the roof," Clint explained.

"That's fine, but you still should have consulted me. It's my cabin, and my money."

"I did what I thought best as your carpenter. If you don't want the roof reshingled, send them back."

Peggy was irritated with his high-handed take-charge manner, and his belligerence when she tried to make him see what he'd done wrong. He was right about the roof, but he should have consulted with her. She was torn between a need to assert her authority in this situation, and the practicality of keeping the shingles. Practicality won, but her pride was a sore loser.

"I'll keep them," she conceded with exasperation. "But next time, consult with me before you make decisions about my cabin and spend my money."

Clint's own irritation over the situation was

clearly expressed in the set of his mouth and the hardness of his eyes. He didn't answer, and they were interrupted before Peggy could say anything more.

"Where do you want this water cooler?" the kid asked in an insolent tone.

"On the roof," Peggy snapped. Instead of rising to her baiting of him, the kid just shrugged and walked back to his truck. "Now, just one minute, young man," she started to chastise him. Clint intervened.

"Stand out of the way," he growled at her, then followed the kid to the truck, climbing up into the bed.

While Peggy watched and seethed indignantly, Clint directed the maneuvering of the truck until it was backed against the side of the addition. Then, with a metallic groan, the entire bed began to raise up on a scissor lift.

"Ho!" Clint yelled when it was level with the flat roof of the studio. The kid climbed up to the elevated bed, and together they carried the crated unit over and set it in the center of the roof. The shingles were also carried onto the roof.

"Come down to the cabin," Clint invited after he'd tacked plywood over the opening for the sliding door. "I brought you something."

"What?"

"Can't tell. It would spoil the surprise."

Peggy was still irritated about the shingles, but followed him. The surprise met them at the door, and he was not happy about being left alone in the strange cabin.

"A cat! Oh, Clint, is this the mouser?"

"He is."

Peggy knelt to scratch behind the ears of the huge gray tabby, all animosity forgotten. He yowled and purred, pushing against her hand demandingly. He yowled at Clint also, rubbing against his leg until he had both of their undivided attentions.

"Affectionate," Peggy commented. "Does he have a name?"

"Uh, no. Name him whatever you want to." Clint couldn't tell her what the boys called the large cat that had fathered most of the ranch kittens. Giving him to Peggy should dramatically reduce the cat population at home.

"Henry," Peggy announced. The cat regarded her through intense golden eyes and yowled again, making Peggy laugh at him. "I don't know if he's correcting me or agreeing with my choice."

"Lock him in the shed for several days with food and water, and a litter box," he added as an afterthought. "Then he'll know that's home and he should stay around."

The last remnants of Peggy's vexation with Clint dissipated as she watched Clint's strong tan fingers stroking the cat. Henry was ecstatically pressing closer, offering as much of himself for Clint's ministrations as he could manage, yowling and quivering to express his pleasure. Peggy felt a damp flush tingle through her. She shook her head to dislodge the disturbing thoughts of those fingers caressing her own quivering flesh.

"So, what's for supper?" she asked, standing up suddenly.

Clint carried Henry up the hill after supper, and Peggy found a moving box for him to fill with sand. She fed him a bowl of the food Clint had brought for him, gave him fresh water, and locked him in the shed for the night.

"We need to do the roof at first light," Clint told her as he prepared to go back to his cabin for the night. "When it gets too warm, we'll come down and do the sliding glass door. Have you read up on laying shingles?"

"No," Peggy admitted. They were standing on the back platform. Clint took her hand and held her eyes with a longing that shook her to her soles.

"I'll teach you all you need to know," he promised, his voice low and seductive.

Peggy stepped back, defensively. "I'll see you in the morning, then, bright and early."

Clint studied her silently for a long moment before answering. "Good night."

Peggy watched him descend the hill, holding the guard rail for support. She felt shaky all over.

*What is wrong with me? Why do I push him away when I want to kiss him so badly, I'm practically drooling?*

*Because, he scares me to death.*

*He cares too much. I care too much.* Peggy knew she could never give Clint her body without giving him her heart, and that would give him the power to break it. It was too soon, the old wounds too fresh, to take that risk. So, what was she to do with him?

It was so complicated. She'd come to New Mexico to simplify her life. Instead, she'd met Clinton Howell.

Henry gave her just enough time to fall asleep, then he began to protest his captivity, in loud wails that came through the caboose walls and refused to be ignored. Peggy got her robe and flashlight and went out to the shed. He ran to her as soon as she opened the door, chastising her with short, quick yowls and insistent rubs against her hands, butting them with his head and biting gently when he didn't think she was diligent enough.

"You're a mess." She smiled and shook her head. He wasn't used to being alone, and clearly didn't intend to allow her to leave him out here by himself. She picked him up and carried him inside.

Henry spent over an hour investigating the entire caboose, frequently emitting pitiful little cries as if he were lost. Each time, Peggy would call to him. He would run to her, yowling and staring at her with his intense golden eyes as if she should understand what he was saying, then resume his prowling. Peggy wasn't sure when she finally fell asleep, but Henry was curled at her feet when she woke up.

"So much for the outside cat," she muttered, stroking his sleek fur. He stretched, then rolled onto his back so she could scratch his stomach. When he'd had enough, he wrapped soft paws around her hand and gave her three quick bites, then licked where he'd bitten.

"You're a beast," she told him, grabbing his head and giving him a playful shake. He brought his hind feet into the game, giving her powerful rabbit kicks that forced her hand off him. "You're tough, aren't you?" She held his back feet with one hand and his front feet with the other. He struggled, then glared at her with a long growl of protest. She released him with a laugh. Henry stalked across the floor, his tail twitching with indignation.

"Henry already thinks he owns the place," Peggy told Clint as she held the door steady while he ran screws into the frame with a power drill. They had spent several hours on the roof, laying shingles, and were now installing the sliding glass door.

"Another male taking over your life?"

She gave him a piercing look. "Yes, it would seem so."

"I would be interested in hearing more of where this phobia of male dominance originated." He spoke lightly while inserting another screw.

"It's a long story, better left for another time." Peggy felt she'd already told him more about Peter than she'd intended, and how did she explain about Kevin? She wasn't sure she understood the situation with Kevin, herself.

"Did you divorce him?" He ran another screw in before she answered him.

"Yes, one of them."

The next screw went in crooked. Clint cursed, reversed the drill and removed it. It suddenly dawned on him how much he'd assumed about her without knowing any facts. *One of them?* That meant there had been two and she was still married to the last one.

"So, you're still married?" He tried for a casual tone and focused his attention on the door. Peggy took his drill when he twisted the head off the next screw.

"I'm not married, Clint. I've been divorced for two years now."

"Oh." He grinned sheepishly and took the drill back. "I just realized how little I know about you, although we've spent a lot of time together." They switched places and he began securing the other side of the door.

"I came out here to start fresh. I'd rather concentrate on the present and the future than the past."

"How do your kids feel about your moving?"

"Mixed. Kevin, the oldest, isn't speaking to me. Megan claims I've abandoned her, and, unfortunately, she has my mother's support on that issue."

"And the youngest, the one you sold the house out from under?"

"Erika is the one who gave me the idea."

"Interesting family." Clint ran in another screw. "There, that's done. Try it out."

Peggy slid the glass door closed, then reopened it. "Very good."

"How about lunch before we start hanging Sheetrock."

Peggy considered the doorway into the addition as she fixed and served sandwiches for their lunch. "Will anything more fit through now that we have the sliding door?"

"We can try, but the hall isn't any deeper than the platform, even though the door is wider."

"I'd just like the refrigerator inside. Not a tiny compact, but a regular refrigerator."

"A small one would fit through from the

hall. There isn't room in here for anything very big."

They were able to bring in her bentwood rocker.

"Until the mattress is out of here, that takes care of the available floor space," Clint observed, sitting in the rocker. The caboose measured twenty-seven feet in length, and seven feet in width. The cupola took up eight feet of the back, and the kitchen used six feet of the front. The pot-bellied wood-burning stove sat in the corner of the living room. Clint was right. There was no more floor space.

Clint insisted on hanging the ceiling first. The bedroom only measured eight feet by nine feet, which took four full size sheets of wall-board, and two half sheets. By the time they were hanging the last piece, Peggy began to realize why most people hired professional dry-wall installers. She gritted her teeth and forced her screaming muscles to hold the heavy sheet tight against the ceiling joists while Clint hammered in the first four nails. She helped him hammer in the rest, then sat down in the chair she'd been standing on.

"Ready to call it quits for today?" Clint

was used to this kind of work, and he was breathing hard, sweat soaking his shirt. He would have quit before now, if it had been his job, but Peggy seemed almost possessed with the need to work until she dropped. Looking down at her, he thought she was close to that point.

"We're not finished." Even as she objected, she didn't think she could get back up.

"I beg to differ with you, madame. I think we are quite finished. We can finish the room tomorrow."

Peggy nodded, then pulled herself off the chair. "How about a glass of iced tea?"

After they'd washed up, Clint filled glasses with ice while Peggy brewed tea in the coffeemaker.

"How about Chef's salad for supper," Peggy asked. "I don't think I'm up to anything much more complex." Meals together when they worked had become a routine.

"Fine with me. I'd like to go back to the cabin and clean up a bit first."

"Yes, that would be appreciated." She pulled a face at his sweaty condition, then gave him a teasing smile. She was as sweaty as he was.

"How long?" Clint rose to leave.

"I plan to soak these sore muscles for an hour."

"I'll return with the wine, in an hour."

"Wine with salad?"

"You're right. I've got a bottle of scotch."

"Yuk. I'll stick to iced tea, thank you."

As soon as Clint left, the thought of a drink while soaking in the tub sounded too good to resist. Peggy poured orange juice over peach schnapps and sipped on it through her bath, while Henry regarded her from the comfortable bed he'd made on her discarded clothes. By the time Clint returned for supper, she was feeling relaxed and mellow.

"How long is it going to take to do the walls?" she asked him after they'd eaten. He had brought the promised scotch, which he was sipping on. She had made another Fuzzy Naval.

"It will take eight full sheets, plus all the partials that have to be cut and fit. We need to be back on the roof before dawn."

Peggy groaned.

"Not sore, are you?"

"Ask me that question in the morning." She grimaced as she stretched her sore arms. "Tomorrow is the last day. The teachers have to be at school all day Thursday and Friday, so I'll only have the weekends to work on the cabin."

"What time is school out?"

"We have to stay until 4:00 when the kids are there."

"That leaves plenty of time to work. How much grading does an art teacher have?"

"I also teach history," she reminded him, acting indignant. "Besides, I have to plan ahead." She stretched her arms over her head, then winced.

"Bring me some lotion, and I'll rub some of the soreness out."

"Uh . . . no . . . I'll be fine."

"It'll help, really. Where's the lotion? In the bathroom?" Clint was already heading toward the door.

"Clint . . ."

"I don't mind. I'll be right back."

*I'll bet you don't mind,* Peggy thought, feeling the nervous trembling beginning within her, and he hadn't even touched her yet.

Clint returned with the lotion, which he applied to his hands before he took her arm, starting at the elbow and working upward with strong hard strokes, using his thumbs.

"Yeow," Peggy winced, as he hit the sore places.

"This would be more effective if you'd re-lax."

*I could relax if you'd stop stroking my arms,* Peggy thought. His hands were strong, and slightly rough, and he was near enough to assault her senses with his warmth, and the spicy scent of aftershave. What he was doing to her sore arms felt heavenly. What he was doing to the rest of her body was most unsettling.

Clint was enjoying the massage as much as Peggy, enjoying having an excuse to stand so near her, to touch her. That he was easing her pain made it all the more pleasurable. When he had rubbed the stiffness out of both arms, he moved to her shoulders.

"Ooo . . . oww." Peggy stiffened with the pain before she was able to relax again. "I didn't realize how sore I was."

"This would be more effective without the shirt."

"This is fine, thank you." She started to get up but Clint laid a restraining hand on her shoulder.

"Sit still. It was only a suggestion."

He used more lotion to massage her neck and Peggy was going to object, but moaned in appreciation instead. She laid her head back against him, and allowed him to work the upper shoulder muscles under her collar. When he was finished, he continued stroking lightly and slowly in order to maintain contact. His hands longed to explore more, but he knew she would break from him if he tried.

"You have marvelous hands." Her voice was warm and liquid. "Where did you learn to do that?"

"Working with horses, actually. I have to remember not to use so much strength on people."

"I feel wonderful, now." She stood and took his hands in hers, smiling into his eyes.

It felt so natural to fold her into his arms. He would have kissed her then, but she tucked her head into his shoulder, not giving him a chance. He savored the closeness, but when she began to pull away, he caught her face in his hand, gently forcing her to look up at him. Her eyes were a dark midnight blue in the fading light, slightly fearful. He gave her a reassuring smile before he lowered his mouth to hers. He had intended to keep the kiss soft and undemanding, but when Peggy groaned and melted into him, he forgot his resolve. He parted her lips with his tongue, and was just beginning to explore her soft mouth when she suddenly broke away from him.

"Clint, this isn't the way to maintain a working relationship."

Slightly dazed, he caught her arms before she could pull totally away. It took him a minute to think clearly enough to come up with a suitable response.

"The working relationship was just an excuse to be near you. My services aren't usually for hire."

She wouldn't look at him. "Then maybe I should find another carpenter." There was reluctance in her voice.

"Only if you're dissatisfied with my work."

"No, I'm not dissatisfied."

"Look at me." He cupped her jaw with his hand. Her eyes were sad as they met his. "I know you don't want involvement right now, when you're trying to get established and settled. Can we at least be friends, until you are ready to succumb to my charms?"

She gave him a weak smile. "I'd hate to have to find another carpenter."

"I'll try to maintain my professionalism, until this job is finished." He let the mischief shine from his eyes. "But after that, all's fair in love and war."

"Hmmm. Be careful. It could be war."

"I'll take my chances." He released her, but not before he stole another kiss.

"I'll be by in the morning and we'll finish up the roof. I'm suddenly anxious to get this project finished."


That night Peggy piled pillows against the wall and tried to read, but couldn't concentrate on the words. She looked up to find Henry regarding her from the foot of the bed, his large yellow eyes scrutinizing her soul.

"I'm being foolish, huh?" She laid the book down with a sigh. "Anyone else would grab this man up in a heartbeat, but not me. I think I have something to prove first. Well, I do!"

Henry meowed. She took it as agreement.

"He's a take charge kind of man. I'd never discover what *I* want to be, what I could be." She waited for Henry's affirmation. He gave it.

"He wouldn't be like Peter, but he would still control my life. He'd probably let me teach school, even paint, but he'd want me to live at the ranch, not here on the lake." She looked around the caboose in the lamplight. "I just got here. It isn't even finished yet."

Henry walked into her lap and began to purr. She rubbed his ears absently. "I owe it to myself to see this through. If it's meant to be, it'll survive the fulfillment of time." She turned out the lamp and slid down under the sheet. Henry lay on her chest, still purring.

"You're too heavy for that, mister." She turned to her side, dumping him off. He verbalized a protest, but settled against her. "Hmmph, some yard cat. You probably don't even know what a mouse is."

She lay awake a long time, stroking Henry's fur while he slept blissfully on.

They finished the roof the next morning, then Clint cut the hole for the water cooler and installed it, tarring around the edge to seal out rainwater. The Sheetrock was hung in a much cooler environment that afternoon. After the full sheets were hung, Clint began measuring and cutting the partial pieces to fit.

He measured the wall space, then marked

the Sheetrock, then made his cut using a Sheetrock knife. He didn't say anything specifically, but from Peggy's perspective, he was the foreman and she was the helper. Since she'd never cut plasterboard before, she allowed it for the first three cuts. When he started measuring for the fourth piece, she pointedly took *her* tape measure out of his hand.

"I think I have the hang of it now, thank you." She gave him a sweet smile, then moved him aside.

"And what do you expect me to do while you're doing that?"

"How about the same thing I was doing while you were doing this."

They both glared at each other for a minute. Clint was as puzzled as he was irritated by her high-handed manner. "I don't understand. I thought you wanted my help."

"I do want your help. I've never done this before, but I want to do it, not tote and carry while you do it."

"You want me to 'tote and carry' while you do it?"

"How would you do this if J.R. were here instead of me?"

"We'd alternate. I'd measure and cut my

piece while he hung his, then hang mine while he measured and cut his next one."

"Then that's what we'll do." Peggy stretched the tape across the wall. "This one's mine."

Clint shook his head, but didn't argue. By the end of the day, the room was finished.

"Do you want a closet in here?" he asked as they surveyed their work.

"Oh, no!" Peggy cried, dismayed. "I hadn't thought of that. There isn't room."

"Let's measure it out."

With the bed against the caboose wall, and the washer and dryer on the outside wall, there was just room for a three-foot closet in the corner. She would be able to just squeeze a small lingerie chest in between the door and the washing machine.

"There won't be enough floor showing to justify buying good carpet," Peggy complained.

"You picked it," Clint reminded her. He showed her how to tape and mud the joints, promising to build the closet when she got finished.

Peggy got a phone call from Megan that evening.

"Michael's had to stay home from pre-school the last two days with a fever," Megan announced, after the briefest preliminaries. "Of course that meant I had to miss work and stay home with him."

"Did you take him to the doctor?"

"It's thirty-five dollars, and that doesn't include any medication."

"Megan, if he's running a fever, he needs an antibiotic."

"I can't afford it, Mother. I told you I've already missed two days of work."

Peggy knew Megan was expecting her to offer to help. There was silence while Megan waited and Peggy thought. She had always helped with expenses where the grandchildren were concerned. With only a high school education, Megan didn't make much, and her ex-husband only helped when it was convenient.

The flip side was that Peggy had moved so far away in order to help Megan become less dependent on her. If Peggy helped her, now, long distance, it would establish a precedent. But Michael needed to see a doctor, and be on medication.

"Take him tomorrow, Megan," Peggy decided with an exasperated sigh. "I'll send you a check. Will one-hundred dollars cover everything?"

"Could you make it two hundred, Mom? The rent's due."

"Your rent isn't due until the first."

"I know. I didn't have it last month. The landlord's been coming around, making ugly threats."

"Megan, that was two weeks ago!"

"I know that, Mom." She sounded irritated.

"What did you do with the money?"

"Really, Mother. If you don't want to send the money, just say so. I just thought you could help us, a little." There was accusation in her voice.

Peggy sighed. It was another old argument. She didn't know why she thought moving five hundred miles away would change anything.

"I'll send you a hundred, Megan," she said tersely. "Anything else?"

"Cheryl threw Kevin out."

"What?!"

"He tried to make it sound like he was the one who left, but I doubt that. He had too much to lose."

"Where's he staying?"

"With Erika. He's sleeping on her couch. Her roommate isn't too pleased."

"Megan, what happened? I thought they were in counseling."

"They were. At least Cheryl was. She went to lunch with her boss and caught Kevin with one of his babes." Megan was obviously enjoying sharing the gossip. "He told her it was innocent, that they'd just run into each other and it didn't mean anything, but Cheryl isn't buying it this time."

The rest of the conversation was more of the same. Peggy listened numbly as Megan gloated over her brother's problems and faults. That night, Peggy sat in the cupola, looking out over the dark water, her thoughts again too disturbed for sleep.

There was no doubt in her mind that this was her fault. Every time Peggy thought about Kevin, the burden of guilt grew. If only she'd divorced Peter earlier. If only she hadn't asked Kevin to handle her stocks, tempting him beyond his endurance. If only. Every time she rehashed the events of last Thanksgiving, the "if onlies" got more creative. *Last Thanksgiving,* she thought sardonically, what a wonderful memory.

\* \* \*

Part of her divorce settlement had included some stock in Pizza Hut, a locally started company that had gone national and whose stock had paid off quite handsomely for those wise souls who'd bought in early. It still made a steady profit, and Peggy, unfamiliar with the stock market, had asked her financially proficient son to manage it for her. A year later, on Thanksgiving Day, after the big family meal, she'd asked Kevin about her profits. She needed some extra cash to buy Christmas presents. He'd looked uncomfortable and tried to talk her out of it. Suspicious, Peggy pursued the issue, and he finally told her there were no profits.

Kevin confessed that he'd sold the stocks in order to buy into a company that had a better gain. An unexpected worker's strike had suddenly caused the stock to drop in value. Now, unless she wanted to lose a great deal, he recommended sitting tight until the strike was settled and the value of the stock rose again, which he assured her it would do.

Peggy demanded to see the stock.

Kevin promised to show her the stock certificates, but they were in a safety deposit box at the bank. He managed to avoid showing them to her until Monday, when she forcefully insisted.

"What did you do with the money, Kevin?" Peggy asked when she finally had the stocks in her hand.

"I was trying to increase your profits, Mom," Kevin insisted. "You told me to use my judgment. I made a few unwise decisions."

"I agree, but I don't think all of them had to do with stock options." Kevin's eyes narrowed in anger, but Peggy stood her ground. "I've looked into a number of things since Thursday, Kevin. You must think your mother is really stupid."

Kevin didn't answer that, which Peggy took as affirmation. The realization made her ill. "You're a full-time student, Kevin, living off your wife's income, paying rent and raising a baby. You drive a new Porsche, wear expensive clothes, and have been seen around town with several women."

"Spying on me, Mother?" Kevin's voice was cold.

"You're not very discreet, Kevin. The first couple of times people told me they'd seen you out with women other than Cheryl, I tried to shrug it off as circumstantial, and probably innocent. But it's not, is it?"

Kevin shrugged, as if it was irrelevant. "I told Cheryl I didn't want any kids until I was out of school, but she got pregnant anyway. Then she got fat. She never has time for me, so I found someone who did."

"That's so gallant of you," his mother said sarcastically. "Who do you think got Cheryl pregnant?"

"I don't live at home anymore, Mother. I don't have to answer to you."

"You are using my money."

"Dad bought the Porsche."

"Your father is supporting two households right now. I questioned that story the first time I heard it. A newly divorced and remarried man does not buy his son a Porsche."

"It's Dad's money," Kevin stated angrily. "You never worked a day of your life. Dad invested . . ."

He never finished. Peggy slapped her son so hard he staggered. She was furious.

"I stayed with your father for your sake. For some reason, I thought a son needed a father. I was wrong. You're just like him, and I divorced him. From now on, you need something, you go to him!" She had taken her remaining stocks, and walked out of the bank. They hadn't spoken since.

Peggy rarely lost her temper, and even more rarely with the children. She had tried to talk to Kevin on several occasions since then, wanting to apologize, but he ignored her, or hung up. Cheryl had threatened him with divorce immediately after that, and only his promise to seek counseling had deterred her. Kevin characteristically blamed his mother for his domestic problems. Cheryl hadn't known anything until Peggy had made a big deal over the stocks. Knowing Cheryl, and from experience, Peggy doubted that, but Kevin had believed it, and kept Hillary, his daughter, away from Peggy in retaliation.

*Cheryl is smarter than I was,* Peggy thought, but her heart went out to her daughter-in-law. She remembered her own pain the first time she'd learned of Peter stepping out on her, and the second, and the third. She wasn't sure when it had quit hurting, when the defensive shell had gotten thick enough that Peter could no longer hurt her.

But there had been no shell against Kevin, and his betrayal had done what she hadn't allowed his father to do. He had broken her heart. Hot tears coursed down her face. If only she'd been more understanding, instead of losing her temper. Now she was going to cry herself to sleep again.

And tomorrow was the first day of school.

# Seven

Peggy had written out her teaching plans over the summer, and sent Clark Graham, the principal, her list of needed supplies. Now she stood in her art room, surrounded by boxes and empty shelves. She'd never set up an art room before, only worked in ones set up by others.

"Overwhelming, huh?"

Peggy turned toward the door and was greeted by a dark-haired woman near her own age.

"Violet Adams. I teach English and history. I hear you're also teaching some history."

"Peggy Thompkins. Yes, two periods. Seventh and eighth grade—New Mexico and American, respectively."

"Good luck. It's a tough crowd."

"History always is. I hated it myself at that age."

"Me, too," Violet agreed. "We always go out for lunch on work days. I wanted to extend a personal invitation. You can meet the rest of the group then."

"Thank you."

After Violet left, Peggy began unloading boxes and grouping supplies. She made a list as she went of things she still needed. The hallway was filled with empty boxes when Violet came by to take her to lunch. They walked the short distance to the Mexican restaurant, where the rest of the group was gathering.

"That must be your van I saw in the parking lot," Ed Cowen, the football coach and physical education teacher commented when Violet introduced him to Peggy. "Only an artist would drive a red van with a phoenix painted on the side."

"Yes," Peggy agreed, "that's my van."

"Did you paint the phoenix?"

"Yes."

"It's very good. Ever consider painting vans as a sideline?"

"Thank you. Yes, I did a few others after I did mine."

"Are you married, Peggy?" The question

came from Joe Cunningham, the basketball coach, who doubled as the science teacher.

"Divorced. Yourself?"

He met her level gaze with a self-confident grin. "The same."

Peggy didn't think Joe looked old enough to be flirting with a grandmother. You never knew about men, though.

"Clark tells us you hale from Kansas." The speaker was young, with frizzy brown hair. Peggy wondered if this was her first year of teaching also.

"Yes, from Wichita, and I hate Toto jokes."

"You shouldn't have said that," Violet warned her. "You'll never hear the end of them now."

Lunch was lively, and Peggy tried to get names and faces together. Fort Sumner was a small school, and most of the teachers taught more than one subject, or taught classes at both the middle and the high schools, which sat side by side.

Back in the art room, Peggy worked diligently through the afternoon, but wasn't finished when Violet stopped by at three o'clock.

"Setting up a room the first time is always the hardest. Next year will be a lot easier."

"I haven't even started on the history stuff," Peggy moaned.

"That won't take but a couple of hours," Violet assured her. "Have you reviewed the books you're using?"

"Yes, Clark sent them to me so I could do my lesson plans this summer."

"So, what's first in here?"

"Clay pots. They are fairly simple, or can be elaborate, while I get to know the kids and where their interests and previous exposures lie."

Violet perched on a desktop while Peggy worked, asking her about where she was living and her family.

"You just graduated?"

"Yes." Peggy smiled at Violet's incredulous expression. "I quit college when I got married, and started back when Erika, my youngest, started college. I took night classes, part-time, so I could watch my grandchildren during the day. Erika and I both graduated in May."

"So you've never taught school before?"

"I've never worked outside the home before," Peggy said with a laugh. "Except for my art, which was mostly a hobby."

"Wow." Violet looked thoughtful for a few minutes. "I keep wondering if that would have made a difference."

"What made a difference?"

"Not working. Being a full-time wife." Violet's eyes looked troubled as she looked up. "My husband and I are separated right now. I'm still trying to understand what went wrong."

"Oh, I'm so sorry."

"Yeah, me, too. How long have you been divorced?"

"Two years."

Violet sighed. "Two years. Does it get easier?"

Peggy thought about her answer for a minute. "Yes, and no. I still don't like being 'divorced.' I feel like 'failure' is stamped on my forehead sometimes, or 'quitter.' How long have you been separated?"

"Since June," Violet supplied.

"You're still in the 'guilt' phase," Peggy told her.

"What's after that?"

"For me, it was anger, at my husband. I began to despise the man, tearing him to pieces in my mind and dwelling on his every flaw. It was easier to deal with it all being *his* fault, with me the innocent victim."

"I like that idea, too." Violet finally smiled. "And now?"

"It doesn't say much for my intelligence if I married a total cad, bore him three children, and lived with him for twenty-seven years. I'm slowly trying to forgive both of us our faults, and realize few things in life are black and white."

"Any regrets?" Violet's eyes matched her name, and they probed Peggy's for the truth to her question.

"Sometimes," Peggy answered slowly, meeting her gaze. "I regret waiting so long to do it." Peggy considered the woman before her, debating how much to share. Violet seemed truly confused, seeking guidance from one who'd been there. Peggy took a deep breath before sharing the rest.

"Peter was unfaithful," Peggy stated flatly, not looking at Violet. "I think the reason for the divorce has a lot to do with whether it's regretted or not." She met Violet's gaze then, and saw understanding. A shrill bell sounded through the building.

"School's out," Violet announced, sliding off the desk. She walked over to Peggy and took her hand. "Thanks. What you've said means more to me than you know."

Peggy gave her hand a squeeze. "People who haven't gone through it don't really understand. I didn't. Staying in an unpleasant marriage made me very critical of those cowards who 'threw in the towel' so to speak. Now I realize I was the coward, staying married out of fear of standing alone."

"Thanks, Peggy. I'll see you tomorrow."

"Will they lock me in the building if I stay?"

"No, you can always get out. You just can't get back in."

"That sounds profoundly philosophical."


It was after six when Peggy pulled the van up to the caboose, bone weary, but feeling like she'd made some headway with the art room. She headed straight to the bathroom, visions of a long soak in scented bath oil uppermost in her mind. Henry met her at the door, and filled her ear with feline protestations and general chatter as he met her step for step, finally tripping her up the steps back to the kitchen.

"Henry!" she screamed, sitting on the

steps and rubbing her bruised shin. "You're driving me crazy!"

A knock on the door interrupted. It was Clint, and he was wearing a most disgruntled expression.

"Where have you been?" he started without amenities. "You said you only had to stay until three-thirty, and it's after six. I thought you wanted to finish taping the bedroom."

Peggy blinked in disbelief, listening to him fuss at her as if she'd stayed out too late on a date. Her eyes narrowed and she gave it right back to him.

"I don't have to answer to you, Mr. Howell. You are my carpenter, not my father. I do not remember making any set plans about when we would finish the bedroom." She held her body rigid, fighting an urge to say more.

"Well, excuse me," Clint drawled sarcastically. "I guess I wasted my day hanging around here for nothing. I do have other things I could be doing, you know."

"Then do them!"

"I will!"

Clint turned and walked back toward his cabin, his back stiff. *Damn the woman! He'd waited around here all day . . . for what?*

*"You're my carpenter not my father,"* he mimicked in his mind. *Carpenter, huh! She could just find another carpenter!*

Clint's black mood continued while he loaded the pickup to go home. There was work to do at the ranch he'd neglected shamefully while he'd been hanging around the lake, acting like a besotted teenager. He'd never allowed the boys to get away with it, when they were dating.

Madame Independence could just stew in her unfinished cabin and enjoy her precious freedom as long as she wanted. Clinton Howell was going home, and would start acting like the mature, responsible, fifty-three-year-old he had been two weeks ago, before a red van with a fiery phoenix on its side passed in front of his cabin.

Stewing was an apt description of Peggy, sitting in her bathtub, too angry to relax. She'd known he was the possessive type. He'd descended on her life with the force of a Kansas twister, and now she had to deal with the aftermath. She should never have agreed to him being her carpenter. She should have hired a stranger and kept the relationship strictly professional.

145

*I did hire a stranger,* she thought ruefully. *I just failed to keep it professional.*

She dressed in a robe and prowled through the unfinished bedroom and studio. The two rooms did closely resemble the aftermath of a tornado. They hadn't been specific about when they would work again. She had mentioned that she would be able to leave the school by three-thirty, and she had indicated often enough how anxious she was to finish as soon as possible. She wondered which one of them she was defending.

An hour and a half of driving with only his thoughts for company cooled Clint's ire somewhat.

*Maybe I was a little harsh. I didn't even give her a chance to explain. Maybe she had trouble with the van. Maybe there was a meeting at the school she couldn't get out of. She opened the door, and I jumped all over her, just like an irate father.*

*Way to go. Made a lasting impression today, yes, siree. Great strategy, hound dog. That vixen won't resurface before Halloween.*

Clint's mood was most foul by the time he pulled up in front of the house at the ranch, greeted by a bevy of barking dogs.

* * *

Friday Peggy worked steadily, trying not to dwell on Clint. She'd been disappointed, but not surprised, when his pickup wasn't parked in front of his cabin that morning. She went to lunch with the other teachers and deliberately tried to learn as much about them as she could, hoping an occupied mind wouldn't have room for other thoughts.

Violet made sure she met the other two single male teachers. Howard Kendall was in his middle forties, divorced, and taught math at both schools. Mark Forrester was in his early thirties, recently widowed, and taught industrial arts, among other things. Although much younger than Joe, whom she'd met yesterday, or Howard, Mark looked like he'd be the most fun to date.

*He could be your son,* Peggy reminded herself. She really didn't want to date anyone. But of the men she'd dated back in Kansas, the ones younger than herself had usually been more fun than the ones her age.

Until Clint.

She gave Mark her brightest smile and asked him how long he'd been teaching, as if she really cared.

* * *

Peggy had already started taping Sheetrock joints when Clint knocked at her door Saturday morning. Neither one of them said anything for a few uncomfortable seconds. Finally, Clint cleared his throat.

"I probably should have called first, but I can get those windows installed today, if that's okay with your schedule."

*So much for an apology,* Peggy thought, slightly miffed. She hadn't slept much for the fourth night running because of this man. She'd been afraid he wouldn't return to finish the job and she'd be forced to find another carpenter—at least that was the excuse she felt the most comfortable with. She stood back to allow him to enter, but he remained on the platform.

"I brought Justin with me. If you'll open the sliding door to the studio, we'll bring our tools in that way."

Peggy didn't know what to make of such stiff formality. She let them in through the other door.

"I'll be in the bedroom, if you need anything," she told them, and returned to taping her joints.

At noon, she made sandwiches and iced tea, then entered the studio to invite them to take a lunch break. Although she'd heard the sawing and hammering, she was amazed at the transformation. Three of the large windows were installed already, and they were working on the fourth. Brilliant sunlight flooded the room.

"It's fabulous!" She forgot her irritation with Clint as she admired the windows, their sashes raised to catch whatever cooling breeze was available.

"Makes quite a difference," Clint agreed, coming to stand beside her. "We'll be finished by this afternoon. We can build that closet today, too, if that's okay."

The way he said it reminded her of their formal status, and she allowed her irritation to show on her face. "That would be fine, but it can wait if you have other things to do."

"I'd like to get this finished."

"Yes, of course. I made lunch, if you're ready to take a break." Not waiting for an answer, she turned and left the room.

Peggy made herself a plate of a sandwich and chips, and took it and her glass of tea into the bedroom with her. She perched on the end of one of the sawhorses, vexed with

Clint for keeping up the stiff formality, vexed with herself for allowing it. Not only that, but she was having some trouble with the tape, and there was no way she'd ask his advice in the present situation.

"Not even going to eat with us?" Clint stood in the doorway, watching her somewhat warily.

"It wouldn't be professional." It was a churlish thing to say, but she couldn't seem to help it.

"I acted like a jackass the other evening."

"Yes."

"Yes? That's it?"

"You made a statement. I agreed with it."

"It was an apology!"

"I must have missed something, then."

"You weren't entirely without fault in this, you know."

"Is that also an apology?" Peggy was trying hard not to smile. His attitude was contrite, but he seemed to be having difficulty with the words. She gathered he didn't do this very often, which didn't displease her. Peter had apologized so often, and with such fluency and insincerity, she would have been more dismayed to discover the same trait in Clint.

"I was worried something had happened to you."

His voice was a growl, and he was glowering at her for making him do this. Peggy was tempted to take pity on him and let him off the hook, but didn't. He needed to understand that he didn't have any claims on her. Letting him off easy now would encourage more of the same, she was certain. She waited, a smile pulling at the corners of her mouth.

"I'm sorry I yelled at you," he stated, the words sounding forced.

The attitude was lacking now, but the words were right, Peggy thought. The least she could do was meet him halfway. "I'm sorry I gave you the impression that we'd work after I got home from school. I didn't even think about it. There was so much to do with the classroom and . . ."

She stopped, frowning at herself. She hadn't meant to justify her actions to him. She didn't have to. The apology should have sufficed.

He smiled at her, and offered his hand. "Friends, again?"

She accepted the hand and smiled back. "Friends."

"For now," he added softly, his eyes darkening. He brushed the Sheetrock dust off her cheek.

Peggy felt the thrill of his touch go through her, and she took a defensive step back. "Have you eaten?"

"No. Come join us. It doesn't feel right, eating at your table without you."

"I'm having some trouble with the tape," she told him, sitting down in the chair he held out for her. "I can't seem to do the corners without wrinkles."

"I'll look at it, after lunch," Clint promised.

He did, and showed her how to cut the tape and apply the mud to make a smooth corner.

"Hang a busy wallpaper, one without any lines in it, and no one will ever notice the flaws."

"Thanks a lot," she grumbled. She took the tool from him and waited for him to leave before she would do the next corner.

"I think I'll go help Justin finish the windows," Clint said as he left, his sigh of long-suffering dramatically loud.

Sunday, with three of them working, the Sheetrock in the studio was hung much quicker than the bedroom. Peggy did all the cuts around the windows, letting the men handle the heavy full-size sheets. She did help them with the ceiling. Clint told her he'd help her cut the trim after she finished the walls.

"You're sure you want to do this yourself?" he asked, meaning taping all the joints.

"I consider it a challenge. It's fun. Really." He didn't look convinced. "If I do a poor job, I'll take your advice and hang busy wallpaper."

"Does your know-it-all book tell you to sand the joints between layers, or wipe them?"

"Sand. I bought lots of sandpaper and a little rubber sander," she told him proudly.

"A damp sponge works as well, and isn't as messy. Try it both ways and see which one you prefer."

"How does a damp sponge work?"

"Joint compound is water soluble. Don't use too much water, though, or you'll wash it all off and have to start over."

"I'll try it," Peggy agreed. "Did you figure out your bill?"

"No," Clint said shortly. "Don't worry about it."

"Clint, please. You've done a lot of work."

"I didn't do it for the money."

"I'm not comfortable with that. Let me pay you, and let's start with a clean slate, no debts, either real or imagined."

"I'll have to think about it. I don't know what the going rate is for carpenters."

"I figured your time. You spent twelve hours as an electrician and forty as a carpenter."

"Four hundred dollars then," he conceded, clearly irritated.

"That's not even ten dollars an hour," Peggy protested. "That doesn't even include your driving time from the ranch and the shopping you did." She got her purse and sat down with the checkbook, writing him a check for an even thousand.

"Peggy, I really don't want that. You're making me uncomfortable." She was making him feel like a gigolo, paying him for something he'd done as much for himself as for her.

"Give it to your daughters-in-law for their next shopping trip. Give it to the church. Invest it for the grandchildren, but please take it."

Clint took it and silently stuffed it in his back pocket. He was really losing patience with her self-sufficient attitude. With luck, it would still be in his pocket when he did laundry. Peggy seemed to read his mind.

"If you don't cash it, I'll deposit it in your account."

"Okay! Can we drop this now?"

"Sure," Peggy purred. "Let the games begin."

"What games?" Clint demanded suspiciously.

"The one you wanted to play as soon as the job was finished." She flashed him her most alluring smile.

Clint's irritation evaporated. "Would you be free for dinner tonight?"

"Yes."

"I'll pick you up in an hour. Dress casual."

Clint knocked on the door exactly one hour later. He carried a picnic basket and a blanket. He handed her the blanket, then offered his arm.

"Shall we go?"

"I don't know. Is it safe?" She eyed the blanket suspiciously, then the basket.

"Hot dogs," he supplied. "How does a wiener roast on the beach sound?"

*Dangerous,* she thought, but out loud she answered, "Nostalgic. I don't think I've done that since Erika outgrew Girl Scouts."

They walked down to the beach and found a suitable location. Clint left Peggy to spread the blanket while he went to gather driftwood. As twilight gathered over the water, they roasted hot dogs over a small cozy campfire.

"How is it that a man who makes his living raising organic beef eats hot dogs?" Peggy asked, licking mustard off her fingers.

"How do you know these aren't organic hot dogs?" Clint's attention was focused on her tongue.

"They taste good." Peggy was busy with her hot dog and oblivious to Clint's attention.

"Well, I didn't say I was a disciple, only a supplier."

"I hope there're marshmallows for dessert."

Clint reached in the basket and pulled out a bag. "Let me guess, you are the type of person who will spend ten minutes toasting a marshmallow until it is perfectly browned on the outside, and all melted on the inside."

"How did you know?" Peggy threaded two of them on her long fork.

"You're the patient, deliberate type."

"And how do *you* toast a marshmallow?"

Clint took his fork and skewered a marshmallow, stuck it near the coals where it caught fire, blew it out, and ate it.

"It figures." Peggy laughed at him. "The impatient type."

"A man of action," Clint corrected.

"Some things are better for the waiting." She pulled a delicately toasted marshmallow off her fork and held it before his mouth. He held her wrist, slowly taking her fingers along with the marshmallow.

"You're right," he agreed, his voice husky. He continued to suck the sticky candy off her fingers.

His hand was strong around her wrist, his mouth warm and wet, his tongue sending delicious shivers through her fingers. His eyes held hers, dark with longing and promise. She felt like a virgin, being awakened for the first time. Her response was painfully intense. A moan escaped her, shocking her, and she jerked her hand back.

She was trembling, and tried to cover it by reloading the basket. Clint sighed, then stayed her hands with his own, waiting until she looked at him.

"I don't want to play games with you. It's too important to me."

"I can't, Clint." Her voice was barely audible and filled with anguish.

"I can respect that, but tell me why. Is it me, or does it have to do with your ex-husband?"

"It's me, Clint. I can't deal with that kind of commitment right now."

"I'm not asking for commitment."

"Yes, you are."

She said it softly, holding his eyes with hers. She could see the pain in them, then felt it as he released her hands and sat back on his heels. He looked out over the dark lake.

"You're right. I have wanted to claim you as mine since you arrived, and you've fought against me every step of the way. Is there someone else you're looking for?"

"Yes," she answered softly. The pain on his face pierced her heart as he swung his gaze back to her. "Myself, Clint. I came here to find myself. I'm forty-nine years old and I don't know who I am, only who I'm part of. If I become part of you, I'll never find out."

He relaxed and laid his hand against her cheek. "It's very important to you, isn't it?"

"Yes."

"Can I help?"

"You already have, being my friend and treating me so special." *Reminding me I'm still a woman,* she thought, not saying it but wondering if he could see it in her eyes.

"I don't want to be your friend," he said, his voice husky. "I want much more than that, but I'll try." He gave her a little rueful smile. "You won't hold it against me if I try a little harder, occasionally?"

"I suppose I'd worry if you didn't," Peggy answered, returning his smile.

They gathered up the food and the blanket, covered the fire with sand and doused it with water from the lake, then walked silently back up the hill to Peggy's cabin.

"Does this search for self involve dating other men?" He couldn't help it. He knew it sounded jealous and possessive, but he had to know.

"If I want to," Peggy stated evenly. "Meeting new people is part of a new job and a new town."

"I see," Clint said tightly. "Well, you'll be in school all week, and I'm going to be busy with the fair. I'll call you."

He sounded so stiffly formal, and she knew he wasn't pleased, but it couldn't be helped. She resented his making her feel guilty.

"I really enjoyed dinner," she told him, her voice cajoling.

"Would you like to go to the fair?" Clint asked suddenly. "I'm judging the calves, but I will be free after that. It's a major function in Fort Sumner. They even let school out on Friday for it."

"I'd better work on the addition," Peggy said, sincerely regretful. "I doubt if I'll get much done this week."

"Dinner then? Saturday night?"

"Okay."

"Until Saturday."

Clint gave in to instinct, pouncing on her suddenly and crushing her against him, his mouth hard on hers, his tongue seeking hers before she had a chance to object. He felt her yield to him, clutching his shoulders for support. He bent her backward over his arm, ravishing her mouth completely before he straightened and released her. She didn't seem very steady, and grabbed the hand rail for support.

"Think of me this week," he said, still standing very near and speaking low. She looked quite dazed. He gave her a last quick kiss, flashed her a smile, and turned to walk back down the hill to his own cabin.

Peggy sat down on the step, trembling from head to toe, her brain foggy with the rush of blood from a painfully accelerated heartbeat. She could hear a distant whistling sound, and knew Clint was feeling as smug as she was rattled. She felt bereft, wishing he'd come back and kiss her again. The trembling increased with the realization that, if he hadn't stopped, she probably wouldn't have stopped him.

*It's definitely time to date other men,* she decided, clutching the railing for support as she rose to go inside. *We need some perspective here.*

# *Eight*

Peggy spent the first four school days trying to learn students' names and interests. While they made coiled clay pots, Peggy talked with each of them. As she had expected, some were quite talented, and some were in there for an easy A. She was pleased with the small class sizes. After student teaching in a classroom of thirty, a classroom with twelve students for art was a gift from heaven. Even her New Mexico history class, which contained the entire eighth grade, only had twenty-four students.

She and Violet shared the same planning period, over lunch in the teacher's lounge. Violet found her there on the third day, frowning over a drawing she was holding.

"Hey, Peggy. What's up?" Violet asked, sliding into a chair with her lunch tray.

"How's your child psychology?" Peggy

held up an incredibly detailed pencil drawing of a man hanging from a noose, his face a gruesome death mask, a vivid line of red ink denoting blood trickling from the corner of his mouth.

"Jack Henning, right?" Violet guessed.

"You know this kid?"

"A fabulous artist, don't you think?"

"Yes, but . . . the subject matter."

"Everything Jack draws has to do with death, violence, and blood," Violet supplied. "He prefers to work with pencil, always using red for the blood against the black and white of the picture."

"Is he violent, or suicidal?" Peggy asked, a little nervously.

"I'm not sure," Violet sighed. "His daddy used to beat him for the least infraction, until he got big enough to hit back. His mama is scared of her own shadow. He doesn't have a very high opinion of himself and doesn't seem to have any friends. He's actually quite bright, when he applies himself, which unfortunately, isn't too often."

"I met him before school started, but I didn't know his name. He brought the stuff out from the lumber yard, and his insolent attitude made me want to slap him."

"That's Jack. How're the other students?"

"What can you tell me about this one?" Peggy held up another drawing. It was of a stick man.

Violet smiled knowingly, and started on her lunch. "Jesus Estavez, right?" She pronounced it *Hey-zeus*.

"You got the Estavez part right, but his name is Jesus. What's his story? What kind of name is that for a kid, anyway?"

"It's pronounced *Hey-zeus* in Spanish. This area is heavily populated with Spanish Catholics, and they take their religion seriously," she said, answering the last question first. "Jesus is testing you with that picture. He's a very popular student, and was probably showing off for his friends. He's a good kid, just a little too full of himself right now."

"He's not the only one."

"Welcome to Middle School."

"One more." Peggy held up a very childish drawing of a house with a family standing in the front yard.

Violet frowned thoughtfully. "What grade?"

"Eighth."

"Jessica Morgan?"

"Wrong."

"Billy Ellis."

Peggy expressed begrudged admiration. "How long have you worked here, anyway?" She laid the drawing aside, picked up her fork, gave a disgusted grunt at the food on her tray, and started with the salad.

"Forever, it seems. I remember when some of them were born."

"Tell me about Billy. Even on the first day of school he wore outgrown, dirty clothes, and I don't think he's taken a bath since then."

"He's a sad one," Violet admitted with a sigh. "His mama is somewhat notorious around here. She divorced his daddy when he was three to marry a playboy from Santa Fe. When that didn't work out, she came back here with him and married Pete Sanders. He owns Pete's Place—you know, across from the hardware store? It's mostly a bar but he serves food. Anyway, she split about three years back, left Billy with Pete. He tries to do right by the boy, but with the business, he isn't home in the evenings. Billy helps some at the bar, but mostly he's left on his own."

"How awful!" Peggy's heart went out to the boy. She set her tray aside, most of her lunch uneaten.

"Is that all you're going to eat?" Violet asked.

"I'm trying to lose weight. It's pointless to eat what I don't want."

"Huh, I wish I had your weight problem." Violet was a little shorter than Peggy and somewhat heavier.

"Twenty pounds," Peggy told her, "then I'll be back to what I weighed before the grandkids came."

"I thought you had to have the baby to gain weight. How does being a grandmother . . ."

"I cooked three meals a day, plus two snacks."

"Oh." Violet finished her lunch, then got up to pour herself a cup of coffee. "Want one?"

"Yes, thanks."

"So," she sat the cup in front of Peggy, sat back down, and leaned close. "Joe asked you out yet?"

"Joe?"

"The science teacher. He hits on every single woman who comes within a hundred-mile radius of this place."

"No, he hasn't." Peggy frowned at the idea.

"He's probably too busy with the fair right now. He will, though. You gonna go?"

"I don't know. He hasn't asked yet."

"I meant to the fair."

"I've thought about it," Peggy said. "Listening to the kids, it sounds like a lot of them have exhibits."

"It's a big deal around here. We could meet at my house and go together," Violet offered.

"I probably shouldn't. I've got so much still to do to the cabin, and I'm not making much progress, working after school. Besides, I already turned Clint down, and . . ."

"Clint Howell?" Violet looked incredulous. Peggy frowned at her response. "Yes. Why?"

"You don't waste any time, do you?"

"I met him out at the lake. His cabin is just below mine. What do you know about him?"

Violet's eyes sparkled as she regarded her friend. "He's just *the* most eligible bachelor in the state. Every widowed and divorced woman in three counties has thrown herself at that man."

"Including you?"

"I'm not divorced," Violet reminded her.

Peggy felt an overwhelming need to escape the closed-in lounge. She stood up and gathered her drawings hastily, knocking over her coffee cup and dropping some of the drawings. Violet grabbed some paper towels and helped her clean up the spill, then handed her the drawings from the floor.

"He has that effect on women," she said in a low, knowing voice.

"Who does?" Peggy silently cursed the tremor in her voice.

"You don't fool me, Peggy Thomkins. If you're gonna go, go for the gold, I always say."

"The only place I'm going is back to the art room."

Violet's laughter followed her out the door.

Peggy took her frustration out on the Sheetrock dope that evening, Henry at her feet, a willing confidant. She had put a jazz tape on, and turned the volume up, but it wasn't doing the job of blocking out her thoughts.

"I really know nothing about the man, except what he's told me. Violet makes him sound like the De Baca County Playboy. No, that isn't exactly true. More like the Prize Bull."

She was aggressively sponging down the joints she'd applied mud to the night before.

It had only taken one joint to convince her that sponging was vastly preferable to sanding. Her next swipe exposed tape. She'd washed off all the mud, instead of just smoothing it.

"Oh, blast it all!" She threw the sponge into the bucket of water, splashing Henry. He darted into the corner and began licking his wet fur indignantly.

"Hal-loo! Anyone home?"

Peggy turned to see Amanda Wilson standing in the doorway.

"I knocked, but figured you couldn't hear me over the stereo. Look at what you've done in here!" Amanda came into the room and admired the walls.

Peggy dried her hands on a towel. "Your timing is perfect. I need a break."

"How's the studio coming?"

Peggy took her into the studio, switching on the light that dangled from a wire in the ceiling.

"Very nice," Amanda gushed. "Clint install the windows?"

"Yes," Peggy answered, her voice tight.

"He does such a good job, don't you think?"

"He's an excellent carpenter." Peggy went

into the caboose and turned down the stereo. "How about a cup of tea?"

"Do you have decaffeinated?"

"Yes." Peggy turned the burner on under the kettle. "Amanda, tell me about Clint. Did you know his wife?"

"Oh, yes. I worked with her frequently on church committees. Such a sweet woman. Her name was Eileen, and she adored Clint and those boys. They took her death real hard."

"Was it sudden?"

"Less than a year after she was diagnosed. Lung cancer. They all smoked. Clint quit with her, and offered the boys a thousand dollars each if they'd quit."

"How long ago did she die?"

"Three years this spring."

Peggy fixed the tea and sat down at the table across from her. "So, is he looking for a new wife?"

"You interested in applying?" Amanda laughed at her question. "Join the line, honey!"

Peggy tried to smile. "No, I was just curious. He's asked me out and, being new here, I don't know much about him."

"Catch of the county. That poor man has

more skirts chasin' him than a dog has fleas."

"I see." Peggy tried to drink her tea, but it was hard to swallow.

Amanda's expression grew serious. "No, I doubt that you do. Clint Howell is a good Christian man. He mourned Eileen for more'n a year before he'd even socialize with folks. He even let his sons and their wives take care of the spring branding. That's a time when the ranchers all help each other, and the wives are expected to provide chow for everyone.

"This is a small community, and most folks have lived here all their lives, so ever'body knows ever'body elses' business, which isn't always a good thing. It's common knowledge that he's been staying out here at the lake more lately, and helping you with this cabin, and there's a lot of speculation. Any courtship takin' place around here is practically done in a fishbowl, but it'll be worse for you, 'cause Clint's family, and you're new."

"Wonderful," Peggy said with a grimace.

"So, there is something goin' on between you two." Amanda was beaming at her.

Peggy sighed. "He's helped me with the cabin, and we're friends. I didn't come out

171

here to get involved with a man. I came out here to get over one. I want a studio and a career, not another husband."

"How about a lover?"

"Amanda! You just told me this place was a fishbowl."

"Don't pay me no nevermind, or any of them either. You just do what's right for you." Amanda finished her tea and stood up.

"You walk down and visit me real soon. Meet the mister. You like flower gardens?"

"Yes."

"I'll help you get one started, if you want. Give you some spring bulbs."

"Thanks. Let me get the remodeling done first."

Amanda turned back after she went through the screen door and laid her hand on Peggy's arm.

"You be up front with Clint, and he'll be up front with you. Don't be messing with his heart if you're not serious about him."

"I won't, Amanda. I respect him too much for that."

"Good." She gave Peggy's arm a pat. "You come see me."

"I will. Good night."

Peggy sat in the cupola again that night, watching the wind ruffle the water's surface and thinking about Clint. Conflicting emotions warred within her. The more she was around him, the closer she came to giving in to him. He was so easy to talk to, to be with. She fed on his admiring gazes, his words of praise. And if she was honest with herself, she longed for his touch. She knew instinctively that he would be a gentle, sensitive lover, putting her needs ahead of his own, and holding her close long after their passion was spent.

It was her knowledge of him that frightened her. He could so easily seduce her into giving him everything, trusting him to know best, turning her life over to his will, regardless of her own. She wasn't strong enough yet. She hadn't had time to establish within herself who she was and what she wanted. When she was with Clint, it was tempting to believe it didn't matter, but when she was alone, like now, and remembered all she'd been through, all she'd sacrificed to get here, she knew it did matter.

She sat, staring at the dark lake, until her body demanded rest. Nothing was solved. The conflict was still there. She wanted Clint too much to let him go. She wanted to accomplish her own goals too much to allow her to have him.

* * *

On Friday school was out for the De
Baca County Fair. Peggy applied the
third and final coat of joint compound to
the bedroom walls. Henry caught three
mice and brought them into the bedroom
to eat. Peggy wasn't sure if he did it to
show her what he'd caught or in retaliation for her not feeding him. He hadn't
caught a single mouse since his arrival,
and Clint had told her he wouldn't as
long as food was readily available in a
dish. He had been quite vocal in his ob-
jection to the empty bowl, but at least
he was earning his keep now. Peggy
tried to ignore the crunching of small
bones while she worked.

Saturday brought letters from Shawn and
Michael, with pictures they'd drawn from the
deer photos she'd sent them. She taped them
to the cabinet door in the kitchen. She spent
the day smoothing the joints for the last
time, making the walls in the bedroom ready
for paint.

Clint called in the afternoon, and they decided to grill steaks at his cabin instead of
eating at a restaurant in town. Peggy dressed
carefully for their dinner. Proud of her slim-

ming figure and tanned skin, she wore a haltered sundress that had previously been too snug. Hopefully, by the time she got the sewing machine set up, she was going to have to take in some clothes. She strapped sandals onto her bare feet.

She carried an unbaked apple pie down to bake in Clint's oven while he grilled the steaks. They ate outside at the picnic table, sheltered from the late afternoon sun by its large umbrella. Clint spent the evening regaling her with stories about judging the junior calf show.

"I felt so sorry for the little guy. That calf weighed more than he did. It was bawling and pulling him around. Dustin was trying so hard not to bawl himself. I don't think we were a very objective judging panel. I think he won more on sympathy than on merit."

"Are you always such a softy?" Peggy asked.

"When it comes to kids and calves—always. Now, around you . . ."

Peggy actually blushed and pushed his hand away.

"Behave. This is supposed to be a friendly dinner."

"That's all I'm trying to be—friendly."

175

Peggy removed his hand from her bare knee. "I saw a road runner today," she told him, attempting to steer the conversation to safer ground. "He made several trips up and down the draw below the caboose. I took his picture."

"Probably chasing a snake. Be careful. The snake could come looking for shelter under the caboose."

"I'll keep Henry inside."

"I could come stay and make sure you're safe." He slid his hand back over her knee, his voice low and husky.

"Who'd keep me safe from you?" She removed his hand again, feeling quite flustered. "I won't give you any pie if you don't behave yourself."

"I'd rather have you anyway." She dodged, but he grabbed her. "You look good enough to eat tonight," he remarked and laid a wet path up her neck with his tongue.

"Clint!"

"I warned you I intended to be persuasive."

"The whole lake can see us."

"Then let's go inside."

"Not on your life."

He released her then, with a sigh of long-suffering. "Guess I'll have to settle for the pie."

"You make it sound like moldy bread."

"Only in comparison to your luscious body." He leered openly at her cleavage.

"I'm a grandmother, for Pete's sake." She felt more like a foolish teenager, fighting off his advances and trying not to respond to the smoldering desire in his dark eyes. She cut the pie and served him a huge piece.

"And I'm a grandfather," Clint reminded her, his eyes hot as he held her gaze.

They took a walk along the beach after eating, and Peggy took off her sandals to walk in the sand.

"That's dangerous, you know," Clint told her.

"Why? Do you have a foot fetish?"

"Yes, actually, but I was thinking about the cuckleburrs. The sand is full of them. Of course, should you encounter one, I'd be more than willing to remove it and carry you home."

"You don't let up, do you?"

"Not unless you tell me there's no hope."

Looking fully into his warm brown eyes, Peggy knew there was no way she could tell him that. He gave her a slow smile.

"I didn't think so," he replied smugly.

He surprised her by letting the moment pass, taking her hand and continuing down the beach. He was thoughtful for several minutes before he spoke again.

"Tell me about your husband."

"Peter?" Peggy's voice reflected her surprise. "Why?"

"So I won't make the same mistakes he did."

"You're a totally different man, Clint, and I'm a different woman from the naive twenty-year-old I was when I married him. Hearing about Peter won't do anything but dredge up ugly memories."

"Are you still friends?"

"No, but I don't hate him. He remarried, almost immediately after the divorce was final, to one of the reasons I divorced him. The kids tell me she is making his life hell."

"Sweet revenge?"

Peggy shrugged. "He's not a bad person."

"Just a bad husband?"

"Something like that. Do you ever talk about your wife?"

"Not usually to women I'm dating. They are intimidated for the most part, if not out-and-out jealous."

"I asked Amanda about her. It sounds like you were happy together."

"Yes, but life goes on. I don't like living alone, but with Eileen as the gold standard, it will have to be someone very special." He said it in such a way that she could not mistake his meaning. Peggy was every bit as special as Eileen had been.

Peggy gazed out over the lake, unable to meet the very charged look in his eyes, uncomfortable with the implication of his statement. "And do you date a lot of women?" she asked, picking up on his earlier comment, hoping to divert the conversation.

"Enough to know what I want."

*So much for diversion,* Peggy thought, as Clint stopped and turned her toward him, holding her shoulders. She laid her hands against his chest, keeping him at a slight distance.

"You're about a year ahead of me, Clint." She met his eyes and faltered. It would be so divine to give in, to melt into this strong, powerfully sensual man, and enjoy the ride for as long as it lasted. He promised to fulfill a part of her that had gone unfulfilled for longer than she could calculate, but that was only one part of her, and she wanted more than the smell of gunpowder when the fireworks were over.

"Give me that same opportunity to discover what I want," she pleaded. "If it's you, you'll be the first to know."

Clint folded her against his chest, just holding her. It was a reasonable request, but one he wasn't sure he could honor. What they had was so tentative, so new, he didn't trust it to withstand the test of time yet. He wanted to show her how great it could be between them, assuring himself that everything else would pale in comparison. Of course he would kill any man who tried to move in on what was his.

His.

Peggy was right, he was possessive, and with the least encouragement on her part he would stake his claim for the whole world to witness. He eased up on the tight embrace, and looked into her upturned face. Her blue eyes were troubled. He tried for a reassuring smile, but it came out somewhat crooked.

"At least give me equal time during your search?" he asked. He felt her relax against him, and bent to take her mouth in a kiss heartbreakingly sweet. It didn't stay that way. He parted her lips and sensually stroked the

180

inside of her mouth and tongue until he sensed her total response. Her hands were clinging to his shoulders before he slowly ended his gentle assault.

Without speaking a word, they turned and began the walk back, Peggy clinging to his waist, and he to hers, their steps in unison as they both tried to regain control of the passion screaming through their bodies.

# Nine

Two weeks after school started, Peggy was beginning to settle into the routine. Most of the teachers ate lunch together in the lounge, in twenty-minute shifts. Peggy and Violet usually ate with the first group, then went into the art room for their planning period. Sometimes they actually got work done. Other times they visited.

"Pat Sullivan asked me to help her with the Junior-Senior Play," Peggy told Violet. Pat taught Speech, Debate, Forensics, and Drama. She was in charge of the two plays the juniors and seniors did for fund-raisers every year.

"What did you tell her?" Violet asked, not looking up from the papers she was grading.

"I'd like to. I worked on quite a few school plays when the kids were growing up, and I enjoyed it."

"But?" Violet prompted, looking up.

"I'd like to finish the remodeling before I take on a new project."

"Is that why you hired Billy Ellis to help you after school?" Violet asked, her pansy blue eyes probing. "Did he really do enough work to merit the forty-mile round trip to bring him home?"

Peggy didn't want to admit the clumsy thirteen-year-old's effort at applying joint compound was going to take her two nights to smooth out. "I need some help, and he needs a job," Peggy defended herself.

"He has a job," Violet reminded her. "Are you sure you're not trying to substitute as his mother?"

"Someone needs to care about him, and it's obvious his stepfather doesn't."

"Be careful, Peggy," Violet warned. "Your helping could be misconstrued as value judgment, and backfire in your face."

"I'm hiring him to help me with the remodeling," Peggy insisted, turning her attention back to the clay she was parceling out for the next class. As far as she was concerned, the subject was closed.

"Where's Joe taking you tonight?" Violet asked, obligingly changing the subject.

"Somewhere in Clovis. He told me to dress for 'a night on the town.' "

"You don't sound very enthusiastic."

Peggy sighed. "You want to hear the confession of a mixed-up woman?"

Violet set her papers aside and gave Peggy her rapt attention.

"I like Joe, but he's not Clint, and that's why I'm going out with him."

Violet gave her a blank look. "Run that by me again. I missed something."

"It doesn't make sense, no matter how many times you run it by. *I* don't make sense."

"Are you using Joe to make Clint jealous?"

"Good grief, give me a little credit."

Violet gave Peggy that probing stare of hers. "What do you feel for Clint?"

"Terrified," Peggy admitted, her voice low. "The man scares me to death."

"Clint Howell?" Violet asked, frowning in disbelief. "Why?"

"He is so sweet, so strong, so everything a woman dreams of a man being," Peggy tried to explain, frustrated with her inability to express herself. "That's why he's dangerous. If I give in to him, he'll consume me."

"Consume," Violet repeated, trying to understand, "as in consummation?"

"No, consume as in consumption," Peggy explained, becoming more agitated. "I was ready for consummation by the second day I knew him, but Clint's not the type of man for a dalliance. He is very . . . possessive, and . . . domineering—all the things I left Kansas to escape."

"I've known Clint a long time, Peggy. From what you've told me about Peter, they aren't anything alike."

"That's what I told Clint," Peggy agreed, feeling miserable.

"Love is a rare thing, a gift from God, so to speak. Some people spend their whole lives looking for it," Violet offered.

"Freedom is also a rare thing. It's taken me forty-nine years to get it."

"And you don't think you can have both?"

"No."

Violet regarded her thoughtfully. "What do you want in life right now, all extraneous factors aside?"

"You sound like my daughter, Erika. She asked me that question, and the answer was this job."

"Are you sorry?"

185

"No." Peggy smiled. "I belong here. And, the answer is the same now as it was then. I want to paint and teach school and find out who I am."

Violet shot her a look of disgust. "That went out with the sixties. Who were you before you came here?"

"Peter's wife, Megan's mother, Shawn's grandmother, even Rita and Bill's daughter. I've never been just me."

"That's garbage, Peggy," Violet exclaimed, exasperated, "an excuse for something you don't want to deal with. You're still all those people. You'll go to your grave being all those people. And they are all who they are because of being part of you. No man is an island, and the few who try to be are the most psychotic people in our society."

"I didn't ask for a lecture." Peggy complained.

"I apologize. I just can't stand to see you throw away happiness in some quest to be a hermit, and for reasons I don't understand. Will being in love take away from your painting or teaching?"

"It did before," Peggy said defensively. Her excuse even sounded lame to her.

"I don't think Clint expects you to give

up your career and raise children. Besides, we're talking love affair, not marriage."

"Wanna bet?"

"He's *asked?*"

"Not in so many words, but it's implied," Peggy said dejectedly. "I want to live in my caboose and paint. If I thought I could have Clint and that also, I would have already grabbed the man. I don't want to be a rancher's wife. I don't even like cows."

The bell rang, signaling the end of the period. They both had a class to teach. Violet gave Peggy an impulsive hug before she left the art room.

"Have fun tonight. Don't compare, just have fun. You want to get together this weekend?"

"I have to go into Clovis tomorrow. Want to tag along?"

"Call me tomorrow. I'd love to."


Peggy and Violet drove over to Clovis the next morning to select carpet for the bedroom and a floor covering for the studio. She put down a deposit and told them she'd call when she was closer to being ready for installation. They shopped for a refrigerator small enough to fit through the door, as well as frivolous things, such as the perfect color nail polish. And through it all, they talked.

"So," Violet demanded, when Peggy didn't offer, "how was the date?"

"Fine," Peggy replied vaguely.

Violet stopped in the middle of the mall, arms akimbo, and glared at her friend. "Either tell me it's none of my business, or spill your guts, but don't give me 'fine.' "

Peggy smiled at Violet's dramatics. "Okay," she agreed, continuing through the mall. Violet fell into step beside her, her head cocked attentively. "We went to a fancy club and ate lobster. Joe was dressed quite handsomely in a dark suit with a white shirt he left opened halfway down his chest."

"Umm hmm," Violet murmured appreciatively.

"They had a band, and we danced. He's quite an accomplished dancer."

"And did you enjoy it?" Violet prodded.

"I enjoy dancing," Peggy said evasively. "It's been a little while since I've been."

"That wasn't the question," Violet stated flatly.

"We talked about teaching," Peggy continued, ignoring her, "and what I liked to paint. Joe has a pilot's license, and he offered to take me flying, to show me the desert and the valley. I told him it sounded fun."

"So you made another date with him," Violet offered hopefully.

"No," Peggy drawled. "He drove me home and walked me to the door. I thanked him for a nice time and told him good night."

Violet stopped again and waited until Peggy met her sharp gaze. Peggy tried to look innocent, her chin raised assertively, but Violet wasn't convinced. "What really happened?" Violet wheedled.

"God, you're nosy," Peggy complained, but she could feel herself smiling, giving herself away.

"He kissed you," Violet accused, lowering her voice and looking around to make sure no one was within earshot.

"Like a masher," Peggy confirmed, her voice equally low. "It was disgusting."

"So," Violet chortled, her eyes sparkling mischievously, "has Clint called?"

"Yes," Peggy answered mysteriously.

"And?"

"I told him we—you and I—were going shopping today and I wouldn't be back until late."

Violet gave her a disgusted look. "I'm

flattered, but I wouldn't turn down a date to be with you."

"Which brings up an interesting point. What *are* you doing here with me? I thought you were going to try to do something with Sam."

Violet made a face. "I threatened him with divorce to shake him up. As far as I can tell, he likes living alone. He can watch two ball games simultaneously without me fussing at him to mow the lawn."

"You don't want a divorce, do you?"

"No." Violet gazed wistfully at the couples walking arm in arm through the mall. "I want the man I married back. He used to chase me through the house, threatening me with the most deliciously decadent things he was going to do when he caught me." She sighed sadly. "Now, he only runs when he's out of beer and he's only got ten minutes before the second half."

"You never had kids?"

"No. Maybe that's why they don't get on my nerves at school."

Peggy was thinking about Sam. She'd never met Violet's estranged husband, but she doubted any man who'd once chased his wife through the house could be completely immune to sexual enticement. They just had to figure out the right enticement.

"Who's Sam's favorite movie star?"

Violet gave her a very suspicious look through narrowed eyes. "He likes Loni Anderson. Why?"

Peggy smiled, a conspiratorial gleam in her eye. "She used to be a brunette."

"I don't think I like what you're thinking."

"You just need to get his attention."

"You don't know Sam."

"But you do. He needs to see you again, and remember why he used to chase you through the house."

By the time they returned to Fort Sumner, late that evening, they had two boxes of L'Oreal hair coloring in addition to their other purchases, and a list of ideas that would tempt Sam away from his TV set. Violet would only agree to dying her hair if Peggy dyed hers also, and she wouldn't commit to when she would do it.

The next day was Sunday, and Violet invited Peggy to her Sunday school class, which she taught. Peggy agreed to come. She had taught Sunday school herself most of her adult life, always children's classes.

She looked forward to attending an adult class.

The First Methodist Church in Fort Sumner was quite large, with around three hundred members. Peggy met a number of families that drove long distances to attend. The outlying ranches were somewhat isolated and she got the impression that Sundays were a time of socializing and catching up on local events as much as a time of worship. The Howells were one of those families.

"Peggy! Welcome!" Clint took her hand, then stood gazing at her, an appreciative gleam in his eyes. She was wearing a navy summer dress, trimmed in white. It was fitted through the bodice with a full skirt that draped becomingly over her hips and showed off her shapely calves. She wore navy and white spectator pumps to complete the outfit.

"You look good enough to eat," he said in a low voice only she could hear.

She was thinking the same thing about him. He had always been handsome to her, wearing casual clothes and tennis shoes. In his charcoal gray western suit and gray eel boots, he took her breath away. She felt small and delicate standing next to his height and broad shoulders. They stood there in the aisle of the sanctuary, silently admiring each other, oblivious to the people around them, until Violet broke in.

"Hello, Clint. Are you here with your family?"

Clint reluctantly released Peggy's hand. "Hello, Violet. Yes, I am."

Clint turned to introduce Peggy to his family. She'd already met the boys, and they were as handsome as their father in their Sunday clothes. Their wives, Tina and Gina, were gorgeous. They were identical, from their hair style to their shoes, petite creatures with dark eyes and dark hair. The children favored the Spanish heritage of their mothers.

"Would you ladies join us?" They all moved down in the pew to make room.

"Thank you," Violet answered before Peggy could decline. She smiled sweetly in response to Peggy's glare as she indicated for her friend to enter the pew first, which placed her next to Clint.

Peggy sang the hymns, sharing the hymnal with Clint, blending her high soprano with his deep baritone. She couldn't concentrate on the sermon, too aware of Clint's warm presence beside her. She tried to distract her thoughts by watching the grandchildren, who kept peeking at her from around their parents, their dark eyes wide with curiosity.

During the closing prayer, Violet irreverently leaned over and whispered in Peggy's ear. "If you don't go to lunch with him, I will not help you paint." She followed up on her threat as soon as the pastor said Amen.

"I see Sam over there. Excuse me, but after our discussion last night, I think I'll invite him to lunch." She slipped away before Peggy had time to say a word.

"I get the distinct feeling you've been set up," Clint said from beside her.

There was amusement in his eyes when she looked up at him. "Yes," she agreed, "and by a woman I thought was my friend."

"I think I've been insulted."

Before Peggy had a chance to reply, Amanda grabbed her arm. "Peggy! I'm so glad you came! Come meet Charlie. I've told him so much about you."

Peggy looked back at Clint helplessly as Amanda dragged her over to meet her husband. He shrugged, as if to say he couldn't help her. Peggy spent just enough time with the Wilsons to avoid being thought rude, then turned to find Clint. To her intense dismay, someone else had found him first.

The woman hanging on Clint's arm and laughing up at him was younger than Peggy, with long auburn hair and even longer legs shown to their best advantage with a bright yellow mini skirt. Peggy felt anger flash through her at the woman's brash behavior. Without thinking about what she was doing, she strode purposefully over to them, and possessively claimed Clint's free arm.

"I'm sorry. Amanda wanted me to meet Charlie." She gave the redhead her most intimidating look. The woman appeared surprised, but didn't release Clint or back off.

"Peggy, this is Corrinne Gallagher." Clint tried to sound composed while the two beautiful women glared at each other over him. "Corrinne, meet Peggy Thompkins. She teaches art at the high school."

The women muttered amenities. Justin interrupted before they had a chance to say any more.

"Dad . . . oh, excuse me . . . hello, Ms. Gallagher, Ms. Thompkins." He gave each woman a quick smile, then turned back to his father. "Dad, we're gonna head back. We'll meet you at the house."

Clint nodded at his son, then turned to

Corrinne. "It was good to see you again, Corrinne." He disengaged his arm from her grasp, then turned amused brown eyes on Peggy. "Coming?"

"I'm ready." She smiled up at him and didn't release his arm until they reached his truck.

"If I didn't know better, I'd say you were a little jealous back there," Clint stated as they headed out of town. It was all he could do not to laugh. He wasn't allowed to be jealous or possessive, but apparently the same didn't apply to her. When Peggy didn't answer, he wrapped an arm around her shoulders and hauled her across the seat against him. He did laugh then, a full rich laugh of arrogant male satisfaction.

"Corrinne would like to be much more than I want her to be. She isn't a threat to you."

"You don't have to explain her to me, Clint. We agreed to be friends, no conditions." She was mortified by her behavior, now that she had time to analyze it. It was useless to try and deny that she'd been jealous. She'd all but scratched the woman's eyes out. Clint tactfully changed the subject, and began to tell her about the valley as

196

they drove past fields laid out patchwork-quilt fashion, across the flat land.

"It looks more like western Kansas than the desert," Peggy commented.

"The irrigated land does. The rangeland is largely grassland, probably not as lush as your Kansas prairie grassland. It takes a lot of range land to raise cattle out here, unless you supplement them with hay. That's what most of the irrigated fields are used for."

It took an hour to get to Clint's ranch, just as he'd said it would. They turned off the dirt road and pulled up to the sprawling white ranch-style house that was set back off the road. From the time they turned into the gate, they were surrounded by a mixed pack of barking dogs. Large barns sat on the other side of the wide gravel drive in front of the house. The drive went further past the house, to where a stable and coral could be seen. Peggy had the impression of space, order, and efficiency.

"Where is the chicken coop you promised to show me?"

"After lunch," he promised with a smile. He came around to open her door, then took her arm and escorted her into the house.

Watching Clint with his family gave Peggy a lump in her throat that was hard to swallow around. It had been a long time since all of her family had gathered together for Sunday dinner. Homesickness threatened to swamp her, especially when she watched the four grandchildren.

The girls had planned their pregnancies to coincide, but they couldn't control the sex of the babies. Clinton, Jr. and Tina had two boys, ages five and two. Justin and Gina had two girls of matching ages. The kids sat at the table with the adults, and lunch was a noisy, happy time. The love they shared was tangible, and Peggy would have been content to just observe and nurse her heartache. They wouldn't allow that, but neither was she singled out. The girls cleaned up after the meal while the boys got the four kids down for naps. Clint and Peggy were shooed out and told they could help next time.

"I like your family, Clint," Peggy told him as they walked outside. "Your daughters-in-law are very special, and the grandchildren are precious."

"They enjoyed you, also."

"Do you have . . . guests . . . for Sunday dinner often?"

Clint laughed and wrapped his arm around her shoulders. "No. Our family time is special, and only special people are ever invited to join us." He lowered his voice conspiratorially. "Corrinne has never been out here."

"I'm never going to live that down, am I?"

"Nope."

"It won't happen again."

"I'm sorry to hear that."

They continued walking toward a stand of cottonwoods. Finally, as they got near, Peggy could make out a long, low building hiding among the trees.

"The chicken coop," Clint announced with a flourish of his hand. "I'd take you inside, but you're not dressed for it." They were both still wearing the clothes they'd worn to church.

"Next time," Peggy agreed. They stood under the shady trees, listening to the chickens clucking from inside the coop.

"I'd like there to be a next time," Clint said softly, reaching for her. She came to him, sliding her hands around his back, and he felt her yield to his hungry kiss. She surrounded his senses with light fragrance and softness in all the right places. Her hands gripped his shoulders as he sought closer contact with her mouth.

Peggy had realized on the drive out that

fighting her feelings for Clint was a losing battle. Their union was inevitable. At the moment, surrendering to the wonder of his kiss, feeling the strength of his large hands on her back, pressing her closer against him, she couldn't remember why it was so important to resist him.

Clint was totally aware of her lack of resistance, and deepened the kiss, running his hands over her bottom and pulling her tight against him. When Peggy finally did try to pull away, he moved to her throat, his hands seeking her thighs under her skirt.

"Clint." He was moving too fast. Peggy felt desire change to panic, akin to drowning. "Clint!" He released her suddenly, then grabbed her back to him. He was breathing hard, and Peggy could feel his pounding heart through his chest, where he held her against him. She was trembling uncontrollably, and feeling weak in the knees.

"You torture me, woman," he groaned. "Either relieve me, or kill me, but stop this agony." He felt her grip relax as she again sought to free herself. He groaned again. "You choose to kill me. You are heartless."

"Clint, slow down. I surrender, but slow down." She laid her palm against his smooth shaven cheek, and tried to give him a reassuring smile. His eyes were so *hungry*. Her smile came across a little weak.

"Let's get to know each other." The raw desire in his eyes threatened to fell her. She tried again. "Let's . . . learn more about each other. We've just met."

"It doesn't matter," he said raggedly.

"Please, Clint," she whispered. She didn't want their first time to be on the ground outside a chicken coop, but she feared if he kissed her again she wouldn't care where they were. It didn't help that the only thing preventing that was her plea for him to wait, and she didn't sound all that convincing, even to her own ears.

His sanity slowly returned, the fear in her eyes finally penetrating the heat of his blood. Reluctantly, he nodded his agreement. They held each other, and slowly walked back to the house.

## Ten

Monday was Labor Day, so there was no school. Peggy had spent the week taping and smoothing all the wall joints in the studio to her satisfaction. Today she planned to be creative—on her bedroom ceiling.

The book on finishing ceilings listed a number of suggestions. She could spray on a thin mixture of spackling compound and particles that gave a nubby texture or, with a specially designed roller, achieve a similar effect without the expense of a sprayer. The other suggestions appealed more to her artistic side. Spackling compound could be sculpted, if not put on too thick, with a variety of tools. It could be combed, swirled, smeared, or applied smoothly then wrinkled by touching the wet surface with a flat tool and pulling it away.

Peggy went out to the shed, followed by

the ever-present Henry, and dug through her boxes of art supplies. Since leaving Clint the night before, she had begun to regard the bedroom in a different light. She wanted it to be impressive. She had sat up late into the night, sketching ideas. It wouldn't be the Sistine Chapel, but then, her motives weren't quite so holy.

After a couple of hours of standing on a ladder working with her hands above her head, she took a break. She seriously considered how she could construct a scaffold to lie on, Michelangelo-style, while she worked on the ceiling. The compound had to be applied with a trowel in areas small enough to work before they dried. Then, with her palette knife, she carved it into the pictures and scenes she'd sketched out. Taping the joints had clued her in that ceiling work wasn't easy, but that had progressed fairly rapidly. Her sculpture was going to take days. She curled up in a ball, stretching out her sore back muscles.

She worked steadily through the day, giving up on the scaffolding idea, taking frequent stretch breaks. As always when she was painting, her mind resented her body's demands. It felt good to be painting again, even if her medium was mud instead of oils.

Actually, she had considered an oil painting across the ceiling, but she liked the subtlety of the monochromatic spackling compound, letting texture project the image, instead of color.

She couldn't deny that the ceiling was for Clint, and wondered what his reaction would be. She tried to decide when to show it to him. *He should see it from the bed,* she thought with a purely physical thrill of anticipation, *after we make mad, passionate love.*

They would be discreet. She had no intention of the whole town knowing they were lovers. As far as the public was concerned, they would be dating. She would have him and her freedom also, if they were careful. Surely at their ages, no one would care, even if they suspected. *Then again, this isn't Kansas, Toto.* According to Amanda, it was a fishbowl. She frowned at the thought. She'd never lived in a fishbowl before.

Then again, maybe she had. After the first couple of Peter's affairs, she had wised up to the fact that most of their friends knew about his mistresses. No one wanted to say anything to her, but she began to recognize the look of knowledge in their eyes.

Then there was Kevin. Where people had

avoided talking to her about Peter, it seemed as if near strangers had found some excuse to call her and "just mention, by the way" that they'd noticed Kevin with this woman or that, and "was everything okay? Cheryl's such a sweet girl, and that precious baby." And they would cluck like hens until Peggy wanted to scream at them to mind their own business.

Peggy looked down at her hand. She was clenching her palette knife so tightly her nails were digging into her palms. She grimaced and forced herself to relax. What was past was past—ashes of her old life. If Fort Sumner was a fishbowl it couldn't be any worse than what she'd already lived through.

Clint called her that evening. He and the boys had spent the day rounding up stray cattle and mending the section of fence they'd escaped through. He sounded as tired as she felt, but it was so good to hear his voice.

"There's a dance the twenty-first," he told her, his voice low and intimate, as it had been through most of the conversation. "It's a private club, local ranchers. We have one about every other month, though I haven't been in a while. I'd like to take you to this one."

Peggy consulted her calendar. The twenty-first was less than three weeks away. With diligence, she would have the bedroom completed by then. "I think that can be arranged," she told him, trying to sound nonchalant.

"It's casual."

*It won't be if I have my way.* Aloud she answered, "Great."

"I want to see you before next weekend."

The timbre in his voice made her want to suggest tonight, but she wrestled herself under control. She was the one who'd insisted on the courtship period. "When?"

"I could meet you after school tomorrow. We could take that boat tour of the lake, now that the holiday traffic is over."

"I'll pack a picnic supper," Peggy offered.

"What? No wiener roast over a campfire?"

"Hmmm, we'll see."

"I'll see you tomorrow."

She had little chance to savor the glow from Clint's call. Cheryl, Kevin's soon-to-be ex-wife, called almost as soon as Clint hung up. Cheryl filled her in on Hillary's exploits, then got down to brass tacks quickly.

"This phone call is about Hillary, Mom. She adores her daddy. Kevin is promising to come to counseling if I'll let him move back in. If it were just me, I wouldn't even consider it." There was a pause as Cheryl realized she was discussing Peggy's son.

"It's okay, Cheryl. I have no illusions about my son."

"No, I guess you wouldn't," Cheryl agreed sadly.

"Do you still love him, Cheryl?"

There was another long pause, then a sigh. "I don't know. I'm too mad."

"But you're considering reconciliation for Hillary's sake?"

"For all his faults, Kevin's a good father," Cheryl admitted. "Hillary misses her daddy. It breaks my heart when she cries for him."

"What does your counselor recommend?"

"Giving him conditions for his return. One of them is attending the counseling sessions with me, before he returns home. I'd like to see him get a job, even part-time, weekends, whatever. Most of his classes are in the evenings. Let him support his own schooling, and prove to me he wants a relationship, not room and board."

"I thought he watched Hillary during the day."

"Until about noon, then he takes her to

the day care. He says she interferes with his studying."

"You have to do what you think best, Cheryl."

"Yeah, but you know men. 'If you loved me,' blah, blah, blah."

The conversation ended with nothing resolved, but Peggy decided Cheryl was looking for a sounding board more than a solution. Still, she wished she could help. On impulse, she dialed Erika's number. Kevin was there, as she'd hoped, but he still wouldn't talk to her. She could hear his voice in the background as Erika offered him the phone.

"She just wants to meddle again," Kevin accused. "Her meddling started this whole thing."

Erika called her brother a name Peggy was shocked she'd use with her mother listening. Seemingly unperturbed by the exchange, Erika asked Peggy about the renovations to the caboose and about her classes. Peggy told her about the mural in the ceiling, but didn't mention Clint. As far as her children were concerned, Clint was her carpenter. As always, Erika cheered her and made her feel there was nothing she couldn't do, if she put her mind to it. She almost made up for Kevin's continued hostility.

Tuesday during their planning period was the first opportunity for Peggy and Violet to talk since they'd parted company at the church on Sunday. Needless to say, not much planning got done.

"You're glowing," Violet told Peggy as they sat down with their lunch trays.

"You're fishing," Peggy said, evading her probing.

"I'll tell you what happened with Sam." Violet's eyes danced as she dangled her bait.

"I'm listening."

"Uh, uh, you first."

Peggy smiled, a very smug, secretive smile. "We're dating."

"And?"

"That's it. We're going to get to know each other better. I had lunch with his family. He showed me his ranch. We went out to the Old Fort museum and Billy the Kid's grave. We ate supper in town and he dropped me off at the church to pick up my van."

"Then why are your eyes sparkling?" Violet persisted.

"He's showing me the lake, by boat, after school. What happened with Sam?"

"He asked me if I was through with this nonsense and when could he come back home. I lost my temper and told him when hell freezes over."

"I see. And where were you when he said this?"

Violet flushed red. Peggy laughed at her.

"I see," she said again, still laughing. "There's hope."


Peggy helped Clint launch the boat from the boat ramp near the dam. Clint expertly backed the boat trailer into the water with the pickup, then backed the boat off the trailer. All Peggy had to do was pull back up the ramp with the empty trailer and park in the designated area. Clint offered her a hand into the boat from the loading dock.

From the water, Peggy took pictures of the cliffs around their swimming cove, and of the caboose, perched on the highest point. From that side, the addition was more obvious than the caboose.

Many of the rock formations were stacks of thin rocks, some of them with such square edges they appeared to have been quarried, instead of shaped by water.

"Sandstone, most of them," Clint explained. "As rocks go, these are fairly soft, and won't take the erosive action of the fluctuating lake levels."

"You mean they're being worn away?"

"Yes, gradually. They'll be here as long as you are, though."

Peggy's thoughts weren't really on rocks. She had discussed Cheryl's conversation with Violet, and the topic of the fidelity of men in general.

"Were you a faithful husband?" she asked Clint suddenly.

"Of course," he answered immediately, then was silent for a minute. "Where did that come from?"

Peggy explained about Peter, and then Kevin. It was the first time she'd really discussed her past with him.

"You stayed with a cheating husband for twenty-seven years?" He was incredulous. No wonder she didn't trust men easily. "Why?"

"Kevin was ten before things got unbearable with Peter," Peggy replied. "Then I stayed for the security, and out of pride. By that time I had three small children, no money of my own, and a demented idea that a son needed his father."

"And now you feel Kevin's behavior is your fault?"

"If I'd left Peter and moved back home with my folks, he would have had my dad for his role model. Instead, he seems to think men should do as they please, and their wives should put up with it."

"Peggy, that's not your fault." They were floating in the area in front of the dam. Clint had turned off the motor so they could talk without shouting. "Kevin is more than old enough to be responsible for his own actions." Clint frowned in thought. "How old is Kevin?"

"Twenty-eight," Peggy supplied.

"What's a twenty-eight-year-old doing still in school?"

"The job he wants requires a master's degree." Peggy felt her ire building. She had gotten to a place where she could discuss Peter calmly, but not Kevin.

"He could have had a doctorate by now," Clint pointed out.

"He changed his major," Peggy stated defensively.

"How many times?"

"Just forget I brought it up, Clint. I

thought you were going to show me the lake." She crossed her arms over her chest and pointedly looked out across the water.

Clint realized he'd overstepped his bounds, and silently cursed himself. He turned over the motor and guided the boat away from the dam. It was obvious to him that Peggy's son was spoiled, selfish, and holding on to his childhood as long as his mother and wife would allow him to. Without his wife, Clint was sure Peggy would be hearing from her son. He was also sure Peggy would take him back, and give him whatever he wanted out of her misconstrued sense of guilt.

The conversation around the campfire they built for the hot dogs was guarded and superficial. Peggy resented Clint's criticism of her son. Of course a man wouldn't understand, especially a man who'd been the model husband and father.

Clint was perceptive enough not to say what he was thinking, but he couldn't disguise his irritation at Peggy's behavior. It was hardly the evening on the lake he'd envisioned the night before, but he didn't know how to repair the damage. He thought about her on the drive back to the ranch. She was right about one thing, they didn't know much about each other. Their bodies yearned for each other with an intensity he had never experienced before, but their minds were light years apart.

"What happened to the glow?" Violet asked her over lunch the next day.

Peggy sighed. "Matt Thomas. He won't do any work in art class. He hasn't cared about anything since class started, except football. He says I'm trying to distract him from his concentration."

Violet laughed at her, then sobered quickly when she saw Peggy's face. "You're serious."

"Of course I'm serious. What am I supposed to do with this kid?"

Violet chewed her lower lip thoughtfully, weighing her answer. "Is failing him not an option?"

"No one fails art!"

"Did it occur to you that he's counting on that?"

"I'll talk to him again. If he'd just try."

Violet really wasn't interested in Matt Thomas. "How was dinner with Clint?"

"I think we had a fight," Peggy confessed dejectedly. She laid her fork down, her lunch half-eaten.

"You think?"

"I tried to tell him about Kevin, and we had a difference of opinion."

"Want to talk about it?"

"No." Peggy had gotten up, and was now giving her full attention to pouring a cup of coffee.

Violet took the hint. "Want to come over tonight and play beauty parlor?"

Peggy sat back down and smiled at her friend. "What made you change your mind?"

"My mirror," Violet stated with a wrinkled nose. "The catch still stands, though."

"What catch?" Peggy asked, feigning innocence.

"You have to do it, too."

"No thanks. Mother Nature is already providing me with natural platinum." She ran a hand through her short blond hair for emphasis. It was generously sprinkled with white.

"Chicken," Violet challenged teasingly.

"I'm too old to fall for that trick," Peggy declared smugly.

"Corrinne Gallagher is forty-five. You think that auburn hair is natural?"

"That is playing dirty."

Violet smiled wickedly.

"Did the whole church witness that childish stunt?" Peggy asked, feeling mortified all over again.

215

"Those who didn't see it, heard about it," Violet stated with relish.

"Amanda's right. This town is a fishbowl."

"I'll meet you in the art room after school." Violet picked up her lunch tray and left the lounge as the bell rang.


The two women faced their fellow teachers the next morning with sheepish faces and dark circles under their eyes from lack of sleep. Violet was almost unrecognizable with her pale blond hair that emphasized her beautiful pansy blue eyes. She looked ten years younger than the salt and pepper brunette she'd been the day before. Peggy had chosen a soft ash blond, close to the color her hair was naturally. In spite of being tired, they were pleased with the results, and the compliments of their coworkers.

Friday, Peggy asked Billy if he'd like to earn some money painting, and promised to pick him up Saturday morning, after she did her laundry. She wondered if he'd be offended if she offered to do a load for him. Life was certainly a roller coaster, and, as if to verify that opinion, Clint called her that night.

216

"Are you free this weekend?" he asked, after they'd exchanged amenities.

"I hired Billy Ellis to help me paint tomorrow."

"Billy Ellis? Pete's kid?"

"Yes. He's so pitiful, Clint. Pete doesn't half take care of him."

"So you've accepted the job." His voice had a clipped, irritated quality to it.

"It's *my* life," she reminded him tersely.

"So it is. I don't know how I forgot. You remind me often enough."

Arguing with Clint made Peggy physically ill. She decided to make the first overture of peace. "I'm free Sunday." The silence from his end of the line almost made her withdraw the offer.

"There's a place I'd like to take you for lunch after church," Clint finally said. "As an artist, I think you'll be impressed."

"Is it fancy?"

"Hauntingly casual, actually. Bring a change of clothes, and whatever artists carry."

Saturday with Billy was another exercise in frustration. For one thing, the kid smelled so bad she could hardly stand to be in the same room with him. For another, he'd never held a paintbrush in his life, and required constant supervision. Peggy gave up trying to do her ceiling while he painted the walls, and ended up doing the brush work while he used the roller. She was grateful the carpet wasn't down yet. Hopefully, the other mistakes would be covered with the second coat of paint, which she would do herself. When she dropped him off at his house that evening, she resisted the urge to encourage bathing. She knew she had to earn his trust before she could make such personal suggestions.

After church the next day, Clint took her to a ghost town called Guadalupe, about ten miles northeast of Fort Sumner. An ancient Catholic church was still cared for by a local family, but the other buildings were rapidly deteriorating. Endless desert stretched flat to the horizon, broken only by the railroad tracks. The empty desolation was almost a presence, making Peggy feel as if she were intruding in something very private.

"Wow," Peggy commented softly, standing in the middle of what had once been the main street. "You can feel the ghosts."

"I've always thought so also," Clint agreed. They walked over the rocky ground, exploring the various ruins. Peggy had brought her camera, and was taking pictures.

"There are several places like this along the railway. They were once train stops, and didn't consist of much more than the station house and sometimes a hotel."

"You were right about this place having artistic appeal. It's incredible. I would love to bring the kids out here."

"I would imagine most of them have been out here, although I doubt art was what they had in mind." At Peggy's blank look he continued, "What else is there to do in Fort Sumner?"

They arranged the blanket in the shade of one of the buildings, and Clint unloaded the basket and the cooler he'd packed their lunch in. Peggy sensed that he was trying to organize his thoughts, and waited for him to speak first.

"I thought a ghost town was appropriate," he finally offered. "We both seem to be dealing with some ghosts of our own." She was listening, wariness visible in her eyes. He frowned. Something was different about her. He couldn't figure out what. He decided to dwell on it later.

"You tried to talk to me about your family, and I passed judgment instead of listening," he finished.

"Is that an apology?"

"You have an obsession with this apology thing, don't you?" Clint said with irritation.

"No, but I get the feeling you aren't real familiar with the concept."

"It isn't something I've found myself required to do very often," Clint admitted, his voice still gruff.

"It must be tough, being perfect."

He was about to take exception to that comment when he caught the gleam in her eyes and the way her mouth was twitching. She was teasing him.

"Yes, it is," he growled. "I don't like it when we're at odds."

"Then let's agree to keep the ghosts in the past. We are the present, maybe the future." She smiled at him, and took a bite out of her sandwich. She vowed not to discuss her kids with him again, either her own or the classroom ones.

"This is good," she complimented him on the lunch.

He returned her smile, but he wasn't as confident. The past was part of what they

were now, and ignoring it wouldn't make it
go away.

## Eleven

Peggy had less than two weeks until the dance, and so much left to do, it made her dizzy. She stayed up late every night, working on the ceiling. She had to start taking pain medicine to get through the days, her back, neck, and shoulder muscles hurt so much. Still, she refused to slack off, determined to make her self-imposed deadline.

Violet again accompanied her into Clovis, where she purchased an Indian woven blanket for her bed, curtains for the two windows, and a dress for the dance. She nearly succumbed to the impulse to purchase a double bed, but decided that was not only too obvious, but with the small bedroom, she'd have to stand on the bed to load the washing machine. She settled for extra pillows instead.

The dress had to be perfect, not too

dressy, not too casual, not too chaste, not too sexy. The final choice turned out to be quite southwestern in style. A full, colorful Spanish skirt showed off her legs. A white peasant blouse embroidered with the colors in the skirt went well with her wide shoulders and full bosom. Peggy was pleased that the skirt had to be two sizes smaller than anything in her closet to fit her waist properly. She splurged on turquoise-and-silver bracelets and earrings to complement the outfit.

It was unlike anything she'd ever worn before, and she marveled at how well it suited her. She purchased similar skirts and blouses to wear to school. She had come to New Mexico to change her image. Shedding her grandma clothes was one step in the process.

The most intimate image change she saved for the last stop of the day, knowing Violet would make too much of it. She did.

"Victoria's Secret?" Violet asked, eyebrows raised.

"I just want to look. I need a new bra to wear under the peasant blouses."

"J.C. Penney's sells bras. We're talking sex here." Violet picked up a lace bra that obviously served no purpose except to entice.

"That's pretty." Peggy took it from her.

Violet gave her a probing look. "After three kids, I recommend something with more support."

The store was crowded with Saturday shoppers, and so Violet reserved further comments until they were in the van driving back toward Fort Sumner. Peggy had bought several silk bras with matching panties, a couple of lacy teddies, and even a garter belt and stockings.

"Panty hose are so restrictive," Violet couldn't help commenting. "I've often considered returning to the comfort and convenience of garter belts and stockings."

Peggy didn't reply. A secretive smile only fueled Violet's curiosity. "Give, girl. What are you doing after school?"

"Painting," Peggy said, all innocence.

"In lace teddies?"

"It's very . . . ah . . . stimulating."

Violet gave up subtlety. "How long have you been sleeping with Clint?"

Peggy was not to be ruffled. Again she smiled secretively. "I haven't."

"Yet?"

Peggy laughed, then agreed. "Yet."

"He's a good man, Peggy," Violet stated, all teasing aside.

"Speaking of which, how's Sam?"

"Sam who?"

Peggy cast her a quelling look.

"Oh, all right," Violet capitulated, making a disgusted face. He is persona non grata as far as I'm concerned. I'm killing myself with aerobics three times a week. I'm starving to death on this stupid diet. I'm wasting good reading time with self-help books when I could be reading Tudor historicals, and do you know what he said to me?" Violet's voice rose with each sacrifice she named.

"What?" Peggy asked.

"He told me I looked like a cheap hussy."

Peggy struggled to keep from smiling. "That certainly explains why he stared at you through the entire church service Sunday. He didn't even pretend to sing, or listen to the sermon. The usher had to nudge him twice with the offering plate."

"He was furious," Violet said flatly.

"He was jealous," Peggy countered. "The only time he took his eyes off you was to see who else was looking, and if looks could kill . . ."

"He would have died years ago," Violet finished, "from the ones I gave him."

"How was your date with Joe last night?" Peggy changed tactics.

"I don't know," Violet answered with a

sigh. "He loves my hair." There was bitterness in her voice.

"Did you have a good time?"

"No."

Peggy shot her friend a concerned look. Violet's mouth was set in a hard line as she stared at the passing landscape. "The masher strikes again?" she queried softly.

"Did courtship go out of style while I was married?"

Peggy took that as an affirmative. "Welcome to dating, divorce-style," she said sympathetically.

"Eating crow and taking Sam back gets more appealing every day," Violet admitted resentfully.

That got Peggy's ire up. "Violet Adams, I'm ashamed of you! There is more to life than men!"

Violet fought sudden tears. "I'm not like you, Peggy. I hate living alone. I miss Sam. I find myself turning the TV on to a ball game, just to pretend he's still there."

Peggy felt tears in her own eyes. How many times had she turned the stereo up louder to cover the silence? Her children hadn't moved out before the grandkids moved in. Taping wall joints, even creating her ceiling mural, didn't warm her heart or her house the way running, excited children did.

"If I had a TV, I'd probably turn on cartoons," she told Violet. A melancholy mood permeated the van, and the rest of the trip home was depressingly silent.


Peggy wouldn't let Clint near the cabin until she was finished with the bedroom. Having made picture frames, she was sure she could handle cutting the angles on the trim for the door, windows, and baseboards. Billy stained the oak trim, as she cut it, using the most goof-proof stain Peggy could find.

"Billy, does your dad have a washing machine?" she finally asked, taking him home Tuesday night.

"Yeah. It's on the back porch."

"Do you know how to use it?"

"Dad does laundry."

"I bet he'd appreciate you doing it some evenings, while he's at work," Peggy suggested. "At least you could do your own clothes."

Billy shrugged, obviously not interested in the conversation. "Don't know how."

"Would you like me to teach you?" Peggy

was losing patience rapidly. It had been a frustrating day, and she was too tired to deal with this.

"Nah, we're okay." He opened the door and climbed out of the van.

Not once since she'd started this personal reform program had he thanked her, or said good night when she dropped him off. As soon as she felt she had his trust, she intended to instill some manners in this kid. She wondered what Pete, his stepfather, was like, then wondered if she really wanted to know.

Wednesday she stayed after school to let the students who'd failed Monday's history test retake it. Clint was hurt that she wouldn't take time off from her remodeling to meet him for dinner, but she was rapidly running out of time. She had made a phoenix stencil that she had intended to use as a border near the ceiling, but she wouldn't be that far before Saturday. The trim had to have the nail holes filled in with wood putty, then be varnished. The first coat of varnish had to be smoothed with steel wool before she could apply the second coat. For the first time, she was grateful it was such a small room.

The carpet was installed Friday, and the effect of the blue carpet on the room raised her spirits considerably. It was coming together, in spite of the setbacks, mistakes, and unfinished trim. The ceiling was impressive, a desert mural of various cacti, mesquite, bluffs, coyotes, roadrunners, rattlesnakes, and even a cowboy on his horse. A narrow creek wound through it, separating the various scenes. She had painted the gray spackling compound with a pale desert sand color, which brought the figures into greater relief. The walls were summer sky blue, the carpet a deeper blue. With the bold colors in the Indian spread she'd bought for the bed, the coordinating curtains, and the phoenix stencil, it would be a stunning room.

She was putting up the curtain rods when Megan called, collect, as always.

"I took the roadrunner picture to school, Grandma," Shawn told her. He was seven, and in second grade. "Brett didn't believe me that it lived with you, so I hit him."

Peggy smiled, even as her heart was squeezed painfully by hearing Shawn's precious voice. "Then what happened?"

"Mr. White sent a note home for Mommy to sign."

"What did your mommy do?"

"Made me sit in my room and think about what I should do next time someone calls me a liar. I told her Mr. White already did that at school, but she made me anyway."

"And what will you do next time?"

"Hit him when the teacher's not looking," he stated with assurance. Peggy heard Megan's sharp reprimand, and Michael took the phone.

"Hi, Grandma. Mommy's yelling at Shawn in his room."

"What are you learning in kindergarten, Michael?"

"M is for Mickey Mouse!"

"That's right! Will you read me a book when I come see you on Thanksgiving?"

"No, Grandma, I can't read," Michael stated, as if she should know that. "I just know alphabets."

"Oh."

"Grandma?"

"Yes, darling."

"I need new shoes."

"What kind of new shoes?"

"Michael Jordan shoes, so I can jump high."

"Wow. What's wrong with your old shoes?"

"They have a hole in the toe, and they hurt my feet!" he stated emphatically.

"Let me talk to Mommy, Michael. I love you."

"Come home, Grandma." The warble in Michael's voice caused tears to spring to Peggy's eyes. "We miss you."

"I miss you, too, Michael. I'll see you Thanksgiving. Have Mommy show you on the calendar."

Peggy waited on her end of the line while Megan encouraged Michael to go watch television. Steeling herself for Megan's familiar plea for financial aid, Peggy was caught off guard by the tremor in her daughter's voice.

"Megan, what's wrong?"

"Dr. Connelley had a heart attack this afternoon," Megan told her in a hushed voice, obviously not wanting the boys to hear.

Dr. Connelley had delivered both of Megan's babies, and she had worked as his receptionist for the last five years. Megan had never referred to him as anything more familiar than "Dr. Connelley," and always spoke of him in awed tones.

"Oh, Megan, I'm so sorry. I know how fond of him you are. How serious is it?"

"I don't know." Peggy could hear swallowed tears. "All they'll tell us is he's 'guarded but stable.' He's fifty-eight years old!"

Peggy wasn't sure if Megan's wail was saying "that's too young," or "that's too old to recover." She tried to sound reassuring. "Youth is in his favor."

"He won't be able to work for months, maybe never."

Peggy felt cold dread wash over her. She hadn't considered that side of it. Megan would be out of a job.

"Don't panic, Megan. Many people recover quite well from heart attacks and return to their previous work. Fifty-eight is somewhat young for permanent retirement. There should be plenty to do for quite a while around the office, billing, phone calls, referrals. He'll be back at work before you even have a chance to take a vacation." Peggy prayed what she said was true.

After she hung up, Peggy sat in the cupola watching the lake reflect the sunset. Megan unemployed would threaten everything. There was no way Peggy could support her daughter's household and maintain her own. Guilt assaulted her. If she'd put Megan through school instead of herself, as her mother had suggested she do, Megan would have a college degree to help with her job hunt. If she'd stayed in Wichita, taught school there, kept the house, Megan could at least move back home with the boys.

"Dear God," she prayed, elbows on her knees, head in her hands, "Let him recover quickly." She grimaced to herself as she realized her prayer of healing was more out of selfish desire than compassion.

# Twelve

Peggy was up with the first light of dawn Saturday. She had stayed awake long into the night, her mind again too jumbled with thoughts to sleep. She rehashed the events with Peter, and with the kids, alternately blaming and exonerating herself for their behavior, and her own. She had also been keenly aware that it was her last night on the mattress on the floor in the caboose. Tonight she would sleep in her bed, in her bedroom.

With Clint.

A thrill rippled through her, again. She wished it were a more sensuous bedroom, one without a washer and dryer in it. She sighed. Seduction hadn't been a consideration when she bought this place.

The mornings were cooler now, but still pleasant. She drank her coffee outside, watching the sun rise over the lake and the deer walk up the draw. She was too restless to stay there for long, though. She had baked a coffee cake, in case Clint hadn't eaten breakfast.

She needed help moving the furniture from the shed into the bedroom and decided to ask Clint to help her. It would mean him seeing the ceiling from the floor instead of from the bed, but she didn't want any other men in her bedroom, and she and Violet weren't strong enough. Besides, since the floor was finished, she wanted to move into the studio also.

Her warm greeting clued Clint in on something happening, although he wasn't sure what. He responded to her exuberant hug, pleased with her good mood, and complimented her on her coffee cake. Watching her as he sat at the table, he was even more convinced that something was going on. There was a glow about her, an almost vibrant energy. She was wearing makeup, he noticed, even though it was Saturday, and they were planning to work all day. She also had on his favorite halter top under a long-sleeved cotton work shirt. There was a light in her eyes that stirred something deep inside him when she looked at him. Yes, something was definitely different today.

"This climate agrees with you," he told her. "You look younger and . . . better . . . since you've been here."

Peggy reveled in his admiring gaze, even as she marveled at his obtuseness. She'd lost ten pounds, deepened her tan, and colored the white out of her hair since moving in almost two months ago. Still, at least he'd noticed *something* was different, even if he couldn't figure out what. She had no intention of telling him what was different. After tonight, though, he would probably assume he had something to do with it.

Before they started moving furniture, Clint wanted to see the room that had deprived him of her company for so many weeks. He stood in the doorway to the bedroom, amazed, taking in the carpet, the walls, and the woodwork. He hadn't looked up yet.

"Well?" Peggy demanded, needing him to say something.

Instead of answering, he walked over to examine her trim joints at the window, moving the curtains aside. His eyes ran critically over the walls, and the baseboards, then finally to the ceiling. As his head rose, his mouth fell open. Peggy smiled with satisfaction as he slowly scanned the entire mural, awestruck.

"You did this?" His tone was hushed as he continued to study the ceiling.

"All by myself," Peggy affirmed.

"I've never seen anything like it." Clint moved slowly around the room to see each scene more clearly. "It's incredible."

"Thank you."

He finally looked at her. She had sounded so casual, but her eyes glowed with pleasure. "I was going to tell you what a good job you'd done on the walls and the trim, until I looked up." He looked up again to emphasize his words. "I can't wait to see what you do with a canvas and oil paint."

"Then we'd better get me moved into the studio."

They went out to the shed, accompanied by Henry, and began moving things into the studio and bedroom as they came to them. Most of the supplies for the studio were boxed and wouldn't be unpacked until the shelves were put up. Peggy set up the wooden easel and placed a bare canvas board on it. Seeing it sitting in her studio sent a thrill through her almost as strong as the one she experienced when she looked at Clint. She smiled. Tomorrow, in the afterglow of love, she would paint the lake at dawn. Maybe she'd give the painting to Clint. She could just imagine his reaction each time he looked at it.

"A smile like that should be reserved for thinking of one's lover," Clint's husky voice startled her out of her musing.

He slid his arms around her from behind, pulling her up against him. She had been thinking about her lover, and now he was nuzzling her neck, making her shiver. She laid her head back into the hollow of his shoulder, allowing him better access. His arms around her bare middle sent a rush of blood to her breasts, and they tingled in invitation. If this continued, her carefully planned night was going to occur before lunch, on the studio floor.

Peggy stepped away from him, trembling visibly. She flashed him a shaky smile and headed toward the door for the next load. Clint slowly followed, but his thoughts were no longer on moving furniture.

By noon, everything was out of the shed, and assembled. Clint had brought the appliance dolly, moved the washer and dryer from the porch into the bedroom, and connected them. Peggy loaded the sheets for the bed into the washer.

"Test load," she explained. Standing in the bedroom with Clint was making her ache for him again. "Let's break for lunch."

"I brought the sledgehammer," Clint told her as they ate sandwiches out on the porch. "It wouldn't take long to knock down the shed."

"That would be great."

They had spoken little all morning, and most of the conversation had been about where to put what. Clint was picking up definite vibrations from Peggy. The sensual energy in the air between them was tangible, and Clint was having a hard time controlling his reaction to it. He hoped the physical exertion of knocking down the shed would help.

"Why don't you go put those sheets in the dryer," he suggested, when their lunch was finished. "I want to make sure the vent works." He went to get the sledgehammer.

Clint loaded the tin from the roof in the bed of his pickup, and together they stacked the wood that had been the walls of the shed in a neat pile to be used as firewood through the winter. The caboose stood free, the metal wheels and short decorative segment of track it sat on now visible. The side bore the scars where the shed had been attached, but once patched and painted, it would be like new.

"Isn't it awesome?" Peggy breathed, as they stood back to look at it. "I knew it would be."

Clint was looking at Peggy, not the caboose. "Yes," he agreed, his voice husky with emotion.

Peggy looked up at him and nearly reeled from the desire that impaled her. They stood, transfixed, gazing silently into each other's eyes, the air crackling between them.

"How about a swim," Peggy said, her voice distant. "I feel grimy from all the dirt."

Clint nodded, not trusting his voice. Maybe the swim would do what knocking down the shed hadn't been able to. At this rate, he was going to be too tired to do anything tonight, if indeed he was reading her signals right. There was still a dance to get through. He nearly groaned aloud as he followed her down the hill toward the lake.

The swim didn't help. Peggy was in a playful mood, and Clint again took advantage of every opportunity to touch her. Instead of swimming in the deep water of the cove, they had decided to swim out from the sandy shoreline below the cabins. It was too late in the year for the summer residents, so they had the beach to themselves. As usual, they were wearing the clothes they'd been working in. Clint had shed his shirt, keeping his shorts. Peggy was also in shorts, the shortest pair Clint had ever seen her wear, and that mouth-watering halter top.

As they swam out toward deep water, Clint pulled her under, sliding his hands along her silky calves before he kicked downward. He released her, and she surfaced sputtering. She lunged at him, and he allowed her to push him under, then kissed her quickly before they resurfaced. He laughed at her inability to overpower him, but instead of getting angry, Peggy flashed him a mischievous grin and dove under again.

Expecting her to grab his legs and try to pull him down, he wasn't prepared for the muddy sand she brought up from the lake bottom, and smeared into his thick hair. He roared and grabbed for her, but she'd already begun her retreat, swimming toward shore with strong strokes. He swam after her, catching her as their feet touched bottom. She screamed as he scooped her up, and with another roar threw her to her back on the wet sand at the water's edge. He pinned her hands beside her head and subdued her with the weight of his body. In the shallow water, he could feel her bare thighs under his.

"Get off me, you're heavy." Peggy was laughing and trying to catch her breath.

"Not until I get revenge."

Peggy's eyes widened, and the laughter stilled as she read the message in his eyes. He lowered his mouth to claim hers hungrily.

"Peggy," he groaned, forcing himself to pull away from her. She wouldn't release him. As soon as he let go of her hands, she wrapped her arms around his neck, trying to pull him back down to her. "This is not a private beach," he reminded her.

"Then let's go back to the cabin. You can help me make the bed."

He studied her face a long moment, wanting to be sure. Her eyes were dark with the passion he'd aroused, guileless and without their usual wariness. She tugged at him until he lowered himself to kiss her again. With a groan of pain, he broke the kiss, pulled her to her feet, and ran with her across the beach and back to his cabin.

"Clint," she protested as he pulled her up the steps to the porch.

"This is closer," he insisted. He closed the door and crushed her to him, his mouth hot and hungry as he silenced any further arguments from her. Once he had her willing response, he picked her up and carried her the remaining few feet to his bedroom.

Peggy gave herself up to the emotions coursing through her with Clint's fevered assault. His mouth was hot against the still damp coolness of her breast, and she could only cling to him as he carried her along on the storm of passion, too long repressed. She was more than ready when he entered her, a scant few minutes after they'd landed on the bed, and screamed out as they climaxed together. Clint rolled with her to his side as they both gasped for air.

It was some time later when the haze cleared, and they began to relax the fierce embrace they held each other in. Clint sought her mouth, giving her a gentle kiss, then smiled at her.

"Are you okay?"

Peggy gave a short laugh. "That wasn't quite the way I had it planned."

Clint hugged her to him. "I'll go slower next time . . . maybe." He released her then, so he could look at her.

Peggy felt shy under his scrutiny, now that

243

the initial passion had passed. She could hardly remember how she came to be naked, it had happened so fast. She reached for the sheet to cover herself.

"Don't do that." He got off the bed then, and took her hand, indicating she should come with him. He led her to the bathroom, turned on the shower, then discreetly left her for a few minutes. He waited until she got in, then joined her.

"Let me." He took the shampoo and began rubbing it through her hair, massaging her scalp. "I wish you'd let your hair grow."

"I cut it off the day I filed for divorce," Peggy said tensely.

"It looks good short," Clint amended quickly. The last thing he wanted to bring up now were ghosts. "Here," he said, handing her the bottle of shampoo. "You put it there, you get it out."

Peggy stretched to reach the top of his head. She smiled, remembering smearing the muddy sand into his hair. Clint bent his head to help her, which put his mouth just above her breast. He teased it with his tongue, then suckled it hard.

"Clint!" She jerked her arms down, barely missing his head with her elbows.

"You're not shy, are you?" He rinsed his

hair under the shower stream, then soaped a washcloth. "Turn around then. I'll do your back."

Peggy did, but he didn't stay on her back. He raised her arms, soaping as he went, discarding the washcloth as he used his hands over her breasts, then between her legs. Not even with Peter, when they were first married, had Peggy known such intimacy. Clint's gentle touch and admiring gaze was arousing her all over again, and she finally took the soap and began to explore him.

His skin was pale and soft where his shirt protected it from the sun. The muscle under it was hard and well developed. Peggy slid her soap-slicked fingers through the springy hair on his chest, circling his flat nipples until they were as hard and tight as her own.

He was a big man, and strong. As Peggy stroked the sensitive skin over his belly, she marveled at the lack of flab. The muscles of his thighs were hard and corded, from riding horses, she imagined. She ran her hands down them appreciatively, then back up over his firm buttocks. She delighted in the feel of him, roving freely with her hands and her vision until it was no longer enough. Pressing her soft belly against his very erect manhood, she lifted her face, seeking his mouth. He met her, having waited patiently until she was ready, and the intensity of their kiss flooded her senses. They were barely dry when they were again in Clint's bed.

Their second joining was a little less frenzied, but not much. Still joined, Clint pulled the sheet over them as they lay on their sides. Feeling totally satiated, Peggy snuggled into him, and drifted off to sleep.

"We're going to be late," Clint's sleep-thickened voice crooned in her ear.

Peggy awakened slowly, reveling in his warm embrace, not wanting to break the bond yet. The light in the room indicated that it was growing late. She looked up into adoring brown eyes and smiled at him.

"Of course we don't have to go. We could stay here and make love all night." His gaze fell to her uncovered breasts and he reached out to cup one. Her nipple tightened under his stroking thumb.

"What time is it?"

"Six o'clock."

That vanquished the fuzzy warmth. Peggy sat up suddenly. "Six o'clock!" she wailed in dismay. She slid out of his embrace and began frantically gathering her clothes, pulling them on quickly, grimacing at their clammy dampness.

Clint lazed on the bed, watching her. "You're acting like a guilty teenager. Who are you hurrying for?"

Peggy felt like a guilty teenager. She hadn't been worried about it at the time, but now she wondered who'd seen their frenzied dash from the beach to Clint's cabin. Now they would be late to the dance, and Clint's kids would undoubtedly give them knowing looks. Her heart sank in consternation. She had intended to be so discreet. Now, the teachers at school would know. Her students would know. The women at the church—Oh, God, she'd never be able to go to church again.

Clint frowned as he sensed her growing panic. He jumped out of bed to catch her before she could dash out. "Are you regretting this?"

She met his scrutinizing gaze, feeling miserable. "I had intended for us to be more discreet."

Clint smiled, remembering their heated kiss followed by the almost desperate run up the hill. "Now the whole county knows you're mine." He pulled her against him and kissed her to validate his claim.

"Clint, they'll judge me," Peggy wailed, struggling to get away. "You've been here forever. They are your friends. I'm the new divorcée in town and will be accused of shamelessly throwing myself at the most handsome bachelor I could find. They'll say I've the morals of an alley cat, but you couldn't help yourself."

"I think you misjudge us," Clint stated lightly. "Is that how people in Kansas think?"

His blasé treatment of her fears only increased her irritation. He stood there, casually naked, his brown eyes sparkling with amusement. Peggy glared at him.

"Let me walk you home. We'll make something to eat and skip the dance." He again tried to pull her close, but again she resisted.

"Just pick me up in an hour—no, make that forty-five minutes." She ran a hand through her hair, which she'd slept on wet, and pulled a distressed face. "I wanted to look so nice tonight."

"Meet me at the door in a pair of red heels, and I'll be quite satisfied."

"Red heels won't go with my dress."

"What dress? I meant *just* red heels." He leered at her.

"Forty-five minutes!" she admonished him, dashing quickly out the door.


"Just explain that we decided to tear down the shed and time got away from us," Peggy coached as they walked toward the community house. At their entrance, which was considerably more than fashionably late, every head turned to watch them. Clint possessively wrapped his arm around Peggy's waist and smiled at his friends. Peggy felt the heat in her face.

The band was out of Roswell, and played a combination of country and slow love songs. The lead singer had a sultry voice that encouraged close dancing. Clint guided Peggy over to where J.R. and Justin sat with their wives, then went with the boys to get them drinks.

"Must have had a lot to move," Gina commented.

As Peggy had expected, she and Tina exchanged knowing glances and amused smiles.

"We decided to tear down the shed." Peggy felt her face flush even as she said it. "We didn't realize the time."

"Umm, hmm." Tina squeezed Peggy's arm affectionately. "I haven't seen Dad so radiant since Jeff was born. Have you, Gina?"

"Maybe when Rachel was born." Seeing Peggy's distressed expression, Gina gave her other arm an affectionate squeeze. "We're happy for both of you."

Peggy was grateful for the men's return. "Would you care to dance?" Clint asked her without even sitting down.

She jumped to her feet. The band was playing "You Decorated My Life" and Clint held her much too close for public dancing.

"I can't wait to get you home," he crooned into her ear.

"Your daughters-in-law practically have us married," Peggy complained.

"Smart girls."

Peggy didn't have a chance to argue as the love song ended and the band quickly shifted into a higher gear. Clint taught her the Texas two-step, and had her laughing and out of breath by the time the number ended.

"I need water," she told him as they left the dance floor.

"Come on. I want you to meet some people."

Clint led her to the bar area for her water, and introduced her to other ranchers from the area. She met the parents of some of her students, which helped make her feel less the outsider. Still, she could feel their intense scrutiny of her.

During the band break, everyone gathered in an adjoining room where the hostess had arranged a lavish feast. People stood in small groups, eating and talking. Tina and Gina stayed close to Peggy, telling her a little about the people she'd met.

"Peggy, you've met Lattie Winegardner," Gina said as a woman near Peggy's age approached them. "The Winegardners own the ranch closest to ours."

"Yes, Clint introduced us earlier." Peggy smiled at Lattie. It wasn't returned.

"What's this Clint tells us about you two getting married?" she demanded, with barely concealed hostility.

"Lattie!" Tina and Gina gasped together. Peggy was too shocked by the question to respond.

"My concern is for Clint," Lattie stated matter-of-factly to the twins. "Eileen hasn't been gone that long, and this one hasn't been around very long. Do you love him?" she demanded of Peggy.

Shock was rapidly giving way to anger.

"Clint is a friend. I don't believe anyone has mentioned marriage."

"I just heard it from the man himself. 'The sooner the better' were his exact words, I believe."

"Excuse me," Peggy said in a tight voice. She ignored the girls' attempts to smooth over the matter and went to find Clint.

"Peggy!" Clint opened his arms to welcome her into the circle of people he was standing with.

"Clint tells us congratulations are in order," said the man on Clint's right.

"You don't congratulate the bride," the woman beside the man admonished him. "You wish her happiness."

"May I speak to you in private?" The comments around her were threatening to push Peggy to the limit of her temper.

"Oh, oh, trouble in paradise, already," quipped another man.

"Short honeymoon," the first agreed.

Clint looked guilty as he walked with Peggy outside where they could talk in private. He started apologizing before she could even start lecturing.

"You've a right to be angry. I should have made a formal announcement with you beside me, but Wendal asked me if marriage was in the wind and I commented that the sooner the better as far as I was concerned. It kind of got out of hand after that."

"Take me home, Clint."

The icy fury in her demand took him aback. "I don't understand. I said I was sorry."

"Now!"

Her attitude was pricking his temper now, and he met her murderous glare with the confidence of a man seldom challenged. "I'll tell the boys," he stated coolly and went back inside.

When they had driven several miles without a word, Clint finally felt calm enough to attempt discussion. "What exactly are you angry about?"

Peggy shot him another drop-dead glare. Her voice was strained with the effort not to rail at him like a lunatic. She feared if she started, she wouldn't be able to stop, not to mention the things she would probably say in the heat of the moment.

"Are you really that obtuse, Clint? You don't know?"

"I asked, didn't I?" he asked tightly.

"I'm not Eileen," Peggy stated. "I would appreciate being asked before announcements concerning my life are made. I guess Kansas is a little more progressive than New Mexico. Women are still asked if they want to get married, instead of being told by the neighbors."

"I've never compared you to Eileen."

"That's not the issue!" She gritted her teeth. She hadn't meant to yell.

"I told you how that happened, and even apologized."

"No you didn't. You don't know how to apologize. You explained to me why you weren't at fault."

"I'm sorry! Happy?"

"Delirious!" She slumped back in the corner of the pickup, arms crossed defiantly across her chest.

The silence in the cab reached suffocating proportions before Clint took a deep breath and tried again. "I really am sorry. I hate it when you're angry with me. We'll do it right with the family tomorrow, make an official announcement, go into Clovis and celebrate if you want to."

"My God," Peggy breathed softly, not sure if it was a prayer or a curse.

"Now what?" Clint was nearing the end of his patience, and it was audible.

"You really don't understand, do you?"

"Why don't you explain it to me?" The sarcasm was heavy.

"Did it ever occur to you that I don't want to get married?"

"No." It was a growl.

"Why?"

"You're not the kind of woman who indulges in affairs. Even you said my asking you to sleep with me was asking for commitment. You were right. I don't treat sex casually, and I happen to like being married."

"I don't. I thought you knew that."

"You were married to the wrong man."

"I moved here to gain my freedom. Why would I throw all that away after two months?"

"I'm sorry you consider being married to me throwing your life away."

Peggy heard the pain through the sarcasm. "You're twisting my meaning. I haven't finished what I came here to do."

"Keep the damn caboose," Clint snapped. "Come out here and paint your heart out. It's a wedding ring, not leg shackles."

"It's not you, Clint," Peggy tried to reason with him. "It's me. I'm not willing to give up my barely attained freedom to be your wife. Why can't we just enjoy each other's company and leave it at that for the time being?"

"It's a matter of trust, Peggy," Clint shared. "You don't trust me. I guess what we had was just a physical need on your part. I hope you're satisfied." He pulled the pickup to a stop at her door.

"That was a cheap shot, Clinton Howell, and I should slap your face off your head for it." Her voice was arctic as she flounced down out of the truck and slammed the door.

She was right. It had been an ugly thing to say, but the conversation had put him in an unreasoning, ugly mood. Clint sat in stony silence until Peggy went inside the caboose. Slowly he put the truck in gear and drove the short distance to his cabin. Inside, he stood in the bedroom, looking at the disheveled bed where their passion had raged only a few hours ago. What had happened?

Deliberately he stripped the bed, using the physical activity to keep from smashing a wall in his frustration. He wadded up the sheets and stuffed them into a laundry basket along with the towels out of the bathroom, his work clothes, and his still damp shorts. Gaining momentum, he packed the clean clothes he'd brought for the weekend and loaded everything into the pickup. There was no use staying here tonight. He wouldn't be able to sleep in that bed anyway. It was doubtful he was going to get any sleep at all.

# Thirteen

Peggy watched the sun rise over the lake Sunday morning from the cupola of the caboose, where she'd sat all night. Sometime in the wee hours of the morning, anger had given way to a numb melancholy. True to her nature, she was replaying the evening, the day, even the last two months, and deciding she had no one to blame but herself. She'd let her priorities get skewed by raging hormones. It wouldn't happen again.

The pale colors of dawn reminded her of the painting she had planned to do, to commemorate the morning after. It wasn't even a particularly noteworthy sunrise, obscured for the most part by gray clouds. She considered painting it anyway. She'd hang it in the bedroom, so she could look at it when she got tired of looking at the ceiling mural.

She climbed down the ladder and went to find her camera.

The nights were cold now. After taking her pictures of the bleak sunrise, which she decided must be done in watercolor rather than oil, she made a pot of coffee and huddled in front of the wood-burning stove. The question now was what to do this morning. If she didn't go to church, rumors would run rampant. She had no idea what Clint would tell people. Surely the man wasn't arrogant enough to believe she'd come around. The thought made her blood run cold. She had to attend church this morning, and act as if nothing unusual had occurred last night.

Violet gave Peggy a long intense perusal when she came into her Sunday school classroom, but didn't say a word. Peggy was wearing more makeup than she'd ever seen her wear, but it still didn't cover the dark circles around her eyes. She didn't say anything when Peggy suggested they sit on the opposite side of the church from the Howells during the worship service, either. Clint was not as generous.

As soon as the pastor dismissed the service

he approached her and took her hand in greeting. It was a typical and perfectly innocent Methodist tradition, but Peggy thought her chest was going to break from the pounding of her heart. He didn't have the option of makeup to disguise his sleepless night. His usually warm, laughing brown eyes showed fatigue, and pain. Peggy kept her focus on the silver slide of his string tie.

"Good morning, Clint." She cursed the tremor in her voice and retrieved her hand as expediently as possible.

"Peggy . . ."

"I apologize for overreacting last night." She managed to get the tremor out of her voice, but she couldn't meet his eyes. "You were right, it was just a statement taken out of context." She raised her voice for the benefit of the curious who were trying not to appear to be eavesdropping. "I hope we can continue to be *friends*."

She finally met his gaze. The hurt had been replaced by a hardness that made her wince.

"If you wish," he answered, his deep voice low and detached.

Peggy could almost hear the shrug of indifference. She'd been wrong to worry about him perpetuating last night's rumors. Clint would never grovel, beg, or manipulate. He gave her a slight nod, a remnant of a more chivalrous time when knights bowed to ladies, and walked away. Peggy bit down on her lower lip hard. She hurried to the restroom. She would not cry, not over another man, and not in front of all these people.

Gina slipped into the deserted ladies' room while Peggy was splashing cool water over her face, heedless of her makeup. Silently Gina handed her several paper towels. Peggy used them, murmuring thanks, then regarded the younger woman. Gina's expression was so tragic, Peggy had to smile.

"I'm sorry I was such a party pooper last night."

"Peggy, please reconsider," Gina begged. "I know you've only been here a short while, but I've never seen two people who belonged together more."

"Whoa, there," Peggy objected, raising her hand for emphasis. "Reconsider? Your father-in-law and I have always been friends, and will continue to be." Peggy turned back to the mirror to try to repair her mascara with the paper towel.

"Marriage was not proposed, Gina," she

261

said to the mirror. "A flip comment was taken out of context and blown out of proportion. I overreacted, that's all." She gave Gina what she hoped was a reassuring smile. "Nothing's changed."

Peggy's smile felt tight. It was an outright lie and she was still inside the church. She sent a brief prayer heavenward, asking forgiveness.

Gina wasn't convinced. "Something's changed, all right. Last night you were both radiant. Today you both look like you spent the night at the wake of your best friend."

"We're fine, Gina."

Gina scrutinized her for a moment, then gave her a hug. "You come out and see us again. Promise?"

"I'll try."

"Promise." It was a demand.

Protective lying was one thing. Being forced to make promises she had no intention of keeping was another. "No, Gina, I won't promise."

The voice was soft, but Peggy's dark blue eyes held Gina's with warning. "Okay," Gina agreed with a heavy sigh.

Peggy finished washing the rest of her makeup off after Gina left. Violet's intrusion wasn't as subtle as Gina's had been. She also handed Peggy a handful of paper towels.

"From streetwalker to ghoul," Violet stated baldly.

"Thanks a lot," Peggy retorted. "I love you, too."

"Want to talk about it?"

"No."

"I heard about the shameless hussy that blew into town and snatched up the poor, unsuspecting, rich widower. Tsk, tsk, tsk," she clucked her tongue disapprovingly, shaking her head.

Peggy was not humored. "Drop dead, Violet Adams, you and this whole damned gossiping town."

Violet flinched at the venom in her friend's voice, not recovering until Peggy was almost out the door of the restroom. "Peggy! Wait!" She caught up with her and tried to grab her arm. "Peggy!"

Peggy jerked her arm out of Violet's hand and continued her march through the church toward the exit.

"Peggy, talk to me." Violet pursued her to the van, where Peggy turned on her again.

"Leave me alone, Violet."

"I was only teasing you," Violet pleaded. "I only heard you came to the dance together, and that there was a misunderstanding about your relationship. No one was cruel, Peggy. I made that up just to tease you." Violet was encouraged by the fact that Peggy hadn't gotten into the van, yet. "Actually, I only heard about it from one person, and she felt bad about possibly causing problems between you two."

"There is no 'we two,' " Peggy stated, climbing into the van. "But there certainly was a 'misunderstanding.' I'll talk to you tomorrow, Violet." She paused, then let her expression soften.

"I'm sorry I cussed you out. I'm not coping very well this morning."

"Come have lunch with me. We won't talk about men at all, if you don't want to, or we can burn them in effigy, whichever."

"Thanks, Violet. I just want to go home and sleep the rest of the day." The tension that had kept her awake all night and even through the sermon was crumbling. Peggy was suddenly, overwhelmingly, tired.

Having no other options, Peggy slept in her bed in her newly redecorated bedroom. She avoided looking at the ceiling. She tried to avoid thoughts of Clint, the fantasies she'd had about him sharing this bed, and her new knowledge of him that far exceeded any fantasies. Even when exhaustion finally claimed her, troubled dreams haunted her sleep.

Monday she waited until the last moment to arrive at school, leaving no time to visit with any of the teachers before classes started. The day proceeded with almost boring normality. Even at lunch, talk was the usual, and no one paid her any special attention, or treated her any differently. Even Violet talked about mundane things, although Peggy could tell it took effort.

"Have you met Bob Parsons yet?" Violet asked her.

"Yes." Peggy remembered meeting the artist and retired history teacher who'd shared so much of the local events of the Fort Sumner area. "I talked to him at length when I first arrived here. He only had two panels done at the time."

"He's almost finished now," Violet told her. "We could drive over there one afternoon."

"That would be nice," Peggy answered vaguely.

Violet took another bite of her lunch, thoughtfully. "Have you met Pete Reeves yet?"

"Billy Ellis's stepfather? No. I hate confrontations, and don't know how to tactfully ask the man to bathe and clothe his son, who is old enough to bathe and clothe himself."

"Want to meet him, off the record?"

Peggy noted the gleam in Violet's eyes and was instantly wary. "How?"

"He owns a legitimate business establishment." Violet gave her a convincingly mischievous grin. "Do you like margaritas?"

"I couldn't go into a bar alone."

"Who said alone? I'd go with you. We could go today."

"That's even better," Peggy commented sarcastically. "Two women in a bar, drinking margaritas in the middle of the afternoon."

"You forget. This is not the big city. This is Fort Sumner, and everyone knows me. We'll go over and see Bob's panels, then drop by Pete's place for a drink. Pete will come over to say hi, and I'll introduce you."

"Maybe another day," Peggy hedged. She picked up her tray when the bell rang for class. "Thanks, Violet."

"For what?"

"For being a good friend." *For not pushing when you're about to rupture from want-*

*ing to,* she thought silently, giving Violet a wry smile before they parted.

She stayed late that afternoon, working in the art room. She had been so obsessed with finishing the bedroom, she'd avoided involvement with school activities. Now, she wished there was something to keep her from having to go home. Pat Sullivan, the drama teacher, found her loading students' clay pieces into the kiln.

"Violet told me you were still here."

"Hi, Pat." Peggy put the last piece in and secured the lid in place.

"These are really good," Pat marveled, picking up a finished terra cotta coyote.

"Yes," Peggy agreed with a flush of pride. "Some of the students are quite gifted."

"Any of them good with paint?"

"We haven't done any painting, yet, but some of the pencil drawings reflect real talent."

"I'm still trying to find workers for the junior-senior play," Pat said. "I thought maybe you could recommend some of the students to paint the backdrop."

Peggy had forgotten the play. Now, it seemed like a tailormade diversion. In addition to keeping her mind off Clint, she would be doing something she enjoyed.

"I'm pretty much done with my remodeling," she told Pat. "I'd love to help, if you're still interested."

"I never turn down volunteers," Pat said. "I'll bring you a copy of the play. It's scheduled for December third."

The play was a murder mystery, of sorts, titled *Who Dunit?* by C.B. Gilford. Peggy took it home and read it that evening. The only stage setting required was the main character's study, which didn't present much of a challenge. Three of the characters were angels. Somewhere in her boxes of patterns she had an angel costume that she'd used in several Christmas pageants. She found it before she went to bed.

Tuesday after school Peggy decided to drive over to the Bowl-A-Matic and see Bob Parsons' progress with the murals. Bob was applying black paint to a steam locomotive when she approached. As before, when he saw her he came down from his ladder to talk.

"So you came back to see what happened to the Comanches," Bob addressed her, wiping paint off his hands with a rag.

"Yes," Peggy answered, amazed that he remembered where their conversation had left off.

"Range wars." Bob gestured to the third panel. Sheep with their shepherds stood on one side, faced off against cattle and cowboys on the other. "Until the white man came with his herds of sheep and cattle, the range belonged to the buffalo, and the Comanches."

Peggy leaned against the brick that divided the panels, settling herself for another history lesson. A natural storyteller with an inborn sense of an appreciative audience, Bob hit his stride quickly. "The sheep came first, under the Spanish rule of this area. However, the Comanche decided they didn't like the sheep, and the herds were lost to Comanche raids. Have you been out to Lake Sumner?"

"I live there," Peggy said.

"This is the Alamogordo Valley, and when it was first created, that was Lake Alamogordo. During a cattle drive, a pair of brothers, named Eddy, thought the valley so beautiful that when they built their railroad town, they named it Alamogordo. As the town of Alamogordo grew, the lake was renamed so as not to confuse people."

"And the railroad made cattle drives obsolete," Peggy supplied, pointing to the last panel that he was still working on.

"Yes," Bob agreed. "Changed Fort Sumner

also. That's why the fort is so far south of town."

"That did puzzle me."

"There was a stage stop here called Resolano. When the railroad came through, the Fort Sumner businesses moved across the street and eventually the town became Fort Sumner. There was already a rail line through New Mexico to California, through the Raton Pass in the north, but winter passage was difficult. The line through Fort Sumner was a shortcut to California. It was only a mile shorter, but the railroad defended themselves by pointing out that the mile they cut off was straight up. Steep mountain grades made using steam locomotives expensive, and so the longest bridge ever built going uphill, was built across the Pecos River." He gestured toward his last panel, where the trestle bridge was depicted in the background. "The southern end is nine feet higher than the northern end.

"Because of the railroad, the valley was once again irrigated, as it had been during the time of the Indians. We could have been the major rail hub, if sufficient water had been available. Clovis got that distinction."

"When was the lake built?"

"The Alamogordo Dam was finished in

1939 by the Bureau of Reclamation. The Corps of Engineers built another dam in 1980, up at Santa Rosa. The lakes were built to collect the snow melt out of the mountains in the north. That's why the lake level fluctuates so much. It fills in the spring, and is emptied through the summer for irrigating the valley. We have to let so much flow through to Texas also."

"They opened the dam Saturday before last, the lake is so full," Peggy commented. "I read in the paper that it's only the second time in twenty years they've had to open the gates."

"We've had one of the wettest summers in recorded history," Bob agreed. "The reason the Pecos bridge had to be so high, was because the Pecos reached such massive flood stages, on the average of about once every ten years. This would have been one of those years."

Peggy promised she would come to the dedication ceremony when the murals were finished, and thanked Bob for his time and for sharing his knowledge. She'd managed not to think about Clint for a whole hour while she talked to him.

* * *

September merged into October, and Megan's boss, Dr. Connelley, continued to improve. The Fort Sumner Vixens, the girls volleyball team, basked in the glory of a championship season. The Fort Sumner Foxes, coached by Ed Cowen, didn't win a single football game. With each loss, the number of players dwindled further. Preparations were begun for homecoming, though without much enthusiasm. Bob Parsons finished his murals, and dedication was set for October twelfth, the Saturday following homecoming.

Peggy enjoyed working with Pat and the kids on the play. She stayed after school frequently to help the stage crew build the backdrops for the set, and then supervised while the students painted them to resemble the walls of a famous mystery writer's study. To encourage creativity, she decided to have a contest for the paintings to hang on the walls of the study. She would let the student body judge the paintings.

Peggy's volunteer staff of students included Billy Ellis, who finally gave in to her coaxing. She also drove in to pick him up on Saturdays to help her finish the studio. Although using him made anything she did take twice as long, Peggy was determined to reach the pathetic boy.

She painted the walls of the studio a soft white, trimmed the windows and the doors, and built shelves along the outside wall under the windows. She sold the furniture she couldn't use, clearing out the porch, and bought a short couch for the caboose that just fit between a side table and the drop-leaf dining room table. She had wanted a hide-a-bed, but with the coffee table that held the stereo and the wood-burning stove on the opposite wall, there wasn't room to pull out a bed. The couch had soft arms in case some poor soul ever did have to sleep on it.

The sewing machine was set up in the studio, with the large chest of drawers that held all her patterns, notions, supplies, and material. She bought a long table with folding legs from a school supply outlet. She clipped the photograph of the "morning after" sunrise to the easel in preparation to painting it. The finished studio smelled of paint and turpentine, radiated sunlight through its large uncurtained windows, and gave Peggy a thrill every time she walked into it.

The lingerie chest and the three-foot closet

didn't begin to hold all her clothes. Peggy built shelves over the washing machine and bought under-the-bed storage boxes. Her bedroom looked like a utility room with a bed in it but saved her having to go into town to the Laundromat, though, for which she was grateful. It also stifled any romantic notions she might toy with. She tried to ignore the ceiling.

Two weeks after his heart attack, Dr. Connelley notified his office staff that he would be closing the office for an undetermined period of time. He had arranged for a colleague to accept his maternity patients, and wasn't even going to consider returning to practice for at least six months. The office would officially close on October eighteenth. Peggy had the date marked on her calendar as the end of the first nine weeks. It was looking like the end to a whole lot more.

Peggy sat in her cupola, watching the moon hanging full over the cold lake, unable to sleep after Megan's phone call announcing the news of Dr. Connelley's retirement. She remembered the events of a certain August night eight years ago with a clarity that belied the passage of so much time. Kevin had been preparing to start his first year of college. Megan had been sixteen, Erika, fourteen. Peter was in Miami on business, as usual.

Peggy had served Stroganoff for supper that night, with green beans, a salad, brown-and-serve rolls, and apple crisp for dessert. She thought it was funny how even the smallest details stuck in her mind about that night. The kids were unusually quiet and kept looking at each other with loaded expressions. Peggy knew something was up. She waited, slightly amused at the signals they obviously thought she didn't see. Finally, Megan put down her fork and cleared her throat. The other two quickly followed suit.

"Mom?"

Looking at Megan's pale face, then at the serious expressions on Kevin and Erika, Peggy's amusement was swallowed by a growing sense of impending doom. She gave her middle child her full attention, putting her fork down also.

Megan wet her lips, looked at her lap, picked up her fork again, then darted a quick glance at Erika. Erika's exaggerated look clearly stated "Just say it!" Megan took a deep breath and tried again to look at her mother.

275

Peggy waited, her heart in her mouth. It was something awful.

"Mom." More fidgeting. An audible swallow.

"Oh, for Christ's sake!" Kevin lost all patience. "The stupid thing got herself pregnant!" Kevin crossed his arms over his chest and glared at Megan in exasperation.

The two sisters erupted, raining curses and admonitions down on their brother's head, while Peggy sat, too numb to intervene. She'd known that's what Megan was going to say. Her friends discussed the possibility frequently, pregnancy and death by car accident being the two greatest fears among parents with teenagers. She closed her eyes to the escalating shouting match going on around her and pressed her fingers to her temples. Suddenly it was quiet, and she opened her eyes to the concerned faces of her three children. At least Megan was no longer so pale.

"Lance?" Her voice squeaked. She cleared her throat and tried again. "I assume Lance is the father?" Lance Bauldin and Megan had been dating almost exclusively since Christmas. Sensing trouble, Peggy had tried to encourage Megan to date other boys also, telling her sixteen was too young to tie herself down to one boy. When that failed, she'd tried to broach the subject of birth control. Megan had turned crimson, responded with "Really, Mom," and fled. Now, Megan was finding something in her lap extremely interesting. She did nod affirmatively to Peggy's question about the father.

Peggy had perused her daughter calmly. Of the three children, Megan most favored her mother's looks. She kept her pale blond hair Gypsy cut and permed in a cascade of curls. She was of medium height and shared her mother's tendency toward plumpness. She'd had on shorts that day, and a loose top. Peggy realized that she hadn't seen her in her usual skimpy attire this summer.

"Since when, Megan?"

"April," came the muffled response from the bowed head.

That was almost as great a shock as the announcement. How had Megan concealed a pregnancy for four months?

"Have you . . ." Again the telling squeak. She started over. "Have you and Lance discussed what you'd like to do?" She silently congratulated herself on handling this like a calm adult. She'd give in to hysterics later.

"We talked about getting married, but that would mean Lance quitting school. I doubt he could support us on his salary at the store."

Lance's father owned a retail furniture store, and Lance worked after school and on weekends delivering furniture. Peggy hated to think of him dropping out of high school. He would be a senior this year, Megan a junior. Peggy was disappointed that he hadn't come to dinner tonight, to be with Megan when she broke the news. She wondered if he was breaking the news to his parents at the same time.

"I want this baby, Mom." Megan finally met her mother's eyes. "With or without Lance, I want to keep and raise this baby." There had been determination and commitment in the dark blue eyes, eyes almost identical to Peggy's.

"Let's start with a doctor's appointment," Peggy had concluded on a sigh of accepting what couldn't be changed.

Lance and Megan had married and moved into the Thompsons' finished basement so they could both finish school. Lance continued to work at his father's store, and had hoped he could move up the ladder into the more lucrative position of salesman. Shawn was born, and Peggy loved him as if she'd given birth to him herself. Michael was born two years later. Peggy kept them both during the day, first while Megan finished school, and then when she went to work for Dr. Connelley.

Lance's hopes for advancement were dashed when his father informed him he would never get out of the warehouse without a college education. The marriage broke up shortly after Michael's birth. Although the divorce settlement included child support, Megan rarely forced the issue, preferring to rely on herself, and her mother. She talked about maybe someday going to nursing school, but Peggy felt it was more for Dr. Connelley's benefit than any serious desire to be a nurse. Lance had worked his way through college, majoring in business, then taken a job out of state. Megan rarely talked about him.

Megan and the boys still lived in the furnished two-bedroom duplex she and Lance had rented after she'd started working. It wasn't large, but it had a fenced-in yard for the boys, sat in a quiet neighborhood, and was close to the grade school. Rent was five hundred seventy-five dollars a month, an enormous sum on a receptionist's salary.

A pitiful yowl from below her brought Peggy's thoughts back to the present. Henry didn't like it when she sat in the cupola. He was unable to climb the steps cut into the wall, and so sat looking up at her reproachfully. Peggy realized she was freezing, in spite of the heavy robe and blanket she was wrapped in. She climbed down and allowed Henry to lead her to bed.

# Fourteen

"I knew I'd find you here."

Peggy looked up from her grade book at the sound of Violet's voice. "What are you still doing here?"

"I could ask the same."

Peggy returned her attention to the grade book. "I live here."

"I've noticed." Violet stood behind her chair and peered over her shoulder at the two deficiency slips Peggy was filling out.

"Matt Thomas and Juan Estavez," Peggy supplied, holding the slips up for her to see. "I offered them an extra credit project, but they weren't interested."

"They failed English, also," Violet supplied.

"Why? They can't play football with failing grades."

"Exactly."

Peggy twisted in her chair to give Violet a puzzled frown. "I don't understand. Ed can't afford to lose any more players. The team needs them—desperately."

"Desperately is right," Violet agreed, then shrugged her shoulders. "I feel bad for Ed. He's a good coach who emphasizes good sportsmanship and the concept of teamwork as well as how to win the game. He doesn't deserve the losing streak the Foxes have had this year. The boys really like him, which is why they've chosen the coward's way out."

"They failed deliberately?"

Violet nodded. "It was easier than quitting, which several others have already done. At least we're past homecoming. Jack do this?" Violet picked up a paper maché mask from a collection displayed on the wall behind Peggy's desk. The face was white, the hair and lips black, with black painted around the eye holes. A gruesomely realistic gash ran blood red from the forehead through the left eye. "Hatchet wound?"

"I'm trying to talk him into doing a painting for the play contest. He's so talented, if he'd just channel it into something . . ."

"More socially acceptable?" Violet rehung the mask. "Who did the wolf?"

"Jesus Estavez."

"No kidding? Quite a comeback from the stick man."

"He's been a welcome surprise."

"Unlike his brother Juan?"

"Juan's talented, he just refused to work."

"How's Clint?" Violet changed the subject so abruptly, Peggy stared at her blankly for a minute.

"Clint who?"

"Uh huh," Violet gave her friend a piercing look. Peggy met it without flinching. "You're acting like one of your students, you know."

"Really? I should have videotaped your performance with Sam last Friday."

Violet had the grace to blush. Sam had come for homecoming and even Violet knew she'd behaved more like an insecure teenager with a crush than a fifty-year-old teacher who'd been married to the man for twenty-five years.

"Sam didn't act any better," she defended herself.

"I noticed."

"At least we're trying. Have you two even spoken to each other? And I don't mean that stilted handshake of greeting you go through every Sunday morning."

"Who two are you referring to?" Peggy persisted.

"Why won't you talk about it?"

"There's nothing to talk about. He fulfilled my every expectation." Peggy stood abruptly, gathering up her grade book, purse, and coat.

"Peggy, I'm your friend," Violet insisted, angry at being once again shut out. She followed Peggy out the door and waited while she locked the art room.

"Then don't bring up subjects you know are distasteful to me," Peggy snarled, equally angry as she glared at Violet. Violet glared back. Peggy felt her anger dissipate almost as quickly as it had appeared. She ran a hand through her hair.

"See you tomorrow, Violet. Thanks for stopping by."

"Any time."

Peggy heard the bitterness in Violet's voice, but didn't know what to do about it. She walked out to the van. Thoughts of Violet, and then Clint, followed her all the way out to the lake.

Clint *had* met her every expectation. It had been three weeks since the dance, and she'd done everything in her power not to think about him. He hadn't come out to the lake, hadn't even called. Apparently, he was also trying not to think about her.

Every expectation. She had expected him to be an incredible lover, and he had surpassed her greatest fantasy. She had expected him to be possessive, and he had surpassed her worst fears. She had known he was stubborn, and proud, but she had thought to hear from him before now. Of course she wouldn't give in to him, but it hurt that he didn't even give her the option. She supposed her cool response to his handshake every Sunday had something to do with his lack of follow-up.

She was wearing herself out trying to keep too busy to dwell on him, but he was everywhere. In a short two months, he had left his stamp all over her life. She couldn't look at the caboose without remembering the afternoon they'd knocked down the shed. Her body betrayed her every time she remembered him, wearing only shorts, shoes, and gloves, his tanned body oiled with the sweat of his exertion, his muscles bunching and rippling as he swung that heavy sledge hammer. She sighed, her body responding as it always did when she thought of that day. She shifted uncomfortably in the seat of the van. It was safer to remember Lattie's accusation at the dance.

Clint's remembered presence haunted her entire house. She'd eaten more meals with him than without him while they were working. He had sat at her dining table. He had sat at the table on the screened porch. He had walked with her along the beach. She'd sculpted the ceiling of her bedroom for him. He'd installed the windows of her studio, and the sliding door.

Even the work she did without him reminded her of him. The miter box she'd used for the trim boards was his. The day she'd used the skill saw to cut the shelves for the studio she'd kept expecting him to dash up the hill and jerk it out of her hands. But he hadn't.

Peggy glared at his empty cabin as she drove past it. That irritated her also. It was cruel of God to make her have to drive past his cabin twice a day. The least He could have done was have him live somewhere else on the lake. There were plenty of cabins she never saw.

Of course, if God were really merciful, she never would have met the man. Maybe he was an abject lesson, and driving past the cabin was a daily reminder. Never again would she let a man near what was left of her heart.

Report cards went out Friday, and Friday night the fifteen remaining Fort Sumner Foxes were once again soundly trounced, in spite of the allout efforts of the players. Both quarterbacks were injured, which dropped the roster to thirteen, mostly freshmen and sophomores. Coach Ed Cowen walked through the school under a black cloud, in spite of the support of the faculty and the students. The whole school seemed subdued. They were scheduled to play Tatum next, the top-ranked team in the state. The situation seemed hopeless.

Tuesday afternoon, Coach Cowen took a vote among the twelve players who showed up for practice. Seven voted to play, five voted to forfeit. An emergency school board meeting that night voted to forfeit. It was a matter of safety, they said.

Peggy had never been a football fan, but she liked Ed, and admired the courage of the boys who'd stuck out a losing season and continued to give their best. She commiserated with the students, but silently agreed with the school board's decision. It was pointless to sacrifice the remaining players for the sake of appearances.

Peggy had problems of her own. Her phone calls with Megan had not been reassuring. What jobs were available did not pay enough to even meet the rent. Megan would receive two more weeks of pay from Dr. Connelley, then would be able to draw unemployment for a while. Peggy promised to help out, but she worried about the situation. There weren't any good options when Megan's income ran out.

The Friday of the forfeited Tatum game, Peggy finally let Violet talk her into having a drink at Pete's Place. Violet assured her there would be a crowd, considering the glum mood everyone was in over the game. She was right. Even at four o'clock, the place was packed. Two men waved at Violet from a dark corner. Violet waved back, then steered Peggy toward them.

The men were dressed in worn jeans and open shirts. They stood as the women approached their table, their dark eyes glinting with approval as they surveyed the two women. Peggy was immediately on guard as Violet made the introductions.

"Peggy, this is Angelo Diaz and Ramon

Estavez. This is my good friend Peggy Thompkins."

The one Violet introduced as Ramon offered Peggy the chair next to him as Violet slid into the one by Angelo. She took it, barely responding to his enthusiastic smile of welcome. She shot Violet a glare of reproach. She'd come here to meet Billy's father, not be picked up by a couple of Hispanic cowboys.

"Two margaritas," Violet instructed the girl who came to take their order. She ignored Peggy's glare and smiled at Angelo. Angelo's expression reminded Peggy of a cat savoring the sight of a cornered bird. Violet seemed to be encouraging him. Peggy felt like the cornered bird. She cast Ramon a quick glance and saw an expression similar to Angelo's on his face. Her heart sped up nervously. This had not been a good idea.

"Any relation to Juan and Jesus Estavez?" she asked Ramon. The waitress sat a large stemmed glass in front of her and she took a quick sip, then nearly choked. She'd never tasted tequila before. The salt around the edge of the glass amplified the astringent effect of the drink on her throat. She looked around for the waitress to ask for a glass of water.

"Cousins," Ramon answered, handing her his glass of water.

Too uncomfortable to be proud, Peggy thanked him and accepted the glass.

"Angelo and I work on the family ranch east of here."

He really was a handsome man, Peggy thought. Very dark, both from heritage and long hours in the sun, his teeth straight and very white in contrast. His hair and full mustache were shiny black, without a trace of gray, although there were sun lines around his eyes. Heavy muscles strained at the light fabric of his shirt and were evident in the bared forearms and work-roughened hands. The interest in his heavily lashed dark eyes made her flush with an uncomfortable warmth. The dense air was difficult to breathe. She tried the margarita again. She noticed Violet's was half gone.

"Are you a teacher, like Violet?" Ramon asked.

"Yes, I teach art and history." The margarita was tasting better with each sip, and Ramon's accent gave his speech a musical quality.

"You painted the phoenix on the red van?"

"She told you about that?"

"Yes, and I have seen it. It is very good."

"Thank you."

"Could you do the hood of a pickup?"

"You want a phoenix on the hood of your pickup?"

"No. How are you with horses?"

"I like to paint horses." She thought of the horse and rider on her ceiling. She wondered if Ramon would like it, then quickly shook her head to dispel the thought.

"Is something wrong?"

He laid a hand over hers. Peggy quickly extracted it to pick up her drink again, laughing nervously. "No, nothing's wrong. What were you saying about a horse?"

Violet and Angelo were getting quite cozy, Violet all but in his lap as she ordered a second drink. The men ordered more beer with tequila shooters. Peggy feared if she finished the drink she had she wouldn't be able to drive home.

"I have a picture," Ramon was saying. She forced her attention back to him. "It's the cover of a book actually, but I'd like to have it painted on the hood of my pickup. Would you be interested?"

Peggy thought about it. With Megan unemployed, extra income would be most welcome right now. She'd gotten five hundred apiece for the two vans she'd done back in Wichita. She could have done more, but the move had prevented it. Five hundred dollars was almost one month's rent. Ed Cowen had also been interested in having her paint his van. She wondered how many others would be. It could be a lucrative side line.

"I've never done a pickup," she answered, trying to sound businesslike. "But it shouldn't be difficult."

The crash of glass hitting the floor abruptly interrupted the conversation. Peggy looked up to find Sam looming over Violet and Angelo, his face suffused with rage. She felt Ramon grab her out of her chair as their own table was thrown to the floor. Sam jerked Violet away from Angelo and began shouting unflattering names at her. Angelo placed himself between them. Sam punched him hard in the jaw. Ramon hit Sam.

Violet grabbed Peggy's arm and they ran for the door as pandemonium broke out around them.

"Wait!" Violet yelled as Peggy opened the door to make their escape.

"What!" Peggy looked at her friend's rapturous expression, then at the focus of her attention. A scene right out of every Hollywood western was taking place before them.

292

Burly men in dirty western work attire were squaring off and duking it out. Bodies flew across the room to smash into tables. Broken glass lay everywhere. A body landed against Peggy and shoved her into Violet.

"Beg pardon, ma'am," the cowboy drawled, then rejoined the fray. Violet didn't seem to notice. Her bright violet eyes sparkled as she watched Sam fight, a mysterious smile pulling at her mouth. He and Ramon were still at it, both of them sporting bloodied mouths and reddened eyes.

"Did you set this up?" Peggy screamed at her over the din.

"Of course not," Violet snapped, never taking her eyes off Sam, "but isn't it wonderful?"

"If he doesn't get killed!"

"Worry about Ramon," Violet stated confidently. But Ramon got in a gut punch that bent Sam over, then knocked him against the wall with a right to the jaw. Violet screamed and dived into the sea of swinging fists and falling bodies.

"Violet!" Peggy yelled as she tried to restrain her friend, but Violet was not to be stopped. She broke free and ran to her fallen husband, leaving Peggy standing in the center of a war zone. Another body slammed into her and she crashed to the floor under his weight.

"Are you okay?" The heavy body was pulled off of her and she was lifted to her feet. Ramon tucked her under his arm and made a dash for the door.

"Violet!" Peggy protested, but Ramon dragged her outside. The wail of police sirens could be heard, and was drawing closer.

"Come on," Ramon yelled, and Peggy was helpless to do more than allow herself to be hustled away. "It'll break up as soon as the police get there." He pulled open the driver's door to a new black Chevy pickup and lifted her in, then climbed in beside her. He started the engine, put it in gear, and quietly pulled around the back of the bar and onto a residential street.

"You're hurt!"

Ramon wiped the blood off his mouth with his sleeve. "I've been hit harder." He grinned at her.

She couldn't help it. She grinned back. "What about your friend?"

"Angelo?"

She nodded.

"He'll learn not to mess with married women." Ramon laughed then, as if the whole thing was great fun.

"Aren't you worried about him?"

"Naw. After Adams hit him the first time, he stayed down. He probably crawled out the back door."

"He left you to fight for him?"

Ramon laughed again, and hauled Peggy against him. "I'm a better fighter. I'm a better lover, too."

His tone was as seductive as his eyes were lustful. Peggy wasn't sure what to make of this whole thing. She had gone to a bar against her better judgment to meet the father of one of her students, gotten in the middle of a brawl, and now was cruising downtown Fort Sumner in a black Chevy in the sweaty embrace of a total stranger, who was coming on to her. She wondered if Clint drove by if he'd force them over and haul her out, as Sam had done. She sighed.

Ramon hugged her tighter, mistaking her sigh. "I got some beer in the refrigerator back at my place." He lowered his voice suggestively. "I'll show you the picture I want you to paint."

Peggy fought panic. She tried to remember she was a school teacher, a grandmother, and nearly fifty years old. She could handle a fresh cowboy.

"Is this the pickup?" Her voice squeaked like a teenager's.

"Yeah. Ain't she a beauty?"

"Are you sure you want to mar the finish with a picture?"

"This picture, yes." He passed the school and was headed out of town.

"Where are we going?"

"To the ranch where I live. I want to give you the picture."

"I need to get back, Ramon."

"Back where? To Pete's? I doubt your friend Violet will appreciate your company right now."

Peggy doubted it, also. "No. I left my van behind the school. I need to get home."

"It's Friday night. Someone waiting for you at home?"

Peggy knew she was taking the coward's way out, but at this point, she didn't care. "Yes, actually. Henry will worry about me."

"Henry?"

Peggy couldn't look at him. "He lives with me." She knew her ploy had worked as his arm slid away from her shoulders and was rested on the steering wheel. "I think maybe Violet took me along this afternoon to set Sam up."

"I wish she'd let me in on the ploy," Ramon answered tightly. He gently rubbed the swollen edge of his jaw.

"Me, too," Peggy agreed. "I have Billy in one of my classes. I wanted to meet Pete, his father, maybe talk to him."

"Huh! Pete's no father," Ramon stated with disgust.

"I understand he's not his natural father, but he's still responsible for him."

"He don't give a shit about that kid, excuse me, but it's true. If I had a kid, I'd be a real daddy to him, whether he was mine or not. World's bad enough when you're a kid, without your parents dumpin' on you, too."

Peggy was surprised at his display of feelings on the subject. "I take it you don't have any?"

"Parents or kids?" he asked, the roguish smile back.

"Kids," Peggy answered, smiling herself.

"I might, but no woman's claimed 'em as mine yet."

"Would you like to have kids?"

"You offerin'?"

The gleam was back in his dark eyes. Peggy flushed warm. "I couldn't even if I wanted to." She smiled at his puzzled frown. "How old do you think I am, Ramon?"

His expression became pained. "Please don't tell me. I'll behave myself."

Peggy laughed then, no longer afraid of him. "Show me your picture, Ramon, then you must take me back to my van."


Peggy tried to call Megan when she got home and was dismayed when a recording told her the number had been disconnected. She called Erika. There was no answer. She checked her watch. It was ten o'clock there, and it was a Friday. No self-respecting single woman would answer her phone at ten o'clock on a Friday night. She dialed her mother's number.

"Peggy! How nice to hear from you."

"Mom, I just tried to reach Megan and her line's been disconnected."

"I'm sure there's been a mistake," her mother assured her. "You know how these computers make such a mess of everything."

"Have you talked to her today?"

"Oh, yes. Your father and I were over there most of the day. They're fine."

Peggy visited a little bit, then hung up. She picked Henry up and climbed into the cupola with him. He settled into her lap as she puzzled over Megan.

"What does she mean, they spent most of the day over there?" she asked out loud, sitting up suddenly. Her mother hated kids, and though she loved her daughter, her grandchildren, and her great-grandchildren, it was a family joke that visits to Grandmother's house were timed with a three-minute egg timer. She claimed small children got on her nerves and raised her blood pressure. It had been that way since Peggy had been a small child. She was sure her conception had been an accident, and that her being an only child wasn't.

With a growing sense of something catastrophic about to happen to her, Peggy watched the road at the top of the hill, where lake residents turned off the blacktop onto the gravel road that wound through the cabins. After sitting transfixed for over an hour, with nothing more notable than a couple of her neighbors coming home, Peggy picked up Henry and climbed down from the observation loft. Her mother was right. It was a computer error. Megan would be calling her collect before the weekend was out.

It had been a long, exhausting day. Henry followed Peggy into the bathroom, where he resumed his nap on her pile of discarded clothes while she soaked in a tub of scented bath oil. The water was cold when a rude pounding on the front door snapped her awake.

The police! was her first thought. Something awful had happened. Who else would knock on her door at this hour? She wrapped her towel around her wet hair and thrust her wet arms into her terry cloth robe. Barefoot, she ran for the door, tying the robe as she went. Caution took over just before she unbolted the lock. What if it wasn't the police?

The pounding came again, nearly causing her to jump out of her skin with its close proximity.

"Who is it?" she demanded, trying to sound tough.

"It's me, Mom," came Megan's familiar voice. Peggy froze in disbelief. It couldn't be.

"Megan?"

"We wanted to surprise you. Come on, Mom, it's cold out here."

Dumbfounded, Peggy opened the door. A very tired-looking Megan stood on the platform, illuminated by the porch light. Instead of letting her in, Peggy stepped out, looking for the boys. Megan's Volkswagen Rabbit sat beside the van, a small U-Haul trailer attached behind it.

"Oh, no," Peggy whispered, her hand going to her mouth.

"The boys are asleep," Megan explained from behind her. "Show me where to put them, and I'll carry them in."

Peggy gave her daughter a blank look.

"Don't I at least get a hug?" Megan asked, looking hurt by her mother's strange behavior. The hug she received was more mechanical than affectionate. "Mom?"

"I was in the tub," Peggy stated lamely, trying to gather her wits. "I'll help you carry in the boys." As soon as she stepped on the rocks with her bare feet she remembered she wasn't dressed. She winced but went on. What difference did it make now?

"Hi, Grandma," Michael murmured sleepily as she laid him in her bed. "We came to live with you."

"We'll talk in the morning, darling," Peggy soothed him. He rolled over and was back asleep. Peggy moved back to let Megan put Shawn in beside him. She shut the door and went back into the kitchen. Megan followed quietly, realizing her surprise wasn't as well received as she'd hoped.

"I don't want any coffee, Mom," she protested as Peggy began assembling the coffee-maker. "It's been a terribly long day and I'm exhausted." Peggy ignored her and continued to prepare coffee. "I'll go get my bag out of the car," Megan stated, wary of her mother's aloof behavior.

When Megan returned, Peggy had combed out her wet hair and was sitting at the table drinking coffee. She didn't look at Megan.

"Where shall I put these?" Megan asked, a suitcase in each hand.

Peggy was trying hard not to rail at her thoughtless daughter, but the question demanded an answer. "I wish you'd asked me that question before you left Kansas, Megan. I could have given you an answer then. I don't have one now."

"I seem to have caught you at a bad time," Megan tried to soothe in a patronizing tone. "It's late, and you're probably as tired as I am. Show me where to sleep, and we'll talk in the morning."

When Peggy finally looked at Megan, Megan took a defensive step back. Peggy rarely got dangerously angry with her children, and Megan's expression was a mixture of fear and confusion as she regarded her mother.

"You may sleep anywhere you like,"

Peggy stated in a cold voice, tight with control. "You may sleep on the floor, in the chair, or in the bathtub. There's even a chaise longue out on the screened-in porch, although it's a little cold out there." Megan looked ready to cry, but Peggy was unmoved.

"I have one bed, Megan, and one bedroom. If you'd ever listened to me about the cabin, instead of whining and wheedling about what you needed from me, you'd have known that before you came. If you'd consulted me about coming, I'd have told you there was no room. What were you thinking of, driving out here unannounced like this?"

"Excuse me," Megan said tightly, and she turned around and went back out the door with the suitcases.

Her first wave of anger spent, Peggy now regretted her outburst. Belatedly, she wished she'd listened to Megan and waited until morning to say anything. It was too late to do anything about it tonight. Megan came back in and headed toward the bedroom, never looking at her mother.

"Megan." Ignored, Peggy followed her daughter. Megan was bent over the bed, scooping Shawn back up. She turned, but Peggy blocked the doorway.

"Excuse me," she said again.

"Put him down, Megan," Peggy said with a sigh. "I'm sorry I reacted so strongly."

"You said what you felt. Coming here was a mistake." She tried to go around, but Peggy stood fast in the doorway.

"Put him down. We'll work something out, and talk in the morning, when we aren't so tired."

"I'll be at the motel in town."

"Megan, be reasonable."

"It's obviously too late for that."

"Put him down." She spoke quietly, but with all the authority of motherhood. With a final glare of defiance, Megan turned and put Shawn back to bed.

Peggy went to the cabinets under the cupola and began taking out blankets and pillows. Megan went back out to the car and brought her suitcases in a second time. Peggy made a pallete on the floor between the bed where the boys slept and the washing machine.

"Sleep as late as you want," she told Megan.

"Where will you sleep?"

Peggy gave her a hug, then cupped Megan's face with her hand. "On the

304

couch." She gestured toward the short couch with a smile. "See you in the morning."

Peggy took the blanket she'd used earlier, and climbed back up to the cupola. Henry greeted her. "So, you can jump this high with proper motivation." Henry regarded her with his piercing gold stare. "Oh, Henry!" She gathered him up, burying her face in his fur before putting him in her lap. "What am I supposed to do now?"

"Yeow," Henry suggested. He adjusted his position several times before he got comfortable.

Peggy sat there through the long night, as she had on the night of the dance, watching the moon dance over the dark surface of the water, and absently stroked Henry. By the time the sun slipped over the horizon, she'd come up with a solution. It wasn't ideal, and it involved supreme sacrifice, but life was like that.

# *Fifteen*

Monday morning Peggy was rudely awakened to the excited clambering of her grandsons.

"Grandma, Grandma!"

"Wake up, Grandma!"

Still half asleep, Peggy grabbed the closest body and started tickling. Michael collapsed in a fit of giggles while Shawn demanded equal time. Soon both boys were laughing helplessly and begging her to stop.

"Okay, how about spankings!" To the boys' squeals and half-hearted efforts to escape, she switched to playful swats.

"Hugs, Grandma!" Shawn begged, grabbing her from behind while she wrestled Michael. She leaned back against the wall and tightly hugged a grandson in each arm.

"I've missed you guys."

"We missed you, too, Grandma," Michael stated seriously.

"But not anymore, huh, Grandma?" Shawn demanded. "Now we live with you."

"Until we get your new house ready," Peggy amended, giving him a final swat. "Go get dressed. You'll be late for your first day of school."

They fled in the direction of their bedroom.

"You're so good for them, Mom," Megan commented from the doorway.

Peggy glared at her daughter. "Don't start again, Megan. You know I love them, but I want to be their grandmother, not their nanny."

"You could be both."

Peggy shook her head. "If I had wanted to be your live-in nanny, I would have stayed in Wichita." She got up and began making her bed.

Saturday morning Peggy had called her realtor. She, Megan, and the boys had spent Saturday and Sunday afternoon looking at the available real estate in the area. Since Megan was not sure what she was going to do, and since Peggy was going to be responsible for the cost if Megan didn't find work before her unemployment insurance ran out,

Peggy decided to look for a cheap place to rent for her. They had found a lake cabin that looked as long disused as the caboose had been. The realtor promised to get in touch with the owner to see if he would be willing to rent the place in return for it being cleaned up.

Megan hadn't brought much with her from Kansas, but the caboose didn't have room for anything. Since the duplex had been furnished, the only furniture she had was the console television set that Peggy had given her and a set of bunk beds for the boys. However, there were uncountable numbers of boxes containing household items, clothing, and toys. Peggy was sorry she'd torn down the shed. Once again the screened-in porch was crammed to capacity.

As a temporary solution to the crowded living conditions until Megan had her own place, Peggy moved her bed into her studio, folding up the long table. The bunk beds were set up in the bedroom. Megan slept on the short couch in the caboose. Peggy kept reminding herself that in more countries than not, their arrangement would be considered spacious. At least she didn't have to look at Clint's ceiling every morning anymore. The boys loved it.

The boys loved everything about Grandma's house. They loved the caboose, especially the cupola. They loved the rock-strewn desert, and already had an impressive collection of colorful specimens. They loved the lake, the beach, and the large rocks that begged to be climbed. Peggy and Megan both warned them sternly about going off by themselves, showing them the wicked cactus and steep ravines and telling stories of huge rattlesnakes that camouflaged themselves in the rocks. Still, Peggy worried about the boys getting hurt.

Megan had brought the boys' transcripts with them and they were excited about en-rolling in "Grandma's school." They rode into town with her in the van. Megan fol-lowed in her car. They made Peggy drive slowly around the lake in case the deer were out, and even slower over the dam so they could see the spillway and the river far be-low.

"There's picnic tables down there, Grandma!" Shawn exclaimed. "Can we go on a picnic there?"

"If the weather stays pretty," Peggy prom-ised.

"Can you fish in it, Grandma?"

Michael's question brought a sudden pain

as Peggy remembered Clint talking about fishing with his boys. His oldest grandson was Michael's age.

"Can you, Grandma?" Michael persisted.

"I don't know how to fish," Peggy answered. If things were different, Clint would probably offer to take the boys fishing. She resolutely shoved the thought aside and smiled at Michael. "I guess we can learn, though, huh?"

Once the boys were enrolled in school, the four of them settled into a routine of sorts. Peggy took the boys with her in the mornings. Megan picked them up after school, since Peggy usually stayed late to work on the play, or tutor students who were having problems.

Megan spent her days looking for a job that included living in, preferably in a city. She had been adamant in voicing her dislike for the cabin Peggy had chosen, and made no secret of her hope that the owner wouldn't go along with the rent proposal. In an effort to sway her mother's thinking, she kept the caboose clean, did the laundry, and had dinner ready every night when Peggy got home.

"You're ruining my diet, I guess you know," Peggy complained one night as

Megan sliced the chocolate cake she'd baked that afternoon. "I'd lost fifteen pounds."

"I've noticed," Megan said. "Don't eat the cake."

"What's eating you?"

Megan finished serving the boys, then sat down. "You've changed, Mom."

"Really? How?"

"You could pass for my sister—my younger sister."

"I just colored the white. It's still my natural color."

"It's not just the hair. You're slimmer, tanner. You dress different. You act different."

Peggy smiled at the backhanded compliment. "Is that a problem?"

"I think I'm jealous," Megan confessed, "Yet at the same time, I don't understand you. You live out in the middle of nowhere, in this absurdly tiny caboose. You don't even have a television!" Megan and the boys had been dismayed to discover their television useless without a special antennae, which Peggy didn't have and refused to buy. The large set was presently taking up a great deal of space in the studio.

"I like it here, Megan," Peggy stated evenly. "You are free to leave whenever you wish."

"I found this today." Megan changed the subject and pulled a paperback book out of the cabinet. "Is this what liberated grandmothers are reading nowadays?"

It was the book Ramon had given her. Peggy snatched it out of Megan's hands. "A man wants me to paint that cover on the hood of his pickup."

"No wonder you moved out of state."

"I haven't agreed to do it," Peggy snapped, irritated.

"What did you agree to?"

The accusation in Megan's voice made Peggy want to slap her. "My personal life is none of your business, young lady." Peggy left the table and ensconced herself in the studio.

*It isn't fair!* she raged silently, surveying the crowded room that had held such promise. Now the large windows she'd installed—that Clint had installed—for light were covered with newspaper for privacy. Her clothes shared shelf space with her art supplies. Her hanging clothes stood in the middle of the room on a portable rack. Even Henry had been crowded out, preferring to spend his days outside, out of reach of small hands. He waited by the sliding door at bedtime, coming in to sleep with her at night and demanding to be let back out in the morning as soon as he heard the boys up.

*I moved down here to avoid living with Megan. I came down here to paint and gain my independence.* The irony of the situation threatened to overwhelm her. It simply wasn't fair. She grabbed her coat and scarf and went out the sliding glass door. She needed space to think, and there was no longer space inside her home.

It was cold outside, and quite dark. Peggy stopped at the van to get her flashlight, and put it in her pocket. She wrapped the scarf over her head and mouth and started down the road past Clint's cabin. It was too dark to risk the trails.

She was startled to see lights on inside the cabin, and Clint's pickup parked beside it. It was the middle of the week, and certainly too cold for fishing. Her heart was racing painfully as she crept by as quietly as possible. She wished he'd step out almost as much as she prayed he wouldn't.

Now instead of her walk centering on Megan, Peggy found her thoughts straying to Clinton Howell. He hadn't called, not once, in the month since the dance. There had been no card, no flowers, no contact of any kind. It was almost as if he didn't care, except that every Sunday, he made it a point to greet her, to take her hand, and to search her face for any sign of relenting on her part. Although he tried to act nonchalant, she could see the pain in his eyes. That pain pierced her heart, and she couldn't meet his intense gaze. And so, he would release her hand, and walk away, and she wouldn't see him or hear from him until the next Sunday.

She wished she could undo that fateful Saturday. At their age, what was passion, compared to friendship? She missed his friendship. Yet, she knew she couldn't deny the passion.

She had reached the beach, which stretched before her in a dark expanse. The water beyond could be heard, and felt, but not seen. She turned on the flashlight to find a rock to perch on, then turned it off, letting the darkness envelop her again. She was so lost in thought she nearly jumped in the lake when she heard Clint's voice behind her.

"I should have known I'd find you here."

"Clint!" It was a startled gasp and it took her a minute to calm her nerves. "Were you looking for me?"

"You weren't at home. I met your daughter."

"You came to the cabin?" She wished she could see his face. His voice wasn't revealing anything.

"I missed you Sunday. Amanda and Violet both told me about your daughter. Aren't you cold?"

Peggy hadn't realized it until he mentioned it. The rock she sat on hadn't warmed at all. In fact, it seemed to have leeched all the heat from her.

"I guess I am," she stated lamely, sliding off her perch. He took her gloved hands and rubbed them between his own, which were also gloved.

"It's a little crowded at your place. Would inviting you over for coffee be too forward?"

Peggy hesitated, unsure of the wisdom of going into his cabin, alone, and at night. She didn't examine what she was unsure of, propriety or her behavior.

"Please, Peggy. We need to talk."

That was certainly true. She allowed him to take her arm and walk her back up the hill, the hill they'd dashed up . . . She shook her head to dislodge the thought.

"How is your family?" she asked.

"Huh? Oh, fine. They're fine." Clint had been thinking about the last time they'd as-

315

cended this hill as well, and unlike her, he had no desire to squelch the memory. He tried to pull his thoughts back to the present. He really had driven out here to talk to her, though the impulse to take her in his arms and kiss her into mindless submission was overwhelming. He wondered what her response would be.

"I thought Megan would enjoy meeting Tina and Gina," Peggy continued. "Also Michael is the same age as Jeffrey and Rachel."

"That implies social contact," Clint teased. "I was under the impression you never wanted to see me again. Or is it just my family that interests you?"

"I never said I never wanted to see you. You never asked." The last was said so quietly, Clint had to strain to hear.

"I guess I wasn't certain of my reception."

"Can't handle rejection?" she teased.

"Not from you."

They stood in front of his cabin, and Peggy could see his serious expression from the light spilling out through the front windows. She didn't know how to answer that.

She looked so vulnerable, Clint gave in to his earlier impulse. She didn't resist when he folded her into his arms and kissed her, gently and hesitantly at first, then hungrily. Even through both their heavy coats and winter clothing, he could feel her tremble. He kissed her once more, deeply and with every intention of arousing her beyond reason. That he was already there was evident when he scooped her up and carried her inside.

"Clint," she protested weakly. "Not again."

"Not again what?" He didn't wait for her answer, but helped her out of her coat, then himself out of his own.

"In front of the whole lake!"

"Your reputation is already ruined," he murmured, kissing her again before he scooped her back up to carry her into his bedroom. "You might as well enjoy what you're being accused of."

This was folly, she tried to tell herself as each kiss carried her further away from rational thought. It wouldn't solve their problem. Her hands sought his hair as his mouth blazed a trail down her neck. They needed to talk. Her body arched in response as his seeking mouth moved over the breast he had bared, and she moaned in surrender. They would talk later.

* * *

Feeling totally boneless, Peggy lay draped languidly across Clint's big body, her head cradled into his shoulder. He had pulled the blanket over them and was so relaxed and quiet, she thought he slept. She smiled to herself, content to lie on top of his sleeping form until she regained the ability to move. *I love this man,* she realized, knowing she couldn't tell him. Admitting it to herself filled her with a sense of peace she hadn't known in months.

"We need to talk," Clint murmured into her ear, breaking the spell.

She sighed. He was right, but she wished he hadn't brought it up quite so soon. She rolled to her side, sat up, and reached for her clothes.

"You don't have to leave," he protested, trying to detain her.

"I remember being promised coffee," she said gently, slipping away from him and into the bathroom.

In the cold light of the bathroom, Peggy tried to analyze the situation. She hadn't been aware that part of the strain of the last month had been an unsatisfied physical longing. Now that she knew, she wasn't sure what to do about it.

Had their month apart mellowed Clint's

possessive character? It hadn't mellowed her craving for independence, so she wasn't sure. Maybe he was hoping she had changed. That would be more in character. She left the bathroom, half expecting to see him making out a guest list for their wedding.

She found Clint in the kitchen, dressed warmly in old sweats with Fort Sumner Foxes blazed across the front. He was pouring coffee into two mugs. He watched her warily, as if fearful of her response.

"Peggy," he started. She stopped him with a warning glare.

"Don't you dare apologize for what just happened."

He grinned, once again the confident rogue. "I never apologize, remember?"

"You wouldn't mean it, anyway," she retorted, but she smiled at him.

"That's a definite." He relaxed then, and joined her on her side of the bar. "Can we start over?"

"I haven't changed, Clint," Peggy warned softly.

"I realized that before I drove out here. So, what is acceptable?"

She blinked at him in disbelief.

"It's been a long time since I made a fool of myself over a woman, and I'm a little out of practice, but I'm willing to try." He took her hand, looking at the delicacy of it encased in his large one. He turned it over and ran his thumb over the calluses on her palm. She withdrew it, embarrassed.

"I've been working a lot lately," she explained.

"Me, too." He turned his own palms up for her inspection. They were rough with old blisters. She searched his face.

"The boys are going to mutiny if I don't get things settled between you and me. I've tried to keep busy, not think about you." He shrugged helplessly. "The ranch looks great."

"And the rancher?" she asked softly.

"Is miserable." Knowing his pride was part of what had driven her away, Clint allowed her to see the pain in his heart. He was most uncomfortable, baring his feelings like this. It was a lot to ask for love, but he was desperate enough to risk it.

Peggy didn't make him suffer long. She gathered him against her. "Me, too."

"Then you'll marry me?" It was asked with the brightness of a boy released from punishment. Peggy shoved him back so hard he nearly lost his balance on the bar stool. He recovered in time to prevent her escape out the door.

"I was kidding!" he insisted. He was lying, but the look in her eyes was unmistakable. Apparently marriage wasn't a safe subject around this woman.

"It's not funny, Clint."

"I'm getting that message."

"It's about time."

Clint clenched his jaw to keep from losing his temper. He'd promised to be a fool for love, but she was pushing it. "What do you want, Peggy?"

She raised an eyebrow at his growled question. He was himself again, arrogant and growling about not getting his way. She almost smiled. This was the Clint she'd fallen in love with, not the man trying to grovel at her feet a moment before.

"I want a modern relationship," she stated matter-of-factly. "You have your life, and I have mine, and when it is mutually satisfactory, we spend time together." His blank expression said her cosmopolitan explanation was going to have to be put in simpler language. "We get together on weekends when it's possible."

"And just what is the nature of our relationship, should someone want to know?" he asked, not happy at all with her explanation.

"What's wrong with 'friends?' "

321

"I don't sleep with my 'friends,'" he commented, unable to keep the sarcasm out of his voice.

"That's no one's business but our own," she stated defensively.

"So are we to flaunt it before the church, or sneak around like guilty teenagers?"

"You act like it's something dirty!"

Clint ran his hand through his hair in a gesture characteristic of Peggy when she was flustered. He'd never had a problem with being old-fashioned, if that's what people were considered who still adhered to morals. Peggy was making him feel foolish. He had the vague impression that his masculinity was being challenged.

Seeing his frustration, Peggy softened. She placed a hand on his arm, letting her eyes plead her case.

"You said it was a matter of trust. You're right. I love you, Clint, but I don't trust you, not with my freedom." He was getting angry again so she hastened to explain. "Give me time. Prove my fears groundless. Show me I have nothing to lose and only more to gain."

It was a challenge, issued with her heart in her midnight blue eyes, and Clint knew he had lost. To press his point now would only prove him to be the very thing she feared, and she would bolt again. He didn't want that, but he was having difficulty being gracious about it.

She helped him out by accepting his silence as acquiescence, and stood on tiptoe to place a light kiss on his set mouth. "It's late, Clint. We'll talk again. Will you be here a few days?"

"I'll stay tomorrow," he growled.

"I'll see you tomorrow, then," she stated sweetly, pressing another kiss to his hard mouth. She slid her coat on and slipped out the door, blasting him with the cold night air.

## Sixteen

Henry was waiting for her when she got home. She opened the door and allowed him to precede her into the caboose. Megan was sitting in the bentwood rocker, obviously also waiting up for her. Belatedly, Peggy realized she should have reentered through the studio, but she'd been too preoccupied to think about it.

"It's about time," Megan stated belligerently. "Don't you have school in the morning?"

Peggy's pink fog dissipated in a rising anger. She'd almost forgotten why she'd gone for the walk. "You are my daughter, not my mother. I'll thank you to remember that, Megan."

Megan switched tactics. "I was scared to death for you. A strange man comes to the door asking for you, and I discover you're not here. It's after midnight, and I haven't a clue where you are. I don't even know if this one-horse town has a police department to report a missing person to."

"Go to bed, Megan."

"Does Clint know about Ramon?"

"Excuse me?" Peggy turned back from the bottom of the landing. She had decided to ignore Megan, but Megan was making that impossible.

"Clint, the man who came looking for you at ten o'clock at night. Does he know about Ramon, or are there others?"

Although the question was confusing, the insinuation in Megan's voice wasn't. Peggy saw red. She marched back up the steps to confront her daughter.

"I don't think I understand the question, Megan. Care to spell it out?"

Megan didn't back down. "What am I supposed to think, Mother? You're reading S & M books given to you by some man . . ."

"S & M?"

"I thought you had a college degree."

"I must have missed that lecture."

Megan looked uncomfortable. "People who get off on whips and chains, bondage, that sort of stuff."

325

"Did you read that book?" Peggy asked incredulously.

"I didn't have to, Mother. The cover was quite self-explanatory."

"It's medieval!"

"The woman is naked and in chains!"

Peggy ran her hand through her hair, not believing the conversation she was having in the middle of the night, and with a daughter who wouldn't discuss birth control.

"Megan," she began with infinite patience. "It is a macho fantasy that a man asked me to paint on the hood of his pickup. I have met the man one time, and we were introduced by a good friend of mine. He liked the phoenix, and asked me if I'd do his pickup. I haven't agreed yet because of the nature of the picture."

"I can't believe you'd even consider it."

"I thought I needed money to keep you in your apartment until you could find a job."

"Well, you don't need that anymore, so you can just tell this Ramon no."

Megan's high-handed attitude snapped Peggy's control. It had been a stressful month, ending with an invasion of her space and her privacy. "I will tell Ramon anything I damn well please," she informed a wide-eyed Megan. "Be careful I don't *accidentally* allow some family resemblance to sneak into the portrait. You could become the reigning fantasy in this *one-horse town!*"

She left Megan speechless, childishly slamming her bedroom door after she stomped through it. Her *studio* door, she corrected herself, seething, standing in the middle of the crush of furniture that had usurped her kingdom. The cramped room was suffocating, and it was obvious she wasn't going to get any sleep tonight anyway. She gathered up her blanket, reentered the caboose, and wordlessly marched past Megan to climb the ladder into the cupola. Henry landed in her lap on his second bound from the floor. He patiently waited while she arranged her blanket before he curled up to sleep. He purred contentedly while she stroked his fur.

*I, too, was purring a few hours ago.* She thought of Clint and tried to recapture the glow she'd felt after loving him. He'd tried to detain her in his bed. If she'd stayed, she would be curled against him now, instead of sitting in the cupola of a derailed caboose, sleeping instead of staring at the dark night, her arms around Clint instead of Henry. She shook her head sadly.

Clint was not the answer to her problems with Megan. She would be trading one bondage for another. She thought of Ramon's fantasy picture. A naked woman knelt in the foreground, a chain around her wrists and neck. Her long blond hair blew wildly around her. She had large, upthrusting breasts with dark pointed nipples, displayed to their best advantage by her position. Her expression was a mixture of fear and resignation. A fierce barbaric warrior sat on a snorting war horse behind her, the end of her chain in one hand, a huge wicked sword in the other.

Peggy's hesitancy in doing the painting wasn't so much its sexist nature, although that was disturbing enough. The painting was also titillating and slightly pornographic. Peggy had done several sketches, slightly altering the original, trying to figure a way to tone it down to something she wouldn't be ashamed to sign her name to. She had almost decided to tell Ramon she wouldn't do it, until Megan had forbidden her to. Now if she didn't do it, Megan would think she had some control over her. She picked her sketch pad up from where she'd left it on the other seat, and looked through her drawings.

A typical male fantasy, she thought. Victorious, dominant male warrior subdues the weaker, voluptuous female and makes her like it. Though more polished than Ramon, Peggy couldn't help but think Clint would also enjoy the fantasy. No, his fantasy would have the beauty across his lap. His arms would be the only "chains" he would need. She began to sketch Clint on the horse, a cowboy instead of a Viking, the woman across his lap with her arms around his neck.

For all his arrogance, Clint seemed to cherish women. They were delicate creatures to be protected and worshiped. His frustration seemed to come from the fact that she refused to be either protected or worshipped. Still, she loved him for wanting to. She just had to get him over his monarchy complex. Though a better monarch than Peter had been, he was still a monarch, and she had already fought her war of independence. It would be a democracy or nothing. She didn't think he would understand her need any more than King George had understood the colonists. However, his motive was love, rather than power, and she was confident of her ability to convert him.

That left Megan. If Megan could find employment around here, she would be able to afford a place of her own. Supplementing her income with painting would allow Peggy to help her, and she could watch the boys on school holidays and through the summer, since she would also be out.

Another sacrifice. She had hoped to work toward her Master's this summer. Raises and job security were based on education and versatility.

*I won't do it,* she decided fiercely. *I wouldn't have been available if she'd stayed in Wichita. I moved five hundred miles away to avoid just such temptation, and I will not let her manipulate me!* It was time for Megan to move out. Peggy made a mental note to call the realtor first thing in the morning. She'd buy the cabin if the owner wouldn't rent it, but Megan was moving out, and the sooner, the better.

School the next day was a disaster. It started off with an argument between herself and Megan over breakfast. The kitchen was entirely too small to house two feuding women. Peggy took her coffee into the studio.

She was tired and snappy at the students, who seemed to sense her weakness like bird dogs after a wounded pheasant. They whispered, passed notes, threw spit balls, and requested hall passes to the restrooms in record numbers. Peggy sent two of them to the principal's office for carving obscenities in the desktops with their keys. By lunch she was a royal bear, one that had been awakened out of hibernation by construction crews, or something of its equal.

"You need a good lay."

"Excuse me?" Peggy looked up from a paper she was trying to grade. Violet was regarding her intently, then she shrugged.

"One of the kids succinctly summarized your problem during English class. Thought I'd pass it along."

"Just what I need, a fourteen-year-old sex therapist."

"It's worth a try."

"It didn't help." She returned to her paper, but Violet pounced, landing in the chair beside her.

"You saw Clint." Her violet eyes were sparkling in anticipation.

"Maybe I saw Ramon," Peggy said evasively, pretending to study the paper in front of her. Violet was already making her feel better. At the silence she looked up to see Violet's horror-stricken face. "I was kidding."

331

Violet visibly relaxed. "Sorry, it's just that he asked me about you."

"Clint?"

"No, Ramon." Violet scrutinized her friend. "He's considered quite good—you know?"

Peggy shot her a look of long-suffering. "You crudely suggest I go get laid, then you shy away from telling me the man's a stud?"

Violet actually blushed, making Peggy laugh. "Get off Ramon. How's your stud?" The color drained from Violet's face and she wilted. Peggy was almost sorry she'd asked.

"Violet, what happened?"

"Sam's been back a whole week and a half, and it's been a week since we made love," she confessed in a low miserable voice. "Football playoffs."

Peggy smiled, a wicked, devious smile. Violet watched her suspiciously.

"What?"

"I never did get to meet Pete."

Now Violet smiled. "What are you doing tonight after class?"

"Avoiding my daughter."

"I'll meet you in the front foyer."

"I'll be there."


Peggy had to admire Violet's communication network. When they walked into Pete's Place, Ramon and Angelo stood up to seat them at their table. Once again Violet ordered margaritas and went into a huddle with Angelo. Peggy could only assume that the same network that had arranged for the two cowboys to be here would also inform Sam that his wife was once again in the arms of Angelo Diaz. What she hadn't expected, was someone informing Clint that she was sitting in Pete's with the notorious Ramon Estavez.

She and Ramon had their heads bent together over the map she was drawing him of how to get to her caboose, so he could deliver the pickup. Her first clue of trouble came in the form of a crushing grip hauling her out of her chair by her arm. She was thrown into Violet's lap seconds before Ramon slammed into the wall.

"Oh my God," Violet groaned, seeing Clint. "Wrong man."

Clint got in two more hard punches before Peggy got her wits about her. She grabbed his arm and pulled with a strength fueled by fear and anger.

"Stop it, Clint!" She knelt beside a dazed Ramon to assess the damage. His lip was split and he was having trouble breathing. She turned back to Clint, furious.

"What is wrong with you?"

"I thought we had a date tonight!" he shouted. "Is he also your *friend?*" The emphasis on "friend" left no doubt what he referred to.

"Yes!" she hissed, right in his face, too angry to care about their audience or the long-term effects of her impulsive retort. "He's my *friend!*"

Clint actually blanched. Peggy glared at him for a full breath, then turned back to Ramon. Jaw set, Clint glanced around the room, then headed purposefully toward the door.

"Clint, it's not what you think," Violet tried to assure him. She caught him by the arm and tried to pull him back, desperate to rectify the mistake. She didn't get the chance. She screamed as Sam jerked her away and threw her over his shoulder.

"Pete!" Sam yelled over Violet's screams of rage, ignoring her pounding fists against his back.

"Yes, Sam?" A short, slightly rotund man came from the kitchen, as if fistfights and truant wives were a daily occurrence.

"This woman is hereby barred from this establishment!"

"Okay, Sam." Pete returned to his kitchen, and Sam carried his outraged wife out the door.

## Seventeen

Megan was in love. She was crazy, deliriously, obnoxiously in love, and she was driving her miserable mother toward a breakdown. Every other word was "Ramon." Ramon knew everything. Ramon had done everything. Ramon was all things every man should be, but never would be, because there was only one Ramon. Peggy's only respite was that Megan and the perfect Ramon went out nearly every night. Peggy tried to be in bed before she came home. She even bought her own coffeemaker for the studio. She set it on top of the unused television.

Ramon had brought the pickup out to Peggy the afternoon after the fight with Clint and swore he was seeing double. When he got over the shock of finding out Peggy was Megan's mother, not her sister, he spent the evening spreading charm with a trowel.

Even the boys were impressed. By the time he left, Megan had stars in her eyes. Even Peggy's droll reminder of the naked woman in chains didn't daunt her. She made some dreamy comment about finding some chains of her own.

At school, the quarrel between Peggy and Clint got a great deal more publicity than the one between Violet and Sam. Both Violet and Peggy were teased unmercifully about being so wild they were banned from Pete's. On Sunday, Peggy slipped out of church by the back door, not wanting to know if Clint planned to greet her or not. She couldn't face the rejection if he didn't.

It was obvious he was still angry. Their eyes had met once, across the sanctuary. His were hard as he held hers. At least he was as miserable as she was, if J.R. and Justin sleeping during the sermon was any indication. He deserved to be miserable, accusing her of sleeping with Ramon in front of all those people. She only hoped the boys held out until he got over it.

Peggy stayed after school almost every afternoon, working on the stage props and costumes for the play. She enjoyed watching the kids rehearse, and was impressed with Pat's direction. Megan stalled on moving out by showing Peggy two ads for a live-in nanny from an Albuquerque paper. Megan sent her resume to the post office boxes listed with the ads, assuring her mother that she and the boys would be moving out soon.

Violet's attitude vacillated between cat-in-the-cream and cat-left-at-home-alone-for-a-week, depending on Sam's behavior. Peggy wanted to wring her neck for basing her happiness on the whims of a man. At this point, though, she knew advice was unwelcome, so she held her peace. In spite of her present state of insanity, Violet wasn't stupid. She'd figure it out soon.

The days passed, filled with monotonous routines that Peggy piled on herself to keep from thinking. The Saturday before Thanksgiving she and Violet drove into Clovis for one of their all-day shopping trips. By the end of the day, Peggy was exhausted, both mentally and physically. She and Violet had discussed the trials and joys of love, marriage, and men in general to the point of saturation. Peggy groaned as Megan came out of the caboose to greet her as soon as she pulled up in the van. She did not want to hear the latest wonderful act of Ramon Estavez.

"Mom, guess what!" Megan gushed, practically dancing with excitement.

"Spare me, Megan," Peggy waved her aside wearily. "I'm glad you had a good time today." She ignored Megan's hurt expression and began gathering her packages out of the van.

"I talked to Erika," Megan told her, with markedly less enthusiasm. "They're coming here for Thanksgiving."

Peggy stopped to give her daughter a sharp look. "Who's coming here?"

"Erika and Kevin!" Some of the brightness returned. "Isn't that great?"

"What happened to meeting at your grandparents' house?" Peggy demanded.

"They had a chance to go on a cruise with a senior citizens' group. Isn't that great?"

"It's very convenient," Peggy grumbled. So her mother had chickened out. She wasn't surprised. "I hope she gets seasick," she muttered under her breath.

"What?"

"Help me carry these in."

They put Peggy's packages on the table, where the boys immediately wanted to go through them and see what she'd bought.

"I thought you'd be pleased," Megan said,

puzzled by Peggy's lack of enthusiasm. "Kevin's coming. Isn't that great?"

"Megan, you say, 'isn't that great' one more time, I'm going to bop you!" Peggy threatened heatedly.

"Look, Mommy," Michael interrupted. "Grandma bought us puzzles!"

"That's really a pretty one," Megan said, watching her mother through hurt eyes. "Let's go in the bedroom and I'll help you work on it."

Peggy stood alone in the middle of the kitchen. Kevin was coming for Thanksgiving. Was it symbolic? Had he decided a year was long enough to punish her? Maybe losing Cheryl and Hillary had made him more aware of the importance of family, and he'd decided to bury the hatchet on the anniversary of the day it had been raised. Maybe Erika had had enough of him living with her and he needed a place to live.

Peggy felt an icy finger of premonition slither up her spine. No, she wouldn't even consider that possibility. He was too close to finishing his degree.

*He's been this close before,* an ugly inner voice reminded her, making her wince. Actually, he'd been this close twice before, but he'd been an undergraduate the two times he'd decided to change majors. Surely this close to getting his Master's degree . . . Peggy shook her head vigorously to dislodge such negative thinking.

*Kevin is coming to apologize for his childish behavior,* she stated emphatically to herself. *He realizes he was wrong, and that family is too important to lose over a grudge. Besides,* she thought with a grimace, *he came out ahead.* She wondered if he would drive the Porsche—the Porsche he'd bought with *her* money.

*It's Dad's money,* she heard him say again, the way he'd said it the day he'd admitted stealing it from her. No, she doubted he was coming to apologize. It didn't matter, she tried to convince herself. She wanted her son back.

With an effort she pulled her thoughts to immediate matters—Thanksgiving dinner, here. She remembered the first time Clint had seen the inside of the caboose. He'd accused her of not being able to cook, the kitchen was so small. And she had confidently answered that she certainly never intended to serve Thanksgiving dinner here.

Where was she supposed to fit two more bodies? The only place left was the cupola, or outside in the van. She looked up at her sanctuary. Two single seats faced each other on either side, with just enough floor space to put your feet. Each seat had its own side rail on the open side, that also served as an armrest. She heaved a mournful sigh. It meant losing the last private place left in the entire cabin, but it could be done. After all, it was Thanksgiving, a time of giving thanks for home and family.

Quite unexpectedly, and without warning, Peggy burst into tears. She sat down at the dining room table, put her head down on her arms, and sobbed her heart out. Her new life was being consumed more completely than the old one, and she didn't think she could rise out of the ashes again.


Thanksgiving Day dawned clear and cold, with highs promised in the middle seventies. With the doors open to the fall-like day and the boys able to be outside, Peggy was coping better than she had thought possible. Kevin and Erika arrived late Wednesday night, in Erika's car, Peggy noted.

Kevin had approached her hesitantly, with the proper blend of repentance and deference, waiting for her to make the first move. Peggy thought he looked thinner, the shadows around his eyes darker. He was a man, now, not her little boy, and the change startled her. He was tall and slender, with Peter's build and Peter's dark hair and sensual mouth. The blue eyes and square jaw came from her. She smiled at him.

"You've grown up," she commented.

"Geeze, Mom, I'm twenty-seven," Kevin protested, visibly relaxing. Peggy opened her arms to him and he bent down to receive her hug.

"I'm sure you've been grown up for some time," Peggy said, releasing him and wiping tears from her eyes. "I've just been too close to notice."

They were all tired and went to bed early. Erika and Kevin slept in the cupola, on beds Peggy had created out of plywood spanning the facing seats and four-inch foam pads. Shawn and Michael had thought them fantastic, begging to be allowed to sleep up there and let Kevin and Erika have their beds, but all Peggy and Megan could see was the eight foot drop to the floor below. The boys had to be content with playing up there, and sleeping in their own beds.

The turkey was cooked in pieces, since a roaster wouldn't fit in the scaled-down oven, and dinner was served outside on the patio table. Peggy was grateful for the cooperation of the weather. The only way six people could have eaten inside the caboose was standing up. Erika loved the place, and let her nephews show her about with the authority of natives. Kevin was more reserved, not saying much as he followed Erika and the boys during their tour.

Over dinner, which they ate around two in the afternoon, Peggy began to mellow. Her three children and two of her grandchildren were here with her, and the day was gorgeous. Kevin seemed to have come for reconciliation, not to move in. He talked about Cheryl and Hillary with such pain in his voice that Peggy's heart grieved for him. He also talked about job offers he was getting, now that he was within one semester of finishing his masters in business administration.

Erika teased him about his personal habits now that he was living with her, setting off a sibling squabble that reminded Peggy more of the children they'd been ten years ago, instead of the adults that sat at her table. Erika talked about her job with an interior decorator, which she loved. She caught Megan and Peggy up on what all of their friends had been doing since Megan and Peggy had left Wichita.

Megan regaled her siblings with stories of Ramon and his ranch. She could hardly talk for the boys interrupting to tell their own stories about Ramon and his horses, and his skill with a lariat. He'd been teaching them, and they were eager to show the newcomers what they could do.

By the time the pumpkin pie was served, Peggy was feeling quite content, listening to her grown children discuss their lives and laughing with them. The bubble burst at four o'clock, when Peggy answered the ringing phone.

"Peggy?"

"Gina? What's wrong?" There was a panic in Gina's voice that gripped Peggy's heart with a cold glove.

"Peggy, it's Dad. It's Mr. Howell," she clarified. "He was thrown from one of the horses."

"Is he hurt?" Peggy sat down hard on the chair beside the telephone, her legs suddenly weak.

"He's been unconscious since it happened. Dr. Roberts is with him. She doesn't know if he'll have to be flown out or not. They're doing X rays." Gina paused before continuing. "I know things aren't real good between

345

you two, but I thought you'd want to know, to pray for him."

*Pray for him?* The cold fear threatening to stop her heart spread throughout her body. He could die. The man she loved could die, and their last words had been so ugly. "Gina, where is he?"

"At the hospital, in the village."

"The village?" Peggy felt the kids gathering around her, silently supportive.

"Fort Sumner. Peggy, please don't drive yourself," Gina pleaded, near hysterics herself. "I couldn't bear it if something happened to you, too."

"I won't drive myself Gina. I'll be there in twenty minutes." She hung up and looked at the concerned faces of each of her children.

"Clint's been hurt. I have to go to him."

# Eighteen

Peggy and Clint were married Saturday afternoon, to the delight of his children and in spite of the disapproval of hers. The simple, private ceremony was held at the First Methodist Church, with the pastor officiating, on the afternoon of Clint's discharge from the hospital. The bride wore a navy blue wool suit and carried a bouquet of red roses. The best man slid the band of marquise diamonds on the bride's finger, since the groom had both arms in casts, with slings crossing them over his chest.

The twenty-minute trip from the cabin to the hospital, Thanksgiving Day, had aged Peggy twenty years, she was sure. Too stricken to do more than silently plead with God, she had ridden in white-faced terror as Kevin pushed the van to its limits on the twisted road around the lake. By the time they arrived at the hospital, Clint had regained consciousness and was growling like a bear. Dr. Roberts had told the family that was a good sign.

Clint had suffered a mild concussion, a laceration to his forehead that required stitches, and had fractured two bones in his forearms. In spite of his age, Dr. Roberts predicted he would only need to wear the casts about eight weeks. Seeing him alive, awake, and robustly irritable had flooded Peggy with such relief she had vowed never to leave his side again.

Kevin, Megan, and Erika didn't have much opportunity to talk her out of getting married, since she hardly left Clint's room after the accident. When they did talk to her, she stubbornly insisted that Clint needed her and marrying him was the only way she could live at the ranch and take care of him. She twisted the truth a little, telling her children that they'd been discussing marriage for a couple of months, but wanted to give their respective families time to adjust to the idea. Erika was skeptical. She reminded her mother that she'd never heard of Clinton Howell until Thanksgiving Day. Peggy was not swayed.

By Saturday afternoon, their attitudes were

mixed. Erika was still upset with the suddenness of the event, but tried to be supportive and open-minded. Megan was resentful. Kevin was silently sullen, until he saw the Howell ranch. He suddenly became very attentive, quizzing J.R. about the various aspects of ranching.

Since J.R. had placed the ring on Peggy's finger, Justin got the privilege of carrying her over the threshold when they got to the ranch. To Peggy's useless protests, Justin scooped her up in a gesture worthy of his father, and carried her into the house. The dining room table was set with china and silver, a large bouquet of flowers, and a small but beautifully decorated wedding cake.

The kids made them go through the ceremony of cutting the cake. Peggy fed Clint his, then placed her bite in his exposed fingers, bending down so he could "feed" her. He growled something about cake crumbs attracting ants inside his cast, but his family only laughed at him. J.R. held his father's glass of champagne while he toasted his bride.

"To trust," he said, watching Peggy with an intensity in his warm brown eyes that caused her to flush.

The afternoon swirled around Peggy with

a cozy sense of family. She and Clint sat in the den in front of a roaring fire, visiting with whomever came through. The boys unloaded Peggy's things from her van. The girls cleaned up the dishes. Michael and Jeffrey got along famously and were mysteriously out of sight most of the afternoon. Rachel shyly took Shawn out to show him the chickens. Kevin and Erika wanted to be filled in on more details of their courtship, since the whole thing had been unknown to them until the trip to the hospital.

Peggy nearly cried when Kevin actually hugged her goodbye, all animosity apparently forgiven. He congratulated Clint, clapping him on the back in a friendly fashion. Megan hugged her mother, then gave her a long perusal.

"I hope you're happy, Mom," she said, somewhat wistfully. "You deserve to be."

Peggy did cry then, and so did Erika as she hugged both her mother and Clint.

"Why are you crying, Grandma?" Michael asked as Peggy nearly squeezed the breath out of him. He was getting upset.

"Grandmas cry when they're happy," she assured him.

"When are you coming home, Grandma?" Shawn demanded.

"It'll be like before, when we all lived in Wichita. I'll come see you at your house, and you can come visit me at mine. Won't that be fun?"

"I guess so," he agreed, not convinced.

Peggy felt a twinge of guilt. Here the boys had just been uprooted from the home they'd had all their lives. Moving in with Grandma had helped the adjustment, some. Now, she had not only left them, she had introduced them to a whole other family they were just supposed to accept. She hugged Shawn tighter. "I'll come see you a lot," she promised. "Take care of Henry for me."

"Henry doesn't like me," Shawn stated.

After everyone left, the Howell brothers took their respective families off to their own parts of the house, assuring the newlyweds that they wouldn't be disturbed before morning. The house was strangely silent now that it was just the two of them. Peggy made coffee and brought it into the den. She settled on the couch beside her new husband.

"This is where I should put my arm around you," Clint stated flatly. He held the casts up with frustration.

Peggy smiled at him. "Does that hurt?"

"Does what hurt?"

"Raising them up."

"No."

She removed the slings, then raised his arms and slid under them, laying her head on his shoulder and wrapping her arms around his waist. "How's that?"

Clint didn't answer. He just savored the feeling of her warmth against his chest, her head under his chin. He breathed deeply of the scent of her clean hair and the light fragrance that she wore. The fire crackled and popped contentedly.

"Any regrets . . . Mrs. Howell?"

"Yes, actually." She lifted her face to his, smiling at his frown. "I wish I hadn't waited until you were handicapped to marry you."

"You had your reasons."

"They seemed foolish when I realized I could lose you."

"And now?"

"I love you. That's really all that matters."

Clint bent his head to kiss her, but doubt nagged at him. It had nagged at him since Peggy had brought up the subject of marriage, in the hospital. He had no doubts for himself, but worried that when her nurturing instincts gave out, Peggy would feel trapped.

She pulled back and regarded him, bringing him out of his reverie.

"I'd appreciate your undivided attention when you're kissing me."

"Sorry." He studied her upturned face, and felt an ache deep within himself. "I just want you to be happy."

"Then pay attention," she admonished him, and pulled his head back down to hers.

The kisses grew deeper and more intense. Clint shifted, sliding down on the couch until Peggy lay on top of him.

"Is this where you intend to celebrate your wedding night?" Peggy asked him.

"I'm at your mercy. Where do you prefer?"

"What's the history of the rug in front of the fireplace?"

"I think my first grandchild was conceived there."

"Any personal history?"

"None."

Peggy eased out from under his casted arms. He watched through smoldering dark eyes as she removed the jacket to her suit. She stepped out of her shoes as she crossed to the stereo. Out of her tape case she selected a tape, snapping it into the machine. Enya's sensuous voice filled the warm room.

Returning her attention to Clint, who still reclined on the couch, Peggy slowly undid the buttons down the front of her blouse.

The fever in Clint's eyes filled Peggy with a heady sense of power. She was in total control. Before when they'd made love, he'd swept her up in a whirlwind of passion, barely giving her time to realize what was happening. She would set the pace tonight. She would take him. Having finished the buttons on the blouse, she undid her skirt and let it fall to the floor. The silky blouse followed closely behind.

Clint groaned appreciatively. She stood clad in the white lace teddy she'd purchased so long ago, and had never worn. Lacy garters held up her stockings.

"These trousers are becoming uncomfortably snug, vixen."

"Really?" She felt her own excitement building as she crossed to him and undid his belt, then the trousers, smiling at the cause of his discomfort. She freed him with her hands, caressing him until he groaned again.

"You're enjoying this," he complained.

"Aren't you?"

"Yes, and no. I'm extremely frustrated that I can't get my hands on you."

Peggy helped him off the couch, sliding

herself under his arms. His kisses were hungry, his tongue plundering, then inviting hers to do likewise. She helped him out of the rest of his clothes. He pulled the straps of her teddy down with his teeth, then attacked her exposed flesh with his mouth.

The rough fiberglass casts bit into her skin as Clint slowly and meticulously worked his way down her body. Control forgotten, she could only hold his head, lacing her fingers through his thick hair, as he usurped her lead. She gasped as he bit into the lace between her legs, and jerked the snaps free. Pulling her down over him, he lay back on the rug.

"Clint!" she protested as he used the casts against her hips to position her.

"Shhh." He coaxed her with his mouth and the pressure of the hard casts. She continued to put up token resistance until his tongue flicked over the most sensitive part of her. She gasped again with the surge of electricity he sent through her body. Rigid at first, she soon was guiding him, then writhing frenziedly as an urgency built within her. She could not contain the moans as Clint continued to stroke her until she thought she would die if she didn't find release. When it came it was violent and explosive, tearing

355

a cry from her throat as she threatened to scalp Clint with the fingers still threaded through his hair.

Still trembling, she moved down to straddle his hips and take him inside her. She cried out again with his penetration. She felt somewhat clumsy in this position, but soon was concentrating more on the rebuilding tension than on her performance. Clint helped her, holding her ribs with his casts. This time he cried out with her as the final thrust shattered them both. Gasping for air, Peggy collapsed on top of his chest.

"I think I need a pain pill," Clint stated after both their breathing had calmed somewhat.

"Oh, Clint, I'm sorry." Instantly contrite, Peggy rose and went to the bathroom. She returned in a few minutes, wrapped modestly in a robe, with a warm washrag, his pills, and a glass of water.

"Don't be sorry," he teased, realizing she really was upset, thinking she'd hurt him. "I'm going to learn not to clench my fists." He smiled at her long face. "I want to touch you so bad." His eyes held hers for a long time. She still looked enchantingly ruffled, and the love in her eyes made his heart ache. He sighed. It was going to be a long couple of months until the casts came off.

Peggy awoke several times during the night. She was in a strange place, a strange bed, and Clint snored. He also thrashed and kicked covers. At one point she was jerked awake by the painful thump of his cast against her bare back. She got up to find a nightgown.

In the pale light from the bathroom, she stood and assessed her husband. He slept on his back, the bent casts flung out to either side of him. Although Peggy shivered in her nightgown, he had kicked off all his covers, and lay sprawled on top of them as if it were summer. The image of this strong, powerful man, now exposed and vulnerable, touched Peggy's heart. He had always wanted her. Now he needed her.

He stirred, tried to turn to his side only to fall back to his back, whacking the casts together across his chest. Peggy winced. He was going to have to sleep in pajamas or neither one of them would have any skin left. The skin over her ribs was red and raw, but she smiled as she rubbed it, remembering their lovemaking.

It had been an impulsive action, getting married. The thought of losing him still made her heart clutch painfully. Looking around the foreign room brought back the doubts, not of loving him, that was never in question, but of the wisdom of marrying him. All her brave talk about making her own life, finding her real self, having a career now sounded like the empty boasts of a child. She had sold out in less than five months. She didn't feel good about it.

But, the deed was done, and this huge man arrogantly demanding three-fourths of the bed was hers, broken arms and all. With Tina and Gina around, she shouldn't be required to contribute much to the ranch. Maybe it would work out. She would keep the caboose, for her studio. She sighed. If she could just get Megan out of it.

Her hopes of not getting involved with the ranch were dashed at breakfast. Since Sunday was all the honeymoon there would be, Clint and Peggy decided to skip church. They were up early, though, and saw the rest of the family off.

"Don't forget the calves, Dad," J.R. mentioned before they left.

"What calves?" Peggy asked when they were alone. They were both still in their robes and returned to the kitchen. Peggy poured a fresh cup of coffee for herself. Clint shook his head.

"It's not the same when you have to drink it through a straw."

"I'm going to make you flannel cast covers," Peggy told him. "I wish I could pad them, too."

"I wish I could take them off," he grumbled. "I can't even scratch my own nose, or anything else, for that matter."

"What calves was J.R. talking about?"

"They're heifers, actually, or they were. I guess they're cows, now."

Peggy gave him a look of exasperation. "Is that the answer to my question?"

"We're on midwife duty." At her alarmed expression he hurried to clarify. "You shouldn't have to do anything more than dial a telephone. If one of them goes into labor and looks like she's going to have trouble, you call the church and tell J.R. to get himself home."

"They're an hour away," Peggy reminded him, not reassured.

"It'll take that long and longer before any

of them get into trouble. None of them were in labor when he checked on them earlier."

"How many of them are there?"

"Six."

"I realize I'm just a stupid city girl, but I thought calves were born in the spring."

"The planned ones are." He smiled at her blank look. "The neighbor's bull got loose while they weren't home. By the time he was noticed missing, he'd helped himself to my heifers. He broke down the fence and scattered heifers over a five-mile area. Took us all day to round them all up. These six were obviously in heat at the time, and so now are calving in November, before they're old enough to do it easily. It's similar to a fourteen-year-old girl trying to deliver. She's old enough to conceive, but not fully developed through the hips, which can make things difficult."

"So you do a C-section?"

"Not exactly." He looked uncomfortable.

"You kill the calf?" She was horrified.

"No," Clint scowled, "You pull it out, if it'll fit."

"Do I want to hear about this?"

"No. How about a shower?"

Peggy considered, then decided she really

didn't want to know about pulling calves. "Okay," she said, agreeing to the shower.

Clint's bathtub was rigged with a hand-held shower head that could also be set into a wall bracket if a traditional shower was preferred.

"How handy," Peggy commented.

Clint paused, wondering about the advisability of explaining why it was set up that way. He'd installed it when Eileen, his first wife, got too weak to manage her own bath. How many times had he bathed her, watching her waste away day by day? And now Peggy was going to have to bathe him. He didn't like the comparison.

"Most men would consider this the ultimate fantasy," Peggy teased him. She was still wearing her robe as she helped him step over the side and into the tub.

"I've never fantasized about a woman in a terry cloth robe," Clint rejoined, pushing Eileen's image forcibly out of his mind. He bent forward and tugged at her robe tie with his teeth.

"Good thing you have your own teeth," Peggy commented, removing the robe and pushing up the long sleeves of her nightgown. She laughed as Clint groaned in frustration. "Here, let's wrap the casts with towels so they won't get wet."

"Now they won't scratch, either," he replied, his voice warm and husky.

Peggy felt herself flush as she looked up at him. His dark eyes were smoldering and his smile definitely suggestive. "I thought you wanted a shower."

"Oh, I do. I'm looking forward to it." The smile became lecherous.

Peggy laughed as she turned the shower on his head. "Maybe I should be using cold water."

"I thought this was my honeymoon." Clint pinned her with a cast and pulled her against his wet face, soaking the front of her nightgown. "That's getting better," he commented. The thin white cotton became clingy and nearly transparent now that it was wet.

Peggy was laughing, protesting and pushing him away with her free hand.

"Wouldn't it be easier if you got inside the tub?"

She finally did, after he'd soaked her completely and most of the floor. She washed his hair while he knelt before her, supporting himself with the casts around her waist. He kissed and licked her bare stomach, delving into her navel with his tongue.

"That tickles." She jerked back from him.

"Why are you all red?" He stopped playing and frowned at the raw skin over her ribs. When she didn't answer he looked up at her, visibly upset. "Did the casts do that?"

She tried to reassure him with a smile. "The towels help a lot. Maybe I'll leave them on."

He hugged her to him. "Why didn't you say something?"

"I don't remember noticing it, at the time." When he didn't release her she sank down to her own knees before him, taking his face in her free hand. His warm brown eyes were filled with chagrin. She kissed the furrow of worry between his brows.

"It's not painful, and it'll heal. We'll learn to manage."

"I don't ever want to hurt you."

"I know that." She smiled, letting her eyes convey her love and trust, then she kissed him again. She pressed tender kisses to his temple, his eyes, the strong bones of his cheeks, his stubbly chin. By the time she reached his mouth, he was ready and waiting, breaking through her gentle kiss with a rising heat and impatient tongue.

Peggy felt a jolt of fire course through her at his sudden assault. She quickly matched his tempo, the shower wand forgotten. Freed, it took on a life of its own and sprayed warm water everywhere. Clint only laughed, lying back in the tub and pulling her over him. He shut the water off with his toes.

When the interrupted shower finally took place, they were both sporting new bruises. Clint decided it was time to renovate the bathroom, starting with a bigger tub. Peggy suggested trying the bed. Most married couples did, she reminded him.

# Nineteen

Peggy and Clint were somewhat surprised to find the ground covered with ice when they went out to the barn to check on the heifers. It was still coming down, a mixture of fine snow and sleet, glazing the ground and making footing treacherous. Adding to the treacherous footing were the five big dogs excitedly crisscrossing their path. Clint yelled at the dogs, ordering them back to the house. Peggy kept a stabilizing hand under Clint's casted elbow, praying he wouldn't slip, knowing she could never catch him.

"The boys shouldn't have gone into the village this morning," Clint commented, looking out across the ice-covered land.

"The village?"

"Fort Sumner, as opposed to the valley."

"What does that make you out here?"

"Way out."

Peggy opened the side door of the barn, allowing Clint to precede her inside. She wasn't sure what to expect. The interior was warm, dark, and steamy, with a powerful smell of manure and hay. The heifers mooed long and low, hearing them come in. Clint waited just inside the door until Peggy found the light switch.

Part of the barn had been partitioned off, and five of the heifers immediately spooked at the sight of Peggy, crowding into the corner of the barn. The sixth one was lying on the hay. She emitted a long bawl that ended in a high shriek. Peggy broke out in a cold sweat, looking to Clint for reassurance. He'd all but promised nothing would happen until J.R. got back.

"Open the gate," he directed, the concern on his face not reassuring Peggy at all. With her support, he knelt behind the prone cow. The cow began to thrash around and vocalize her distress. Peggy instinctively backed up.

"She's frightened of you," Clint told Peggy. "Go back through the gate for a minute."

Peggy didn't have to be told twice. Once on the outside, she noticed the other five cows huddled in the far corner of the barn, staring at her with huge frightened brown eyes. Peggy backed further away.

"Peggy!" she heard Clint shout. "I need you to come check the position of this calf."

"How do I do that? She won't let me near her."

"She has no choice. I'll try to get her head in my lap."

Peggy approached warily. As before, the cow began to thrash in agitation. Clint talked to her in soothing tones, keeping his voice low. He had crawled to her head on his knees. Peggy could see a mixture of frustration and concern on his face. He shifted clumsily to a sitting position, wiggling his legs under the heifer's head and pulling her into his lap with the casts. The heifer fought him, smacking him in the face with her nose. Clint grimaced, but held fast, still talking to her in soothing nonsense. With the same voice, he instructed Peggy.

"Stay behind her, so she can't see you, or kick you. I need you to put your hand gently inside and tell me what part of the calf is coming out first."

Peggy looked at him with horror. There was no way she was putting her hand *inside* a cow. The slimy, bloody discharge running out was enough to turn her stomach. She would throw up if she touched it.

"I can't," she stated, barely audible. She shook her head for emphasis, her eyes entreating Clint not to ask again. It didn't work.

"Would you prefer I try to do it with my feet?" His voice remained calm for the heifer's sake, but his eyes were hard with warning.

Peggy looked back at the cow's bottom, and a shudder of revulsion rippled through her. The cow kept thrashing and lowing her protest, then suddenly she bore down with the strength of her entire being. More bloody fluid poured from her, but nothing of the calf, not even a bulging. Peggy felt panic and looked at Clint. He was totally occupied with calming the mother.

Peggy had borne three babies of her own. It had been a long time ago, but she remembered it had involved pain, and hard work. She had been surrounded by comforting people, Peter, a caring nurse, a physician she trusted. She had known more what to expect after the first one, but she remembered being terrified with Kevin, not knowing what was going to happen. Clint had compared this heifer to a fourteen-year-old, brutally raped by the neighbor's bull during her first heat. She kept feeding this image, trying to build a level of compassion to override the revulsion. The heifer pushed down again, straining with all her might. Again no progress.

"Peggy," Clint stated softly. "The calf will die if we don't get her help."

"Why can't I just call for help?"

"I need to know whether to have them bring the vet with them. If it's breech, we need the vet. The sooner you check, the sooner you can go call for help, unless you plan to pull it yourself."

That did it. Fighting the bile that rose to her throat, Peggy hesitantly reached her hand toward the slimy passage. The cow pushed again, making her jerk her hand back.

"Do it while she pushes!"

Not giving herself time to think, Peggy quickly did as Clint commanded. She had her whole hand inside, and half her forearm, before she encountered a soft nose. She nearly jerked her hand back out, but then she felt the length of the calf's nose. It moved under her hand. She actually smiled triumphantly.

"It's a nose! And he moved!"

Clint slumped with relief. "Okay, he's alive then. Go call J.R."

"Clint? Does she have an hour? Does the calf?"

"Go call, then we'll decide."

Peggy rinsed her hand at the water trough, then hurried to the house, sliding several times on the icy path. She dialed the church with trembling fingers. The clock on the stove showed it was nearly eleven o'clock.

"They've already left, Peggy," the church secretary told her. "They were afraid the roads would get too bad if they waited."

"How long ago?"

"Maybe ten minutes."

"Thanks." She hurried back to the barn, relieved that help was on its way.

Time passed with excruciating slowness, measured in episodes of bearing down on the part of the suffering heifer. Each effort cost her energy, and after an hour she was perceptibly weaker, no longer struggling against Clint, who still held her head and tried to soothe her. Peggy sat with her back to Clint's, supporting him, wringing her hands and praying.

"How much longer?" she asked plaintively.

"Two minutes less than the last time you asked."

370

"I'm scared, Clint," she whispered, as if the heifer could understand, ignoring Clint's sarcasm. "What if the calf dies while we wait?"

"It's a risk."

"How can you be so cold?" She twisted around to look at him, then regretted her accusation. He looked terrible, as if it were he who suffered instead of the cow he held.

"It's wait for J.R. or talk you through the delivery."

Their eyes held for an eternity while Peggy wrestled with the idea. It was broken by another effort from the heifer to push the stuck calf from her body. Peggy couldn't stand it anymore.

"What do I do?" The terror she felt at the idea was audible in her trembling voice. Maybe J.R. would get here before she had to do much.

"You must push the head back up between contractions, and try to pull the front feet forward. The feet must come first, with the fetlocks straight, and the head midline between them."

Fear caused cold sweat to trickle under her arms and between her breasts as Peggy once again positioned herself behind the heifer's back. Again she held the tail with

371

one hand and with a grimace slid her other hand up to the calf's nose. He hadn't come down any in the hour since she'd last felt him. She stroked him, praying for a sign of life.

"Okay, I'm on his nose." The heifer thrashed again, then began to bear down.

"Just wait," Clint instructed, trying to soothe the mother again.

Peggy could feel the pressure of the contraction against the calf's head, but he didn't come down. He did twist his head slightly, as if in protest of the pressure.

"He's alive!" she shouted. The mother thrashed violently and mooed in fright. Clint threw Peggy a quelling look.

"Sorry," she whispered. "I was just so afraid he wouldn't be."

"Push him back up," Clint instructed, "Until you feel a leg."

Peggy pushed, gently at first. For three contractions she made no progress. "He's stuck."

"Of course he's stuck. That's what you're trying to fix. You're probably trying to be gentle. Please consider that this mother weighs approximately six hundred pounds and that calf close to fifty. Forget gentle.

372

You're not strong enough to hurt either one of them."

Taking a deep breath, Peggy gave the next push all her strength. She felt the calf budge a little.

"He moved!" The mother jerked and hit Clint in the face again.

"Sorry," she whispered again as he glared at her. "I keep getting carried away."

Peggy's arm was shaking with fatigue before she got the head high enough to find a foot. Again she cried out and had to apologize, although the mother was losing a lot of her fight by this time.

"Do you feel hoof or joint?"

Peggy assessed carefully. "Joint, I think."

"Keep going until you find the hoof, then straighten it."

Easier said than done, Peggy thought. She was in almost to her elbow by this time. She had to wait through a contraction before she was able to straighten the leg.

"Now find the other one."

The other foot was higher, and took several tries before she was able to bring it down and straighten it out. The mother pushed and Peggy felt the calf slide down.

"He's coming!" She remembered not to

shout, but she could hardly contain her excitement.

"Make sure the head is between the feet."

Peggy reached back inside, past the feet, and found the nose. He was straight now. She removed her hand, giving Clint a tired smile of triumph. "He's lined up."

But the mother was exhausted by this time. She mooed pitifully and was barely pushing with the contractions.

"You're going to have to pull while she pushes," Clint informed her. "She's going to give out on us."

Peggy's shoulders slumped. She felt exhausted herself. She worked the trembling muscles of her right hand and elbow and watched the cow's feeble efforts at pushing. With a resigned sigh she reached in and found the small feet of the calf.

"Hold behind the fetlocks, the ankle joints, and pull with all your might when she pushes."

The mother pushed, and Peggy pulled. Her hand slipped off the calf and she nearly toppled over backwards.

"You can use a rope," Clint suggested.

Peggy gave him a horrified look. She got a better grip on the calf for the next contraction.

"The vet uses a chain."

Peggy pretended not to hear him. They made some progress with the next push. Three pushes later, Peggy could see the hooves. She was too tired to cheer. She gave Clint a weak smile.

"You're beautiful, d'you know that?"

"The blood hides the wrinkles," she answered, but she felt a strengthening warmth flood her. "Come on, little mama," she encouraged the heifer through the next pull. "Come on, you can do it." Peggy could finally see the calf's pink nose through the opening, spread open by the protruding feet.

Clint, too, was coaching, and soon the nose was outside, then the whole head, then the whole calf. Peggy held him against her and cried, praising God, praising the mother, praising the calf himself. With Clint's instruction, she helped him stand on wobbling legs and brought him to the mother so she could lick him dry. The mother was weak, but she gave her calf a few licks.

"Now what?" Peggy asked Clint, helping him up. He'd been sitting for so long he wasn't standing any better than the calf.

"We need to get the mother up to her feet, and let the calf nurse as soon as possible."

"Really, Clint," Peggy chastised him. "She's just been through a rough delivery. Give that baby a bottle and let her sleep."

Clint fixed her with a tired look of long-suffering. "She's a cow, Peggy, not a human. If she doesn't bond with her calf now, she will reject him. Unless you wish to be wet-nurse as well as midwife, I suggest you encourage her to get to her feet."

"Men," Peggy muttered. She had no clue as to how to encourage a six-hundred-pound mother cow to stand up. Fortunately, the cow still didn't trust her, and struggled to her feet in an attempt to get away from her, taking her calf with her. They joined the group still huddled in the corner of the barn.

"Some gratitude," Peggy grumbled, standing with her hands on her hips. The newly delivered mother let out a bawl, which the others took up. Her calf, now licked mostly dry, had found her udder and was feeding greedily.

"I'm grateful," Clint's low voice assured her from near her ear. He bracketed her with his casts. "I'm also hurting like a son-of-a-gun."

"Oh, Clint." She turned and hugged him close. She thought he was trembling as much as she, but it was hard to distinguish.

She released him to help him into his coat, but he refused.

"I'm a disgusting mess, and I don't want to have to clean the coat. Let's just get back to the house."

Peggy was a worse mess than he, but the cold against her wet clothes made her wrap her coat around her shoulders at least. It was still snowing, the ground white and slick. The wind sliced right through her. By the time they got into the house, she was positive she was frozen. She ran warm water over her hands.

"I'm worried about the kids," Clint commented. He took the pill she gave him and allowed her to strip him out of his nasty clothes.

Built with practicality in mind, the utility room was accessible from the outside, with the washer and dryer, and a bath with a shower. Peggy put their clothes directly into the washer, then stepped into the shower. It took a lot of water and soap before she felt warm and clean again. She wrapped Clint's casts in towels, and got him cleaned up also. They were both too tired, and worried about what had happened to the kids, to reenact the events of the earlier shower. To Peggy, it seemed like a lifetime ago.

Dressed in clean clothes, they tried to decide the best course of action.

"With the icy roads, I'd guess they were off in a ditch somewhere between here and the village," Clint stated. "If we go after them, we could end up in a ditch of our own."

"You don't have a vehicle that can manage icy roads?" Peggy asked.

"The truck is the heaviest. You could put the chains on it. Ever attach chains?"

"I'm from Kansas, remember? It snows there."

"Okay, let's do it."

When Clint mentioned "truck," Peggy was thinking "pickup." What he led her to was a *truck*.

"I can't drive that," she objected.

Clint sighed with exasperation. "It's that or load gravel into the pickup for weight."

Peggy shivered with the cold. It had been almost three hours since the kids had left the church. The grandkids were with them. The shiver turned into a shudder as Peggy thought about the little kids stranded in the snow.

"I'll try."

Clint showed her where the chains were kept. She arranged them behind the dual

378

tires of the old truck, then climbed in to start it. She'd never dealt with a clutch before, and she and Clint both became frustrated as he could only talk her through it, rather than demonstrate. Reverse was the most difficult gear to find, and Clint was ready to attempt it with his teeth before she finally found it. Fortunately, as far as applying the chains, she only had to move the truck a few inches. It jerked back that far before it died, nearly pitching Clint to the floorboard.

"Just attach the chains," he gritted out, "then we'll deal with using the clutch."

She killed the engine six more times before she got the big truck backed out of the equipment barn, then killed it again when she hit the brake.

"Look, Peggy, it's not your fault." Clint tried to regain his patience. "It's a cantankerous old truck and you've never driven with a clutch. Let's just take it slow."

Peggy restarted the truck and found first gear. Biting her lower lip until she tasted blood, she eased out on the clutch and felt the monster begin to move forward. She raced the engine and managed to get rolling with only a little hopping.

"It probably was time to replace the

clutch anyway," Clint muttered grimly, bracing his feet tight against the floorboard. "Okay, try second."

Second was easier than first, and third was easier yet. Unfortunately, she had to start all over at the gate to pull out onto the road.

Peggy drove slowly, never exceeding thirty miles an hour. They found the kids where the ranch road turned off the highway. J.R. had been driving and hadn't quite made the turn on the ice-slicked road with the unwieldy van. Another car had stopped on the shoulder, and the women and children sat in the warmth while the men tried to dig the van out of the ditch. Peggy pulled the truck over to the shoulder in front of the other car, put it in neutral, set the brake, and slumped with relief.

Clint smiled at her. "You're something, Mrs. Howell."

"If this is your idea of a honeymoon, Mr. Howell," she retorted, "I don't want any part of one of your workdays."

No one was hurt, and with the truck and a chain, the boys were able to pull the van out. Justin drove the truck home, with Peggy in the center between him and Clint. She sagged against her husband as a remote part of her noted how easily Justin managed the clutch and the gears. She didn't care. She just wanted a nap. She wanted someone to promise her that never again would she be left alone on the ranch. Closing her eyes, she silently screamed, *I just want to teach school and paint!*

# Twenty

In spite of the impulsive nature of Peggy's decision to marry Clint, she had given it some thought beforehand. Being the new lady of the manor involved living with the beloved ghost of the former lady, as well as usurping the role jointly held by the twins for three years. Peggy had successfully managed a household for twenty-seven years, and considered herself capable of the job; but she'd never managed a ranch. She'd also never tried to manage a household while holding down a full-time job. Living with the Howells was not quite what she'd imagined. By the end of the first week of marriage, she was feeling more an outsider than before the wedding.

"Honeymoon over already?" Violet asked her on Friday. They were spending their planning period in the art room, as they frequently did when they wanted privacy.

"It's hard to explain," Peggy said, frowning.

Violet put down her papers and came to sit across from her. "Try me," she invited.

"It's not Clint," Peggy hastened to clarify. "He's wonderful." She paused to let the warm glow fill her that thinking of Clint always produced. At least that part of married life was working out.

"Good sex, huh?"

"Violet!" Peggy was yanked out of her reverie to catch her friend grinning at her. "Well, yes," she admitted with a smile and a slight blush. "He's quite resourceful."

"I'll bet." Violet laughed with her, then sobered. "It must be difficult living with his entire family."

"He has a great family," Peggy defended softly, but she could feel the frustration closing back around her.

Violet touched her arm supportively and waited until Peggy looked at her. "Whatever you say will never be repeated," she promised.

Peggy gave her a weak smile. Violet was a good friend, and even though she usually knew the latest dirt on any subject, she wasn't a gossip.

"It's not really scandalous," Peggy assured her, "just . . . confusing." Violet waited silently. Peggy took a deep breath and plunged in.

"I don't fit in. Except for the clothes in the closet, nothing in that house is mine. Eileen decorated the house twenty years ago and it's never been changed. Tina and Gina do all the cooking and housework, insisting that I have worked all day and should relax and spend time with Clint. Even Clint doesn't seem to need me. He spends his days with the boys and doesn't come in until I do. I was going to give up my work on the play to take care of him, but the one day I went straight home after school, he didn't come home until dark. They'd been out mending fences."

"I thought he had two broken arms," Violet interjected.

"He does. He doesn't actually do the physical work. He sits in the pickup or walks around and supervises while the boys work."

"Oh, I bet that doesn't fly for long," Violet predicted.

"Hmmm." Peggy had been so wrapped up

in her own adjusting, she hadn't given much thought to Clint's—or the boys'—adjustment to Clint's change in status. Violet was right, the boys wouldn't stand for their father's straw-bossing for long.

"So what *do* you do?" Violet asked, bringing her back to the original topic.

"I help Clint with his shower before supper. We . . . ah . . . talk." She could feel herself blushing and bit her lip trying to keep from smiling. "I tell him about my day and he tells me about his."

Violet was laughing at her by this time and Peggy couldn't contain the smile any longer. "Well, we do talk," she insisted.

"Oh, I don't doubt it," Violet said, pausing to wipe her eyes. She looked at Peggy and they both started laughing again.

"I'm just jealous," Violet stated when she could breathe again. "Maybe I'll break Sam's arms."

"Try joining him in the shower a few times," Peggy suggested. "Hopefully you won't have to resort to violence. However," she rubbed a bruised hip gingerly, "I can think of softer surfaces than a porcelain tub."

Peggy went home that night feeling better, even though nothing had been resolved. After

385

dinner, she suggested entertaining the grand-children while Tina and Gina cleaned up the dishes, since they wouldn't let her help. With Clint advising one two-year-old and Peggy the other, the children played a board game in relative harmony, until their mothers came to get them for their baths.

"Thanks, Peggy," Gina said, extracting little Cindy from her lap. "It was so much easier without the kids underfoot."

"Goodnight, Grandma. Goodnight, Grandpa." Hugs and kisses were distributed among the four children before their mothers herded them off. Clint didn't like the grand-children calling her Peggy, so they called her Grandma as Shawn and Michael did. The older children had only been two when Eileen died, and didn't remember her. With the children at least, Peggy had a place.

Saturday morning Peggy insisted on cook-ing breakfast. While she enjoyed the compli-ments from the family on her culinary skills, it wasn't as satisfying as she'd anticipated. The kitchen was not familiar to her. Even when she'd moved into the caboose, she'd brought her favorite pans, utensils, dishes, potholders, and especially her collection of coffee mugs, most of them gifts from the children and grandchildren. Instead of cooking breakfast making her feel more at home, it made her feel like she was a guest in someone else's house; a welcome guest, one the family was comfortable enough with to allow them such liberties as cooking, but a guest nonetheless.

"Drive out with us to feed the cattle," Clint invited after breakfast. "I'll introduce you to the girls."

Intrigued, Peggy got her coat. The "girls" turned out to be a large herd of pregnant cows, divided between two pastures. Peggy was grateful for the protection of the pickup as the cows crowded eagerly around, bawling impatiently.

"They know they're going to get fed," Clint explained. J.R. got out and unloaded the sacks of cattle cubes, talking soothingly to the cows as he moved through them to the feeding trough.

"There are a lot of them," Peggy commented, concerned as J.R. disappeared into the midst of them.

"Two hundred on this pasture, another two hundred on the other pasture," Clint supplied. "And that is just the breeders."

In spite of Peggy's rash statement that she didn't like cows, she found herself watching them. There was a layer of snow over the pasture, heavily trampled where the cows were gathered. Steam rose in a cloud from their mingled breaths and warm bodies. "What's the difference between the black ones and the red ones?" she asked Clint.

"Different breeds. The solid red ones are Red Angus. The red ones with the white faces and white feet are Herefords. The black ones with the white faces are a cross-breed called black baldies."

"I like the Herefords," Peggy decided, not sure why. "When will they deliver?"

"End of January, early February."

"Isn't it still cold?" Peggy turned a worried expression to Clint.

"If it's too cold, we keep a close eye on them," he assured her. "If we let them deliver too late in the year, then we're dealing with roundup in the heat of summer."

"Roundup?"

Clint smiled indulgently at her ignorance. "When the calves are about two months old, we round them up for branding, dehorning, and castrating. If enough ranches cooperate, you can usually do the entire herd in one morning."

"Branding?" Peggy searched the cows milling around the pickup. Sure enough, each bore a neat brand on their right hind-quarter. She tried to make out the design.

"It's a state law," Clint said. "Each time an animal changes owners, it must be branded with that ranch's brand. My cattle are fortunate in that I raise my own breeding cows, and keep my market steers from birth to feed lot, so they are only branded once."

Finally Peggy made out one of the brands. It was identical to the symbols over the entrance to the ranch, three cascading H's, joined by their vertical legs. "Three H's for three Howell's?" she asked.

Clint laughed before answering. "The brand is considerably older than the three of us. No, it stands for 'High Howell Hacienda.' My great-grandfather started this ranch in 1918. My father added most of the acreage, in the fifties. I started dabbling in organic beef during the late sixties, as a side line. I went into full production fifteen years ago, when I proved to my father it was profitable and not just a passing fad. The chickens were Tina and Gina's idea."

"How big is this ranch?" Peggy asked an hour later when they were driving back toward the house after feeding the second group of cows.

"It's somewhat broken up, but there's forty

sections altogether," Clint supplied, watching for her reaction.

"You don't think I know what a section is, do you?" Peggy asked smugly. "Well, I've taught enough Kansas and New Mexico history to know that most of the plains states are laid out in grids, one mile by one mile being called a 'section.' Each section contains six hundred forty acres." She smiled triumphantly, then frowned as what she'd just said sank in. "You own forty *sections?*"

Clint and J.R. both laughed at her. "It sounds impressive until you realize it takes forty acres to feed one cow/calf unit unless you supplement," Clint said. "I'd like to have another five-section pasture, if I could find one in this area."

Peggy shook her head, too amazed to even respond.

The Junior-Senior play was performed to a packed house on Tuesday night. Peggy had taught oil painting to the more advanced students, and four of the best efforts hung on the wall of the main character's study, where most of the action of the play took place. Peggy had been proud to award Jack Henning the Students' Choice prize for the best painting. It was another one of his dark and gruesome subjects, but the play was a murder mystery and the main character in the play was a mystery writer, so it seemed appropriate. Besides, his talent was undeniable.

The next evening, after the younger families had retired to their own apartments, Clint invited Peggy into the study.

"You've been so tied up with the play, we haven't had time for business," Clint said after they'd both taken seats at his desk. "I'll have one of kids bring me to town tomorrow after school. We need to get your name on my account and have you sign a signature card so you can write checks if you need to. The boys are both on the ranch account, so I'll let them take over paying the bills and handling the ranch transactions."

"I'm not to be involved?"

Clint frowned at the cool tone to her question. "In running the ranch? Why would you want to be?"

"Because I'm your wife," Peggy stated pointedly.

"There's no need," Clint said, missing the warning in Peggy's voice. "The boys need to be learning the paperwork part of the ranch, and this will be a good opportunity for them." Clint acted as if that was the end of it. "Now as to my personal . . ."

"Is there a dowager house also?"

"What?"

"A dowager house. You know, where the mother-in-law moves after the lord of the manor dies and turns the estate over to his son."

"What are you talking about?"

"A medieval monarchy. Only the men have brains. The women are just around to cook, clean, and produce more sons."

Clint's exasperation was evident in his expression. He didn't even defend himself.

"You asked me once to tell you about Peter," Peggy reminded him, "so you wouldn't make the same mistakes. Peter managed our household, paid the bills, took care of major purchases. I was given a household checking account for groceries and school expenses for the kids, and charge cards for clothing and household needs. I was called to account for each purchase I made. It was a Sunday afternoon ritual," she added grimly, "before he went back out of town on Monday."

"You are comparing me to Peter because I want to let the boys manage the ranch?" Perplexity furrowed Clint's brow.

"No, I am comparing two male chauvinists who consider simple mathematics too complicated for a woman to understand."

"I never said that!"

"No, but that's what you think!"

The accusation hung in the air between them. "You are my wife," Clint finally stated quietly, with restraint, "and everything *I* have is yours. The ranch is co-owned with the boys, and has been for over six years. It passes to their children, not their wives, although surviving wives are provided for, as you will be.

"We try to operate as a business venture," Clint continued. "Profits are divided among us, with a set percentage being put back into the business. 'Bonus money' is voted on, by everyone. Sometimes it's divided, sometimes it's used to purchase something for the ranch, or to build on with. When the last two children were expected, we voted on that van, so we could all go places in one vehicle."

Peggy was silent, but her expression was guarded. "I will be glad to go over my personal assets with you," Clint assured her, "and add your name to any of them. My question to you is, are you willing to share what is yours with me?"

His dark eyes regarded her intently. Peggy

felt a sick realization flood through her. She hadn't thought of that. In an effort to prevent another tyrannical marital relationship, she had come out looking like a jealous, greedy fool, and it was going to get worse. In her one-sided campaign, she hadn't considered what would happen to what was *hers*.

Instead of gloating over her lack of defense, as she had done with him, Clint was saddened by Peggy's lack of trust. "I don't want my name on your caboose, Peggy, or your van, or your checking account."

"Then don't put my name on anything of yours," Peggy said, quite subdued now.

"I need you to be able to write checks, Peggy." Clint held his casts forward.

"Let J.R. do it. It's different the second time around, isn't it? Especially when we both have children. What's yours belongs more to your children than to me, and what's mine belongs more to my children than to you."

"Speak for yourself." Clint gave her a wry smile. "I'm not done with what's mine, yet, and they can't have it until I am."

"And what was I to do differently?"

394

Peggy demanded, taking his comment personally.

"About what?" Clint asked, not understanding.

"About Megan, about Kevin. Should I let my daughter and grandsons live on the street? Should I bring legal charges against my son?"

"Whoa! Hold it! It was just a flip comment. I just meant I'm not ready to die and leave everything to the children. I was not criticizing."

Peggy was mollified, somewhat.

"Can we go over the accounts, now?" Clint asked, the exasperation back in his voice.

Clint showed her how his personal finances were set up, and how the ranch accounts were handled differently from their personal accounts. Peggy was impressed with his business acumen, and when he was finished, she showed him how she'd set up her own.

"It's never wise to have only your name on a title, or an account," Clint told her. "If something happens, no one can touch anything until it's gone through the courts. Do you even have a will?"

"Yes, of course I do." Peggy didn't tell

him that the only reason she did was because her divorce lawyer had explained the need for one to her.

"A New Mexico one?"

"New Mexico lawyers are different from Kansas lawyers?"

"No, but the courts are. I'll send the will you had drawn up to my lawyer, and he'll make the necessary adjustments."

"What adjustments?"

"To make it legal in New Mexico," Clint stated through clenched teeth. "Will you stop being so suspicious of me? Why did you insist on getting married if you didn't trust me?"

Yesterday Peggy had known the answer to that question. Now, it was obvious that her loyalties still lay more with her children than her husband. She also still felt a powerful need to demonstrate her independence. She looked at Clint, sitting there like a bull with a scowl on his handsome face and his casted arms crossed over his chest. She felt an ache, deep in her chest.

"I do trust you, Clint," she said, entreating him with her eyes. "I'm just having trouble with the transition back into married life. I've tried so hard to make my own way."

Clint opened his casts in invitation. Peggy

went into his embrace, kneeling in front of his chair.

"I should have insisted we wait," he spoke into her hair. "You explained your need to find yourself first. You asked me to give you time."

"I'm the one who insisted we get married," Peggy argued, her voice muffled against his shirt.

"You were coerced."

"You needed me."

"I needed you before I broke my arms."

Peggy pulled back to look at his face. His eyes were dark and warm and looking into them spread that warmth through her entire body. He gave her a funny half-smile.

"Help me up," he instructed. "I've sat in this chair so long, I'm . . . stiff." The smile widened wickedly.

"Re-e-ally?" Peggy drawled, looking down.

"Better yet, take off your clothes and sit in my lap. Let me see what I've been missing all these years being a rancher instead of an executive with a secretary to play with."

One of the few advantages of having Clint's arms in casts was he was almost totally at Peggy's mercy, which she loved taking full advantage of. Instead of taking her clothes off, she undid his, slowly, teasing his bare flesh with her fingers, lips, and tongue. Finally, she removed her clothes and offered her breast to his mouth, straddling his thighs in the chair.

"Turn around," he suggested, the awkwardness of the chair apparent. Peggy turned and sat on his lap, guiding him inside as she did. "Umm," he murmured appreciatively, "maybe I'll let you do the books after all."

"Nothing would come out right," Peggy objected, somewhat breathlessly.

"Maybe not the numbers," Clint agreed. He discovered that with his arms crossed over her chest, he could reach one breast with his fingers. Encouraged, he leaned forward, reaching and stretching slowly with the other hand.

"Oh," Peggy gasped, then began to help as she realized where he was trying to go. "Oh! Clint!"

"We'll try this on a horse as soon as I get the casts off," Clint promised into her ear, when he could talk again. "It's only fair to compare both sides of the question."


Now that she lived forty-five miles from Fort Sumner, Peggy had to confine her project of reforming Billy Ellis to school hours. After being banned from his father's business establishment for lewd behavior and inciting a riot, she didn't feel comfortable approaching Pete as his son's teacher to discuss his son's lack of supervision. Pete would probably comment on her lack of supervision, losing what little credibility she still had with him.

"He needs a woman," Violet advised when Peggy was discussing her concern about Billy's lack of hygiene.

"Thanks a lot," Peggy snapped. "Last time I looked, I thought I qualified in that role."

"You know what I mean—one his own age. A man in love will do anything to please the object of his affection."

"Even carry her out of a bar over his shoulder?" Peggy asked, switching the subject.

Violet blushed prettily. "It worked. Sam doesn't trust me now, so he doesn't ignore me."

"And you encourage it."

"Of course. Now instead of dieting, I see a manicurist once a week." Violet extended her fingers, flaunting the newly sculpted nails that were painted a vivid red.

"And the hair?"

Violet coyly flipped her platinum blond hair back away from her face. "Drives him crazy. He keeps begging me to change it back, but he loves it. Yesterday, he wouldn't even let me go to the grocery store without him."

"Sounds stifling to me," Peggy commented, shaking her head.

"Not as much as two broken arms," Violet neatly turned the topic back to Peggy.

"I didn't do that."

"No, Clint did. If I remember correctly, he was the one wanting to figure a way to get you in his camp." Violet grinned wickedly. "Desperate, but effective."

"He didn't do it on purpose," Peggy stated with a frown.

"Probably not," Violet agreed, "but he sure used it to his advantage."

After Violet's prediction that the boys wouldn't put up with Clint's interference for long, Peggy started trying to prevent an inevitable conflict. On the weekends, she asked Clint to stay with her when she babysat the grandkids, insisting that they minded him better than her. She took him for drives around the ranch so he could tell her more about the cattle, the operation of the ranch, and to get him away from the boys for a while.

In the evenings after supper, Peggy massaged his sore shoulder and neck muscles. Though she'd rather be doing other things, she sat with him while he watched television, or she read to him, curled up in his lap, imprisoned by his casts. She kept them padded now. The night in the office chair had resulted in fresh abrasions across her ribs.

Her attention to him usually cajoled him out of his surly moods, but it didn't change the fact that someone had to help him perform almost every task; from the most mundane, such as pulling off his boots before he entered the house; to the most personal. He missed riding horseback. He missed driving himself where he wanted to go. He missed swinging the grandkids up onto his shoulders. He wanted to hold Peggy while they slept.

Friday night Clint's tolerance of his imprisoned arms and the boys' tolerance of their frustrated father hovering over them while they worked ran out simultaneously. The family gathered for supper as usual. Tina cut Scott's meat into tiny pieces and put it on the tray of his high chair. Two-year-old Cindy was teething and fussy. Each bite Gina tried to coax her to eat only raised the pitch of Cindy's cry and increased her struggling to get down. J.R. was explaining to Peggy about the state's water rights, since it was once again a political issue, raising his voice over Cindy's wailing. Trying to listen to J.R., Peggy inadvertently fed Clint a bite of baked potato that burned his tongue.

Clint hollered and cursed, something he rarely did. When Peggy tried to give him a drink of iced water, she dribbled it down his shirt in her haste. He exploded, standing up and kicking his chair to the floor behind him.

"I feel like a two-year-old! I might as well sit in a high chair and wear a bib!" Cindy stopped her whining and stared at her grandfather. "At least they can feed themselves!" Clint finished his tirade. He stomped off toward his bedroom.

No one at the table moved for several seconds. A final blasphemous curse echoed through the house just prior to a loud crash accompanied by the splintering sound of wood.

"The door was closed," Peggy groaned, laying her head in her hands.

"I've had enough of this," J.R. announced, getting up from the table.

"J.R., leave him alone," Peggy advised. "Talking to him now will be useless and you'll probably get into a major fight."

"Damn right! He's been looking for a fight for the last two weeks!"

"Peggy's right, J.R." Tina tried to lay a restraining hand on her husband's arm but he jerked away.

"No, J.R.'s right."

"Justin!" Gina's plea went unheeded as Justin followed his brother toward their father's bedroom.

"Let's take the kids to the kitchen," Tina suggested with a sigh, picking up Scott, high chair and all.

Peggy couldn't eat, and she didn't want to stay and hear the shouting match she was sure would ensue. She excused herself and went outside, grabbing up her coat and car keys on her way out. She got in the van and drove out of the driveway, heading toward town—the village, she reminded herself. She wasn't sure where she was going until she got to the turnoff toward Santa Rosa, and the lake. Then she knew.

She was going home.

# Twenty-one

Megan came out of the caboose when she heard the van pull up outside. "Is everything all right?" she asked.

"Everything's fine," Peggy stated, giving her bewildered daughter a hug.

Peggy entered the caboose, then stood in the middle of it, slowly turning and taking it all in. Homesickness swamped her, bringing unwanted tears to her eyes. Here was her kitchen, her table, her stereo, her bentwood rocker, the cupola. Most of all she'd missed sitting in the cupola, looking out over the lake and sorting out her thoughts. The beds she'd made for Kevin and Erika's visit were still where the benches had been. A sob escaped her, and the tears flowed down her cheeks.

"Mom!"

Alarmed, Megan hugged her mother to

her. Peggy didn't resist, but allowed herself to be held and mothered by her daughter. Henry came running in from the addition, yowling and rubbing Peggy's ankles. Peggy bent down and scooped him up, burying her tear-streaked face in his fur. She took several deep breaths, regaining her composure.

"Do you have some coffee?" she finally asked, putting Henry down and wiping her eyes with the backs of her hands.

"I'll make some."

"No, Megan, wait. I want to make it."

Megan sat quietly watching from the table while Peggy lovingly opened the cabinets and went through the steps of making coffee. Peggy sighed as she touched each familiar cup, then chose her favorite.

"Mom, what's going on? Did you and Clint have a fight?"

"No, not a fight really. I just got homesick."

Megan silently observed her mother for a minute before she spoke. "You're talking about here, aren't you, not Wichita."

"Yes. I miss my caboose, the lake. I never got to finish the studio." She poured the coffee, offering to make one for Megan.

"No, thanks. Unlike you, I never learned to drink coffee and go to bed."

"Are the boys in bed?"

"Yes. Do you know what time it is?"

Peggy checked her watch. It was ten o'clock. She looked at the wall clock in the kitchen for verification.

"Oh, Megan, I'm sorry. I had no idea. I drove around for a while before I came here. I had no idea," she repeated. She picked up her purse to leave.

"Sit down, Mother," Megan instructed with an indulgent smile. "You might as well drink your coffee."

Peggy sat down. Megan chatted about the boys, about Ramon, waiting for her mother to signal that she was ready to talk. Peggy drank her coffee, stroking Henry, who sat in her lap, then a second cup, seemingly content to just listen to Megan.

"Ramon asked me to marry him," Megan finally announced, since her mother didn't seem inclined to talk.

"Megan, that's wonderful!"

"I'm very happy about it. He's a wonderful man, and the boys worship him. He wants me to stay at home, be a housewife, a mother, have more kids, someday."

Peggy smiled at Megan, noting the way her face lit up and her eyes sparkled as she talked about it. From the beginning, all

Megan had ever wanted to do was devote herself to her kids. It looked like she would now be able to.

"When?"

"Christmas."

Peggy felt her smile fade. Christmas was two weeks away!

"Christmas?"

"It's perfect, Mom. Erika and Kevin can come back then. Maybe Grandmother and Grandfather would even come. You'll be out of school and can keep the boys. Ramon wants to honeymoon in Santa Fe. He says it's just beautiful there in the winter."

Peggy didn't hear anything past, "you can keep the boys." She was beginning to understand why her mother insisted kids got on her nerves and refused to have them around for long periods. Six kids. Six kids, out of school, cooped up inside because of the cold weather. Clint was as grouchy as a bear with a splinter in each foot and she was going to have six small, running, rowdy kids in the house for two weeks. Her Christmas break. She'd rather teach history to seventh graders.

"We could use your studio as our bedroom . . . hang curtains across all those windows," Megan was saying when Peggy tuned her back in. "He'll store all my extra stuff out at the ranch. He even said he could rig an antennae so we can hook up the TV."

"You're planning to live here?"

"Weren't you listening, Mom? We're gonna build a house on his land. It's connected to his parents' ranch."

"Where does he live now?" Peggy asked, feeling first imposed on, now invaded. Where did it end? Would Kevin ask to move in after Megan moved out?

"In his parents' house," Megan answered. "We can't move in with his parents."

*You moved in with me,* Peggy thought, glaring at her inconsiderate daughter.

"I didn't think you'd mind," Megan said uncomfortably. "It's not like you live here now."

"What would you do if I did?" Peggy asked coolly.

Megan blinked, taken aback by her mother's hostility. "I guess we'd do something else," she replied vaguely.

"Then I suggest you find that 'something else,'" Peggy suggested. "As the realtor recently demonstrated, there are plenty of available places to live, all of them larger than this." Peggy got up from the table and began taking linen out of the cabinets built under the cupola.

"What are you doing?" Megan asked, clearly alarmed.

"Spending the night," Peggy answered, climbing the ladder to make up one of the beds in the cupola.

"You can't!" Megan gasped. Peggy caught the anxious glance she cast toward the addition.

"This place is still mine, Megan." She returned to the floor and gave Megan a level gaze. Megan refused to meet it. "Ramon can either slink out the studio door, or I'll see him at breakfast."

Megan's face flushed with guilt, but Peggy ignored her. "There are some things I want to take out to the ranch. We'll talk in the morning." She gave Megan a superior smile that dared her to challenge her.

Megan returned the smile, looking somewhat ill. "See you in the morning," she said meekly.

Peggy called the ranch before she climbed up to bed, telling Gina where she was and that she'd be home sometime the next morning. Henry missed his jump, sinking claws into the foam pad of the bed, scrambling madly for a foothold for his back feet.

Peggy reached down and pulled him the rest of the way up.

"You're out of shape," she admonished him, settling him into her lap. With the unflappable arrogance of a true cat, Henry acted as if he'd done nothing unusual. He curled up in Peggy's lap and began to purr contentedly.

Peggy sat up most of the night, watching the moonlight play across the cold water, stroking Henry. She wouldn't be belligerent, she decided, but she would be firm. Megan could stay in the caboose until the wedding, but then she and Ramon would have to find their own place. Her instinctively coming here tonight showed she needed a place to get away by herself occasionally.

Poor Clint. She was sure he felt the same way. He'd only been in his casts for two weeks. He had six more weeks to go—at least. It was amazing the number of things people did with their hands and arms, mostly without thinking about it. He probably suffered from a multitude of itches, irritations, and discomforts rather than ask someone to scratch his nose, adjust a waistband, feed him a snack. He couldn't even go to the bathroom unless she or one of the boys was around. Peggy wondered if she

411

would have lasted as long as he had before exploding with frustration.

They both needed time away, Peggy decided. They were rarely alone. Courting in Fort Sumner wasn't near the fishbowl that being married at the ranch with the whole clan in residence was. Now, it looked like she'd have the boys over Christmas break.

Christmas was two weeks away, and neither she nor Clint had done any shopping. She'd never seen Albuquerque, where the girls loved to shop. Perhaps a weekend retreat would take care of several problems: shopping, distance from both of their children, and time alone with each other. Peggy went to sleep with pleasant thoughts of honeymoon suites and shopping malls dancing in her brain.

Shawn and Michael were excited about having Grandma for breakfast. Ramon sheepishly joined them, fully dressed and unable to look Peggy in the eye as he accepted a cup of coffee from her.

"Welcome to the family," Peggy said, not releasing the cup.

Ramon finally looked at her, grinning guiltily. Peggy smiled at him, somewhat amused at his behavior; the cocky playboy, brought low by an impending mother-in-law.

"Where are the dishes you brought from Wichita, Megan?" Peggy asked, allowing Ramon to enjoy his coffee out of the limelight. "I want to take some of my dishes out to the ranch, and you'll probably need to use yours until you move into your own place."

"Why don't you leave your stuff here, Mom?" Megan recommended. "You said you wanted to keep the place. What are you going to use when you come out here?"

"I just want a few things," Peggy said, taking mugs out of the cupboard. "Most of it I will leave." She hadn't taken out very much when it became obvious there wasn't enough counter space for what she was doing, especially with Megan trying to cook breakfast.

"I'll get a box out of the studio," she announced, heading that way.

"Uh, Mom . . ." Megan tried to stop her.

It was too late. Peggy stood on the threshold into her studio, shocked. There was no studio. Megan had already hung the curtains over the windows; long floor-to-ceiling white drapes that covered two entire walls, hiding her shelves. The floor was carpeted with a thick blue shag. A double bed, night stand,

and dresser now occupied the room, along with the television set. An antique armoire had been added, since the studio didn't have a closet. The boys lounged in the middle of the bed, watching the TV. Obviously, the antennae had already been installed.

"Look, Grandma," Michael called to her. "Ramon fixed the TV!"

"So I see," Peggy said through tightly clenched teeth. She turned on Megan, who shrank away from her, white-faced.

"How dare you?" Peggy demanded, stalking her retreating daughter. "My studio, Megan! Where is my stuff?"

"Ramon couldn't stay here and share that little bed," Megan defended herself feebly. "Surely you see that. With you living out at the ranch, I really didn't think you'd mind us living here." None of her arguments were making a dent in her mother's angry expression.

"Where is my stuff, Megan?" Peggy repeated in a voice arctic and tightly controlled.

"On the porch," Megan replied meekly.

Peggy shoved past her daughter and marched out to the porch. Her art supplies were all out there, back in their boxes, along with her sewing machine, the chest of drawers, and her dismantled single bed. Her daughter had moved in and relegated her to the porch.

"Mom?" Megan's tremulous voice broke into Peggy's black fog.

Peggy turned on her daughter, and felt her anger slip a notch. Megan stood watching her mother, tears welling up in her eyes. Ramon stood nearby, looking helpless and unsure of what he should be doing.

"You've always helped me, Mom," Megan tried to explain. "I really didn't think you'd want the caboose anymore, now that you've remarried. We'll put it back."

"Just like it was," Ramon assured Peggy, taking Megan's arm. "I'll even paint the outside for you—call it rent."

Looking into Megan's tear-streaked face was like looking at a reflection of herself, twenty years ago, Peggy realized, feeling her anger slip another notch. Kevin and Erika both favored their father, but Megan was almost a clone of her mother. Although she loved all her children, she was closest to Megan, not just because of the physical similarity, but because Megan had always needed her most.

Kevin had been strong-willed and defiant from the beginning. From refusing to accept her feeding and sleeping schedule to defying her attempts at potty training, Kevin had set the pattern of resisting her influence over his life from an early age. Erika was the strong one, quietly independent and always more mature than her years. Now that she was grown, she counseled her mother more than she sought counsel.

Megan needed Peggy. Physically, financially, and emotionally, Megan depended on her. Even with Ramon standing at her side, offering support, it was Peggy she needed reassurance from. Peggy shook her head at the whole situation, then gave Megan a wry smile.

"All right," she capitulated, opening her arms to Megan. "You're forgiven." Megan came and held her mother fiercely.

"We'll put it back just like you had it," Ramon repeated, still hovering.

"You'd better," Peggy admonished firmly, releasing Megan, "or I'll move in with you."

The crunch of tires on gravel turned their attention toward the road.

"It's Clint," Peggy stated unnecessarily as the pickup pulled into view. She went out through the screened-in porch to greet him.

"I'm sorry, Peggy," Clint apologized before

she even helped him out of the truck. "I wasn't mad at you."

"I know that," Peggy assured him, giving him a hug.

A long low whistle of admiration came from Justin, who'd gotten out of the driver's side of the pickup. Peggy and Clint both turned to see what he was whistling at. Justin stood in front of Ramon's black pickup, looking down at the painting blazoned across its hood.

"So this is the 'chained lady,' " he commented, more to himself than anyone.

Ramon, always willing to accept the admiration of others for his truck, moved to stand with him. Peggy smiled indulgently as Ramon's chest swelled at Justin's awed expression. Clint pulled away from her embrace to see the painting for himself. Instead of admiration, a look of shocked disbelief crossed his face. Clint stood, open-mouthed, staring at the painting on the hood of the black pickup. It was the first time he'd seen it.

"You painted that?" he all but shouted at Peggy.

Ramon stepped back, wary now. He glanced down at Clint's casts, as if for reassurance that the big man couldn't hit him again.

"You painted *that!*" Clint did shout this time.

Ramon and Justin both moved away from the pickup. Peggy stood her ground as Clint glared at her. A good fight was just what she needed, had been spoiling for, as J.R. had so aptly described Clint's mood the night before.

"Yes, I painted that. Most people are very impressed. It's even better than the phoenix, don't you think?" She smiled at him, daring him to disagree, tossing down the gauntlet. He didn't disappoint her.

"The damn phoenix isn't *naked!*"

"Of course she is," Peggy argued, approaching him, her voice still sweetly taunting. "There isn't a stitch of clothing on that bird."

Clint saw red. If he had use of his arms, he'd shake her. The glow in her eyes dared him to try. He struggled to regain control.

Peggy watched him draw several deep breaths. His jaw muscles were clenched so tight they were twitching. His fists were balled, the knuckles white. She wondered if maybe she'd gone too far. She should have shown him the picture, at least prepared him.

"I'll head on back to the ranch," Justin interrupted, heading toward his pickup. He wanted out of the vicinity before his father exploded. Last night had been enough for him.

An evil imp within Peggy didn't heed her own warning that she'd pushed Clint far enough. She smiled at Justin. "What do you think of the painting, Justin?"

The look Justin gave her clearly asked, "Are you out of your mind?" and warned her to quit while she was still alive. Peggy's confidence faltered a little. Justin was as big as his father and could be equally intimidating. She decided to give up the game.

"I'll bring your father," she assured Justin. "We'll be along in a minute."

Justin looked from his father to his new stepmother, assessing the situation. Finally he nodded and climbed into his truck. "See you back at the ranch."

"We'll discuss this later," Clint told Peggy through clenched teeth.

Back inside the caboose Peggy announced Megan and Ramon's wedding plans to a quietly smoldering Clint while she finished gathering up the items she wanted to take back to the ranch.

"You're invited out for dinner Friday," Ramon

said after Peggy's announcement met with silence. "My parents wanted a chance to meet you before the wedding."

"That will be fine," Peggy accepted uneasily. She picked up her box of things and her purse. "I'll talk to you tomorrow, Megan," she said, giving her daughter a quick hug. She hugged Ramon also, but wasn't sure what to say, so she gave him a brief smile before turning to help Clint down the steep steps out of the caboose.

As they drove toward Fort Sumner, Peggy wasn't sure which issue to bring up first.

"Is meeting the Estavezes Friday okay with you?" she finally broke the silence by asking.

"I know the Estavezes," Clint commented in a flat voice.

"Well, of course you do," Peggy acquiesced quickly. "You wouldn't have to go, what with your arms and all. Megan's my daughter."

"And what am I, Peggy?"

His voice was cold and his eyes hard. Peggy shivered involuntarily. Her stomach was in a knot from the stress of the last two days. She wasn't sure how much more she could take.

"You're my husband, Clint. I didn't mean

to imply you weren't. I just thought after the incident last night . . ."

"And is a husband's reputation not considered before you parade your pornographic paintings before my community?"

"Pornographic? *Your* community?" Peggy's voice matched his now. "I thought I lived here, too."

"Apparently you don't care what people think of you."

"Of all the people who've seen Ramon's truck, you're the only one who's thought it was pornographic!" Peggy's former chagrin had given way to indignant fury.

"The woman is naked!"

"Nothing shows!"

"That's irrelevant!"

"You wouldn't think so if I'd painted it the way Ramon asked me to!"

"That's another issue. Just what kind of relationship did you have with Ramon that he would ask you to paint such a thing?"

Peggy hit the brake, so angry she was shaking. She jerked the van over to the shoulder of the highway and came to an abrupt stop.

"Get out, Clint," she instructed, her voice tight with suppressed rage.

"I would love to, my dear," Clint stated

in a calm, deliberate manner, "but as in every other area in my life lately, I seem to require some assistance."

Peggy slung open her door and stomped around the van to the passenger side. She opened Clint's door. He merely sat there, facing forward, refusing to acknowledge her. Peggy began to feel somewhat foolish. They were acting like children.

As if sensing her cooling ire, Clint finally looked down at Peggy, who was still holding his door open. "If you would kindly release my seat belt, I will get out now."

"And do what, walk home?"

"If you wish."

They held each other's eyes for a long moment. There was a sadness in his brown eyes that tore at Peggy's heart. He was a proud, stubborn man, and she loved him.

"I should make you, you know," she said, no longer angry.

"You couldn't do it."

"You're awfully sure of yourself," she commented, raising one eyebrow.

"I know you."

"Really? It didn't sound like it a few minutes ago."

"Why did you paint that picture, Peggy?" His voice was soft now, almost pleading.

"Income, mostly. I agreed to do it when I was trying to keep Megan in Wichita. It took me a while to make it into something I would sign my name to."

"It's my name, too, Peggy."

"It wasn't when I did that, not that I would have consulted you. My art is my own."

"You will not sign the Howell name to pornography." His voice was hard again.

Peggy released a sigh of resignation. "So much for trust. You don't trust my behavior, or my judgment, and now you want to dictate what I will paint, an area you promised not to interfere with. What's next, Clint? Do I have to quit teaching and learn to ride a horse?"

"That painting is embarrassing. I would never do something that I thought would embarrass you."

"Oh, really? Starting a fistfight and accusing me of sleeping with Ramon Estavez in front of the whole village must not be your idea of embarrassing."

"I reacted without thinking," he growled, frowning.

"Well, I didn't. I gave that painting a great deal of thought before I did it. When I show you the original, you'll see that. The original was pornographic. I altered it enough that it is now merely sexist."

"She's still naked." There was defeat in the statement, as well as in the slump of his shoulders.

Peggy smiled to herself, grateful Clint wasn't looking at her. She didn't think he was ready to see the humor in their argument. "How do you know?"

He threw her an exasperated glare. Not only was she winning the argument, now she was mocking him.

"I doubt if Lady Godiva had as much hair as I painted on that girl."

"Do you have any other paintings lined up?" he demanded, letting his irritation show.

"As a matter of fact, I do." She gave him a wicked smile as she closed his door and walked around to the driver's side.

"Well?" he demanded when she acted as if that was the end of the discussion.

Peggy fastened her seat belt and pulled back out onto the highway. When she was up to cruising speed, she glanced at Clint's glowering face. A mischievous imp danced within her, and she smiled at him. "Ed Cowen asked me to do the side of his van."

"With what? Naked cheerleaders?"

"It would serve you right if I let you

think that. Honestly, Clint, what kind of marriage are we going to have if that is the type of trust you display?"

"Okay, you wouldn't do naked cheerleaders. What's his fantasy?"

"He doesn't want a fantasy. He wants a life-sized football player, in full uniform, I might add, rushing down the field with the ball."

Clint flushed guiltily.

"You're taking some serious chances accusing me of painting pornography, you know," Peggy continued. She had the upper hand now and couldn't let go. "I ought to paint the original lady on the hood of your field truck."

"You wouldn't dare," was in Clint's mouth, but he bit it back. If he dropped it, she would. The invitation to dare her fairly glowed in her eyes. He shook his head with a smile. "That old truck needs a new paint job. I think I'd prefer a solid color, though, if it's all the same to you."

## Twenty-two

The first thing Peggy learned about the Estavez family was that they did not consider themselves Hispanic, but rather New Mexican. They were descended from Spanish nobles who had settled in New Mexico when it was still under Spanish rule. To be considered of the same stock as the Mexican immigrants was an insult to them. Peggy wondered how many people she had insulted since living in New Mexico.

Ramon had three brothers and five sisters. The two Estavez brothers that Peggy had in her classes were his first cousins, children of Ramon's father's brother, who also lived on the vast ranch. Ramon's maternal grandmother lived with them, and most of the ranch hands were related in some way. Angelo Diaz was Ramon's first cousin on his mother's side.

Peggy's main concern, the family's acceptance of Megan and the boys, was put at ease almost immediately. They seemed to love Megan and her children as much as Ramon did. Peggy was reassured as she and Clint drove home.

"How long does it take to drive to Albuquerque?" she asked.

"It's about a hundred and fifty miles, about four hours from the ranch because we're so far from the interstate," Clint answered. "Why?"

"Would you be interested in a honeymoon weekend? We could do some Christmas shopping. You could show me around, take me out to eat—or order room service and eat in. Some bridal suites come with hot tubs." She made her voice as coaxing and suggestive as possible.

Clint thought about it for a minute. It wasn't a bad idea. With Peggy's working and their living with his family, their private time had been limited and overrun with day-to-day commitments. "I'll ask the girls where they recommend staying," he agreed to Peggy.

"I'm looking forward to it. Let's leave Friday, as soon as I get home. Then we'll have all day Saturday."

"How about I have someone drive me in and meet you after school," Clint suggested. "That'll save at least two hours."

Christmas fell on a Wednesday. Friday was Peggy's last day of school before the Christmas break. They made plans to stay in Albuquerque until Monday night. Kevin and Erika were due in on Tuesday. The wedding was scheduled for Christmas Day.

Since the Estavez family was strictly Catholic, Megan did not want to offend them by marrying their son in the Methodist Church. The living room and dining room at the Howell ranch had been built with entertaining in mind, and the Howell clan all insisted that the wedding should be held there. Tina and Gina were in their element, assuring Megan that they would take care of every detail. Peggy and Clint were instructed to enjoy their honeymoon and stay out of the way.

Peggy and Megan compromised on Megan's moving out of the caboose. She and Ramon preferred to live in one of the ranch's line shacks, closer to his work and his family than in one of the lake cabins. The line shack required a bit of cleaning and repair before it would be habitable for more than patrolling cowboys needing a roof for the night. Megan promised to be out of the caboose by February first.

"A line shack?" Peggy had queried skeptically. "Megan are you sure that's a good idea?" Peggy had visions of a dilapidated one-room shack, leaning in the wind.

"It'll be great," Megan assured her. "It's bigger than the caboose."

That wasn't saying much, Peggy thought. She'd seen bathrooms bigger than her caboose.

The long-awaited bell Friday afternoon was accompanied by a visit from Clark Graham, the principal. Peggy's anticipation of meeting Clint and getting on the road early, turned to a sickening sense of dread when she saw Clark's face. He greeted her mechanically, then sat down in a chair across from her desk.

"All ready for the big day?" he asked conversationally. He wouldn't meet Peggy's eyes.

"Yes, the girls seem to have everything under control." Peggy watched him uneasily.

"I hear you and Clint have a big weekend planned."

"Yes, we're going to Albuquerque. Clark, is something wrong?"

"Not wrong, really, just changes. They affect you, I'm afraid." He took a deep breath and plunged in. "Are you familiar with Carol's Spanish classes in Clayton?"

"Vaguely. I know she teaches them through a video hookup that allows her to interact with the students there."

"Right. Right. It was a pilot program this year, financed by the phone company. They are promoting it to a lot of the small school districts as a way of keeping down costs and sharing resources. The school board has been very impressed. Although it is expensive to set up, it really is quite cost effective in the long run."

"And this is going to affect me?" Peggy knew at a gut level that her job was at stake. She felt faint.

"We haven't had an art teacher at Fort Sumner for several years, Peggy," Clark said, finally looking at her. "I personally begged the school board to let me hire one. I'm very pleased with what you've done. We have some talented students."

*But,* Peggy thought. *Here it comes.* She waited, watching a sheen of perspiration break out on the principal's forehead.

"The school board has looked at the teachers at Clayton, trying to decide what Clayton has that they could reciprocate with the Spanish classes we have, and they voted for the art classes."

"Art!" Disbelief dispelled the dread. "Art taught over television hook-up? History I could understand, but *art?*"

"Peggy, I realize this comes as a shock. . . ."

"A *shock?* No, Clark, it's an outrage. You cannot teach art over a television. You cannot fax artwork over a phone line. You cannot talk a student through something that is done with your hands!"

"It's being done at other schools, Peggy, and successfully, I might add," Clark stated softly.

Peggy sat speechless for a minute. The whole idea was so ludicrous she couldn't even imagine it. Then she realized the personal implications. "When?"

"Not until the fall." Clark was brisk and jovial again. "You'll get to fulfill your contract for this school year."

"And next year? I teach history also, remember." She tried to keep her voice impassive. It would do her no good to alienate the principal.

431

"You just got married, Peggy. You're a rancher's wife, now. That's a full-time job in itself."

Fury started as a hot coal in her belly. She drew herself up erect in her chair and glared at Clark, who looked uncomfortable again. "I'm a *teacher,* Mr. Graham."

"Yes, well, of course," he stammered. "You could go back to school, get certified in other subjects."

"And what other subjects do you need teachers in?" Her voice was cool, totally without sympathy for the principal's discomfort.

"I'm not sure, English, maybe."

"There are no openings here, are there, Mr. Graham?"

"Well, we usually have openings every year. I just won't know until contracts are signed."

"Next summer," Peggy stated flatly.

"I wanted to give you time to think about it. A lot can happen between now and summer," he stated optimistically. He met her eyes briefly then looked toward the door.

"Well, Merry Christmas, Peggy." He stood up to leave. "Enjoy Albuquerque."

"Thank you, Clark," Peggy answered with saccharine sweetness. "You've certainly done everything in your power to make it more enjoyable."

Clark cast her a warning look that reminded her he was still her principal. Peggy forced the smile to remain on her face, although at this point she really didn't care. She felt like screaming at him and telling him he could plan to set up his television class over Christmas break because she wouldn't be back. She wanted to tell him what she thought of his dropping this on her right before Christmas. She wanted to beg him to reconsider, to let her go before the school board and explain why art couldn't be taught over a television set and a fax machine.

Clint found her still sitting at her desk, idly drawing on a sheet of paper.

"Problems?" He leaned over her shoulder to see what she was drawing. "I thought you said Jack had quit drawing death pictures."

"He has," she answered sullenly. "This one's mine."

"Nice. Anyone I know?"

"Clark Graham."

"I especially like the red blood dripping off his shirtcollar."

"Thank you. Maybe I'll nail it to his door."

433

"I've got a pocket knife. It's not as effective as a dagger, but it's all I've got." Clint tried to coax a smile from her.

"I've been fired," Peggy announced without expression.

"Fired?" Clint turned serious. "For what?"

"Replaced, actually, by a television set." She gave him the details in a defeated monotone. "It's not really Clark's fault. He's just the scapegoat." She wadded up the picture she'd drawn and tossed it in the trash. "He's the reason I even have a job. It was the school board's decision to use the television hook-up."

"Come on. We can talk about it while we drive."

Slowly, mechanically, Peggy gathered her coat and purse and went with Clint out to the van. J.R. was waiting in the pickup. He'd already loaded Clint's gear into the van and was just waiting to see them off.

"You kids have fun," he teased them, giving Peggy a hug goodbye. If he noticed Peggy's morose mood, he didn't say anything about it. She forced a smile and even managed a wave as they drove off.

"This could actually be a blessing in disguise," Clint offered after they'd driven in total silence for several miles.

434

"What?" Peggy pulled herself out of her reverie.

"Losing the job, it could actually be a blessing."

"I'd considered taking summer classes, anyway," Peggy stated thoughtfully. "I was just thinking about what subject interested me. Clark recommended English, which is okay. I enjoy literature and writing. It would go well with history."

"What about your art?"

"I'd still be an artist. I've painted all my life without benefit of a college degree. After Megan gets back from Santa Fe, I'll have my studio. Maybe I'll do private lessons."

"Where would you go back to school?"

Peggy shrugged. "Portales, at Eastern New Mexico. I had planned to work on my masters this summer. Now I'll get certified in another specialty first."

"What about another option?"

Peggy's guard was up immediately. "What option?"

"Not teaching next year."

Peggy felt her hackles rising. "Of course. I should have known. Let me guess, I could stay home and learn to be a rancher's wife, right?"

Clint groaned, realizing his mistake too

435

late. He had no choice but to finish what he'd started. "Before you get in a wad and start calling me names, would you hear me out?"

"I'm listening," Peggy stated tightly.

"Ranching is a full-time job, one that requires a lot of people. So far you've only seen the winter side, the dormant side, so to speak. Come spring, the pace picks up considerably. There're calves to roundup and brand, bulls to castrate, baby chicks to raise. In the summer we have alfalfa fields to irrigate, cut, and bale. We breed next year's calf crop. There's cattle and chickens to get to market. There's the horses to breed and train. There's always pastureland to maintain, sick animals, the unexpected weather to deal with."

Even in her irritation, Peggy marveled at the animated enthusiasm with which Clint talked of ranching. It was obvious he loved what he did and couldn't understand why everyone wasn't trying to get into it. He waved his casted arms in abbreviated gestures.

"You would still be an artist," he continued. "In fact, you would have more time to paint. We can build a studio out at the ranch, free-standing if you want. I'll move

436

the caboose out there, if that's what you want."

"I want the caboose at the lake," Peggy stated evenly.

"That's fine. I'm just trying to show you that I'm flexible. I want you to be happy."

"But you don't want me working." It was an accusation.

"I'm trying to show you it's unnecessary. You no longer need to work to support Megan. It's an hour drive into the village each day, and another one home. You are a valuable member of the family. We'd enjoy having you work with us."

"As what, Clint? Babysitter? Cook? Maybe I could paint murals on the sides of the barns. What if I *want* to teach?"

"But if the position in the village isn't available . . ."

"Then I go where one is."

"I can't leave the ranch!"

"I'm not asking you to."

Clint sat silently digesting this for a few minutes. He knew they were dangerously close to saying things they would later regret. He shouldn't have tried to discuss the issue today, when she was still smarting over the news of being replaced by a television set.

437

They had married so quickly, there had never been a proper reception. Clint was proud of his standing in the community, and was certain Peggy would be, too, once she was made aware it. She needed to meet the other ranchers.

Suddenly he was sorry Megan and Ramon had chosen to have a small family wedding. The Estavez family was as prominent in ranching as the Howells. A large wedding would have been the perfect setting for introducing Peggy into New Mexico society. It was too late for that, but maybe not for a reception to celebrate his own marriage. He vowed to discuss it with Tina and Gina when they returned home. Maybe he'd call them from the hotel.

"What are you thinking?" Peggy asked suspiciously, seeing his smile.

"That you should make some phone calls, write some letters, see what's available," Clint said magnanimously. "We can tour the University of New Mexico campus while we're in Albuquerque, if you'd like."

"Why the sudden change?"

"There's no harm in research. You have time yet, to decide what you want to do."

What Clint did not say was that he hoped by summer she would see how important a role she had at the ranch, and that the long drives to anywhere else were not worth it. He was confident in his ability to persuade her.

"You're smiling like the proverbial cat with canary-in-mouth."

"Actually, it is the smile of a man, alone with his new wife, heading toward a motel room in Albuquerque for a three-day orgy of uninterrupted sex."

"I thought we were going shopping!"

"Oops," Clint feigned dismay. "I didn't mean to let that slip until I had you safely locked in the room."

Peggy gave his casted arms a pointed look. "And how did you plan to manage that?"

"I know the bell captain personally," he assured her with the roguish leer that always made her flush.

It was hard to stay angry with him when he teased her like this, flooding her with the liquid heat of desire. When he turned smoldering brown eyes on her or leered at her as he was doing now, or sneaked up behind her to assault her neck with his mouth, she turned to helpless jelly.

Being handicapped had not slowed him down much, at least in his pursuit of her. It hadn't hampered his ability to overwhelm her senses, either, making her lose total control of her body and the situation. No matter what she started, he always ended up dominating the finale. She always gained in the losing, but it had become a personal challenge to her. She smiled, plotting strategy for the three days ahead.

"What are you smiling about?" Clint demanded.

"I was just wondering about the selection of Christmas gifts that would be left in the Fort Sumner stores come Tuesday morning."

Clint laughed then, a full arrogant laugh of male satisfaction. "We'll make it up to them on New Year's," he promised. "Can't you drive any faster?"

Peggy laughed at his impatience and applied slightly more pressure to the accelerator. In spite of their flirtatious conversation, though, the knowledge that her goal of teaching school was in serious peril was not far from her mind.

## Twenty-three

Bill and Rita Hogan, Peggy's parents, drove into the driveway of the ranch right behind Erika and Kevin just before suppertime on Christmas Eve. Peggy brought the whole family running with her glad cry. By some miracle, Kevin had brought Hillary with him. It had been a year since she'd seen her youngest grandchild, who was now three years old. Peggy would have sat and held her all evening, but Hillary preferred to study her grandmother from afar, staying close to Shawn and Michael, or her Grandfather Bill, Peggy's father. Although it tore at her heart, Peggy realized the whole situation was more than a little daunting to the child, and so she tried to be content with whatever Hillary would allow her.

Supper was a hasty affair, then the young people loaded into the Howell's passenger van and drove to the Estavez ranch. Megan and Ramon had been the guests of honor for Christmas Eve dinner.

Once family obligations were met, the young people planned to separate into male and female groups, and commence the bachelor parties. Peggy and Clint were left to entertain Peggy's parents and supervise their collective seven grandchildren. Although somewhat overwhelmed, Peggy wasn't complaining.

Clint and Peggy's father hit it off immediately. They sat in the den in front of the fire, watching the kids run wild and talking while Peggy took her mother on a tour of the house. Within an hour, Rita complained of being tired from the long drive, and retired to the room Peggy had prepared for them. Peggy was certain seven small children, ranging from seven years old down to two, wore her out more than the five-hundred-mile drive. Bill stayed to help them settle the kids down for sleep.

Since it was Christmas Eve, the most festive solution was to bed them all down in the den, on pallets made from sleeping bags and quilts. Bill restoked the fire, and it crackled cozily while he and Clint took turns telling Christmas stories until they were hoarse. Finally by midnight, they had them all asleep, and Bill retired to his own bed.

Peggy curled up on the couch with Clint, spoon-fashion, content to watch the fire and the sleeping children. She rested her arms on top of Clint's casts, which he crisscrossed against her chest. He even managed to position one hand over her breast, which he caressed with his free fingers.

"This is as close as we get to heaven on earth," Peggy commented, her voice thick with contentment.

"Why is that?" Clint asked, nuzzling her ear.

"Heaven is love, harmony, peace. I have my parents, my children, and all my grandchildren together with me again. And now I also have you, and your family. I can't remember a more perfect Christmas."

"I thought you left Kansas to avoid all this," Clint reminded her.

Peggy smiled to herself. "I don't want them to stay. Part of the pleasure is knowing it's temporary. It wouldn't be Christmas without family." She paused, remembering.

"Two years ago I learned about Christmas divorce-style," she shared with Clint. "I had the kids Christmas Eve, without Peter, for the first time in twenty-seven years. He and his new wife got the kids Christmas Day. I spent the day with Mother and Daddy by myself for the first time in twenty-seven years. It gave me a new respect for holiday depression."

Clint didn't know what to say, so he just held her close. Peggy returned the hug, then continued.

"Last Christmas Kevin wasn't speaking to me." Her voice caught on a lump in her throat that formed with the memory. "He even sent the presents I'd bought them back to me, unopened."

Clint sighed. Peggy would have fallen off the couch from the depth of it if he hadn't been holding her so tight.

"It's okay," she told him, resettling herself. "This year I have them all back together in addition to you and your family. It's going to be a wonderful Christmas."

Clint remained thoughtfully silent. He had a strong suspicion that the peace in Peggy's family came at a price, at least where Kevin was concerned. He was sure they would know what the price was before Kevin went back home.

"I get the distinct feeling you're not sharing my bliss of this moment," Peggy complained, twisting around so she could see his face.

"I was just wondering if we were going to spend the night here," Clint responded evasively.

"I thought we'd let Megan sleep here when they get back," Peggy said, snuggling back down against him. "Her kids and Hillary will be frightened waking up in a strange place and Hillary is more familiar with Megan than with me."

Clint could hear the sadness in her voice at that admission. He decided to pursue the issue. "How do you suppose Kevin talked Cheryl into letting Hillary come so far, and at Christmas?"

"Cheryl has never approved of Kevin's punishing me by keeping Hillary away. I guess she is as relieved by the reconciliation as I am, even though she and Kevin are separated. I should call her tomorrow and thank her. I'm sure Kevin didn't call and let her know they'd arrived okay."

"I'm sure he didn't," Clint agreed. He was thoughtful for a minute before proceeding. "Seems to me, if anyone should have been punished, it should have been Kevin."

"I'm the one who practically disowned him," Peggy stated defensively. "I was so angry at the time. I was sorry, of course, after I'd cooled down, but the damage had already been done. I hurt Kevin terribly, throwing his father's behavior up to him, then telling him never to come to me for anything ever again. He decided to take me at my word, and I'm the one who suffered."

"Still," Clint argued, "he's not without guilt."

"He never forgave me for divorcing his father," Peggy explained. "He blamed me when Peter remarried." She gave a short, mirthless laugh. "He blames me even now for his father's unhappiness. If I hadn't divorced him, he wouldn't have married that awful woman and she wouldn't be making life hell for him now."

"Yet he's divorcing his wife," Clint pointed out.

"Oh, no," Peggy disagreed emphatically. "Cheryl's divorcing him. It's her fault. Just ask him."

*Kevin needs to grow up,* Clint thought silently, knowing better than to voice his opinion out loud.

"I plan to talk to him while he's here," Peggy said. "He's blaming Cheryl and me for his problems instead of trying to work them out."

"I'm glad you see that. Do *you* still think you're to blame?" Clint asked, hoping to steer Peggy's thoughts the right way and make it sound like she'd arrived there on her own.

"I suppose I always will," Peggy admitted with a sigh. "You try to do the right thing, and it still comes out wrong. By the time you realize it's wrong, it's too late to undo the damage."

Clint gave up subtlety. "As long as you continue to accept the blame, he will continue to blame you. Kevin is a grown man. His behavior is his choice. I hope you tell him that."

"Maybe," Peggy conceded. "I'm just grateful he's here, and Hillary's here. I don't want anything to spoil it right now."

Clint was silent, continuing to hold her as he studied the coals glowing from beneath the fireplace grate. The fire was nearly out. It was too late to add any more logs.

When the young people arrived home, Clint was startled awake and made aware of an uncomfortable crick in his neck from falling asleep on the couch. Peggy stirred from her position on his chest, then slowly extracted herself out from under his casts.

"What time is it?" she asked Megan.

"Two a.m. Good idea," Megan commended, indicating the pile of children on the floor.

"Yes, well, I hope you still think so in the morning. I'm assigning you the remainder of the night watch."

Megan giggled, and Peggy looked at her suspiciously. "How much did you drink?"

"Not nearly as much as the men," Megan defended herself. "It was a bachelor party, Mom. Lighten up. I'm the bride." She giggled again.

"It's a long drive back out here, too," Peggy chastised her, thanking God they'd made it back safely.

"Gina didn't drink. She drove."

"Smart girl," Peggy conceded, somewhat mollified.

"Really, Mother, give us some credit. We're hardly kids." She giggled at that, too. "We all have kids." She laughed then, as if she'd told a hilarious joke, and headed toward the bathroom.

"I'll check on the boys." Clint followed Megan out of the room.

Peggy made up the couch for Megan. Tina and Gina each came in to check on their respective offspring, and thanked Peggy for keeping them. With a kiss to Peggy's cheek, they headed for their own beds.

"Are you going to set the alarm?" Clint asked when they were finally in bed themselves.

"No," Peggy stated emphatically. "We babysat while they partied. We earned the right to sleep late while they deal with their children, their hangovers, and Christmas morning."

Clint chuckled. "I have every confidence that they'll keep the children quiet and out of our room, allowing us to sleep as late as we wish."

Peggy had to laugh too. The kids would be up with the dawn, demanding to open their presents and rousing the entire household. In spite of her statement earlier, she wouldn't miss it for the world.

The children were indeed up with the chickens and dancing with impatience as the red-eyed adults dragged themselves out of bed and gathered around the coffeepot. The youngest needed to be fed, which was nearly the undoing of the older ones, who were much too excited to be concerned with food. The sadly hungover men went to the barn to escape the noise and try to clear their heads with the cold morning air. Although Kevin tagged along, Peggy doubted there was much in the way of ranch chores he would be willing to attempt.

Bill was down early as well, hoping for a tour of the grounds and the stables. He ended up helping to feed Hillary. He informed Peggy that her mother would be down after her bath. Peggy smiled knowingly and her father winked at her. It would be a long bath.

Finally, the children were fed, the chores done, Rita's bath completed, and the turkey put in the oven. The newly expanded Howell family gathered in the living room, where the available floor space had been grievously compromised by an enormous Christmas tree surrounded to suffocation with brightly wrapped presents. In spite of the children's impatience, Clint, as head of the family, insisted Christ be given first billing instead of Santa Claus. Peggy held the Bible while Clint read the Christmas story to a fidgeting audience, followed by a brief prayer of thanksgiving for home, family, and financial welfare.

After a pious Amen, Clint solemnly intoned, "Let the destruction begin."

It took two hours to lay waste to a month's worth of careful shopping and wrapping. Clint ceded the task of passing out the gifts to J.R., but insisted they be done one at a time, so everyone could see what everyone else received and the giver could be acknowledged and thanked. Clint let the children take turns opening his own gifts.

Peggy had agonized since the wedding over what she would give Clint. She knew she wanted it to be a painting, but choosing the subject had been difficult. By some unspoken agreement, Clint and Peggy unwrapped their gifts to each other last. When he had Shawn unwrap it for him, she knew from the expression on his face that she'd chosen well. Clint stared at it in openmouthed astonishment. The others quickly gathered behind him to see it.

The family photo album was filled with pictures of Clint and the boys on horseback. Peggy had found three that would blend well together, adjusted the faces to reflect their present ages (using some photos she took herself for just that purpose), and had done her painting. Clint and his two boys rode casually across the sparse New Mexico grassland, Clint pointing at something in the distance, the two boys watching where he pointed.

Clint's eyes met Peggy's over the top of the frame, their dark brown depths liquid with pride, pleasure, love, and a warmth that suffused through her like warm brandy. She finally blushed at the intensity of his gaze and the profuse compliments of his family. Her own children just looked on quietly, smugly deflecting their mother's compliments by saying it was nothing more than they had come to expect, having seen her work many times in the past. Bill refused to be modest, praising his daughter to all who would listen.

"Your turn," Clint insisted to Peggy, nodding at J.R. meaningfully.

J.R. was grinning as he reached under the tree and withdrew a fairly large box, handing it to Peggy. It contained a handsome pair of tooled and richly embroidered black leather ladies' western boots.

"They're beautiful," Peggy told him, thinking she had no idea what she was to wear them with, or to. Nevertheless, she tried them on. They seemed to fit, but never having worn western boots before, she wasn't sure. They felt stiff.

452

"There's more," Clint announced, his own excitement barely contained.

The next box was heavy, and when she opened it, she almost gave herself away before she quickly smiled with forced enthusiasm. It was a bridle, and that could only mean one thing. Somewhere there was a horse, and Clint expected her to learn to ride it.

"Should you give me these in front of the children?" she joked, hoping to cover her dismay. Clint's puzzled frown conveyed his lack of understanding. "Whips and chains?" She jingled the metal pieces by the leather straps, trying to look vampish.

Megan laughed, then squelched herself, until she and Peggy exchanged glances. Then they both started laughing.

"It's a bridle," Clint told her, which only caused them to laugh harder, now at Clint's not getting the joke.

"I'm sorry," Peggy tried to apologize, giving him a hug. "It wasn't that funny."

"Doesn't anyone want to know what the bridle goes to?"

"I certainly do," Rita said.

Peggy tried to look enthusiastic, but felt sick. There was only one thing a bridle went to, and she wanted no part of it. Horses were beautiful creatures, and she loved to paint them, but up close, they were rather spooky. They had strange eyes, huge teeth, and sharp hoofs. To Peggy, horses were right up there with lions and snakes—best admired from a distance, preferably through photographs.

She was surrounded by a family who had all learned to ride simultaneously with walking, however, and who remembered their first horse more fondly than their first car. The four smallest Howells were the most eager to escort their new grandma out to the barn. Peggy found herself being fought over, Shawn and Michael not about to have their positions usurped by newcomers.

Clint forcefully demanded quiet as they approached the barn. He instructed everyone to wait at the corral fence, except J.R., who he sent in to bring out the gift. He edged out the children to stand near Peggy. She gave him a weak smile.

"Her name's Heather," Clint told her as J.R. led out a pale gray Appaloosa mare.

Peggy watched the horse walk sedately beside J.R. and knew Clint watched her, waiting for her pleased response. She avoided looking at him until J.R. brought the mare over to the fence. J.R.'s proud expression

454

turned puzzled as Peggy just stood there, looking at the horse.

"Don't you want to pet her?" J.R. asked, holding the mare's head steady.

"I don't think Peggy is pleased with my surprise," Clint stated dryly.

Peggy winced at the disappointment she knew she was causing, and finally met Clint's hard gaze. "She's a beautiful mare, Clint, I'm just not sure I will ever get up enough nerve to ride her."

"She's eight years old, and as sedate as a rocking chair," Clint insisted. "That's why I bought her. She's a perfect first horse. Hillary could ride her."

"Oh, no," Peggy gasped, horrified at the thought.

"I want to ride her, Grandma," Michael begged, tugging on Peggy's pant leg.

"That's a good idea, Michael. Show your grandma how easy it is."

"Clint, I don't think that's a good idea," Peggy tried to intervene, but Michael was already climbing the corral fence, and J.R. had him on top of the horse before Peggy finished her protest.

"Me, too, J.R." Shawn was right behind his brother.

Peggy stood rigid, biting her thumbnail as

Heather circled the corral with the two boys on her back, J.R. holding her lead rope. She didn't even object to Michael's enthusiastic thumping of her sides with his heels, urging her to go faster.

"You going to be shown up by a five-year-old?" Clint challenged her. "Scott and Cindy want to go next."

Two years old, or five years old, it didn't matter. It was obvious that if she intended to live on a ranch, she was expected to learn to ride a horse. The best she could hope for was postponement.

"I insist that you be the one to teach me."

Clint frowned at her thoughtfully, then realization dawned. "Okay," he conceded, ruefully shaking his head. "Riding lessons commence in one month, as soon as the casts come off."

"As soon as Dr. Roberts says it's safe for you to be back on horseback," Peggy amended.

Each of the children got a turn on Grandma's new horse before the group headed back to the house. Tina, Gina, and Megan started dinner preparations. Peggy and Clint took her parents and the children back into the living room to start carrying out the gifts and picking up the wrapping paper. The young men stayed outside with the horses.

"I guess I should have bought you a fur coat," Clint said, once again the helpless bystander as Peggy began gathering up paper and bows.

"It was silly of me to think I could live on a ranch and avoid horses. I'll enjoy going with you on horseback." Peggy prayed it was the truth. "Heather appears to be as docile as you promised."

"But you don't like her."

Rita and Bill had left to carry a load of gifts out for Shawn and Michael. Peggy handed Hillary the sack of bows she was collecting, instructing the child to find the rest of them. She slid under Clint's casts, giving him a kiss, and smiled into his troubled brown eyes. "I like the horse. I have to like the horse, because I love the cowboy."

"I'm a cowboy, too, Grandma," Michael insisted, running into the room. He was decked out in his new cowboy gear, complete with hat and boots.

"You sure are, darling." Peggy reluctantly extracted herself from Clint and gave Michael a hug.

The Estavez family arrived for Christmas dinner, which was to be served at one o'clock. The Guntners, Tina and Gina's family, also came. Both families brought enough food to feed the entire huge gathering, which they added to the enormous layout Tina and Gina had to start with. Seeing all that food, Peggy was sure they could have invited the entire county and still had leftovers.

Peggy met so many new people, her head swam. Women talked nonstop while carrying dishes to and from the kitchen. The pastor and his wife came and fit right into the crowd, seeming to know everyone there. Children of every age ran underfoot and begged for a taste, or were pulled away just prior to putting dirty fingers into the tempting array of pies and cakes. Peggy enlisted Megan and Erika, and they herded the entire group into the den. The older ones were sent outside with Bill and Clint and given strict orders not to set foot back inside until called. The rest of the men escaped to the outer regions, mostly around the corral.

Amazingly enough, the entire group of fifty men, women, and children sat down together for dinner, and quiet reigned long enough for Clint to say a prayer of grace and thanksgiving. After his Amen was repeated around the table, chaos resumed.

From that point on, the day became a blur for Peggy.

Megan and Ramon were married at four o'clock, in the living room, in front of the tree. The photographer took pictures of all the wedding party, the family members, and the reception. It was dark when they finally made their getaway in Peggy's van, leaving the lavishly decorated pickup sitting in the middle of an outraged crowd of shaving cream artists. It was close to midnight before all the guests were gone, and the house restored to some semblance of order.

The next morning, a bleary-eyed group of adults once again gathered around the coffeepot, trying to injest enough caffeine to countermand the night before. Erika and Kevin had to get back to Wichita, Erika to her job, and Kevin to return Hillary to her mother. Rita and Bill were going back also. Peggy opened the refrigerator to find something to feed them for breakfast.

"How does turkey and dressing strike you?" she asked, staring with dismay at the packed interior of the refrigerator. She wasn't sure she could find the carton of eggs if her life depended on it.

"I'll settle for a piece of pecan pie," Kevin suggested.

Peggy looked at the rest of them.

"I'll take chocolate," said Erika.

Clint groaned in revulsion. "Can you find the butter?" Peggy did, holding it up to him triumphantly. "Make some toast and I'll eat the turkey."

Hillary wanted no part of leftover dinner. She demanded Corn Pops.

Bill said he'd join Clint in the turkey and toast. Rita declined breakfast altogether, returning upstairs to pack.

"So, Kevin, what will you do come January?" Peggy asked as she fed Clint and herself.

Kevin cleared his throat and put down his fork. "Um, well, Mom, I was going to talk to you about that."

Clint refused the next bite, resting his casts on the table, watching Kevin intently. Kevin glanced at him quickly, then at his grandfather, then back to Peggy. He seemed nervous.

"I only have one semester left," Kevin spoke to Peggy, "And then I'll have my MBA. I'm already receiving job offers."

"That's good, Kevin," Peggy encouraged.

"I'd like to go ahead and finish—full-time,

you know?" He waited, hoping for an offer instead of having to beg.

"That's understandable," Peggy agreed. "What are your plans?"

"Well, I, uh, I thought, that is, now that Megan's married . . ." He trailed off. Peggy sat, waiting expectantly for him to tell her his plans. Kevin shot a quick glance at his sister.

"Erika's roommate isn't too happy with my living with them," he stated, changing tactics. "I need a place of my own."

"I didn't think that would last too long," his mother agreed. "What about Cheryl?"

"Aw, Mom, Cheryl's being real stubborn. She's been seeing some marriage counselor, and it's a woman. I'm sure she's divorced and hates men. They're trying to make me into a trained lapdog." Kevin let all his frustration out as he spoke.

"What does she want you to do?" Peggy asked softly.

"Ridiculous stuff!" Kevin stood up and began pacing the large kitchen, waving his arms for emphasis. "She won't even talk to me, just issues ultimatums. It's not even Cheryl talking, it's that damn b—"

"Kevin," Erika interrupted, her voice a warning.

461

Peggy looked from Kevin to Erika, watching their silent signals. It was obvious the two of them had talked at length, enough that Erika knew that where Kevin was headed wasn't wise. Peggy stifled a smile. If Erika only knew the words she heard, now that she taught school. Still, her daughter's efforts to protect her were amusing.

She glanced at Clint to see if he was also amused and was startled to see the hard way he was watching Kevin. She'd forgotten what a chivalrous knight he was. No, he wouldn't find Kevin's language amusing. She looked at her father and was surprised to find him watching her, his face unreadable. She frowned in confusion, then looked back at Kevin.

"It's okay, Kevin," Peggy reassured him. "Go on."

"She's being brainwashed," Kevin finished.

"By someone other than yourself?" Peggy asked, amused at his assessment of the situation.

"What the hell's that supposed to mean?" Kevin demanded, glaring at her.

"Sit down, Kevin!" Clint and Bill said, almost simultaneously.

Kevin glowered, first at his mother, then at his grandfather. Finally he looked at Hillary, who had quit eating and was staring at him, a worried look on her little face. He sat down sullenly.

"Erika, why don't you take Hillary upstairs and finish getting ready," Peggy suggested quietly.

"That's a good idea," Kevin agreed. "I would really like to talk to you alone, Mom, but there hasn't been any opportunity." He tried to look pointedly at Clint, but couldn't hold the man's gaze. He looked back at Peggy. "Could we talk—just you and me?"

"No." Clint spoke with icy finality.

"Now, see here!" Kevin exploded, jumping back to his feet. Peggy restrained him by holding up her hand.

Peggy looked at Clint, who met her questioning gaze without blinking. He also didn't explain.

"This is between me and Kevin, Clint," she said, trying to convey her displeasure at his interference.

Clint realized the situation was extremely volatile and was getting out of hand quickly. "Can we talk alone first?" he suggested, his voice low and restrained.

"Oh, that's great!" Kevin interrupted, turning away from them with frustrated gestures. "Clear it with your husband before you talk to your son. Who's it gonna be, Mom? Huh?" he demanded, coming to stand so that Peggy was between him and Clint. "Me or him?"

Peggy looked from her son to her husband, feeling trapped. Kevin's eyes were wild, his expression challenging. Clint's eyes were probing and his mouth set in a grim line as he waited for her answer to Kevin's question. She closed her eyes and took a deep breath to gather her wits. When she opened them she gave Clint an entreating look.

"This is not a matter of choosing between you," she insisted. With a sinking heart she watched Clint's jaw clench and knew he didn't believe her. "Let me talk to Kevin. We'll talk later."

Clint didn't answer her. His gaze was hard as he studied her, then he turned and left the room.

# Twenty-four

Peggy watched Clint walk out, torn between running after him and standing her ground. She looked to her father for support. Bill was watching her with sad eyes.

"He doesn't understand," Peggy maintained.

"Do you?" her father asked, rising to his feet. When Peggy didn't answer he turned to Kevin.

"You will speak with respect to your mother," he warned in a quietly authoritative voice. "I'll go help your grandmother load the car."

Peggy watched until the swinging door came to rest before she turned to her son. "What is this all about?"

"Jesus, Mom," Kevin exclaimed.

"Is that a prayer?" Peggy asked, warning him.

"No," he admitted, forcing himself to calm down. He sat down and took a sip of his coffee, then made a face. He got up to pour it out, then made a new cup.

"Want one?" he offered.

"Sure," Peggy said, sighing with frustration.

"Mom, you know how I feel about Cheryl, about Hillary," Kevin started, sitting back down with the two cups of coffee. "But what can I do? She won't even talk to me."

"What did she ask you to do, Kevin?"

"She's not being reasonable. She's being guided by that bimbo, and her lawyer. Do you know who she hired? Grant Wallace! Really, Mom," he eyed his mother accusingly, "did you give her his name?"

Peggy took a sip of coffee to keep from smiling. When she had decided to divorce Peter, she had done some research. Grant Wallace had the worst reputation in town— for taking men to the cleaners, right down to their skivvies. His name was cursed and reviled among divorced men, and praised and blessed among divorced women. Peggy had hired him, and he'd more than lived up to his reputation.

"No, I didn't give her his name," she finally answered. "He's well known, however."

"No shit," Kevin stated bitterly. He ignored the glare from his mother.

"You hope Dad's miserable, and you hope I'm miserable. To you, we're only getting what we deserve."

"Why do you think that, Kevin?" Peggy asked tightly.

"You refuse to help me."

Peggy blinked, too astonished to respond.

"I've been living with Erika for three months now," Kevin continued. "You helped Megan. You've been supporting Megan all her life, and her two kids. When Megan lost her job, you gave her your house, your precious caboose. That's all I've heard Erika talk about since you moved down here, but as soon as Megan gets in trouble, you hand it over. When I get thrown out, you don't offer me shit!"

"You will show me respect, young man," Peggy demanded, her lowered voice trembling with her effort not to shriek at him. "If you feel slighted, you can talk to me. If you have a need, you can come to me, but you will not talk to me this way."

Defiance emanated from Kevin like heat waves off hot asphalt. He looked so much like his father as he stood there, mentally calculating the most prudent avenue to take, the best way to get around her. Peggy stood her ground, matching him glare for glare.

Kevin's defiance began to crumble. The hardness left his eyes, and he dropped his gaze to his hands. His tight mouth began to quiver, a gesture so unexpected Peggy forgot part of her anger. The rigid shoulders sagged, the clenched fists fell to his side, and his entire long length dropped defeated into the chair, his head falling into his hands. With horror, Peggy realized he was crying.

"Kevin?" She went around the table. When she touched his shoulders, he turned into her, burying his head into her torso, holding her around the waist.

"Kevin?" She smoothed his hair back. He had Peter's hair, silky, dark, and curly. For all his faults, he was her son, her firstborn, a piece of her heart and her life. Peggy felt hot tears flood her eyes and drop onto her hands as she caressed his hair and held him.

"I'm sorry, Mom," he apologized in a strangled voice which further tore at her heart and caused more tears to flow.

"Shh, it's okay," she crooned. "We were both angry."

"I guess I got jealous," he admitted, his voice muffled against her. "Daughters are allowed to need their mothers. Sons are expected to stand on their own, even support the women. I've failed all of you."

"No, Kevin, no, you've not failed anybody."

"I've failed Cheryl, and Hillary."

"You are such a good daddy, Kevin. Anyone can see that. And Cheryl still loves you. You've hurt her, badly."

"She wants me to get a job, Mom. She doesn't believe in me. I'm so close. One more semester—five months—and I'll be able to show her. In five months I can be making fifty thousand a year."

Peggy was skeptical, but she didn't say anything. She continued to stroke his hair.

"Can you help me, Mom? Just for five months, I could pay you back, once I'm working."

Kevin turned luminous blue eyes up to her, his thick dark lashes spiked with moisture.

"What is so bad about working, Kevin?" she chided him. "Most twenty-seven-year-old able-bodied men work."

"You, too?" he accused, pulling away from her.

"Do you want your family back, Kevin?"

469

"Of course I do," he stated impatiently. He stood up to find a tissue, brusquely wiping at his eyes.

"All Cheryl wants is an indication that you're willing to share the load." Peggy wiped gently at her own eyes, trying not to smear mascara.

"I'm trying to get an education so I can get a better paying job," Kevin explained with exasperation. "What good is my working at Pizza Hut for minimum wage if it compromises my studying and costs me in grade point average?"

Kevin blew his nose and recomposed his features. Within seconds, all evidence of his earlier tears were gone. Peggy wished her own face would clear up that quickly. She wouldn't look normal again for hours.

She went to the sink and wet a paper towel to blot against her eyes. Kevin refilled the coffee cups and sat back down at the table.

"I'm willing to help," Peggy informed him, taking her own seat, "but you have to do your share."

"Like Megan did?" Kevin asked, the sneer back in his voice.

"Megan did all my housework, cooking, and errand running," she informed him sharply, "plus drew unemployment from when she did work."

"She likes that kind of stuff," Kevin grumbled, but he backed off.

"What are you willing to do, Kevin, for your family and your career?"

Kevin stared sullenly at his coffee cup.

"What about all those job offers?" Peggy suggested. "Would they be interested in hiring you now, before you graduate?"

"Most of them aren't even in the state of Kansas, much less Wichita," Kevin stated with exasperation.

"I see. So you'd want to move after graduation?"

"If that's what it takes to get the best job."

"Have you discussed this with Cheryl?"

"What does she have to do with it?" Kevin challenged, losing patience. "If she wants to be my wife, she'll go where I go."

*Just like I did,* Peggy thought bitterly. "Kevin life is not the same as it was thirty years ago when a man could get away with statements like that. You've got some choices to make here, son, and they are going to impact on the rest of your life."

"Are you going to help me or not?" Kevin demanded.

"Are you going to do anything to help yourself?" Peggy came back.

"I'll look for a job," he conceded ungraciously.

"You'd better," his mother advised, "because I don't have enough to support you until you're out of school and gainfully employed as an MBA. I've got to go back to school myself."

Kevin listened, unimpressed, to her abbreviated tale of losing her job. "So what's the problem?" he asked when she finished. "You're married to Clint now. You don't need to work."

"I want to be a teacher," Peggy stated tightly. "I *am* a teacher, and I *will* teach."

"Okay, Mom, okay," Kevin held up his hands defensively. "It's not a big deal."

"Yes, it is, Kevin. It's a very big deal, even if I'm the only one who thinks so."

"I'll get a job," Kevin promised. "I just need a couple thousand to live on until I do, and even then what I can make won't be enough to keep an apartment on."

"A couple thousand?" Peggy asked in disbelief.

"I really need more like three thousand to start," he amended. "An apartment is six

472

hundred a month and they always want two months in advance."

"Megan paid that much for a house with a fenced-in yard," Peggy objected.

"It's more expensive to live near campus," Kevin insisted.

"Can't you share?"

"Everyone I know is married, or shacked up. It's for five months, Mom. I'll study better without the distraction of a roommate."

"And the rest?" Peggy asked weakly.

"Food, utilities, gasoline, clothes, tuition, books," he ticked items off on his fingers, "oh, and I almost forgot, car insurance. That's another thousand."

"One thousand dollars for car insurance?" Peggy was incredulous.

"It comes due in January. Foreign cars cost more to insure."

"You're still driving the Porsche?"

"I'd lose more money selling it than I'd gain. I have to have a car, Mom, and I already have that one. At least it's paid for."

*Yeah,* Peggy thought, *with my money.*

"I'll give you three thousand, Kevin, to pay your insurance, get you into an apartment, and cover your school expenses. After that, I'll pay your rent. Everything else is up to you."

"I'll make it work, Mom," Kevin assured her, getting up to leave. "You'll see, you and Cheryl both."

*Will we?* Peggy wondered, watching him go.

Peggy tried to talk to Clint after everyone had left, but he asked J.R. to drive him out to check on the cows. She tried again after supper, but he pretended to be totally absorbed in a movie on television and only responded in vague monosyllables. Finally, she gave up.

*Stubborn man,* she declared to herself, and devoted herself to spending time with Shawn and Michael.

"I know you're awake," she said into the darkness that night as she and Clint lay together, not touching, in their bed. "I did not choose Kevin over you."

"All I asked was to talk to you before you talked to him," Clint's cool voice answered her. "You refused me."

"He's *my* son, Clint," Peggy begged for understanding. "I felt like I needed to handle it alone."

"You gave him money," Clint accused.

"It's my money," Peggy reminded him softly.

"He's got you buffaloed, Peggy, and you know it." The mattress heaved as Clint worked himself onto his other side so he was facing her. "He's not even trying to carry his own weight."

"You don't know anything about it," Peggy defended Kevin hotly. "He's going to get a job and he's going to pay me back."

"I know a con artist when I see one," Clint argued, unconvinced. "He's twenty-seven years old, Peggy. He needs to grow up, learn responsibility. Even your dad recognizes it."

"I don't interfere with you and your sons," Peggy retorted, turning on her side away from him. "Please don't interfere with me and mine."

"I won't," he replied with soft finality. Peggy clung to the side of the bed as he heaved himself away from her again, rocking the bed as if it were caught in an earthquake.

Clint was distant with Peggy over the next few days, which was fine with her since she was still feeling a little resentful. She still did the things for him that she always did, but instead of the teasing and flirting that usually accompanied their routines, they were both coolly polite. Shawn and Michael grew more jealous of Clint's grandchildren living with their grandma as the week went on, vying with them for her attention and time. They even became jealous of Clint. It seemed to them that everytime they finally had their grandma to themselves to read a book, play a game, or work a puzzle Clint needed her to do something for him. Peggy began to think she had eight grandchildren instead of seven.

Peggy called Violet to talk to her about the job situation with the school. Violet had gone to Eastern New Mexico State for her master's degree and was able to tell Peggy how many credit hours she would need to be certified in language arts as well as history.

Frustrated with Clint, frustrated with the grandchildren, frustrated with her career, Peggy decided to unpack the boxes she'd brought out from the caboose two weeks earlier. In one box she found a book she'd bought before she'd left Kansas, and never read.

Bedtime had always been Peggy's favorite

time to read. Married to Peter, that hadn't been a problem, since he was away from home four nights a week. Although it hadn't been a good marriage, she'd never before realized how much freedom she'd had in it. Once the children were fed, bathed, and put to bed, she had been free to sew, paint, or read a book.

She had no personal time now. She had a full-time job and a live-in husband. The books she read to him were westerns and spy novels. She preferred historical novels and biographies. The only painting she'd done since they'd gotten married had been his Christmas present, and she'd done that at school, mostly on her break. She didn't even take a bath alone anymore.

She had left Kansas because of the demands on her life. Megan had wanted her house. Kevin had wanted her money. The grandsons had wanted her time. Now, she lived in New Mexico. Megan had her house, Kevin had her money, and the grandsons had her Christmas vacation. Maybe she should have surrendered in Kansas, she thought bitterly, while she was still ahead.

Peggy was still in this self-absorbed, self-pitying fog when Michael brought her a deck of cards and asked her to play a game with him. He had just dealt the first hand when Clint interrupted.

"Peggy, I need to change clothes so I can go into the village with J.R.," Clint announced, coming through the door of the den.

Michael didn't wait for Peggy's response. He threw the cards down on the floor, then scattered them further with a kick of his foot. "I hate this place!" he yelled. "I want to go home!" He ran out of the room before Peggy had a chance to stop him.

"Peggy!" Clint demanded when she rose to follow Michael. "I have to change."

"Can't it wait a minute?" she asked, exasperated. "Michael's upset."

"Michael's throwing a tantrum to get your attention. If you go to him now you're just rewarding him for misbehaving."

"Michael is five years old and feeling threatened by all the people moving in on what was once his exclusive domain," Peggy corrected him. "I know exactly how he feels."

"What's that supposed to mean?"

"It means we all need more room to breathe." Peggy hadn't thought about what she wanted to do until this moment, but now it came to her clearly. "I'm going to take the boys to the caboose for a couple of days," she announced calmly. "I need to check on Henry anyway, and it'll make things easier on everyone."

"What about me?" Clint asked defensively.

"There are four able-bodied adults living here who can take care of you quite well," Peggy stated. She turned and went to find Michael and Shawn.

Peggy Jo Thompkins Howell was running away from home—again.

Peggy sat in the cupola of the caboose, watching the water in the moonlight. Henry was thrilled to have her back, and was already stationed in her lap, idly purring to her absentminded stroking. Shawn and Michael were asleep in their beds below.

Peggy had realized on the drive out that she was running away again. Now that she had time to think about it, she further realized it wasn't going to do her any more good this time than it had the last time. She couldn't run away from herself.

She had known Clint was a dominant, chauvinistic male, but she had married him anyway. She had known Megan was manipulative and clinging, but she'd let her stay in the caboose, and she'd let her dump the boys on her for the whole week of Christmas break. She'd known Kevin was not responsible when it came to money, but she'd given it to him out of a sense of guilt. She had no one to blame but herself.

Even school. If she'd used her brain she would have chosen a larger school district where art was more stable as a teaching position. Instead, she'd chosen a tiny school where art hadn't been taught in five years and she could only teach three classes. She'd been so wrapped up in getting as far away from her family as possible, she was grateful Alaska *hadn't* offered.

*It could be worse,* she thought. *I could be stuck in an igloo with Megan and both of us unemployed. We'd probably marry fat Eskimos just to keep warm.* The humor of the image finally pierced through her self-pity and made her smile.

"Oh, Henry," she admonished the boneless pile of fur in her lap. "We've got to do something about that woman in the chains. It's time for her to sit on the horse for a change—to take control of her life."

## Twenty-five

The next morning Peggy unpacked the airbrush and paint, and changed the scene on the hood of Ramon's pickup. She put the woman on the horse, dressed, with the sword and chain in her hands. The man didn't have hair to cover his naked condition, but covered himself with his chained hands. His expression was one of astonishment.

Clint came out when she drove into the driveway the evening of the next day.

"Is that how you feel?" Clint asked her when he saw the altered painting.

"Yes," Peggy stated defensively, prepared for a fight. "It's time for this woman to take charge of her life."

"You've had me in chains since the day I met you," Clint admitted, surprising her with his candidness. "Chained and vulnerable, and at the mercy of your sword."

"What sword?" Peggy had expected him to be angry with her for being gone for two days. Instead he was sharing his heart with her.

"The sword of your words. When you are angry with me, it hurts me. I didn't like the first painting, and I don't like this one, either. Men and women were meant to be partners, side by side, not one in bondage to the other. If you feel like this marriage is a form of bondage, then something is wrong."

"I definitely feel bound," Peggy admitted, "By you, by Megan, by Kevin, by Shawn and Michael, now even by the school. There's nothing left for me."

"They cannot take what you do not give."

"I've already reached that conclusion," Peggy admitted, giving him a slight smile. "It's time we all grew up. I'll pay Ramon to have his truck repainted; solid black this time; but I had to unchain that woman."

"I don't like being lumped in with your kids, Peggy," Clint said as they walked toward the house. "I didn't ask you to marry me to take care of me. I've got two sons and two daughters-in-law who could do that. You chose to get married."

"You want me to quit teaching and ride a horse," Peggy accused.

"I want you to be my partner, riding out with me to check on the calves. That's my greatest pleasure, and I wanted to share it with you. As far as your teaching, I want you to do it because you want to, not because you feel you have to for financial reasons. If you want to be an artist, or an art teacher, that's what I want you to be. Not teaching school would give you more time to paint."

"Then I wasted all that time and money getting my degree."

"Education is never a waste."

Peggy thought about that. She *had* gained more than a degree. She'd regained her self-confidence, enough that she could file for divorce finally, enough that she could leave home for the first time and follow her own dreams. Then she'd met Clint, and gotten sidetracked.

"I need some time to think, Clint, and I can't think here."

"Where then?"

"I want to go home, to the caboose, when Megan moves out. I want to put it back right, finish the studio, sort out my feelings."

"You consider that home?" Clint asked, letting her see how much that hurt him.

483

"I don't fit in here, Clint."

"So you're running away," he accused flatly.

Peggy had to smile at that, even though it wasn't particularly funny. "That's what my mother accused me of when I left Kansas."

"Were you?"

"I guess I was."

"And did you gain anything by it?"

"No." Peggy shook her head sadly. "They followed me."

"They'll keep following you, as long as you let them."

"I want time to think, Clint."

"You're your own worst enemy, Peggy," Clint stated sadly. "You've been hurt by those you loved and trusted, and I think you're afraid to love and trust again. I want only your happiness, not your enslavement. I want a partner, not a servant. When you want to be my partner, I'll be here."


Megan and Ramon returned New Year's Day, and came out to the ranch to exchange vehicles and pick up Shawn and Michael. Ramon screamed as if in pain when he saw what Peggy had done to his fantasy woman. She refused to discuss it, but handed him a check for five hundred dollars, to reimburse what he'd paid her to paint the first scene. Megan looked at her mother strangely and assured her that they would be out of the caboose by the following weekend.

Peggy called Eastern New Mexico State in Portales and made an appointment to talk with one of the counselors before school reconvened. She came back with a schedule for the spring semester, and an announcement that she knew Clint wouldn't understand.

"I'm going to live at the caboose during the week while I go back to school." She knew he had heard her, although he continued to watch the news as if he hadn't. "I'm going to enroll in night classes in Portales, on Tuesdays and Thursdays, and it's too far to drive back here that late, then back to school the next morning."

"And the other nights?" Clint asked, without emotion, never taking his attention from the weather forecast.

"I'll have studying to do, papers to write. It'll be easier this way."

He looked at her then, and she cringed under the scrutiny. She watched the weather forecast to avoid his eyes.

"So you've decided teaching school is more important than being married."

"I'm asking for some time."

"I got married because I wanted a wife." Clint's voice raised slightly in anger. "Why did you get married?"

*Temporary insanity,* Peggy thought, but didn't say it.

"Remember the night after the wedding?" Clint asked, softening his tone. "You told me you loved me, and everything would work out. Do you no longer love me?"

Tears burned Peggy's eyes and swelled her throat at the vulnerability Clint was allowing her to see. She swallowed hard and studied the floor at her feet. "That's not the problem," she choked out.

"Then why can't we work it out?"

"I have to do this, Clint," Peggy said with anguish in her voice, finally looking at him. "It's been a goal for so long. To quit now and admit defeat . . ." She shook her head for emphasis. "I can't do it."

"I don't remember asking you to," Clint said softly.

"But that's what you'd like," she accused.

"I was a widower for three years," Clint said, coming to stand in front of her. "In that time every single woman with designs

486

on being a rancher's wife let me know that she was available for the job, and even a few who were married. If all I wanted was a good woman to help me with the ranch, I had a large selection to choose from. I didn't need another ranch hand. Tina and Gina do an admirable job of handling the feminine side of the ranch. What I missed most, was my soul mate."

Clint stood very close to Peggy, letting her see the love in his eyes as he looked down into her troubled blue ones. "I recognized you the first day I met you. I allowed you to marry me for the wrong reasons, hoping to show you what I already knew. We're good together, Peggy. Whether you teach school, fly airplanes, or rope cattle, you're the woman I want to share my life with."

"You hate my son."

"I disagree with your methods."

"You bought me boots and a horse."

"So? Buy me a set of paints."

"You don't think I should go back to school."

"I was only trying to show you it wasn't necessary if you didn't want to. Obviously, you feel that it's important."

"It's too far a drive back out here from Portales, Clint."

"Then stay at the caboose on those nights, and come home on the others."

"I'll come Friday through Monday," Peggy compromised.

The first day back at school Peggy was dismayed to see Billy Ellis dressed in his usual filthy, ragged clothes. His hair was long and greasy, his face marred with a fine raised rash, his teeth unbrushed, his hands unwashed, and his bare feet erupting from the toes of his battered tennis shoes. He slumped at his desk, dozed through most of class, and barely acknowledged Peggy's greeting when class was over and he walked by her desk toward the door.

"Come here, Billy," she instructed, barely able to contain her irritation. He came, but stood sullenly beside the desk, looking at the floor.

"Did you have a nice Christmas?" she asked. He answered with a shrug of his shoulders. "Did you give your father a gift?"

"Yeah," he muttered, still looking at his feet, which he shuffled restlessly.

"What did you get him?" Peggy prodded.

"A watch."

"That's nice," Peggy praised. "What did he give you?"

"Money."

"For clothes?" she asked hopefully.

"I bought some tapes, played some games."

"I see." Peggy tried to hide her disappointment.

"I gotta go, Mrs. Howell. I'll be late for class."

Peggy sat at her desk while the next class filed into the room, trying to think. She'd tried the subtle approach to no avail. It was time for the direct one.

As soon as school was dismissed she drove to Pete's Place. She sat in the van, stoking up her courage, before she got out and went in. This early on a Monday afternoon, the place was nearly deserted. She asked for Pete as soon as the hostess greeted her.

Pete came out of the kitchen and assessed her suspiciously. He wasn't quite as tall as she was, and although he wasn't really fat, his waistband rode low under the paunch of his stomach. His once white pocket T-shirt stretched over the expanse, and smelled strongly of fried food. He might have been a handsome man once, but now he looked tired and dejected.

"Mr. Ellis?" Peggy asked. When he didn't deny it she extended her hand. "I'm Peggy Howell, one of Billy's teachers."

"What's he done?" Pete demanded, not accepting her hand or offering to sit down and talk.

"Could we talk?" Peggy had been nervous to begin with, and his behavior was not putting her at ease. Finally he gestured toward a table and she gratefully sat down. He sat across from her and waited. Now that she had the opportunity to talk to him, she wasn't sure what to say.

"Billy's not in any trouble, Mr. Ellis," she assured the man scowling at her.

"Name's not Ellis," he corrected. "That's his name. Everyone calls me Pete."

Peggy remembered Violet telling her he wasn't Billy's natural father. That had been a stupid mistake on her part. "I apologize, Mr., um, Pete." He continued to regard her as if she were from the Internal Revenue Service.

"Um, well, I know you're trying to raise Billy by yourself, and run this business, and it isn't easy." *What a cold man,* she thought, unable to keep eye contact and not sure how to break through to him. "I tried to help Billy last fall, hiring him to help me with remodeling my cabin. I'm sorry I wasn't able to continue, but I had some family situations arise and . . ."

"You the teacher started the riots in here?" he demanded suddenly, and Peggy felt her stomach wrench.

"I'm a friend of Violet Adams," Peggy confessed. "I was here with her."

"You married Clint Howell, has a ranch southwest a' here?"

"Yes, but . . ."

"You think my son's a charity case?" The menace in the man's hard eyes goaded Peggy's temper.

"I think your son's neglected," she answered boldly, even as her hands trembled and she felt trickles of sweat run down her sides. "I realize it's not easy raising a boy alone . . ."

"So you thought you'd meddle," he finished with an ugly sneer.

"The boy needs a bath and decent clothes," Peggy snapped.

"Why? 'Cause he don't meet your standards? You listen to me, Mrs. Howell"—he stood up—"how I raise that boy is nobody's business but mine and his. He ain't sufferin' and he ain't complainin'."

"But you aren't helping him," Peggy tried to point out.

"Mind your own affairs, Mrs. Howell. From what I hear, you ain't managin' them too well." He walked away from her, back into the kitchen.

Peggy felt humiliation burn in her face. She'd handled this whole thing wrong and had lost control of the situation. She stood with all the dignity she could summon, refusing to slink away with her tail between her legs like a whipped dog.

"I was only concerned about Billy, that you might want more out of life for him," she shouted toward the kitchen door. She didn't know whether he heard her or not. She picked up her purse and left the restaurant, her head held high.

Peggy thought about her conversation all the way back to the ranch. Was Pete right? Was her campaign to improve Billy really a form of prejudice, a desire to make him conform to her standards? Was she interfering; meddling, he'd called it, the way she'd accused Clint of interfering?

*It's not the same,* she decided, the more she thought about it. *Clint and I are arguing about parenting methods, with common goals. Pete has no goals for Billy, and Billy has none for himself.* She vowed to continue her campaign to show Billy there was a better way, if he wanted it.

Through January Peggy lived at the lake Tuesdays through Thursdays. Fridays after school, she drove back to the ranch, where she spent the weekends. The calves began to deliver by the middle of January, and in spite of herself, Peggy began to look forward to the drives out to check on them. Clint got his casts off the end of January, and began doing exercises to try to regain the strength in his arms and hands lost during the two months of immobility.

As soon as possible, Clint was back to riding his range on horseback, and reminded Peggy of her promise to let him teach her to ride. Heather proved herself to be the "rocking chair" Clint had promised she would be, and never spooked, or shied, or even complained about her inexperienced rider. She did what Peggy told her to do, even if it didn't make sense, or stood patiently when Peggy gave her mixed signals, waiting until Peggy figured them out. By the second weekend of lessons, Peggy was riding beside Clint to see the new calves, and decided the view from horseback was better than the one from the pickup after all. Clint never gloated, but smiled with satisfaction at his booted and jeans-clad wife riding beside him across his ranch.

By February Peggy began to wonder if she hadn't taken on more than she was capable of dealing with. In trying to complete the requirements for accreditation in English before school started in the fall, she'd taken eight hours of upper level Language Arts courses. The heavy load required extensive reading and several papers, two of which were due simultaneously the first week in February.

"Neither professor will budge on her deadline, either," Peggy complained to Violet during their lunch break. That was the only time they saw each other now, and Peggy tended to eat lunch with a book in one hand, frantically trying to stay caught up.

"What are you going to do?" Violet asked.

"What can I do?" Peggy lamented. "If I don't sleep any this weekend I might be able to make it. I've driven back over to Portales to work in the library every night this week.

I have an impressive pile of information, I just have to organize it into two papers."

"I wish I could give you the papers I did for that class, but I'm afraid the references are sadly out-of-date."

"Thanks, but I have to do this on my own," Peggy stated.

"It's okay to let people help you, Peggy," Violet said, concern in her voice. "Maybe not give you papers, but there are other ways of helping."

"Such as what?" Peggy demanded.

"Take some of your personal days. Let a substitute teach on the days that get too deep in commitments," Violet suggested.

"Huh, and let Clark Graham know I can't hack it?" Peggy asked disdainfully. "No way."

"I just worry about you. You're so intense about everything you do. There's more to life than teaching school or getting your degree."

"That's easy for you to say. You have your Master's and enough years here to have confidence in job security." Peggy scrutinized her friend. "And don't you dare say it's not like I need the job."

"I would never say that," Violet assured her.

*No,* Peggy thought to herself, *but you're thinking it, you and everyone else I know.*

Peggy came to school glassy-eyed the following Tuesday after staying up all night to finish the two papers. Violet gave her concerned glaces, but wisely didn't say anything. Determination was all that got Peggy through the long day. Clint met her after school.

"What are you doing here?" she demanded, too tired and irritated to even be civil. "I have to get to class."

"I'm driving you," he informed her. "You stayed up all night, didn't you?"

"I had to get done."

"And how did you plan to drive to Portales and back tonight on no sleep?"

Peggy held up the thermos bottle she'd filled in the teacher's lounge. "That's what God made caffeine for."

"He also gave you a brain," Clint stated, exasperated. "Did it ever occur to you to ask for help?" He took her arm and led her toward his truck.

Peggy followed docilely, too tired to object. She woke up in Portales to Clint's gentle nudging. She directed him to the building where her classes met. He handed her the thermos and her briefcase, and promised to come back when class was over.

"Violet was right," she admitted in a defeated voice during the drive back.

"About what?" Clint asked.

"Asking for help. I should have taken today as a personal business day, let a substitute teach my classes. It just seemed so important to make Clark see how serious I was about teaching."

"Was it worth risking your life for?"

"No. I wasn't thinking too clearly last night. I didn't think I had a choice in the matter," Peggy said tiredly.

"You have several choices," Clint stated quietly.

"I won't quit!"

"Why do you keep assuming that's what everyone wants you to do?"

Peggy looked at his hurt expression in the dim green light from the dash. She had ignored him most of the weekend, bringing her typewriter out to the ranch and working almost nonstop. Even at that, she hadn't finished by the time she'd left for school Monday morning. She'd spent Monday night at the caboose, knowing she had too much left to do to finish in time without pulling an all-nighter. She'd been so tired by the end of school, she had been physically ill, but still she'd been determined to drive herself the eighty miles to Portales.

"I didn't like being fed, bathed, and dressed for eight weeks," Clint said. "But I had no choice, short of living in a cave and starving to death. I also knew I would do the same for you, or any of the kids. That's love, Peggy. That's what family means to me.

"You've always done the giving in your family," he continued. "Everyone else takes. You don't know how to ask for help, maybe because you've never had anyone to ask. I don't want that kind of relationship with you. When you need something, I want you to ask me. I want to be your partner."

"You have a ranch to run."

"I'm not foolish enough to try to run it by myself. And I'd rather drive you to Portales when you need it than attend your funeral and be consoled by people telling me about your independent spirit, if you don't mind."

"I'll try to remember that," she answered softly.

"Promise?"

She looked up into his dark eyes. "I promise. Clint?"

"Hmmm?"

"Thank you."

"Any time."

Peggy began to look forward to Tuesday nights. Clint met her after school, drove her to Portales and back, and spent the night with her in the caboose. When he kissed her goodbye in front of the school on Wednesday mornings, before returning to the ranch, Peggy always felt like she'd spent the night with an illicit lover instead of her husband.

"I think I'm jealous," Violet commented one morning, meeting Peggy inside the door. "Can I borrow the caboose on the weekends, when you're out at the ranch?"

"No way," Peggy stated emphatically, shaking her head. "Now that I have it back, I'm not ever giving it up to anyone, ever again."

"So selfish," Violet commented peevishly. She turned to walk away toward her classroom, then turned back. "The least you can do is tell me about it over lunch."

"Get out of here!" Peggy waved her away, laughing as she headed toward the art room.

Peggy was called out of class that afternoon for a long distance phone call. Already prepared for the worst by the time she walked to the office, Peggy's hand shook as she took the receiver.

"Hello."

"Mom?" It was Erika. Peggy sat down hard in the secretary's chair behind the desk. Who was dead? Her mother? Her father? "Kevin's been in an accident." *Kevin. Oh, God.*

"He's going to be okay," Erika reassured her, "but I knew you'd want to know. Want to talk to him? He's right here."

"Hi, Mom!"

"Are you all right?" Peggy felt light-headed with relief, hearing his voice. "What happened?"

"Pulled out in front of a dump truck," Kevin stated. Peggy thought he sounded proud of it. "He was moving faster than I thought."

"Are you okay?"

"Just . . . bruised. Broke my arm against the door. Hit my . . . head."

"Let me talk to Erika," Peggy demanded. She was beginning to suspect he had been drunk.

From Erika Peggy learned that the Porsche was considered totaled, hit at an angle from the rear on the passenger side and thrown into a ditch. Kevin had been alone, and wearing his seat belt. He'd hit his arm and head on the driver's door and window when the truck hit him. Everyone was telling him how lucky he was to be alive and relatively unharmed. They'd given him something for pain, which was why he was acting so silly. They were waiting for an orthopedic surgeon to set his arm.

After talking with Erika, Peggy called Clint. He insisted she fly rather than drive back to Wichita. Peggy refused.

"When are you leaving?"

"As soon as they can get a substitute here for the rest of my classes. I'll pack some clothes at the caboose."

"You're not coming home first?"

"There's no need," she explained patiently. "I'll call you from Wichita." She replaced the receiver on its cradle before he had a chance to argue further.

## Twenty-six

Peggy went straight to the hospital when she arrived in Wichita. The nurses allowed her to peek in on Kevin, who was sound asleep under sedation. They assured her that he was fine, the orthopedic surgeon said surgery didn't look necessary at this time. The skull X rays proved he had a hard head and there was no apparent damage there. Peggy drove to her parents' house much relieved. She still had a key, and let herself in quietly, tiptoeing back to her old bedroom.

"Welcome home."

Peggy whirled at the unexpected sound. "Dad!" Bill Hogan stood in the doorway in his robe, looking pleased with himself. "You scared me half to death!" She went to give him a hug.

"Thought you could sneak in after curfew, did you?" he teased her, squeezing her hard.

502

"Never could before, and I'm sadly out of practice."

"Did you stop and see Kevin first?"

"Yes, but he was sleeping. The nurses said he'll be fine, though."

"Want some coffee?"

Peggy was torn between fatigue and a desire to sit up and talk with her father. Sentiment won out. It had been a long time since she'd been able to talk with her dad, just the two of them. Usually her mother was hovering nearby, and it wasn't the same.

"Kevin's in some trouble over this," her father told her, after the coffee was brewed and they were sitting across from each other at the kitchen table.

"I knew it was his fault," Peggy said. "I guess they issued him a ticket for reckless driving. What's the fine going to be? Have you checked into it yet?"

"There's more to it than that." Bill fiddled with his coffee cup before meeting his daughter's eyes. "He was driving without insurance."

"But I gave him the money . . ." Peggy couldn't finish, feeling suddenly ill. He'd lied to her again.

"How bad is it?" she asked, fearing the worst.

"I don't know yet. He doesn't have a driver's license either. When Kevin is able to deal with it, a patrolman will be around to talk to him. The cement company who owns the dump truck can press charges also. The driver was treated and released, but he'll lose a couple of days of work because of it, not to mention the damage to the truck."

Peggy held her head in her hands, wearily wishing it would all go away.

"I'm sorry, honey," her father consoled. "I had no idea he was driving that car without insurance."

"It's not your fault, Dad. I should have checked up on him. I gave him the money believing he'd do what he said. I know better."

"Did he tell you what Cheryl wanted him to do?" Bill asked instead.

"He said she wanted him to get a job. When I talked to Cheryl earlier she said something about going with her to counseling also."

"That's exactly what she asked. He went to counseling with her once, pronounced the counselor a man-hating, uh,—"

"Bitch?" Peggy supplied.

"Yes," Bill admitted, giving her a disapproving look. "Anyway, Cheryl offered to change counselors, but he said it didn't matter, he wasn't going." He sighed and shook his head sadly. "He wouldn't even discuss the job issue."

"One of the conditions of the money I gave him was he had to find a job," Peggy supplied, feeling defeated.

"After what he did with your stocks, why did you give him money?"

"So he could finish school," Peggy stated defensively. "I tried to help him just like I've helped Megan." She got up to leave the table.

"Sit down," he ordered, keeping his voice low. "I'm not done."

"I'm tired. It's two A.M. and I just drove five hundred miles."

"Sit down and listen to what I have to say. You're not going to flounce off in a huff until you hear the whole story."

Peggy sat down, glaring at her father. She held her body rigid at the edge of the chair.

"Kevin's bright," Bill began. "He comes over here and we talk about investments, and the best stock gambles, and the economy. He watches companies, knows which ones will grow and which ones will go bust. He's going to make an incredible investment broker someday, if he can keep his hands off other people's money. But not with his present attitude."

Bill leaned closer, resting his weight on his forearms, his manner intense. "Kevin has the intelligence to get himself out of this mess, but he won't use it unless forced to."

"How?" Peggy asked, angry, but listening.

"He's going to try to talk someone into getting him out, and he's going to use everything from his broken arm to not being able to graduate. We can't give in."

"What about Peter, his dad?"

"Peter's wife just filed for divorce. Adultery," he added with a wry smile. "She's planning to clean him out of anything you left him. She hired that same fellow you used, Grant Wallace."

Peggy had to smile. Poor Peter. He was a slow learner.

"How's Cheryl doing now?" she asked.

"Without Kevin to support, she's doing fine, at least financially. Kevin gets Hillary every Sunday. He brings her by here a lot. That's the one day he acts responsibly, so I know he can do it.

"Now," he returned to the former subject, "Will you let him face this alone?"

"I'd be a pretty poor mother if I did," Peggy retorted.

"Okay, I'll rephrase it. Will you let him be responsible for his debts, without financial assistance from you?"

"I'm out of money, Dad," she confessed sadly. "I gave him the last of it so he could finish school. The only way I could help would be to mortgage the caboose or the van. I'm probably going to have to do that anyway to go to school myself this summer."

"Won't your husband help?"

"I want to do it on my own." She ran her finger around the rim of her cup, avoiding his scrutiny.

"Why?"

Peggy threw him a quick glance. Challenge glowed in his eyes. She frowned at him. "What do you mean, 'why?' "

"I want you to tell me why it is so important for you to do this school thing on your own, without asking anyone for help, including your husband, or your father."

"I don't know." Peggy waved her hands in frustration. "It just is."

"Think about it," Bill persisted.

Peggy chewed her lower lip and studied the coffee in the bottom of her cup. "To prove I can, I guess," she finally replied, thoughtfully. "I moved to New Mexico to prove I could stand on my own, be successful. I haven't proved that yet, and if I let Clint help me, then I didn't do it, he did."

"It's called 'pride,' " Bill said with a satisfied smile. "Self-esteem." He leaned forward again. "You're denying your son the very thing you are fighting for."

Peggy sat back in her chair and looked at her father in disbelief. "But he . . ." She shook her head.

"Asked for help?" Bill supplied. "Of course he did. It's easier that way. Didn't you ever take the easy way out, even though you knew it wasn't the best?"

Watching her father sitting there with his gray head cocked wisely made Peggy flush guiltily. "Peter," she admitted.

"For starters," Bill agreed. "It's also easier to do for your kids than let them suffer through learning how to do it themselves. Kevin was a tough kid to raise. I'm sure it became easier to just do things rather than battle to make him do them. What you lacked was a motivating factor."

"Why didn't you bring this up about twenty-five years ago?" Peggy demanded, getting angry again.

"It's taken me some time to see it myself. When your kids were little I was still working, and didn't see much of them. I remember being more concerned about your happiness during that time than your parenting skills. You are a good mother, Peggy, don't get me wrong. But Kevin isn't going to grow up until you cut the apron strings, and neither one of you are going to be happy until you do. You've got the perfect motivator right now."

"What's that?" Peggy asked dejectedly, unhappy with the conversation.

"He has no car."

"He has to have a car," Peggy objected. "It doesn't have to be a Porsche . . ." She stopped because Bill wasn't listening. He was shaking his head emphatically. "Dad!"

"We have an excellent bus system here in Wichita," Bill told her. "He can get anywhere in the city from the hours of seven A.M. until ten P.M. He can go to school, to work, to Cheryl's, all through the metro bus line. There're also taxis, but they cost more."

"You expect Kevin to ride the bus?" Peggy couldn't believe it.

"Without a driver's license, he won't have much choice," Bill pointed out. "I guarantee it won't be for long. That boy will find a way to have a car by the time his license is reinstated. And he'll move up to Porsche level before the year is out. He puts too much store by his image to settle for anything else." He paused, then smiled.

"Let's go to bed. Nothing has to be decided tonight." Peggy gave him a hug and left him setting the pot back up for breakfast.

Peggy went back to the hospital the next morning. Kevin was awake, propped up in bed with pillows and in a surly mood.

"Good morning to you, too," Peggy told him, giving him a hug and a kiss in spite of his unwelcome scowl. "How do you feel?"

"Like shit, how do you think I feel?" he growled, viciously grinding his thumb into the nurse call light on his console. When the voice came over the intercom, asking if she could help him, he reminded her he'd asked for a pain pill twice in the last thirty minutes and still didn't have it, embellishing his complaint with several explicatives.

"If you asked me for help like that, I would see that it was an hour before you got it," Peggy told him, her eyes narrowed in disapproval at his language and his rudeness.

"Nobody asked you," Kevin stated baldly.

Peggy stood up. "Maybe I'll come back when you feel better."

"What, so you can gloat? I'm sure Grandfather's filled you in on all my crimes."

"I came because I love you, Kevin," Peggy said softly, trying to diffuse his anger. "I wanted to see that you were all right."

"I have a broken arm, Mom. Did I mention that the car's totaled? What am I supposed to do?"

"Use your brain, Kevin," Peggy said, standing up to leave. "If you'd used your brain prior to yesterday, you wouldn't be lying here with a broken arm and a totaled car." She gave him a kiss and ruffled his dark hair affectionately.

"I love you, Kevin. I'm disappointed in your behavior, but I love you. I also know you'll do what you want to do. If you want that MBA, you'll get it. If you want to stay out of jail, you'll clean up your act, including your language, before you go before the judge. If you want a car to drive when your license is reinstated, you'll get a job. If you want your family back, you'll get off your high horse and make things right with Cheryl. The choices are yours."

"Where are you going?" Kevin demanded, pulling himself up in his bed.

"I'm going home," Peggy answered calmly, turning back from the door. "If I don't dawdle, I'll make it back in time for my class. If you need me, call me. I'll do what I can, but I will not give you any more money." She stood, looking at her son, wanting him to understand that she meant what she said. "I'll call you tomorrow and see how you're doing."

"You're not going to stay?" Kevin asked incredulously. "Who's going to take care of me? I have a broken arm!"

"Kevin, you broke your left arm and you're right-handed. I think you're more than capable of taking care of yourself." She walked out of his room, feeling confident that she'd done the right thing with Kevin at last.

Peggy took her ticket at the turnpike gate and remembered the last time she'd driven out of Wichita, heading for New Mexico. Seven months ago she'd run away because she couldn't say no to her children. Unable to boot them out of the nest, she'd abandoned the nest. The problem, at least in the case of Kevin and Megan, was that instead of learning to fly, they'd come running after her.

*I want it all,* Peggy thought to herself. *I want to teach school. I want to paint. I want to be independent, free to make my own choices. I want to be married to Clinton Howell and share the joys and sorrows of life with this incredibly strong, stubborn, wise, and loving man.*

*So, who's stopping you?* she demanded of herself. Certainly not Clint. Not the Clint who'd helped her hang Sheetrock when he always hired it done himself, then rubbed out her sore muscles afterward. Not the Clint who'd driven her to class when she'd so foolishly stayed up all night writing papers. Not the Clint who'd insisted she learn to ride a horse then challenged her to teach him to paint. Their painting sessions were almost as enjoyable as their rides out to see the calves, Peggy thought with a full heart.

That left her children. Kevin had enough problems of his own to keep him busy for years. She hoped he had enough pride to show her he could do it without her help, but if he didn't, she felt confident that she was now strong enough to do what was best for him, even if it meant letting him suffer a little.

Megan was too wrapped up in marital bliss to pay her mother much attention, although when she did look at her mother, there was a new attitude of respect and just a little awe. She no longer made assumptions about Peggy's time or property. When Peggy told her no, she didn't even whine anymore. She still sighed, Peggy thought with a smile, but she no longer argued.

Peggy arrived in Portales in time for her classes, but barely heard the discussions, still preoccupied with her earlier thoughts. Driving back toward Fort Sumner after class, she pulled over to the shoulder when she got to the turnoff toward the ranch. She should have been exhausted after the events of the last two days, but she felt strangely elated. The last thing she wanted to do was spend the night alone.

There was no hope of quietly slipping in without waking anyone up. Barking dogs escorted her from the gate and Clint met her at the door. He was wearing blue jeans, the top two buttons undone, his chest and feet bare, his hair rumpled from sleep. He was the sexiest man she'd ever laid eyes on.

"You okay?" he asked, his voice low and husky, his brows drawn down in concern.

"I am now," she replied. He overwhelmed

her still, this big burly cowboy she'd married. She smiled up at him as she laid her palms against the hair of his chest. He felt wonderful. He smelled wonderful. He surrounded her with a heady warmth and strength and desire. He searched her face, brows still furrowed with concern.

Peggy slid her arms around his neck and pulled his mouth down to hers, wanting to taste him, consume him. He groaned, deep in his throat, and pulled her hips against his, communicating his growing interest. Peggy pressed her full length against him, offering all.

"Dad? I heard the dogs. Anything . . . oh . . . hi, Peggy."

"Lock the door, Son," Clint instructed, scooping Peggy up in his arms.

"Clint!" Peggy objected, embarrassed in front of Justin, who was watching them with sleepy-eyed interest.

"Hush, woman, we're married," Clint admonished, carrying her toward their bedroom.

Their lovemaking was slow and achingly sweet, a savoring of sensations, of touch, of taste. The goal was not for a climax as much as it was for a union, a joining of bodies and souls. They lay together for a long time, quietly holding, touching, being as one.

"I missed you," Peggy finally said.

"I'll have to send you to Kansas more often," Clint teased, still holding her close.

"Do you know what I thought when I got to Fort Sumner?"

"What?"

"I thought, 'I want to go home.' "

"To Kansas and Auntie Em?" There was teasing in his voice, but Peggy heard the uncertainty.

"Kansas wasn't even in the running," she murmured, stroking the furry pelt across his chest. "I was trying to decide whether to go to the caboose, or come out here."

"And you decided to come home?" Peggy could hear the hope, but he needed confirmation.

"I wanted to come home." She kissed him on the mouth. "So, I came home."

"I love you, Peggy Howell."

"It would be nice to hear it occasionally."

"You haven't given me much opportunity."

"I'll try to do better."

He kissed her slowly, sliding his tongue ever deeper. When he'd coaxed her into responding in kind, he paused long enough to ask, "Did you tell the school you'd be back tomorrow?"

"I didn't say when I'd be back."

516

"You won't be back tomorrow."

"And why is that?" She knew the answer, but she wanted to hear it.

"You need your sleep," he responded, and proceeded to keep her up the rest of the night.

## Twenty-seven

Spring came to the desert with violent thunderstorms, warm weather, and an explosion of color from the numerous varieties of cactus plants. Peggy came down with a severe case of spring fever, torn between the desire to stay out all day trying to capture nature's beauty with oils and watercolors, and do her duty to school, both the one she taught and the one teaching her. In the end she tried to content herself with photographs to paint from at a later date. She did manage to take her watercolor art class out on several field trips to let the students paint the cactus.

Spring break fell on the last week of March. She hardly saw Clint the whole week. He and the boys were up at impossibly early hours to be at neighboring ranches before dawn to help with roundup. They were in bed shortly after dinner every night. Peggy had a project in mind, and spent the time he was away working in the equipment barn with her airbrush.

Roundup on the Howell ranch was scheduled for the end of the week. The men spent the day before in the pastures, making preparations. Tina and Gina spent the day before at the grocery store. Peggy was amazed at the amount of food they bought.

"You didn't buy this much for Christmas," she exclaimed as she helped them unload the van.

"We didn't feed working cowboys at Christmas," Gina explained. "By the way, Clint requested apple pie. I suggest you start tonight. We'll need at least six of them, and the ovens will be tied up tomorrow."

"Six pies?"

"At least. Even with six I'm not sure there will be any left for us."

"Six pies," Peggy repeated in disbelief. It would take her all night to peel the apples. "How many cowboys are we talking about?"

"Around twenty-four," Tina supplied. "We'll feed them breakfast before they get started, around four A.M., then lunch when they're done."

Peggy was grateful for Tina and Gina's

expertise, never having dealt with the feeding of twenty-four ranch hands before. Again feeling somewhat the outsider, she made her pies and took mental notes while the two younger women organized the kitchen and the house for the next morning. The adult portion of the Howell household gathered around the coffeepot the next morning at two A.M. Peggy couldn't remember getting up at two A.M. since Erika had started sleeping through the night.

"There's something obscene about getting up this early," she grouched, her attitude not improved by the excited bustling of the rest of the family. She was content to nurse her coffee at the kitchen table and watch for a while.

"Come here," Clint coaxed, taking her arm. He led her outside the house.

The night air was cool and fresh as Clint led Peggy away from the house. The dogs barked briefly, then joined them in silent escort. They walked to the corral fence, away from the lights of the house. As Peggy laid her arms along the top rail of the fence, a dark furry body brushed against her arm.

"Good morning, Henry," she addressed the cat, who immediately began to purr in response.

"You're up early." Peggy felt much more awake now.

"Probably still up from cattin' about all night," Clint speculated sourly.

"If you'd let him stay in the house, he wouldn't cat about all night," Peggy admonished him.

"I've never had a cat in the house—"

"—and you're not about to start now," Peggy finished for him. They'd been arguing about Henry since Peggy had brought him home from the caboose.

"Spoil him when he goes to the caboose with you," Clint said. "When he's here, he's a barn cat, just like he used to be."

"Meany," Peggy pouted.

Clint pulled her back into his embrace, taking her away from Henry. "I brought you out here to enjoy the moonlight, not argue about the cat."

The waxing moon was bathing the open expanse of grassland in silver, casting shadows from the low scrub trees and the fence. It was so bright, only the brightest stars were visible.

"It's beautiful, isn't it?" Clint asked.

Peggy had to agree. The house and its various outbuildings had been built on top of a slight rise. The stable and corral sat at the west edge, overlooking a vast plain. Peggy felt like she could see for miles.

"My first night in New Mexico, I watched the moonrise over the desert," she told Clint. "I felt as though I'd found a kindred spirit."

Clint hugged her tighter against his chest. "I felt like that the day I met you."

Peggy turned in his embrace, leaning back to try to see his face in the moonlight. "I haven't been much of a partner," she murmured sadly.

"Doesn't sound like you've had much experience."

"No, I guess not, but I'm learning."

"I'm afraid you'll learn a lot today." Clint hugged her close, savoring what he knew would be the last quiet moment of the day.

"I talked to Kevin last night," Peggy said, her cheek against his chest.

"His court date was yesterday," Clint remembered. "How did it go?"

"He won't get his license back until June, and his accumulated fines total three-hundred-seventy-four dollars. The court set him up on a payment plan. If he misses a payment, he goes back before the court."

"Incentive to stay employed," Clint commented.

"That and Cheryl," Peggy agreed. "He moved back home last night."

"I hope it works," Clint said sincerely.

"At least he's working on making it work. I'm proud of him. He's eaten a lot of crow the last two months, and knowing Kevin, it's not getting easier with practice."

"I guess we have to attend his graduation," Clint stated with feigned reluctance.

"I wouldn't miss it for the world," Peggy told him, then continued with mock sternness, "And you'd better not either."

"Yes, ma'am," Clint acquiesced meekly. He turned toward the house, keeping her wrapped under one arm. "Coffee break's over, partner," he addressed her. "Time to go to work."

As Gina had predicted, the ranch hands began to show up for breakfast a little before four o'clock. "Morning, Mrs. Howell," Peggy heard over and over from the men as they entered the house. Only Ramon greeted her as Mom, giving her a kiss on the cheek. Even Jay Estavez, Ramon's father, who was older than Peggy, called her Mrs. Howell.

Peggy helped Tina and Gina serve the huge breakfast of biscuits, ham, sausage, hashbrowns, two kinds of gravy, their choice of eggs, orange juice, and gallons of coffee.

In much less time than it had taken the women to prepare the meal, it was consumed and the men were out the door. Peggy stood in the center of the kitchen with the twins, surveying the damage.

"No matter how liberated we think we are, it still boils down to the women stay home and cook and clean, the men go off to hunt," Peggy observed wryly.

The twins made quick eye contact with each other before giving Peggy identical expressions of knowing amusement. "You just haven't been a rancher's wife long enough to find out," Tina told her. "Have you noticed you don't see many bachelor ranchers?"

"Rancher's wives are held in high esteem out here," Gina added. "They are treated with respect by the other ranchers, which is why they all called you Mrs. Howell."

"We're worth our weight in gold," Tina bragged.

"A ranch wife is much more valuable than a hired hand," Gina agreed. "It's amazing the things we're called upon to do."

"Like pull calves?" Peggy asked.

"Yeah," Gina grinned at her, "and drive trucks, and rescue stranded motorists from ditches."

"We consider this catering," Tina said,

waving her hand around the kitchen. "We've actually hired out to ranches that didn't have someone who could handle preparing meals for such large groups."

"We decided to do home school this year rather than send the kids to kindergarten in the village because it's an hour bus ride each way to school."

"We bottle-feed any calves who are sick, or whose mother is sick, or whose mother hasn't bonded with them and so won't feed them. Just like human babies, it has to be done round the clock when they are real small."

The girls continued to take turns telling Peggy about the duties of ranch wives. "Then there's heifer watch, when you set the alarm every two hours and go see if any of them are in labor."

"And in the summer the ditch master calls and announces you have an hour to get over to the valley and open the gates if you want your field irrigated that month."

"Of course the men are in the far pasture and the kids just went down for their naps when he calls."

"And the tractor always breaks down while we're in the middle of cooking supper, but one of us must drop everything and run into town for the needed part."

"But we always get blue ribbons on our chickens," Gina mentioned, on the positive side.

"And the men let us go shopping in Albuquerque without the kids at least twice a year."

"Tina and I feel quite lucky to have each other to help share the load. We feel even more blessed now that you've joined us."

"Yeah, I'm a great babysitter," Peggy agreed.

"Don't discount that," Tina told her. "If we're here, the men don't think about the fact that we've been home with them all day. They're tired and just want to clean up and relax."

"Your entertaining them after supper saves us thirty minutes clean-up time," Gina agreed. "It seems a simple thing, but the men never thought to do it."

"We are ranchers, Peggy," Tina stated. "It's what we know, and what we love. Before the kids came, we even helped herd the cattle during roundup. We don't have the physical strength to handle the calves, but I can stay in the saddle on a cutting horse, and that's no small feat."

"I've stayed up on labor watch with Justin countless times. I've pulled my fair share of calves."

"How many women do you know that can feed twenty-four cowboys a full breakfast at four A.M.?"

Peggy smiled. "Not many. Most of the women I know would serve them doughnuts and coffee."

"We should try that one year," Gina suggested to Tina, giggling at the thought.

"Huh!" Tina snorted. "We'd be doing roundup by ourselves." To Peggy she added, "Most ranchers are willing to help you in any way they can, but they expect to be fed, and fed well."

"It's a team effort, Peggy. The men could no more run this ranch without us than we could without them. She needs to see roundup," Gina told her sister.

"I suppose you feel the best qualified to educate her," Tina mocked her twin.

"You make better rolls than I do," was Gina's excuse.

"Flattery from you is never without ulterior motive," Tina quipped. "Okay, but not until the dishes are done and I get first nap."

"First nap?" Peggy questioned Gina as they walked toward the stable an hour later.

"After everyone leaves, we take turns with the kids and try to catch a nap to compensate for getting up so early," Gina explained. They saddled the horses, and rode together out to where the men were working the cattle.

The holding pen was a large fenced-in area in the middle of the pasture. Gina and Peggy sat on their mounts outside the fence to watch.

"I want you to see the team effort roundup requires," Gina began, pointing out across the pasture where two mounted cowboys were herding in a group of cows and their calves. "Those men were at the fence line before first light. As soon as it was light enough to see, they started herding the cattle in their section in toward the holding pen. There's another pen in the other pasture. Half of the men went over there with J.R. to do those calves.

"Dad, J.R., and Justin herded some of the cattle into the holding pens yesterday, so the branding could get started while the rest of the herd is rounded up and brought in. Watch Justin," she instructed. Justin was energetically pursuing a calf through the group inside the large holding pen, lariat in hand.

"That's a cutting horse," Gina informed Peggy, her eyes sparkling as she watched her husband. "Wherever that calf goes, that horse will follow. It takes a good seat to stay in the saddle of a working cutting horse." Gina's eyes darkened and her smile became sensual. "Justin has a fine seat," she purred.

Peggy laughed at Gina's admiration of Justin, but watched him, entranced. The tall young man hugged his mount with his knees and thighs, twisting his body to follow the sudden direction changes as they gained on their darting victim. Flanking the running calf, Justin threw his lariat and caught the calf's hind legs. He pulled the rope up, and working in unison with him, the horse backed up, taking the slack out of the rope. Slowly they dragged the bawling calf over to where a group of five men waited by an open fire.

Two cowboys grabbed the calf, one the head, the other the back legs, releasing Justin's rope so he could go get the next one. Three other men moved in and worked over the calf. Peggy strained to see around all the broad backs of the cowboys, but whatever they were doing was largely shielded from her by their bodies, and the calf was back up so quickly, Peggy had trouble following all of it.

"It takes two men to hold the calf," Gina continued her lesson. "Dad's got the branding iron."

Peggy hadn't realized the man welding the iron was Clint. She'd been too focused on the calf.

"That's Larry Winegarner dehorning and Jay Estavez castrating the bulls. They are both very good, and quick, which is important. The calves are released before they hardly know what has hit them. Then they are returned to their mothers and allowed to go back to the pasture."

"Is all that necessary?" Peggy questioned softly, watching the calf bound to his feet, somewhat dazed. "Must they be dehorned?"

"They will hurt each other if the horns are allowed to grow. Some people do leave the horns on, but if we have to use antibiotics when one gets hurt, he's no longer marketable as organically raised."

"It still seems cruel."

"They have a brief moment of pain now, to save greater pain later."

That sounded profoundly philosophical

somehow, and Peggy again looked away from the calves and at Gina. She was watching Justin again, that secretive smile back on her face.

"The calves aren't near as much fun to watch as the cowboys," Gina stated.

Rather than watch Justin, Peggy preferred to watch her own husband. Clint wore leather chaps over his jeans and leather gloves over his hands, as did the other men. Their hats were battered and soiled, their boots scuffed. Thin cotton shirts stretched over hard muscles as they labored. Although it was early and the morning still cool, the men's shirts were already damp with sweat. Peggy felt transported back in time. She doubted if roundup looked any different one hundred years ago.

"I was supposed to be showing you the teamwork," Gina remembered. "It would take our men weeks to do the work that's being done today. Instead of roping and holding the calves, they would have to use chutes, which squeeze the calf so he can't move. The ranchers working together makes everyone's roundup more efficient, and more fun."

"Tell me, Peggy," Gina turned away from the men and looked at Peggy. "Did you enjoy the work you did on the caboose more when you worked by yourself, or when Dad was there?"

Peggy didn't even have to think about her answer. She couldn't have done the work on the caboose without Clint. If Clint hadn't been there, she would have had to hired another carpenter, and she knew the camaraderie wouldn't have been there. "We had such a good time working on that caboose," she said out loud.

"One of the joys of love is sharing," Gina philosophized. "Tina and I could have demanded our own homes, kept our families separate, but we didn't want to. It's much more fun to work together, and we aren't both wasting time doing duplicate jobs. Why should both of us cook dinner? To impress our husbands on our abilities as cooks? It wasn't just flattery when I told Tina she made better rolls. She does. She can't touch me on fried chicken, though," Gina bragged with a grin. "And after eating your apple pie, I doubt either one of us ever attempts to make another one.

"I know it's been hard for you, finding your place among us," Gina said with understanding. "You're used to running your own house, planning meals, cooking, shopping, and all the millions of tasks that are involved in the role of wife. When you married Dad, you married into a household that didn't need you in that role. Look at it this way, that's our job. You are a school teacher, we are, among other things, homemakers. Together, we improve both our lives."

"How have I improved your lives?" Peggy asked skeptically. "Outside of babysitting, I don't know the first thing about ranching."

"You're learning, and you help more than you think. When you ride with Clint to check the calves, you free up one of us. No one is allowed to ride out alone, not even the men. The ranch is too big, and too many things can happen.

"And quit discounting watching the kids," Gina scolded. "Tina and I never both get away, unless the boys watch them, or Dad. They love you, and we don't worry when they are with you. It's been so much fun to go riding together on Sunday afternoons, the four of us."

"Anybody can watch kids," Peggy demurred, but she basked in Gina's praise.

"As we mentioned before, no one ever did. Speaking of which, they'll be up by now and Tina will be after our heads for leaving her for so long."

Shortly before one o'clock twenty-four tired, hot, dusty, hungry cowboys returned to the house. Veterans of roundups, Tina and Gina were ready for them with galvanized tubs of warm water, soap, and towels, set up outside. They removed their chaps, gloves, and hats, and carefully wiped their boots off before coming into the house. Lunch was roast beef, mashed potatoes, gravy, brown beans, three kinds of vegetables, and home-made dinner rolls with butter. Naively, Peggy doubted any of them had room for the six pies she'd baked.

"Mrs. Howell, I accused Clint of bragging on his new wife when he told us about your apple pie." The cowboy held up his plate for his second piece while he spoke. "No wonder he grabbed you up so fast."

Peggy served pie and refilled iced tea and coffee, and basked in the compliments. Clint's eyes were filled with pride as he watched her from his position at the head of the table. But the compliment that made her day was not over her apple pie.

Lee Estavez detained her when she refilled his coffee cup. He was Ray's youngest brother and therefore Ramon's uncle. "You have my son Jesus in your art class," he told her. "I think he's got talent."

"I agree," Peggy said, somewhat surprised. "He's done some really original things, especially with clay."

"He wants to take more art," Lee told her. "Will you be there next year?"

Peggy's smile faded. "I don't know, Mr. Estavez."

"You'd better call me Lee. Half the county answers to Mr. Estavez."

Peggy laughed with him, then sobered again. "They are changing the art format next year. I hope to stay and teach language arts in addition to history, but I won't know until summer."

"I'm sorry to hear that," Lee said sincerely. "I know for a fact that you are directly responsible for Jesus' interest in art. At first, he only took the class to goof off."

"Thank you," Peggy responded with a modest smile. "It means a lot to hear that."

"He's wanting to buy some tools and clay, so he can do some things at home this summer. Where can he find those?"

"I'll bring him a mail order catalogue from one of the art supply houses," Peggy promised.

The men dawdled around the table, talking,

arguing, teasing, and letting their food digest. Then, as if on a signal, the whole group rose to leave. Their compliments to the women for the food were lavish as they filed out of the house. The women cleaned the kitchen while the men loaded their horses. By midafternoon, the house was quiet and the fatigue of the adults apparent.

"Can you handle one more event today?" Peggy asked Clint, intercepting him before he reached the recliner in the den. He had showered and shaved, and she knew if he sat down, she would never get him back up.

"Aren't you tired?" Clint protested.

"Yes, but it's important. I've been working on it all week, and I want to show you now." She tugged insistently on his arm. With a whine of being forced under duress, he allowed her to pull him out the door.

"Sit here," she instructed, indicating a bench in front of the porch. "I'll be right back."

Clint lounged on the bench and watched Peggy walk away through half-open eyelids. She disappeared into the machine barn, and he heard the large doors being slid open. When he heard the old truck start up, he sat up, fully alert and wondering what she was up to.

The truck backed out of the barn, Peggy at the wheel, her full attention on the side mirrors. The tall wooden side of the truck's bed was covered with a large sheet, secured top and bottom. It rippled slightly in the breeze, but gave no clues as to what it hid.

Clint stood up, fear constricting his throat. He wondered what he'd done to deserve what was under that sheet. There was no doubt in his mind. Peggy had painted his truck, just as she'd vowed she would, and he wasn't going to like it.

Gears ground gently as Peggy wrestled with the transition from reverse to first. By the time she maneuvered the truck around to the drive in front of the house, the rest of the family had gathered with Clint. Public humiliation, he thought, glancing at the openly curious faces of his sons, daughters-in-law, and grandchildren. He wondered if there was any spray paint out in the shed.

"Peggy learned to drive the truck," J.R. noted, picking up a clambering two-year-old.

"She's been practicing all week," Tina supplied, "But she won't let us see what she painted on it."

"Some form of superior female standing over her vanquished male foe," Clint guessed in a dejected voice.

"Why?" Justin asked, clearly perplexed. "I thought you two were getting along."

"No way," Gina countered. "The painting, I mean. This one's special."

"She's been too excited about it," Tina agreed.

Peggy stopped the truck in front of her audience, carefully set the brake, and turned off the engine. Then she grinned at Clint expectantly. His return smile lacked enthusiasm, and Peggy's faded with disappointment. She opened the door and got out, then shut it firmly.

"I thought you'd be pleased," she appealed to Clint. She stayed beside the truck.

"I am," Clint assured her, trying to force some credibility into it. "I'm just so . . . surprised."

"Not as much as you will be," she promised, her smile returning.

"That's what I'm afraid of," Clint murmured, mostly to himself.

Peggy didn't hear him, her back turned while she freed the sheet up along the bottom. Then, with a theatrical flourish, she jerked it away. As it fluttered to the ground, she watched Clint's face for his reaction.

He was stunned. His jaw dropped slightly as he gazed up at the life-size portraits of

Peggy and himself, riding side by side on their horses. They were looking at each other, their hands gesturing as if deep in conversation; They were riding along the beach, a familiar cliff in the background with the red caboose perched on top of it. A strange bird flew in the sky above them. It was a long time before he could look away, at his wife's radiant face.

"It's incredible!" Justin finally spoke for the group.

"I think they want to be alone," Gina suggested, taking Justin's arm and tilting her head back toward the house. He gave the painting one final admiring look, then gathered up Cindy. He punched J.R. one on his way in, tilting his head as Gina had. J.R. grinned and followed, carrying Jeffrey. The girls took the hands of the older children, and they all disappeared into the house, shutting the door.

Once alone, Peggy approached Clint. The approval in his eyes intensified as he focused on her.

"Partners," she explained, her voice soft.

"As it should be," Clint concurred.

"It needs an inscription, though," Peggy said thoughtfully, "but until this morning, I didn't have one I liked."

"I like 'partners.' "

"This morning Gina told me, 'The joy of love is in the sharing.' "

Clint smiled his agreement. He reached for her. "I love you."

Peggy's heart suddenly felt too full to contain it all. "I love you," she answered against his shoulder, her voice tremulous. "I still have trouble believing it."

"That you love me?" Clint asked, pulling back from their embrace.

"No. That in my search for myself, I found you."

Clint gazed into her dark blue eyes, suddenly serious. "And did you find yourself?"

"Oh, yes," Peggy stated emphatically, her eyes smiling. "I'm a teacher, an artist, a mother, a grandmother, a rancher, and Clinton Howell's wife. I am a contributor to each of these areas of my life, just as they contribute to mine."

"I already knew that." Clint pretended to be unimpressed. "I could have told you that the day I met you."

"But I had to find it on my own," Peggy insisted.

"I like your translation," Clint praised her, turning back to the painting. "Does the bird mean something? What is it?"

"The phoenix, of course," Peggy informed him proudly. "I altered the legend."

"Tell me."

"It's not the fire of destruction that causes rebirth, but the burning fire of love." She pulled Clint's head down and kissed him with all the fire in her heart and soul.

"I'm a believer," Clint murmured against her mouth, then he scooped her up and carried her into the house, his fatigue forgotten as he entered their bedroom and pushed the door closed with his boot.

## Afterword

There are not words sufficient to thank all the people who helped this book come about. Rita Gay Mitchell, my friend, neighbor, and chief critique read every page of every draft, sometimes right off the monitor. She knew my characters better than I did, sometimes, and frequently said to me, "Peggy wouldn't do that." She was usually right.

From the Fort Sumner area, C.W. and Janean Grissom from Taiban provided invaluable ranching and farming information. Linda Waller taught history at Fort Sumner, and shared her knowledge with me. Joan Trotter, a photographer who lives on Lake Sumner, provided *tons* of wonderful photographs of the area. Bob Parsons, retired history teacher and artist, provided the town's history. He is an actual person, and the murals on the Bowl-A-Matic were painted the year the story was set. I thank him for permission to include him in my story. Dr. Joyce Roberts is also a real person. She is Fort Sumner's only full-time physician, and allowed me to use her name in the story.

I would like to include Lois Hudgens, Faye Taylor, Judith Speck, Donna Deeb, and Gin Ellis for reading the rough manuscript, and sharing their thoughts, as well as giving me their support.

To my long-suffering family, who lived in a dirty house and fended for themselves for meals on countless occasions; thanks for believing in me. My children, Justin and Erika, wanted to be in the story. My husband, Rocky, is a real cowboy, from Dodge City, Kansas. He not only cooks, he frequently served me meals at the computer. That's love.

This book was inspired by my mother, Peggy Jo Hughes, who lived in Fort Sumner for ten years, teaching school and painting the desert. From her I gained my love of books. She believed in me as a writer, submitting my first short story when I was sixteen. This is not her story, but she is the epitome of *On Wings of Love*.

## About the Author

Fay Kilgore lives in Atlanta, Georgia, with her husband, two children, three cats, and a dog. She has a bachelor of science degree in nursing from Wichita State University, and is working on her Master's degree in nurse midwifery at Emory University. She currently works in the office of an OB/GYN.

Fay has used writing as a creative outlet most of her life, and considered pursuing it as a career instead of nursing. Now, with her first publication through Zebra, she feels she has the best of both worlds.